D0489179

Josephine Cox was born in Blackburn, one of ten children. At the age of sixteen, Josephine met and married her husband Ken, and had two sons. When the boys started school, she decided to go to college and eventually gained a place at Cambridge University. She was unable to take this up as it would have meant living away from home, but she went into teaching – and started to write her first full-length novel. She won the 'Superwoman of Great Britain' Award, for which her family had secretly entered her, at the same time as her novel was accepted for publication.

Her strong, gritty stories are taken from the tapestry of life. Josephine says, 'I could never imagine a single day without writing. It's been that way since as far back as I can remember.'

For information about the Josephine Cox newsletter, please see page 359 and visit www.josephinecox.co.uk.

For exclusive updates on your favourite HarperCollins authors, visit www.AuthorTracker.co.uk.

Also by Josephine Cox

JOSEPHINE COX

~

The Loner

HarperCollins*Publishers*

HarperCollins*Publishers*
77–85 Fulham Palace Road,
Hammersmith, London W6 8JB

www.harpercollins.co.uk

Published by HarperCollins*Publishers* 2007
1 3 5 7 9 8 6 4 2

A catalogue record for this book
is available from the British Library

ISBN-13: 978 0 00 724412 6
ISBN-10: 0 00 724412 6

Typeset in New Baskerville by
Rowland Phototypesetting Ltd, Bury St Edmunds, Suffolk

Printed and bound in Great Britain by
Clays Ltd, St Ives plc

Mixed Sources
Product group from well-managed
forests and other controlled sources
www.fsc.org Cert no. SW-COC-1806
© 1996 Forest Stewardship Council
FSC

My thanks to my large and wonderful family for all the love and support you have always given me. And to my many friends, including the ones who read my books and write to me. What would I do without all of you? Stay well, be good, and if you can't be good, be naughty!

CONTENTS

PART ONE

~

Blackburn, 1955

The Road to Ruin

CHAPTER ONE

S HE MADE A ghostly figure as she silently wended her way through the dark, shadowy streets.

Late again, she thought. But there was little regret as she recalled the fun-filled evening, with good company and a man's arms about her. Why should she feel guilty? What was so wrong about her having a good time? She was still relatively young and vibrant. The men liked her and she liked them, and there was more to life than sitting at home and being a good little wife. Life was too short for that.

As she turned into Derwent Street, she thought of young Davie. Only then did she feel ashamed. She hoped he wasn't waiting up. She didn't want to see the sadness in his eyes when he saw her arrive home at this late hour, giddy with booze and caring for nothing or no one, except him, her darling son.

'You're a bad woman, Rita Adams,' she told herself. 'You should have been home hours ago.' She gave a small, nervous laugh. 'There'll be sparks flying, you'll see.'

Her unsteady footsteps echoed eerily against the pavement as she continued her way past the row of terraced houses. At this hour, most people were in bed and only one house was lit up. This was her home. This was where her family would be waiting and watching. She thought of her child again, and the guilt was cutting, 'Davie's a good boy. He doesn't deserve a mother like you.' There were times when she hated herself.

Shivering in the cold night air, she clutched the lapels of her coat and drew it tighter about her. 'Remember now,' she muttered, 'you've spent the evening with your old friend, Edna.' Such lies, she thought. Such badness. She reached her gaze towards the twitching curtains and saw the shadowy figure of a man. 'He's waiting for you,' she whispered nervously. 'Best not let him guess what you've been up to.' She giggled. 'Best have your story good and ready.'

Each time she had a different excuse, and each time she became a better liar. Tormented, she thought of her long-suffering husband, and her ageing father whose house they lived in. But it was her son she mostly feared for: Davie was a fine and loving boy who did not deserve a mother like her. These three wonderful people were her family and she loved them with a passion, and God help them, they loved her too; more than she deserved.

After an evening of laughter and drink she remembered how it had been, in the back alley, the thrill of being in the arms of a stranger. She didn't know his name, nor did she want to. They simply met, talked and laughed, shared a moment of frantic excitement, and then he went on his way.

No money ever changed hands on such occasions. It was the excitement, that was all she craved. Brief and sordid, the encounters meant nothing to her. She adored her husband; she cherished her family. But sometimes, for some mysterious reason that she didn't understand but was powerless to resist, Rita Adams followed the urge to abandon her responsibilities and lash out at life.

If she lost control, it wasn't her fault she told herself – *it was not her fault.* Life was wonderful, and then it became too mundane, and then she began to wander. But it was wicked. *She* was wicked; a loose and shameful woman. And afterwards, she was always sorry. But 'sorry' was never enough. She knew that.

Having searched for a plausible excuse for coming home so late, Rita had hit on the idea of Edna Sedgwick. She had been meaning to go and see the old dear for some long time now, and what was more, Don knew that. He was aware that her old friend had been poorly. She'd tell him that she'd rushed round there when she heard that Edna had worsened . . . and had spent more time with her than she should have.

Plain and outspoken, with a mop of bleached hair, Edna had been a good neighbour, and when she moved away, the whole family had missed her. It was the most natural thing in the world for Rita to go and see the sick woman.

Surely her Donny wouldn't argue with that?

Rita felt a pang of guilt at using Edna as an alibi to lie her way through this night – not only because she had promised not to lose touch, but somehow, two long years had passed since Edna and Fred had left the street, and Rita had never found the time to pay her old friends a visit.

Her part-time job at Michelle's Hair Salon, doing all the perms and the rest of it, kept her occupied. It was murder on the feet though, she thought, fishing for a cigarette in her handbag. Somehow, she managed to strike a match and light it. Taking a deep drag, then stumbling on, she said loudly, 'I will come and see you soon, Edna mate, I really will. I'll be on your doorstep tomorrow, an' that's a promise.' A hollow promise, she knew.

In that moment, between three and four a.m., she felt as though she was the only person in the whole world. But then suddenly, it was as if this world was awakening; house lights were going on as people got ready for early shifts, and dogs were let out to relieve themselves against the lamp-posts. Best get home, Rita thought, quickening her steps. Falling this way and that, she found it highly amusing. 'Yer drunken beggar, our Reet,' she giggled. 'Stand up straight, will yer.'

Squaring her shoulders, she pushed on, one hand steadying herself against the walls of the houses and the other keeping her coat tight about her.

In the distance, she could hear the faint clatter of horses' hooves against the cobbles. That would be Tom Makepeace, on his way to the Co-op Dairy depot to deliver his milk churns from the farm and to collect the crates of bottles for his round. Tom knew all and sundry hereabouts, and everyone liked the man, Rita included. Her son and Tom's daughter Judy were the best of pals.

The clattering grew louder until he was right there beside her. 'Good God, Rita love, what are *you* doing, wandering the streets at this time o' the morning?' he asked, reining the big horse to a halt. With a gruff manner and his homely face worn by the elements, Tom was in his mid-forties and as decent a man as could be found anywhere. Like most folks he had heard the rumours that circulated about Rita, though he had learned never to make hasty judgment. All the same, he suspected she would have a plausible lie in answer to his question.

'I've been to see Edna Sedgwick,' she fibbed. 'Got talking – you know how it is.'

'Oh, aye, I know how it is, and I heard she'd not been well. Has she improved at all?' Tom knew something about Edna that Rita obviously didn't, but he played along with her lies.

Anxious to get home, Rita cut short the conversation. 'Oh, yes, she's a lot better, thank God . . . only I spent more time

with her than I should've. Got to be getting home now.'
Moving on, she made every effort to walk with dignity, but
her head was whirling inside and her feet seemed to go every
way but forwards. Instead of sobering up, she felt worse than
ever, and what's more, her hangover was kicking in now. Rita
Adams, you're a born liar! she thought. One o' these days
it'll be the death of you.

Feigning a smile, she called after him, 'Bye then, Tom.
Stay well now.'

Turning his head, Tom noted how she swayed from side
to side. 'Drunk as a skunk and a liar into the bargain!' He
clicked the old horse on, and shook his head forlornly.
'Some folks never learn.'

He thought of his own family, and felt like a millionaire.
Although his wife Beth was neither flamboyant nor striking
in her looks, like Rita, she owned the prettiest eyes and a
smile that could light up a room. An admirable cook, despite
all the rationing they'd had to get used to, during and
straight after the war, she thought nothing of cracking him
over the head with the mixing spoon whenever he got under
her feet. He chuckled out loud. Many were the times she'd
chased him down the path after catching him with his finger
in the mixing bowl or pinching some crust off a newly-baked
loaf.

Their daughter Judy was an added blessing. Deeply thoughtful and gentle in her manner, her laughter was like music to
his ears. But she could also be outspoken and strong-minded.
When championing any particular cause, she possessed a temper that could shake the foundations of the earth. Her friendship with Davie Adams was deep and abiding; he was the
brother she had never had, the apple of her eye. It was a good
job the young 'un took after his father, Don, and not his
mother, Tom thought.

Beth and Judy. These two were the pivot of Tom's existence. And he thanked the Good Lord for them, every day of his life.

Glancing after Rita, Tom recalled the heartache she had caused her family. What a foolish woman she was. She had a loving husband, a fine son, and a generous father who had taken them in after she and Don had lost everything in a failed business venture. Yet time and time again, she put them all through the mill.

He flicked the reins to gee up the horse. 'God knows how they put up with her,' he grumbled. ''Cause I'm buggered if I would!'

CHAPTER TWO

FROM HIS BEDROOM window, young Davie Adams watched his mother come stumbling down the street. Her beautiful dark hair was wild and dishevelled; he heard the raucous laughter and her quick defiant shouts, and his heart sank. 'Drunk again,' he murmured. 'Oh, Mam! Why do you do it?'

He sneaked out to the landing and looked down. In the light from the parlour, his father's anxious figure threw a shadow over the carpet as he paced up and down, waiting for her, obviously worried about her. The boy knew that his dad loved his mam, and forgave her every time. But what if this was one time too many? His young heart thudded with fear and misgiving.

'Go back to bed, lad. Don't be out here when she comes in.'

The boy almost leaped out of his skin. 'Grandad!' Turning, he saw the old man standing behind him. Once tall and straight, with looks that could entrance any woman, Joseph Davies was now slightly stooped, his dark hair marbled with grey, and a look of desolation in his blue eyes. 'Will she never learn,' he asked gruffly. 'God forgive me, what kind of daughter have I raised?'

'Don't get upset, Grandad,' Davie whispered. 'You'll see, it'll be all right. It always is.'

Smiling fondly, the old man laid his hand on the boy's head. 'You're a good lad, Davie. An example to us all.' He nodded. 'Happen you're right. Happen the both of us should get back to our beds.' He gave a stifled little cough. 'Afore we catch our death o' cold, eh?'

He paused at the sound of someone fumbling with a key in the front door lock, then the banging of fists against wood, and then her voice, loud and angry. 'What the devil are you lot playing at in there? Thought you'd lock me out?' There was a crude laugh and then she was yelling, 'OPEN THIS DOOR, YOU BASTARDS! IT'S BLOODY FREEZING OUT HERE!'

Joseph's face crumpled with disgust. 'Drunk and shameless . . . cares for nothing and nobody, least of all us.' He had long heard the gossip, and for a while he had chosen to ignore it. But little by little, the truth had hit home: his daughter, little more than a streetwoman.

Suddenly she burst in, muttering and swearing when she lost her balance as she turned to slam shut the door. 'You buggers locked me out – left me in the cold like some mangy old dog.' Grovelling about on her knees, she continued to moan and curse, 'Thought you'd keep me out, did you? Unfeeling, miserable bastards . . .'

'Stop that racket – you'll wake the boy! Nobody locked you out.' Don was unaware that his son was already out of bed, a witness to everything.

Startled that he was so near, Rita scrambled to her feet and looked up. Standing before her was a man of some stature, his handsome features set hard and his dark Irish eyes tinged with sadness. Where he had once been proud and content, there was lately a nervousness to him, a sense of despair had gradually etched itself into his heart and soul, and it showed – in the eyes and the deepening lines on his face, and in the way he held his shoulders, bowed down as though he had the weight of the world on them.

Everyone knew how it was between him and his wife. His workmates knew more than most. Some had even bragged of bedding her. They goaded and tormented him, until he was forced to defend both himself and his wife. Twice he'd been involved in fierce fighting, and each time it was he who took the blame and got sent on his way.

After a time he had learned to keep his head down and get on with his work There seemed no point in trying to defend her any more, and though he evaded the jokes and innuendos, the shame was crippling, but he was a man trapped in the wonderful memories of how it used to be. Even now he loved her with a passion that frightened him. But now, at long last, his love for her was overwhelmed by another more powerful feeling; a feeling of utter, crippling revulsion.

'Hello, Donny, my big, handsome man.' Unsteady, unashamed, she opened her arms and went to him, her clumsy fingers tousling his brown hair. 'You needn't have waited up. I meant to be home earlier, only I went to see Edna Sedgwick. We got talking – you know how it is . . .'

He pushed her away. 'Don't lie to me, Rita.'

'I'm not lying.' She could look him in the eye without the slightest compunction. 'I'm telling you the truth! Why do you never believe me?'

He smiled then – a slow, sad smile that made her feel guilty. 'Because I'm not the fool you take me for,' he answered in his soft Irish lilt. 'I've learned the hard way so I have.'

When again she prepared to lie, he bristled with anger. 'For God's sake, Rita, look at the state of you. You've been out on the town . . . again! Booze and men, that's what you've been up to! Who was it this time, eh? One of the men from the factory, was it? One of my new workmates, is that the way of it, eh? Will I go into work on the morrow and have 'em all staring at me, . . . sniggering behind my back and pitying me? Is *that* how it'll be?'

'NO!' The guilt was written all over her face, and still she defied him. 'You don't know what you're saying. I would never do a thing like that.'

'Liar!' He looked down on her face and adored every inch of it. But if he didn't stand up to her this time, he never would. 'I know what you've been up to. You'll not squirm out of it this time. I've had enough of being the town laughing-stock. It's all over now, so it is. You've played the dirty on me once too often.'

'I already told you, I was with Edna.' She had learned to lie handsomely. 'We were in her house all night.'

When she came closer, reaching up, he got another waft of her tainted breath, and it sickened him. 'I want the truth.' He pushed her away.

'I already told you – I went to see Edna.' Rita yawned. 'She was right glad to see me, Donny – she asked after you and the boy, and—'

'For God's sake, Rita, will ye stop!' Suddenly he had her gripped by the shoulders. For what seemed an age he looked her deep in the eyes, and what he had to say next shook her to the core. 'So, you went to see Edna, did you? And what would you say if I told you that *Edna Sedgwick died two days ago.*'

Throwing her aside, he looked at her with contempt. 'Fred called here earlier to tell us the news.' The bitterness in his voice was cutting. 'Poor Edna's been at death's door this past week, and you didn't even know, or care. In the two years since she moved away, you couldn't find the time to go and see her once – not even when you knew she'd been

12

ill. So I'll ask you again: who were you *really* with tonight?'

Genuinely shocked to hear the news about Edna, Rita knew her lies had found her out. A sob rose in her throat as she looked pleadingly at her husband.

He hardened his heart. 'I don't suppose you even know who you were with. Lifting your skirts to some stranger you might never see again. I dare say he thought you were a woman off the streets. And where did ye go this time, eh?' The big Irish man could have wept as he said the ugly words to his beautiful wife, who degraded them all with her actions. 'Down the alley, was it?' he persisted. 'Or did you find some filthy room at the back of a pub?'

When the awful truth of his words hit home, Rita's heart sank. So Edna had died and she didn't even know. She and Edie, as she had always called her, had been the best of friends, shared many a giggle as Rita did her neighbour's hair of an evening, accepting one of her homemade sponges in return. Innocent days, simple pleasures. Remorse settled on Rita like a cloud. What was she doing – to herself, to her family?

'Don't talk like that, Donny,' she pleaded. 'You know it's you I love.' She couldn't help what she did, but she *was* sorry. She was always sorry. 'I won't do it again, I prom–'

'No more promises!' Don Adams came to a decision that had been months, if not years, in the making. 'You're not the woman I married,' he told Rita. 'Sure, I don't know you any more. I don't want you anywhere near me. I don't want you in my bed, and I don't need you in my life.' Suddenly, though his heart ached with love for her, he felt as if a great weight had fallen from him. The endless torment was over. He strode towards the door.

There was something about his manner that frightened Rita; a kind of finality in his threat she had never heard before. He was talking of not wanting her, not needing her. Oh, but he'd said that before during their rows, many times. But this time he seemed different and she was afraid. He was her life, her one and only true love. She could never survive without him.

'First thing in the morning,' he went on, 'I'm away . . . me and the boy. As for you . . .' He turned, just for a moment, staring at her, seeing a stranger. 'It's finished, Rita. I've had enough. From now on, you can do what you like, because I don't give a sod!' Ignoring her wailing and her excuses, he left the room.

He was halfway up the stairs when he heard her scurrying after him. 'Don't leave me, Donny. I'll be good . . . Don't stop loving me!' She grabbed him by the trouser leg, pulling him back.

Frustrated, he swung round and snatched her to him. 'How can I ever let myself love you again?' he said, on a shuddering breath. 'Dear God, Rita! There was a time when I would have willingly died for you, I would have fought the world for you – and I *have*. But not any more.'

'Don't say that.' She saw her life ending right there. 'Please, Donny, don't forsake me.'

'What – you mean in the same way you've forsaken me?' There was a break in his voice. 'You've shamed us all. You've shamed me and the boy, and your father – the only one who would take us in when I lost my business and couldn't pay the rent.' He despaired. 'Time and again, I gave you a second chance. Like a fool, I thought you might come to your senses.'

Thrusting her away, he said harshly, 'Why do you need to be with these other men? Aren't I man enough for you? Don't I treat you well – provide for you, love you as much as any man *can* love his woman?'

He thought back to the time when their love was young. Oh, but it had been so wonderful – exciting and fulfilling for both of them. They had met fifteen years ago, when Joseph had come into the firm of carpenters where young Don, waiting for his call-up papers, was working. It was Rita's half-day off from her apprenticeship at the hairdresser's so her daddy had brought her along for a bit of company. The young Irishman and the seventeen-year-old girl had fallen for each other at first sight.

Don sighed deeply, all these thoughts rushing through his brain while he held his wife's body close to his, feeling her heart beating wildly against his own.

When had it all started to go wrong? he asked himself. Maybe if they had had more children . . . but it wasn't to be. More likely, it was when he'd gone overseas with the Army in 1942. A lot of people had changed during the war – and not for the better. Good marriages had gone bad all the time. He knew that Rita resented being stuck at home with baby Davie, and that bitch of a mother of hers, Marie, had encouraged her to go out drinking and dancing and doing God knows what.

It had all led up to this. And he couldn't take it any longer.

'What is it with you?' he asked brokenly. 'You're fortunate to have three people in your life who give you all the love they can, and yet time and again you throw it all back at us.'

Supporting her by the shoulders he looked at her sorry face, now swollen with the drink, her once pretty eyes drugged and empty, and the tears rolling down her face. And his heart broke. She looked so vulnerable, so sad, he wanted to press her to him, to hold her so tight and love her so much that she would never stray again, and for a moment, for one aching moment, he almost forgave her.

If only she would mend her ways, he thought. If only she

could be a proper wife and mother, like she used to be. But she couldn't. That woman had left them all behind long ago. 'No, Rita.' The sadness hardened to a kind of loathing. 'Sure, I can't forgive you any more.'

In that moment, when he turned from her, he felt incredibly lonely, and more lost, than he had ever been in his whole life. And yet he still loved her. He always would.

~

From the top of the stairs, Davie and his grandad saw and heard everything. 'Come away, boy.' The old man slid an arm round his grandson's shoulders. 'You don't need to listen to this.'

As his father walked up the stairs, a broken man, Davie looked into his eyes. 'You won't really leave, will you, Dad?' he asked. 'You can't leave us.'

'I'm not leaving *you*, son.' Davie was his pride and joy. The boy was conceived before Rita went bad, so he had no doubts about being the boy's real father. Moreover, Davie had a way with him that reminded Don of his own boyhood, in his manner and his thinking, and in that certain, determined look in his eyes. Yes, this boy was his own flesh and blood, and through the bad times when Rita neglected them both, it was Davie's strength and nearness that kept him sane.

He looked at the boy, with his shock of brown hair and his quiet dark eyes and he saw a man in the making.

Taking him by the shoulders, Don told him, 'You must go back to bed now. In the morning, you and me are away from these parts.' He glanced up at his father-in-law. 'I'm sorry, Dad. I've tried my best. She's your daughter. I hope to God you can talk some sense into her.'

The old man nodded. 'And if I can . . . will you come back?'

Don thought for a moment, before shaking his head. 'No.'

Through his anguish, the older man understood, though he did not underestimate the ordeal ahead of himself.

'No, Dad!' Davie had never been so afraid. 'She needs us. I'll talk to her . . . I'll make her see. She won't do it again, I promise.' He tried so hard to hold back the tears, but he was just a child and right then, in that moment, his whole world was falling apart.

Then, seeing how determined his father was, he clung to his grandad. 'Don't let him go!' he sobbed. 'Tell him, Grandad, tell him she'll be good and she won't hurt us any more. *Tell him*, Grandad!'

Suddenly Rita was there, shouting and yelling and going for Don with her claws outstretched. 'You cruel bastard! So you'd leave me, would you!' Wild-eyed and out of her mind, she went for him, hitting out, tearing into his flesh with her nails, and it was all he could do to defend himself and at the same time keep the pair of them from toppling down the stairs.

'ENOUGH!' Enraged, the old man threw the boy to safety, before lashing out at her with the back of his hand. 'To hell with you! You're no daughter of mine!'

When she stumbled and slid down the steps in an oddly graceful fashion, the boy lurched forward and ran down the steps after her. At the bottom, when he went to help her up, she threw him off. 'LEAVE ME!' she screamed.

Then, seeing the agony on his young face she was crippled with guilt. 'I'm sorry, son. It was my fault, all my fault.'

Struggling with her, he managed to sit her up. 'Where are you hurt, Mam?' His voice trembled with fear.

Composed now, she smiled resignedly. 'I'm not hurt. Give me a minute to get my breath.' She chucked him under the chin. 'He can go if he wants to. You can make your mammy a cup of tea and the two of us will talk until the sun comes up – what d'you say to that, eh?' She didn't tell him how her back felt as though it was broken in two, nor that her arm had bent beneath her at a comical angle, and the pain was excruciating. She felt strange. Drunk, yes. But there was something else, a frightening thing, as though all the life and fight had gone out of her in an instant.

Horrified, and riddled with guilt, Don ran down the stairs two at a time. 'For God's sake, Rita, are you mad?' He stretched out his arms to help her. 'What possessed you to start a fight at the top of the stairs like that? You could have been killed!'

Seeing her like that, he couldn't think straight. He loved her, hated her, needed to stay yet had to leave. The look on young Davie's face tore at his heart. Where did it all go wrong? Was it after Davie was born? Maybe she couldn't cope when money was tight and he found it difficult to get a job? Was the badness always in her? Or did he somehow cause it? But how could he blame himself? What did he do that was so wrong? And could he really stay here now and keep his sanity? Did he still love her enough?

'We don't need you!' Her spiteful voice pierced his thoughts. 'You bugger off!' She waved him away, angry with him, angry with herself. 'Go, if you like, and don't come back. Me and Davie can do well enough without you.'

For a long moment he looked at her, at the dark, lifeless hair that long ago shone like wet coal, and the eyes that were once alive and smiling but were now dull and empty. He recalled the years of happiness they had shared. But then he thought of the many times he had given in and gone another round and each time it ended in arguments. This time had been the worst, when her own father had lashed out and sent her hurtling down the stairs.

It was no good. He knew that their lives together were over and, though it was a wicked shame and he would have done anything for it not to be so, it was time to realise that they had no future together.

'I thought I told you to bugger off!' She kicked out at him, gritting her teeth at the pain that shot through her.

'All right, Rita.' The sigh came from his boots. 'But I'm taking the boy with me.' He knew if he left Davie with her, their son would only be taking on a thankless responsibility, one, which even he himself could no longer cope.

'I'm not coming with you! I'm staying with Mam!' The boy looked up, his eyes hard and accusing. 'If you won't take care of her, I will'

'No, son. She'll only break your heart. Whatever you do, and however often you beg her to give up her bad ways, she'll never change.'

'She will!' Tears stained his young face – angry, hopeless tears that tore his father's heart wide open.

Don shook his head. 'You're wrong, son. She'll carry on the same way, with the men, and the booze . . . and she'll make all kinds of excuses. She'll tell you lies until you start to believe them. She'll shame you, make you lose all your friends, until in the end you can't hold your head up. She'll make you feel life isn't worth living.'

'NO!' Seeking reassurance, Davie turned to his mammy. 'You won't, will you? You won't tell me lies and make me ashamed?'

She shook her head. 'No, son, I won't do that to you.' God forgive me, she thought. I should let him go – let them both go – and leave me to suffer the consequences. But she was weak, and frightened, and she couldn't bear to relinquish her child.

'And you won't go with all the men, will you, Mam?'

'No, son, I won't do that ever again.' False promises and lies! Too many lies, too often, until now she didn't know any other way.

~

For a while, the household settled to an uncomfortable calm. Davie helped his mammy into the sitting room where she slumped into a chair.

The sound of Don moving to and fro, packing his case in the bedroom overhead, could be heard. There was a buzzing behind Rita's eyes and her whole body was trembling; Davie sat holding her hand.

About a quarter of an hour after he had disappeared upstairs, Don came downstairs, carrying his case. Setting it down in the doorway, he paused to ask one more time: 'Can you change your ways, Rita? Can you be the woman you once were?'

Some last crazy impulse made her taunt him: 'For my son, yes. But not for *you*.'

He did not reply, but merely nodded. It was confirmation to him that the wife he knew was long ago lost to him. Looking at his son, he said quietly, 'I'll make us a good life, Davie. I want you to come with me. Will you do that for your daddy – will you?'

The boy shook his head stubbornly. Torn two ways, he knew that every word his father said about his mam was the truth. He knew how often she had lied; he sensed she was lying to him now. But still he couldn't bring himself to leave her.

'I have to stay here.' His head told him one thing; his heart another. And being a child who had not yet learned the way of life, he gave the only answer he could. 'Mam needs me.'

The man looked from the boy to the woman, and back again at the boy, who had a man's heart, and he felt an overwhelming sense of pride. His sorry eyes went across to his father-in-law who had come down stairs and was now hunched at the table looking as though the end of the world had come.

That was what Rita did, Don thought. She had sucked the life out of everyone here, and it was never her who paid the price. It seemed to give her some sort of twisted satisfaction. Well, as far as he was concerned, the spell that had held him captive for so long was well and truly broken.

'Don't blame yourself, Dad,' he told the old man. 'Don't let her destroy you! Joseph, do you hear what I'm saying?' He waited for the old man to look at him, and when he saw his quiet smile, he returned it with a nod of the head; reassured that they now understood each other.

Taking a piece of paper from his pocket, he handed it to the boy. 'If ever you need me,' he told Davie, 'contact this man. I was in the Army with him. He'll know how to find me.'

The boy took the paper and laid it on the ground. 'I don't want you to go,' he whispered, his uplifted gaze like a knife in the man's heart.

Without a word, Don flung his arms round his son. Choked with emotion, he embraced him for a long moment, before releasing him. 'I wish to God it could be different, son. But your mam's made her choice, and now I've made mine.' He held the boy at arm's length. 'I don't want to leave you behind. Please, Davie, get your things and come with me.'

The boy shook his head. *'I can't.'* Everything was disintegrating, and there was nothing he could do. 'Don't go, Dad. Please, please don't leave us.'

Don looked at his wife and saw the angry set of her mouth, and he knew his decision was right. 'I need to go, son,' he answered wisely, 'just as you need to stay.' With her lies, she had even won over his son. May God forgive her for this, for he could not.

'Don't forget,' he reminded Davie. 'I'll always be there for you, whenever you need me.'

For her too, he thought. Even though she had destroyed their lives, he would not cut off all ties with her. For the boy's sake, he thought. That brave, loyal boy who truly believed his mother would keep her word.

~

When the door closed quietly behind him, the boy clung to his mother. 'We don't need him,' she said tiredly. 'I've got you now. We'll be all right, Davie. We'll look after each other.'

He was startled and alarmed when she had one of her sudden mood-swings. 'Bastard!' Grabbing the cushion from behind her, she flung it across the room. 'He's a wicked man, Davie. All I did was have a drink and enjoy a good time – an' what's wrong with that, eh? What harm was I doing?'

Dipping into her handbag, she took out her packet of Park Drive and a miniature bottle of Booth's gin, and took a long swig from it. 'He'll miss me, you'll see,' she declared, lighting a ciggie. 'He'll miss his old Reet and he'll soon be back, you mark my words.'

'Shall I put that in the cupboard?' Reaching for the bottle,

Davie was disappointed when she snatched it out of his grasp, smacking his hand away.

'I can't let you do that,' she told him. 'I've had a bad shock. I need my strength.' On seeing his downcast face she tapped him more gently on the arm. 'Go and make your mammy a cup of tea, there's a good boy.' She was angry – angry at her husband for leaving; angry because she was in pain and nobody cared. And she was very angry, that a boy not yet fourteen should think he could tell her what to do. 'Go on, then. Shift yourself!' She sucked on the cigarette and blew out a long plume of smoke.

Concerned and afraid, Davie insisted. 'I don't want you to have any more of that.' He pointed to the bottle. 'Please, Mam, let me put it away.'

'DO AS YOU'RE BLOODY WELL TOLD!' she screeched, lashing out with the back of her hand.

With no choice, Davie left her there and went into the kitchen, where he stood for a time by the pot sink, his fists clenched, head hanging low and his eyes closed. He felt rejected, with a deep-down sadness that was like a physical hurt. He had to ask himself, how many times had his daddy felt the same way he felt now?

In the next room, Rita remained slumped in the chair; she was hurting badly from the fall, but she didn't want pity. She wanted her life the way it had been. With Donny gone and her father turned against her, all she had left was Davie, but he was just a boy. How could he look after her? The time was fast approaching when she would get the sack from the salon, as she kept erratic hours – and what would become of them then?

When the sadness threatened to overwhelm her, she fumed at how cruel Don had been in leaving. Then there was her father . . . her own flesh and blood. If Joseph had been any kind of a man, he would have given Donny a bloody good hiding. 'You let him desert me, Dad, and I'll never forgive you for that.' Her shrill voice sailed through to the kitchen where he was now leaning against the pot sink, his pained eyes staring out at the long dawn.

Still a strong, capable man, despite long years in the foundry, and a heart battered by bad memories, the old man heard her relentless abuse and knew exactly how he had spawned such a degraded creature. She was made from the same mould as her mother.

Moving to sit by the kitchen fire, and adding a bit of coal to it, he ran his hands through his thinning hair, trying hard to turn a deaf ear to his daughter's rantings. His son-in-law's departure had cut Joseph to the quick. Yet it only reinforced his belief that what he was about to do *had* to be done – because if he relented now, she would be the death of him – and what of the boy? Someone had to give her a jolt – make her realise what she was doing, get her off the road she was travelling. Sometimes you had to be cruel to be kind, and that was the way of it.

She'll blame everybody else, like she always does, he thought crossly. She's done the damage to herself and torn this family apart, and God help us, she still hasn't learned. His mind flew to his wife, dead of TB these ten years, and although he still grieved for her, his life was peaceful now, after long years of torment due to her faithless ways.

His mind was made up. No one else should have to suffer like that. Davie would come off worst . . . that fine young lad who would love his mother whatever she did. Good or bad, he would only ever see Rita as his adored mammy.

In the next room, the vicious tirade was unending. The whole world was against her, Rita raved. Her father was bloody useless and besides, he had always been a thorn in her side, lecturing her about the rights and wrongs of parent-hood, and how she should be a better wife and think of others. What a bloody cheek – when he himself had been unable to control his own wife, who used to disappear for weeks at a time with her latest boyfriend. Rita had hated and loved her mother in equal measure.

For one dizzy moment, Rita thought she could smell her mother's perfume – Attar of Roses – mixed with something far more heady, a scent that the girl later recognised as gin, now her own favourite tipple.

Thinking of her mother now filled her with rage. 'GO ON, THEN!' she bellowed. 'YOU CAN ALL CLEAR OFF – AND SEE IF I CARE!' Taking hold of the poker, she smashed it into the grate. Then the bottle was thrown, spill-ing its contents across the half-moon rug. Struggling to her feet and sobbing with the effort, she clung to the standard lamp.

Laughing wildly now, she saw the boy watching her, white with fear. When he darted forward to take hold of her, she drew back her hand and slapped him hard across the mouth, gasping when the blood trickled down the side of his chin. And oh, the way he was looking at her . . . as though she was the Devil incarnate. Taking the heavy poker, she laid into the mantel-piece, sending the clock and ornaments shattering across the floor.

Then she was crying. 'I'm sorry, son,' she gabbled. 'It's the drink and whose fault is that, eh? Your dad's left me and you know I didn't deserve that.' She swayed, her hand at her mouth, feeling sick as a dog.

'*I want you out of this house.*'

Joseph had come into the room and had witnessed everything.

'What? You can't do that!' Fear marbled her voice. 'Look, Dad, I'm sorry. It was an accident. I've always had a temper, you know that. I'll put it right. I won't do it again. Look, here!' Reaching into her purse, she shook out a handful of silver coins. 'I've got money, I'll get you some new ornaments and—'

'I want nothing from you!' The old man stood tall. 'I don't care about the damned ornament, but you can never replace that clock. It was precious to me – a gift from your mother – all I had left of her.' His gaze fell to the money in her hand. 'Earn that, did you?' His voice thickened with disgust. 'Half an hour in the alley, was it? Well, you can keep your filthy money, you trollop, because I don't want it. What I want is you, out of this house . . . NOW!'

'But Grandad!' The boy came once more to her defence. 'Mam's already said she won't do it again.' Inside he was in turmoil, but he had to be strong for her.

Seeing Davie's downcast face, and knowing how he must be hurting, the old man said kindly, 'Not you, son. I don't want you gone from here. It's *her* I want out of my house. She's had her chances time and again, and each time she's promised to change her ways.' He slowly shook his head. 'It's like your grandmother, all over again. My Marie was just the same, God rest her soul. You see, my boy, I just can't go through it all again. We've allus given in, but not this time. I'm too old and tired to take it any more. It'll be the death of me.'

'But you can't send her away!' The boy panicked. 'Where will she go?'

'Back to the streets where she belongs.'

'That's fine.' Rita struggled to stand. Holding on to the back of the chair, she told them both, 'I'm a proud woman, and I don't stay where I'm not wanted. Help me, Davie. I know where we can go, me and you. We don't need this hovel. We can do better, you and me!'

'Not you, Davie!' Just as Don had pleaded with Davie, so now did the old man. 'She's not worth it. Let her go and find her own sort. You stay here.' He lowered his voice. 'Please, Davie, don't go with her. Stay here, with me.' Truth was, at this moment in time, he needed the boy more than ever.

But the boy's answer was the same as before. 'I can't leave her, she's my mam. We'll take care of each other.'

'So, you mean to desert me as well, do you?'

'I have to look after her.'

'No, Davie!' Somehow, he had to stop the boy from going. 'You're not listening to what I'm saying. Your father tried to warn you, and now I'm begging you . . . *don't go with her.* She'll take you down the road to ruin. Stay here with me . . . please.'

The boy was steadfast. 'No, Grandad. She needs me.'

'What? And you don't think *I* need you?'

The boy shook his head. 'Not as much as Mam does.'

'Right!' Desperation heightened to anger. 'Go on then! If that's what you want, you can bugger off the pair of you, out of my house and out of my life. And I pray to God I never see either of you again!'

For a long, shocked moment, the boy looked him in the eye, not wanting to believe what he'd just heard.

'Come on, sweetheart.' Rita stubbed out her cigarette and tugged at his sleeve. 'We don't need him. We don't need anybody. You and me, we'll be fine on our own.'

The old man lingered a moment longer, silently pleading with Davie to see sense and change his mind. But he knew how loyal the boy was, and he had seen how his father leaving had made him all the more protective of his mother. And he realised he had lost to her, yet again.

Without a word, he went upstairs, where he sat on the edge of his bed, saddened at what his own daughter had become, and worried about Davie: there was no telling where Rita might take him. God only knew where it would all end.

A few minutes later, Davie came upstairs to collect a few things. He paused at the old man's door. 'I'm sorry, Grandad,' he said.

But there was no forgiveness in the old man's heart, only fear for the boy, and hatred for his daughter. 'Go away,' he grunted.

'I don't want to leave like this.'

For a fleeting moment, the old man almost relented; for the boy's sake, perhaps he should give her another chance. But how many chances would she need before she saw what she was doing to herself and others? *No!* The mixture of old and new anger was still burning, and he deliberately turned away, his heart like a lead weight inside him.

After a while he heard the boy move away, heard his footsteps dragging down the stairs – and it was all he could do not to go after him and catch him in his arms and tell him they would have a home here for as long as they wanted.

But he had been through it all so many times with her, just as he had with her mother, and each time she sank deeper into the swamp. Then there was the gossip and the sly looks in the street. You couldn't go on like it, and she wouldn't change her ways. Why couldn't Davie see her for what she was?

The slam of the front door shattered his thoughts. Slowly and heavily, he went downstairs to the front room and looked out of the window. As he watched them go down the street, his daughter limping – from the drink, he assumed – he could hardly see them for the tears scalding his eyes.

'Look at you,' he murmured. 'A mere scrap of a lad, and yet you take it all in your stride.'

He saw how the woman leaned her weight on the boy, and how he took it, like the little man he was. 'God help you, Davie,' he muttered. 'She'll use you and then she'll desert you.'

He was bone-tired, and his heart full of sorrow.

When they were out of sight, he left the window and went back to sit down, holding the broken bits of the clock, the tears he'd managed to hold back now flowing down his face. It was all such a mess. What a dreadful night's work this had been. 'I'm sorry, Davie. I *had* to send her away,' he whispered. 'I've done my best, but I'm too old and frail to put up with her bad ways.'

He glanced out at the waking skies and he prayed. 'Dear God, keep them both safe. Let her realise the harm she's done. And keep young Davie under Your divine protection.' He hoped the Almighty was listening.

The rage inside him was easing and now, with the coming of the dawn, there was another feeling, a sense of horror and shame. What in God's name had he been thinking of, to do such a terrible thing?

Suddenly he was out of the front door and shouting for them to come back. 'We'll give it another go! We'll work at it! We'll try again!' His lonely voice echoed along the early-morning street.

He paused to get his breath, then he hurried up to the top of Derwent Street and round the corner, and he called yet again, but the pair were gone, out of sight, out of his life, just as he'd ordered them to do. And it was more than he could bear.

~

Wearily, he made his way back. In his troubled heart he feared for them both.

But even Joseph could not have foreseen the shocking sequence of events that were about to unfold.

CHAPTER THREE

O N LEAVING THE house, Davie did not look back. With his mother leaning heavily on his arm and stumbling at every turn, he threaded his way through the familiar streets of Blackburn, his heart frozen with shock at the night's events and his mind swamped with all manner of torment.

He suspected his grandfather had been watching from the window, and he knew how bad he must be feeling. From past experience and having been on the receiving end of the old man's kindness countless times, he knew the calibre of the man, knew how it went against Joseph's loving nature, to have thrown his own daughter out onto the streets. Davie readily forgave his grandfather. He did not want Joseph to feel guilty, because he had always done right by Rita. Over the years, he had done right by them all.

Twice the old man had taken the whole family in; once, a few years back, when a little business Don had set up after the war, had gone bust, and then again, more recently, when Rita had squandered the rent money and they were evicted. Most of her own wages and tips went on drink and cigarettes, these days.

Through it all, Joseph had supported them. No man could

have done more for his family. And who could blame him for turning her away? The neverending fights and arguments had tired the old chap to the bone.

'Where are we going, Mam?' The boy knew she was hurt and he was anxious. 'Maybe we should go straight to Doctor Arnold's house? He'll be up by now.'

But Rita would have none of it. 'I'm not going to no bloody quack!' she retorted. 'We'll pay a call on a good friend of mine. Jack will help us, I know he will.' She chuckled fruitily. 'Lord knows, I've done *him* enough favours in the past.'

She instructed her son to head for Penny Street. 'Third house on the right – number six, as I recall.' She gave a deep sigh. Her whole body was becoming numb. 'Once we've rested, we'll get away from Blackburn Town and never come back.' There was hatred in her voice. 'If I never see that old bugger, or your father again, it'll be too soon.'

As they went slowly towards Penny Street, her footsteps dragging, she slurred, 'My Jack's an obliging fellow. He'll not turn us away.'

But turn them away he did.

When they got to number six, the lights were out. 'Jack!' Rita's voice sliced the morning air. 'It's me . . . Rita.' Banging on the door, she yelled through the letterbox, 'The old sod's chucked me out on the streets and I've nowhere to go. Let me in, Jack! I've got my boy with me. I'm hurt. I need to rest . . . a few days, that's all. Then I'll be gone and I'll not bother you again.'

Suddenly, the door was flung open. 'For chrissake, you silly cow, will you shut up!' Sleepy-eyed and unshaven, the man was bare to the waist. 'What the devil d'you think you're doing, banging on my door this time of the morning! Clear off and bother somebody else. I want no truck with you!'

'*Send the old slag on her way!*' a woman instructed, shouting from the upper reaches of the house. 'If you don't, I will!' Her harsh mutterings could be clearly heard. 'Thought I wouldn't find out about the pair of you, did you? Worse than the dogs in the street, you are, carrying on the minute I'm away to see my poor sick sister ... *Now I'm warning you, get rid of her, or I swear I'll have her eyes out!*'

Half-closing the door, the man called Jack lowered his voice. 'Jesus! She'll be scrambling her clothes on to come and face yer,' he warned Rita. 'She can be a right bastard when the mood takes her. Soonever she got back from her sister's, the neighbours couldn't wait to tell her about us.' He shifted his attention to Davie. 'Sorry, son, but it's been murder, trying to stop her from coming after your mam. You'd best take her away, and the quicker the better. There's nothing for you here.'

When Rita refused to leave, the man rounded on her with a vengeance. 'For God's sake, Rita, take a look at yourself. What the hell are you thinking of, wandering the streets at this time of a Saturday morning with this young lad in tow? Have you no shame at all?' He felt guilty. 'Aw, look, I know we had a bit of a fling, but you mean nowt to me ... I told you that from the start. We had our fun and now it's over.'

'She'd best not be there when I get down the stairs!' His wife's angry voice sailed from the rafters.

Afraid of the consequences if his wife should suddenly burst in on them, he hastily pushed Davie aside. 'Get her away from here. Go on! Make yourselves scarce, the pair of you.' Desperate to be rid of them, he slammed shut the door.

As they went away, Davie and his mam could hear the argument raging inside. 'Let go of me! She needs a damned good leathering, and so do you! I can't believe you took that dirty slut to our bed the minute my back was turned. Christ Almighty! She must have been with every bloke in Blackburn.'

Davie tried to block his ears, but the voices followed them down Penny Street. The postman stopped to listen, curtains twitched, and a dog in a nearby house began to bark.

'If I had any sense I'd pack my bags and be out that bloody door!' The wife raved on. 'Another feather in her cap, that's all you are. She's trash, that Rita Adams. She'll flutter her eyelashes and the blokes'll gladly tip up the price of a drink for a knee-trembler wi' that one down a dark alley. Fools, the lot of 'em! An' I thought you were different, our Jack, but you're just like the rest of 'em, a dirty dog sniffin' after a bitch on heat.' There was a muffled cry before she was shouting again, 'Let go of me. I'll have the skin off her back when I catch up with her.'

'I was sure he'd help us.' Rita sank onto the nearest door-step, her face deathly white and her limbs all atremble. 'I really thought I meant summat to him.' Out of all the men she had slept with, Jack had been the special one, or so she thought. He had really listened to her, bought her small gifts, seemed to be her friend.

Gathering her strength, and holding onto her son, she carefully hoisted herself up. 'Make for the church, love.' Her head on his shoulder, she urged him on. 'They'll not turn us away.' The smallest of smiles crept over her features. 'We'll rest there for a while, and then we'll think what to do.'

'It's too far, Mam.' Davie could see how that tumble down the stairs had really hurt her, and now this humiliating rejection seemed to have taken the heart out of her altogether. He was ashamed of what she had become, could have sat down and cried at the pity of it all. How she could have given herself to that married man Jack, when she had his own lovely father, Don, was a mystery to him.

'What about your other friends?' he asked kindly. 'Couldn't we go to one of them?'

'I lied, son,' she confessed. Unable to look him in the eye, she hung her head. 'There are no friends. There's just you and me.' She gave a wistful smile. 'Nobody wanted to know me when I was your age.' She shrugged her shoulders. 'Even at school, I always found it difficult to make friends.'

In that revealing moment, she saw herself as she really was, that quiet, lonely girl from a troubled background, the daughter of an unstable woman, and now, herself, a wife who time and again had cheated on a good man and brought trouble to her own doorstep.

'You mustn't blame your grandad for throwing us out,' she told Davie. 'You hardly knew your grandma, but she was a difficult woman.' She shuddered as the rain predicted by the weather-forecaster began to fall. 'Your poor grandad had a lot to put up with, all those years ago, and when he saw me going the same way as *her*, he couldn't bear it.' Shame flooded her soul. How could she have let herself follow blindly in her mother's footsteps?

She raised her gaze and looked at her son, made to bear a heavier burden than young shoulders should ever carry. 'I'm sorry, Davie . . .' She could say no more, for now she was sobbing, all the pent-up grief of the years being released, and he was holding her, and she felt more comforted than she had ever been in her whole life.

'It's all right, Mam,' he murmured. 'I'll take care of you now.'

Together they went along Addison Street and through the empty marketplace, and now as they cut along towards Church Lane, he asked her if she was all right. 'I'll be fine,' she answered brightly. 'You'll see, once I've had a proper rest and time to sort it all out, I'll be off again like a spring lamb, and you won't be able to keep up with me.' But her sight was growing dim, and the numbness was creeping up her body.

Not altogether reassured, Davie crooked his arm round her waist and pressed on, the rain soaking through their clothes and slowing down their progress.

~

They were entering the spinney when one of Rita's dragging feet got caught in the bracken; as she lurched forward, Davie was taken with her, rolling down the incline and into a shallow ditch, where she made no move to get up. 'I'm hurt,' she gasped. 'You'll have to leave me, Davie. Go and get help . . . Hurry, Davie. Get help.'

At first he tried to lift her, to get her to safety and out of the cold and rain. But the more he tried, the harder she fought.

'No, my lovely. Leave me be.' She had the strangest feeling; the pain had gone and she was in another place. But her son was here, and he was frightened. She roused herself. 'Get help, Davie,' she repeated. 'Quickly!' And then she was silent and he was frantic, and as he struggled to raise her into his arms, she gave a shudder that chilled his heart. In that moment, he was mortally afraid.

Laying her gently down, he took off his coat and draped it over her. 'Stay still, Mam,' he sobbed. 'I'll run as fast as I can, and I'll be back before you know it.' Ducking his head against the rain, he ran up the bank, down through the spinney and out into the lane.

As he ran, a kind of dread stole over him, making him weep unashamedly. Desperate for help, he hurriedly wiped away the tears with the cuff of his shirt-sleeve. 'Can anyone hear me? My mother's hurt. We need help!' Yelling at the top of his voice, he could hear the animals scuttling in fright all about him, and when, breathless, he broke through the trees, he paused to search both ways along the winding lane, but there was no one to be seen.

Taking to his heels, he began running, suddenly pausing again when he thought he heard a sound in the distance. For a minute he couldn't make it out, but then he recognised the clippety-clop of horse's hooves, and to his immense relief, saw the familiar milk-cart rounding the bend. 'Tom? Tom, stop. It's me, Davie!'

Drawing on the last of his strength, he raced towards the cart, his heart at bursting point as he prayed to God above for his mammy to be all right.

'What the devil's going on, lad?' Tom drew the cart to a halt, while Davie was bent double, gasping and crying, and telling Tom how he needed help and that his mammy was badly hurt.

'All right, I hear you.' He patted the seat beside him. 'Climb up here. You can tell me about it as we go.'

Dishevelled and in a state of panic, Davie wasn't making too much sense as he clambered onto the wagon. 'We went to the man and he told us to clear off, and there was nowhere else to go and we were making for the church . . . then she fell and I couldn't get her up. Hurry, Tom. Please hurry!'

'Calm down, lad, take it easy. We'll see she's all right.' Sending the horse into a trot, the little man kept his eyes on the ruts and dips in the lane. 'What's happened?' He needed to know. 'It's your mam you say? Last time I saw her, she was heading home, a bit the worse for wear, but fine enough. She should have been back hours ago. What in God's name were you doing out here, the pair of you?'

But Davie wasn't listening. He was hellbent on getting to

his mother, and realising this, Tom concentrated on the way ahead. 'How far?'

'Here!' Suddenly they were at the point where Davie had broken through from the woods. 'She's down there.'

Before the horse had slowed down, Davie was already jumping off the side of the wagon. 'We have to get her home as soon as we can,' he gabbled. 'Grandad threw us out but he'll take her back now, I know he will.' That said, he was away and into the woods, calling Tom's name as he went. 'Quick, Tom, this way! She's in here.'

From some way behind, Tom followed, his mind full of questions. How had this come to pass? Davie said his grandad had thrown them out. Dear mother of God, why would Joseph do such a thing? But then again, hadn't it been on the cards, and wouldn't Tom himself have been tempted to do the same thing if *his* daughter had turned out to be such a bad lot . . . giving herself to all and sundry and making a mockery of her hardworking husband. Any other man would have shown her the door long ago.

As he hurried after the boy, Tom decided that the questions would have to wait. There were more important things to attend to now. Poor Rita was hurt and she needed help. For now, that was all that mattered.

~

A few minutes later, his face torn by overhanging branches and his ankles sore where the thorns and bracken had proved a hindrance, Tom was shocked to see Davie's mammy lying crumpled in a shallow ditch. 'Step aside, lad.' Falling to his knees beside her in the wet leaves, he took hold of her hand, taken aback by how cold she was. In the slimmest shaft of light filtering through the umbrella of trees, he saw how pale and still she lay. 'We'd best get her out quick.' His quiet, decisive manner gave Davie a sense of calm, and hope. But not peace of mind. Too much had happened this night. Too many bad memories would follow him, and he thought he would never again know peace of mind.

Between the two of them, they set about getting her up, and when she cried out, they stopped to give her a moment. 'Shh now. It's all right,' Tom reassured her. 'You're safe. We've got you.'

All the same, it was a slow and painful operation, but at last they had her out and up on her feet, albeit unsteadily. 'Crook your arm under hers,' Tom instructed. 'She's in no fit state to take her own weight, and I can't get the wagon down here, so we'll have to carry her out the best we can.'

As they took her step by careful step towards the lane, she dragged her feet and murmured incoherently, and as the horse snickered, sensing something amiss, they lifted her gently onto the bench set into the back of the wagon. 'There's a rug under the driver's seat. Fetch it, will you, lad?' Tom grunted.

While Davie went to get the rug, Tom made Rita comfortable. 'It's no good taking her back to your grandad's house,' he said quietly. 'It's the Infirmary she needs.'

Davie gave no reply. Instead he sat beside his mother while Tom tucked the blanket around her. When she began shivering uncontrollably, Davie held her closer, trying to warm her, intent on making her safe.

'Right, that should do it.' Tom nodded. 'Keep her as still as you can,' he said as he climbed down. 'We don't know what injury she suffered when she fell.'

Thankful that soon they would be on their way, Davie glanced down, astonished to see his mother looking straight back at him. The rain had stopped, and in the brightness of a new day, her eyes were incredibly beautiful. 'I'm sorry, Davie,' she said. 'You're a good boy.' She then gave him a look of absolute love. 'And I have been a bad mother. A bad . . . mother. Don't hate . . .' Her voice faded away.

Davie felt her convulse in his arms, and then she was still, her wide eyes still turned on him, and in that moment he knew. But he could not accept the truth, and in his overwhelming sorrow, he screamed out for Tom to help her. 'HURRY! WE HAVE TO GO NOW! Hurry . . . oh, please hurry, Tom.' The rending sobs tore through him and he couldn't speak any more. Instead, he held her close, the scalding tears running down his face and onto hers. 'Don't go, Mam. Don't leave me . . .'

Tom drew the milk-cart to a halt and turned round. He saw, and it broke his heart.

'She's gone, lad.' Inching close, he took hold of the boy's arm. 'There's nothing we can do for her now.' Tremulously reaching out, he placed his fingers over the dead woman's sightless eyes and closed them. 'Come away, son,' he urged softly. 'It's out of our hands now. We'll take your mammy where they'll look after her. They'll know what to do . . .'

Suddenly startled when the boy leaped off the wagon and sped into the woods, Tom called after him, 'No, Davie! Come back, lad!'

Time and again, Tom called after him, but Davie was quickly gone, and Tom was afraid this might be the last he would ever see of him. 'COME HOME TO THE FARM WHEN YOU'RE READY.' He cupped his hands over his mouth. 'MY HOME IS YOURS. I'LL BE THERE WHENEVER YOU NEED ME, DAVIE.' His voice fell. 'I'll always be here for you, son. You must never forget that.'

With a heavy heart he returned to cover Rita's face. 'The lad's tekking it hard,' he murmured as he wound her into the blanket. 'It don't matter what badness you've done, lady, he can't help but love you.' He made the sign of the cross over her, and prayed that she might find a kind of peace elsewhere, for she had found none on this earth.

As he climbed into the seat, he stole another glance into the trees, but there was no sign of Davie, and no reply when he called his name. Licking his wounds, poor little bugger! Oh, but he'll be back, God willing. You'll see, when he's all cried out, he'll turn up at the farm, looking for his friends. And we'll be there to help him through.

Drawing a long deep breath through his nose, he held it for a while, before the words eased out on the crest of a sigh. 'He'll come back.' He turned his head to look on the dark shadow that lay in the back of his cart. 'I can only promise you, that when the lad does come home, we'll take care of him.'

Davie had a special place in his own family's affections. Since toddlers, Davie and Tom's own daughter, Judy, had played together, sharing every experience that youngsters share – learning to ride the ponies; chasing the rabbits into the hedgerows; laughing at secret nothings that no mere adult can ever understand, and as they grew and blossomed so did their friendship until they were virtually inseparable.

'Come home, son,' he murmured. 'Come home, where you belong.'

Slowly shaking his head in despair, he clicked the old horse on; this time at a sedate and dignified pace.

After all, with the way things were, there was no hurry now.

CHAPTER FOUR

'LOOK, MAM, HE'S home. Dad's home!'

Tom's daughter Judy had been watching for him these past two hours. Now, as she saw the old milk-cart turn the bend in the lane, she took to her heels and ran to open the gate of Three Mills Farm. Her dad was back, and she needed a hug.

Tom saw her coming and his heart burst with pride. How had he come to father such a lovely creature? Small-boned, with long willowing sunkissed hair and eyes soft and grey as a dove, she was like a rainbow after rain to him.

Right from when she was a toddler, Judy had been behind him everywhere he went, and now at the age of twelve, it was the same; whether he was milking the cows or stacking the hay, she was there. Most days, before and after school, she helped him in the fields or the barn, and when he was painting the house, she went before him, washing the picture-rails inside or the window-sills outside, or holding the ladder in case it slipped and he broke his worthless neck.

And when she wasn't helping him or her mammy, she was running across the valley with the local dogs at her heels. Other times she would sit quietly with the fishermen at the river, thrilled when they caught a fish and put it back, and sad at heart if they took it home to cook it.

From a tender age, Judy was drawn to the water at every turn; Tom and Beth daren't let her out of their sight in case she slipped into the river. So, when she was little more than a year old, they took her into the water and, as they expected, she loved it. Swimming had come naturally to her, until she was as much at home in the water as the fish themselves. 'Should've been born with a tail and fins,' her parents joked.

When she wasn't swimming or watching the fishermen, the little girl was running down the towpath, racing the barges as they made their lazy way alongside. She was kind and curious, totally fearless, and wherever she went, her smile went with her. Although her parents grieved that no other babbies had come along after her, to keep her company, they idolised their precious gift of a daughter.

'Where've you been?' When the cart was slowed down, she scrambled up. 'We've been looking out for you.' Wrapping her arms about his neck, she gave her dad a long, affectionate cuddle. 'Mam says you've been down the pub having a crafty pint.'

'Does she now?'

'Yes. She said you'd be talking and drinking and forget the time.'

He laughed at that. 'Another time she might well have been right, but not today, lass.'

'So, where were you then, Daddy?'

His smile fell away; his mind full of images he would rather not recall. 'I didn't get the milk-round done as quickly as I might have. Y'see, I were held up with summat entirely unexpected and it threw me right out of the routine.' What with finding Davie's mammy and taking her to the undertakers, then the police quizzing him, and afterwards serving his loyal customers and finishing the deliveries before going back to look for Davie, the day had sped by without him realising.

'You promised to take me fishing. Did you forget?'

'No, lass, I didn't forget. Like I said, I had urgent business to attend to.'

'What kind of business?' Clicking the horse on, she let it amble towards the stable.

'It's not summat I want to talk about just now, our Judy.'

Seeing his downcast face, she drew the horse to a halt. 'Has something bad happened?'

'Get along with you now,' he urged tiredly. 'It's been a long day and I've a need to talk with your mammy.'

Something in the tremor of his voice made her keep her silence. She wanted to know what had upset him so, but for now she could wait. And so she clicked the horse on again. 'Mammy's got the dinner all ready,' she promised. 'It's your favourite – steak and onion pie.'

Normally he would have smacked his lips at that, but not today. Today, Judy sensed he had something deeper on his mind. She realised it must be something very serious, otherwise he would have told her.

For now though, she wisely left him to his thoughts and concentrated on the way ahead.

~

Just as Judy promised, Beth had the meal all ready to serve. 'Late again, Tom Makepeace!' She tutted and fussed, and wrapping the tea-towel round her hands she took the meat pie from the oven. 'It's a wonder this pie isn't burned to a cinder, and as for the vegetables, I wouldn't be at all surprised if they've turned to pulp.' She might have continued with her good-natured scolding, but his thoughtful mood made her cautious. 'What 'ave you got to say for yerself then?'

'Not now, love.' Heartsore and weary to the bone, Tom

washed his hands at the sink. After drying them on the towel hanging from the range, he dropped himself into the arm-chair. 'I'm beaten, lass,' he muttered. 'It's been the worst day.'

Making the pie safe on the table, she wiped her hands on her pinnie and came to him. 'Whatever's wrong, Tom?' She knew her man all too well, and she knew there was some-thing troubling him deeply.

He glanced anxiously across the room at Judy who had returned from the stable. 'Come here, lass. There's summat you both need to know.' He recalled how deeply devoted to Davie she was, and he feared the effect his news might have on her.

With trepidation, Judy came to her mother and the two of them waited for Tom to explain. 'It's bad news,' he warned grimly. 'I'm sorry, but there's no easy way to tell it.'

And so he told it straight; how Davie's mam had come home drunk and abusive once too often, and of how, after too long being patient and forgiving, her husband had walked out.

'Oh, no!' Beth was shocked. 'What about the boy and his grandfather? Couldn't they persuade him to stay and give it one last try – for Davie's sake if not for theirs?'

'Is Davie all right?' Judy's anxious question turned Tom's heart.

'Hear me out, lass. I'm not done yet.' He enveloped them both in the sweep of his gaze.

Instinctively clinging to her mother, Judy fell silent; and Tom continued.

Firstly he answered Beth's question. 'From what I could gather, Don didn't want to leave without Davie, but the boy decided to stay behind, with his mammy.' He paused and sighed, then quietly continued. 'It seems the grandfather had come to the end of his tether, too. There was a row of sorts, and after Don left, the old man threw Rita out, bag and baggage.'

He quickly imparted how the boy had decided to go with his mother and look after her as best he could, though his grandad didn't much care for that idea. In fact, old Joseph was so upset that he told them both to sling their hooks and good riddance, more or less.

And then he relayed the worst news of all.

'I was driving past the woods during my round when I heard young Davie shouting for help. His mammy had suffered a fall and hurt herself badly. By the time I got to her, she were drifting in and out of consciousness.' He recalled the sad sight of her, and cleared his throat. All day long, he had wanted to make his way back home to Three Mills Farm, and confide the news to his wife, for it was she he always turned to when in times of trouble. But events had taken over and, as it turned out, there was little opportunity.

He described how he had followed the boy and how, when he came to Rita, he could tell straightaway that she was in desperate need of hospital treatment.

'We managed to get her as far as the cart and lay her down, when she drew her last breath. It were a matter of minutes, that's all, and she was lost to us. And there was nothing either of us could do to save her.' He blew his nose loudly.

'What about Davie!' Shocked at the news, Judy's immediate thoughts were for her friend. 'Where is he? Why didn't you bring him home with you, Dad?'

Tom shook his head. This was going to be hard. 'Seeing his mammy go like that, it was a terrible thing for the lad to witness, especially after seeing his father walk out and then his grandfather turn against his own flesh and blood. He held her close until she'd said her last words to him, then before I knew it, he'd leaped off the cart and was running into the forest, as if old Nick hisself was after him. Oh, I called for the lad time and again . . . told him to come along of us and that we'd take

47

care of him, but I haven't seen him since. I had to get his mammy away, don't you see? There was the police to deal with and all sorts. Afterwards, I went back, and I scoured the woods, calling and shouting and begging him to come home with me. But there was neither sound nor sight of him.'

'Poor little chap.' Beth was appalled by the news. 'What will become of him, d'you think? Where will he go? How will he survive – a lad of his tender years?'

Judy was distraught. 'We've got to go back! We have to find him. Please, Dad, we can't just leave him.'

'He's not there any more, child. I searched and called and there was nothing. He'll be long gone by now.'

Tom recalled how brave Davie had been and how, through a bad sequence of events and none of them his doing, he had been made a man overnight. 'He'll get through this,' he said decidedly. 'Young though he is, the lad's already come through one bad shock after another. I'm sure he'll think long and hard about which way to go. Don't worry, lass. Happen when he's had time to consider everything, he'll come back of his own accord.' In reassuring his daughter, he failed to reassure himself, however, although he was certain of one thing. 'Davie knows he'll be safe enough with us.'

But Judy couldn't let it drop. 'When you've eaten and rested, will you come back and see if he's there?' she pleaded. 'He might have been hiding when you called for him. He might not have wanted to talk – perhaps he wasn't ready then, but he'll listen to me, I know he will. Please, Daddy, please come back and try again.'

Knowing how determined she could be, Tom worried that she might take matters into her own hands. Deciding it was wiser to pacify her, and being anxious himself as to Davie's whereabouts, he relented.

'All right, lass. Once I've had a sit-down and a bite to

eat, we'll go and search for him. But first we'll call at his grandfather's house. The police will already have been to see him, to inform him about poor Rita's death. I told them everything I knew and they said to leave it with them.' At the back of his mind he wondered. 'It wouldn't surprise me if we didn't find young Davie there. After all, when you think about it, where else would he go, but home?'

'I wouldn't count on it,' Beth warned. 'It was his grandfather who threw them out, wasn't it? So, for all we know, Davie might be blaming him for what happened to his mammy.'

'Davie would never do that!' Judy sprang immediately to his defence. 'Davie thinks the world of him. It was his grandad who took them all in when they lost their home and everything.'

'The lass is right,' Tom agreed. 'Young Davie is not the sort to lay the blame where it doesn't belong. The truth is, Rita brought it all on herself, God help her.'

At that point, Beth served the meal and they sat at the table, each thinking of Davie and praying that he would be all right, out there, God knows where, grieving for his mammy and with no one to comfort him.

After a few mouthfuls of the pie, Tom pushed back his plate. 'Sorry, love, I haven't the stomach for it,' he told his wife. 'If we're going to search for the lad, we'd best get off now. But first we'll stop off at Derwent Street – check on Joe, and see if the boy has turned up there, before we go off on a wild-goose chase round the woods.'

Beth and Judy readily agreed. They put on their coats and stout shoes and waited at the door while Tom got the Morris Minor out of the barn. 'I didn't think it would start,' he said as they climbed in. 'I can't recall the last time I had this motor-car on the road.'

'Hmh!' Beth gave him a wry glance. 'I'm not surprised,

because whenever you take me and Judy out, it's always on the blessed cart! I'm surprised the motor-car hasn't seized up altogether,' she grumbled. 'Then we'd have turned up at Joseph's house in that smelly old cart. And what would folks think, eh?'

Going down the lane at a steady pace, with the engine spitting and complaining, they sat quiet for a while, each engrossed in their own thoughts, thinking of Rita and the way things had turned out. Mostly their thoughts were for young Davie, because in truth he was the one who had suffered most in this tragedy.

Judy was certain that Davie would not hold his grandfather responsible for his mammy's death. For one agonising moment, she put herself in Davie's shoes. He had loved his grandfather; and it must have come as a shock when Joseph turned against him. She also knew that, although he would forgive him, he would never be enticed back, even if his grandfather changed his mind. If Davie was anything at all, he was proud, and fiercely independent.

When they turned the corner into Derwent Street, they were not surprised to see the neighbours emerging from Joseph's house. 'The news has spread,' Tom declared respectfully. 'I expect he's had folks in and out since the police came to see him.'

As they got out of the car, one or two of the neighbours nodded to them, and they nodded back. They didn't speak. What was there to say?

'He'll need all the support he can get,' Beth replied. 'Rita's reputation was known throughout Blackburn. She lost respect and many friends through her degrading antics. Time and again, she brought trouble to the door; first to poor Don, and then to her own father, even though he had been so good to her.'

'You're right, lass,' Tom remarked under his breath. 'She managed to heap shame on the only three people who truly loved her.'

'Hmh! There'll be them as say she deserved what she got.' Beth gave a long, shivering sigh. 'All the same, I can't help but feel saddened by what's happened to her, so young an' all.'

'I know what you're saying, lass.' Tom felt the same. 'But now she's gone, it's the old man we have to concern ourselves with, and the boy especially. Folks round here will no doubt keep an eye on Joseph but the boy has no one. He's out there somewhere, God knows where, without a friend to talk to, and no roof over his head.' He glanced sideways, seeking reassurance from this wise woman of his. 'It's a bad thing, don't you think, lass?'

'It is,' Beth concurred. 'But you did the best you could, and a body can do no more.' She touched him softly on the arm. 'Don't fret yourself, Tom. You can't be responsible for what's happened; none of us can. All we can do is hope the boy is safe . . . wherever he might be.'

'We have to find him.' Judy was determined. 'If he's not here, we have to search and search, and not give up until we can take him home with us.' She had visions of Davie curled up somewhere, alone and shivering, and frightened. She longed to be with him, to give him consolation. Like her daddy had said just now, it was a 'bad thing'.

They found the old man seated in the parlour, his head bent low to his knees and his hands clasped over his head, as though trying to fend off some vicious attacker. Rocking backwards and forwards, he didn't even hear them come in. 'Joseph?' Tom laid his hand on the man's shoulder. 'It's me, Tom, and my family. We've come to see how you are.'

It was a moment before Joseph looked up. They had been prepared for him to be deeply shocked by the news of what had happened to his daughter and grandson, but even so, they were taken aback by the stricken look in his eyes. His face was marked with angry red streaks where he'd scraped his fingernails down his cheeks, and the skin hung in curious folds over his features, as though the substance had been sucked away from underneath. 'Oh, Tom.' He began rocking again. 'What in God's name have I done? Rita, my own flesh and blood. I sent her away, thinking she might get herself in order and come back to live a decent life, and now she can't *ever* come back.'

Plump teardrops pushed over his eyelids and ran down his face. 'My daughter was a wilful woman, ran right off the rails at times, but she didn't deserve to be struck down. Dear God, she had so much to live for, so much to make up!' He rolled his eyes to heaven. 'I turned her out on the streets . . . her and the boy with her. May God forgive me. I should lie in hell for what I did!'

When he began sobbing, Beth whispered to Judy to help her in the kitchen. 'Stay with him,' she told Tom, 'while me and Judy see if we can't make us all a cup of tea.' That was typical of Beth. A cup of tea would put so many things right. But not this time, she thought. Not this time.

'Will Joseph be all right?' Never having witnessed such grief, the young girl was feeling scared.

Beth held her for a moment, taking comfort from the girl's warm body against her own. 'It'll be terrible hard for him,' she said emotionally, 'but he's got friends. And maybe when Davie's come to terms with what's happened, he might be of a mind to make it up with his grandad, and find his way home.'

'No, Mam. Davie will never come back here, not now.' Judy Makepeace was unsure about a lot of things in her young life, but of this she was 100 per cent certain. Wherever Davie went, it would be far away from the house in Derwent Street.

CHAPTER FIVE

WHILE HIS WOMENFOLK busied themselves in the kitchen, Tom tried to get the grieving man to say something, but Joseph had fallen into such a deep silence, he seemed unaware that anyone else was there with him.

When, a few moments later, Beth and her daughter returned with a pot of piping hot tea, Tom revealed his concerns. 'I don't know what else to do,' he said in a low voice. 'I've tried everything to coax him into talking, but all he does is rock backwards and forwards, his eyes fixed in a stare to the floor. It's like he doesn't even know I'm here.'

As was her way, Beth took matters into her own hands. Setting the tray down on the table, she knelt in front of the old man. 'Joseph?' Her voice was silky soft. 'Joseph, it's Beth . . . look at me, dear.'

When he seemed not to have heard, but instead kept rocking back and forth, back and forth, faster and faster, she raised her hands to his face and made him be still. 'JOSEPH! It's me, Beth. I've made you a hot drink. I want you to take it, and then we'll sit and talk, you, me and Tom. Will you do that for me?'

Now, as he turned away, she persevered. 'You, me and Tom,' she repeated. 'The three of us like old friends, just

53

drinking and talking, and helping each other. Do you think you can do that for me?'

Joseph looked into her eyes and saw the kindness there. But it seemed an age before he answered, and then it was just the slightest nod.

Beth smiled at him. 'All right, that's what we'll do then, eh? The three of us . . . talking and drinking, and helping each other. Yes! That's what we'll do.' Greatly relieved, she could see he was coming back to her, but he was still in shock, and in her brightest voice she teased, 'D'you know what, Joseph? I don't know about you, but if you've got any old brandy hidden away, I wouldn't mind just the teeniest drop in my cup of tea.'

She gave a deliberate sigh. 'Oh, but I don't suppose you've got any such thing, eh? So we'll just have to go without, won't we?' Beth knew full well that Joseph always kept a bottle of brandy in the cupboard. 'It would have been nice, though, don't you think? A drop of the good stuff to warm our cockles?'

Slowly but surely, a glimmer of understanding crept over Joseph's sorry features. 'You artful devil, Beth Makepeace,' he said in a croaky voice. 'You know exactly where it is.'

He rallied round. 'You can fetch it, if you like.'

$\sim$

The brandy did the trick. By the time Joseph had drunk three cups of tea with the 'teeniest' drop in it to give it a kick, he was beginning to talk freely, though the sadness was all too evident. 'I've got you to thank for looking after her,' he told Tom. 'God only knows what might have happened if you hadn't heard Davie calling from the woods. Oh, and where is the lad?' He grabbed hold of Beth's hand. 'Where's my Davie? Did you know, I threw him out . . . lost my temper. I couldn't see owt but what she'd done, and he was willing to go with her and leave me on my own.'

His voice trembled. 'I turned against him – lost my head. He'll never forgive me, will he, eh? Surely he knew I'd change my mind the minute he was out the door, and I did! I went after him, but he were gone. They were both gone, and it was too late. Too late.' His voice broke, and for a moment he was quiet, then when he was composed, he looked at Tom. 'Why doesn't he come home, Tom? He needs me . . . we need each other. Where in God's name is he? What's going to become of him?'

'I don't know,' Tom answered truthfully. 'Happen he'll think things over, and when he's come to terms with what happened out there in the woods, he'll turn his mind to you, and he'll know you didn't mean it when you spoke harshly to him.'

Unconvinced, Joseph's next question was directed at Judy. 'I reckon you know him better than any of us, lass. Will he come home, d'you think? When he's cried himself out, will he make his way back to his old grandad? What d'you reckon, pet?'

The girl said cautiously, 'Maybe.' Davie loved his grandad, she knew that for sure. But what she didn't know was how deeply he had been affected by what had happened to his mammy. And for his grandad to turn against him was un- thinkable. Davie would be taking it hard, she knew that well enough, but she revealed nothing of her thoughts. What would be the point? She'd only upset the old chap further.

'It's a lot for the lad to deal with.' Joseph was thinking aloud now. 'First his mammy comes home drunker than I've ever seen her, then there's this terrible fight and his daddy walks out, and as for me . . .' He took another swig of his tea. 'I threw him and his mammy out onto the streets. And that was *after* I had damn near pushed her down the stairs. She must have hurt herself badly but she didn't say owt, you see? Oh, my Rita. My stubborn little girl!' He sobbed anew. 'What kind of monster am I?' He took another swig. 'The lad saw his mammy die out there in the woods. God Almighty! I wouldn't blame him if he never wanted to set eyes on me again.'

For a split second there was an uncomfortable silence, before Judy flung her arms round the old man's neck, saying passionately, 'He loves you! Davie would never think bad of you – never!'

Startled by her sudden show of affection, the old man looked up to see her crying. 'Oh, lass,' he said huskily. 'It's no wonder our Davie took you for a friend. You're a caring, kind young thing, and if you say he'll forgive me, then I'll take your word for it.' If only he could turn back time. If only . . . 'I'm hoping our Davie won't forsake me, any more than I could forsake him,' he wept, 'and I hope you're right, bonnie lass, when you say he'll come home. But I was harsh on him . . . on both of 'em. I turned my back on the lad when he needed me most. Happen he'll never forget that. Happen he'll never forgive me for it neither.'

Taking another swig of his tea, and for the first time, Joseph told them about his late wife, Marie. 'My wife was a real beauty, just like Rita,' he said fondly. 'Unfortunately, she started the boozing soon after having Rita. An' then our second child – baby Matty, we called him – died in his sleep one night, and there was no consolin' her. Poor little Matty – an' now Rita, too. Both me childer dead an' gone.' He gave a long, shuddering sigh. 'At first I thought I could help my Marie to be rid of the booze and the men, and live a decent life with me and with our beautiful daughter Rita. But for all my efforts, it didn't happen. Lord knows how hard I tried to change her. Many a man would have walked out on her, but I couldn't do it. I loved her, y'see, and when she was sober she had a mischievous and lovable nature, just like Rita.'

As the Makepeace family listened respectfully, Joseph paused. The bad memories had, by now, brought a scowl to his face. 'Oh, but when she'd been at the booze, by God, Marie was the devil incarnate.'

He explained how Rita seemed, in time, to have naturally followed in her mother's footsteps. 'I can't blame the lass for what she became,' he said regretfully. 'She grew up adoring her mammy, living in her shadow, seeing her kind and loving one minute, and in the next how violent and cruel she was.'

He took a moment to remember. 'I should have left her then,' he said gruffly, 'but I loved her too much. I kept on hoping she'd come to her senses for the child's sake, but she never did. And when the TB took her off when she was still in her prime, it seemed like my Rita took on her mother's character . . . up and happy one minute, then down and shameless the next.'

He spoke of his son-in-law. 'She were just a kid when she met Don, and oh, I was that pleased for her. I thought, here's a good man, hardworking and decent. They will be happy together, not like Marie and me. Aye, he loved her as much as any man can love a woman, but when she went wrong, he couldn't change her, any more than I could change her mammy.'

He hunched his shoulders. 'I don't blame him for walking out, and nor should anyone else. If I'd walked out, all them years back, I might have saved Rita from copying her mammy's ways. In truth, Rita became worse than my Marie ever was. She went with men openly. She even did her dirty work with blokes who worked alongside Don at the factory.' Growing emotional, he took a moment to compose himself. 'There were snide remarks and cruel taunts, and my son-in-law would retaliate, like any other normal man would. But then there'd be fights, and he'd lose his job again and there would be no money coming in.

'They say you shouldn't speak ill of the . . .' Unable to say the word, he closed his eyes, then quickly opened them again, and now his voice was stronger. 'It pains me to say it, especially now she's gone . . . but my daughter was a slut of the worst kind. There was such badness in her – almost as though her mammy had passed it on with a vengeance. And good man that he was, Don stuck with her, till his patience was tried too far. I knew it had to happen, and somehow I reckon I also knew that one day it would end in tragedy. She was like a runaway train, my Rita, heading straight towards a cliff-edge.'

'Have you any idea where Don was headed?' Tom wondered if the man had been informed of the situation – his wife dead, and his son missing.

'No idea at all.' Joseph had been thinking along the same lines. 'When he left here, it was on the spur of the minute. He was in such a state, I don't reckon he knew where he was headed himself. Although, he did give a slip of paper to young Davie, with someone's name on it. The boy must have gone off with it.'

'Well, Don will have to be told, won't he?' Tom queried. 'He'll need to know what's happened. His wife is beyond his help now, but the boy needs his father.'

'Yes, you're right.' Sad at heart and not knowing which way to turn, Joseph revealed, 'I told the police the whole story, from beginning to end, and they promised to do what they could to find him.'

'But they're not really duty bound to do so, are they?' Beth intervened.

Joseph agreed. 'Happen they've done their duty in telling me about the accident, and mebbe it's up to me to do the rest.'

'But what about Davie?' Judy persisted. 'The police will have to find him, won't they?'

'I hope so, lass. After all, he's only just coming up to fourteen. I told them how much he thought of his mammy and how badly this whole business would have affected him. Let's hope they find him, eh? Aye, let's hope they do. As for him going after his dad, he doesn't have a penny piece on him, and the mood our Don was in when he left, it wouldn't surprise me if he hasn't already left the country – jumped on a ship at the docks mebbe, and gone to sea. They can always use a good carpenter on board ship.'

Tom was interested. 'Was that what he hankered after?' he asked. 'Making for foreign parts?'

'Yes. Right from when he went abroad with the Army he had an appetite to see the world. Said as how he'd like to join that scheme to emigrate to Australia . . . with all those wide open spaces where a man could breathe. Then again, he might have gone back to Ireland. I understand he has an old aunt there, although, as I recall, he hasn't seen her in years.'

He yawned, and said sleepily, 'Aye, happen that's where he'll be headed . . . Australia, or Ireland. One or the other, I'll be bound.'

All talked out and exhausted from grief and the effects of the brandy, he began to nod off, and when he closed his eyes, Judy whispered to her mammy, 'Can we go and look for Davie now?'

Carefully, without waking him, Tom helped the old man onto the sofa, where he promptly fell into a deep sleep. Judy ran to get a blanket and Beth laid it gently over him, and when they were certain he would be safe, they left the place, securing the door behind them.

Beth tapped at the house next door to let them know that Joseph was sleeping soundly. 'Will you keep an ear out for any disturbance, Patsy?' Beth asked the young woman who opened the door. She knew her vaguely from her visits here to collect Judy or pick up Davie.

'I'll be glad to.' With her lank hair tied back with a grubby ribbon, the woman appeared to have her hands full with a multitude of children clamouring round her ankles. 'It's no bother at all,' she assured them.

Thanking her, Beth explained, 'He should be fine now, but I thought it best to let you know he's on his own.'

Patsy agreed to look in on him within the hour. 'Don gave me a spare key last winter, when the old man went down with pneumonia. There were times when Rita wasn't . . . well, you know what I mean.' A look of repulsion flickered across her features. 'The boy needed looking after when his dad was at work. I just popped in from time to time to make sure everything was all right. Don't worry, I'll keep an eye on old Joseph,' she promised.

Beth was relieved. 'Thank you so much.'

As she turned to walk away, she saw what she took to be the woman's son, standing further back in the passageway. Tall and well-built, with dark eyes and longish dark hair, he was a good-looking boy. 'This is my son, Lenny.' To his embarrassment, the woman pushed him forwards. 'He's a handy sort.'

Thinking that was an odd thing to say, Beth smiled and nodded, and he nodded back, and as she went away Beth heard his mother reprimanding him for not keeping the children out of her road while she dealt with the visitor at the door. However, satisfied that Patsy and her husband Ron would take care of Davie's grandfather, Beth returned to the car. 'Apparently Don gave them a key when Joseph was ill last winter,' she said, getting in beside Tom.

'Very wise too,' Tom declared, starting the engine. 'What with Rita boozed out of her mind half the time and trawling the streets for men the other half, I expect he was concerned that someone should keep an ear out for the boy and his grandad.'

Feeling guilty, he addressed himself to Judy. 'We'll be on our way now, lass.' Waiting for Beth to settle herself in the seat, he then pulled away from the kerb. 'I know we could have gone back to search for Davie first, but I was worried about Joseph. I knew it would come as a shock when the police arrived to see him, and I just needed to make sure he was all right. And there was always the chance that Davie might be there.'

Judy understood. 'It's what Davie would have wanted,' she said. 'He must be worried about his grandad too.'

'Well, at least old Joe is resting now.' Tom gave his wife a sideways wink. 'After the brandy your mammy plied down him, I dare say he'll sleep till the cows come home. Matter of fact, if the Almighty Himself came knocking at the door, I don't reckon Joseph would hear a thing.'

~

Some short time later they arrived at the spot where Davie had run out onto the lane. 'This is it.' Pulling over to the verge, Tom got out of the car to collect a torch from the boot.

'You'll need to stay close,' he warned, 'but like I say, I don't think we'll find him. I went round and round these woods, calling out his name and looking into every nook and cranny, to no avail. So don't go expecting miracles.'

Judy was the first out of the car and away. 'Come back here, child!' Startled, Beth brought her to heel. 'I know you're keen to find him – we all are – but I don't want you wandering off into them woods by yourself. You're to stay close at all times.' Though anxious for Davie, the fear for her own flesh and blood was instinctively stronger.

They spent almost two hours searching. Tom led them to the spot where he'd found Rita, and from there they covered a wider circle, calling out Davie's name and leaving no stone unturned. But at the end of it, they were disappointed.

On the way back to the lane, Tom had his arm round his daughter's shoulders. 'You're not to be too disheartened, lass,' he said kindly. 'He'll turn up when he's ready.' Though he gave Beth a look that said different, because after what young Davie had been through, he doubted whether the boy would ever again be seen round these parts.

~

Judy was quiet all the way home. From when they left the spot where Tom had first seen Davie, her troubled gaze was strained to catch a glimpse of him, through the lamplit streets, along the darkened lanes, down by the river and alongside the canal, and now as they drew ever closer to home, her heart sank like a lead weight inside her. The thought of never seeing Davie again was unbearable.

Tom drew up at the battered five-bar gate with its hand-painted sign reading *Three Mills Farm*. He got out, opened up, drove the old Morris Minor through, then got out and closed the gate again. He patted the bonnet approvingly, then went to change into his wellies and old coat to check on the animals.

Beth made her and Judy a mug of cocoa. 'There y'are, lass.' She placed the drink and a slab of fruit cake in front of Judy, who was sitting at the table, looking forlorn. 'Come on now, love,' Beth said. 'Davie's a strong, sensible young man. Wherever he is, I'm sure you'll find he'll come to no harm. Now, drink your cocoa, there's a good girl, then you must get yourself ready for bed. It's been a long day today, and we've a hard day ahead of us tomorrow, what with having to help round up the sheep and a load of other jobs. Your daddy will need all the help he can get.'

They had just finished their cocoa as Tom walked in the door. 'That blessed fox is about again!' he grumbled. 'It's already had two o' my chickens . . . best layers an' all! By! I nearly had him just now.' He shook his fist in the air. 'If I ever get close enough, he'll feel the heat of my shotgun up his backside an' no mistake!'

Red-faced from the chase he fell into a chair, thanking Beth when she handed him a freshly made cup of milky cocoa.

'Get that down you,' she advised with a chuckle. 'Chasing after foxes, in the dark an' all, it's a wonder you didn't go head over heels in the dungheap. What's more, you're too slow an' heavy in the belly to go running after foxes and the like. They must be sittin' laughin' at you, Tom Makepeace.'

'What's that, woman?' he asked indignantly. 'Are you saying I could do with losing some weight?' He took a huge bite of his cake.

Beth cocked a snook. 'If the cap fits,' she said wryly with a mischevious glint in her eye.

Judy was the first to go to bed. 'Good night, my beauty.' Tom hated seeing her so quiet; it wasn't in her nature.

'Good night, love.' Beth held her a moment longer. 'Remember what I said . . . you're not to fret about young Davie. He'll be all right, you mark my words.' All the same, she too was worried. He was only a boy, after all.

'Good night, Mam . . . Dad.' Judy kissed them both and headed off upstairs.

~

An hour or so later, lying in bed, her mind filled with thoughts of Davie, Judy heard her parents going into their room. 'Ssh! Pick your feet up, man,' Beth chastised her husband when he tripped over the mat. 'We don't want to wake the lass.'

Judy smiled when she heard her father arguing with Beth as to why she'd put a fringed mat on top of the landing. 'Every blummen night, I trip over that damned mat.'

'Will you give over with your moaning!' Beth retaliated. 'That mat's been sat there these past six years, and nobody but you has tripped over it yet.'

With Davie strong in her mind, Judy couldn't sleep. Climbing out of bed, she went across the room to perch on the windowseat. She would sit here for an age when her thoughts were troubled, and they had never been more troubled than they were tonight. Of all the forces of Nature, it was the sky that seemed to soothe and embrace her; day and night she never ceased to marvel at its changing moods. There was something especially beautiful about the autumn sky tonight; moody and magical, bathed in soft moonlight, it seemed more haunting than she could ever remember.

But then, Judy Makepeace lived within Nature itself; she walked it and felt it, and her every breath was tuned into it. Her only close female friend, a girl of her own age called

Annie, would laugh at her, saying, like Tom and Beth did, that she should have been born a bird or a fish.

While other girls were already dreaming of dating boys and dressing up for Saturday afternoon at the pictures, Judy had never really craved those things. It wasn't that she didn't enjoy them, because she did. Like any other adolescent girl, she liked to look in the shop windows at the latest fashions, and when the boys in the picture-house started flirting and teasing, she would giggle in response. She could give as good as she got, though she would blush to her roots if a boy tried to kiss her.

Once, when her mam and dad took her to a local barn dance, Annie's older brother Philip had kissed her full on the lips. She had wiped her mouth afterwards, when he wasn't looking. He made her feel scared, somehow, but she put it down to her own shyness and inexperience.

Life was good, and there were so many things she wanted to do. But always in the forefront of her mind was Davie Adams. If she didn't have him in her life, nothing would be the same. It was Davie she turned to whenever she needed advice, and it was Davie with whom she loved to walk along the river, or across the fields, or when they were bringing in the hay and it was all hands to the task. He was her hero, and she loved him.

Her love for Davie and the love she felt for her parents was not the same. The strength of love was the same, but it was as though they lived in different parts of her heart. The part where Davie lived had always been there, but now there was something else, a deeper feeling, and she did not know how to deal with it.

There had been moments when she thought she might talk about it to Annie, but something stopped her. She didn't think the other girl would understand.

Sitting cross-legged on the windowseat, her thoughts shifted to other things. She sat for a time, her eyes closed and her mind going over the day and, after a while, with the sleep beginning to draw her down, she stretched her limbs and eased herself off the seat.

As she stood up to pull the curtains closed, something alerted her, some quick movement down in the yard. Leaning towards the window, she stared out into the darkness, but there was nothing to be seen, except a lone cat prowling the area for a mate.

Turning away, she crossed the room, stumbled into bed and drew the blankets over her. In a matter of minutes she was fast asleep.

In the other room, having talked themselves into exhaustion, Beth and Tom also were asleep.

It had been a worrying day for them all.

CHAPTER SIX

SETTLING DOWN IN the barn, Davie thought he had
caught a glimpse of someone at the window. He wondered if it might be Judy, but he daren't draw her attention.
If he was discovered here, he knew how Tom would want to
return him to his grandad, when all he needed was to hide
in a quiet place where he could be left alone to think things
through.

At first he had thought that maybe he might go and see
Tom and thank him for what he had done. But then, as he
got closer to the farm, he decided against it. Sometimes,
when a kindness was so big between two people who understood each other, saying thanks was far too small and insig-
nificant.

After searching around, he found the old Tilly lamp hanging above the window; another search in the semi-darkness
revealed a box of matches hidden on the shelf alongside.
Aware that the light might be seen from the house, he took
the lamp and the matches, then from a safe corner, he lit
the lamp, keeping the flame low and shielded, while he
made himself a bed in the hay.

'Don't you worry.' Peeping over the stable door, the old
shire horse had been watching him with big curious eyes.

'I'm not moving in on you.' Davie stroked its long mane. 'I just need somewhere to bed down for the night. I need to think, and plan. I have to know where I'm going from here.' His voice and spirit dropped. 'I feel hopelessly lost,' he confided. 'I miss my grandad, and I need to be near Judy and her family. But if I stayed I might hear bad talk about my mam, and I wouldn't like that at all.'

At the thought of his mother being slandered, a wave of anger rushed through him. 'I know she did bad things, and I know she caused a lot of unhappiness for the family, but if I hear anybody calling her names, I swear I'll kill 'em!' Tears filled his eyes. 'I'll never know why she did those terrible things . . . shamin' us an' all. But I don't think she meant to hurt us. I don't think she could help herself.'

Gulping back the tears, he quickly composed himself. 'I need to look for my dad.' He gave a great heave of a sigh. 'But where do I start?' he asked the wide-eyed creature. 'And if I was to find him, would he thank me for it?'

Deep down he desperately needed to locate his father and be reassured. At the same time he believed his father would rather be left to find his own way through what had been a difficult time for all of them, added to which, Davie was reluctant to burden his father with the knowledge of the terrible sequence of events following his sad departure.

Because of the angry, wounding words born out of despair, Davie was sensible enough to realise that it would take time and distance for everyone to reflect on what was said and done. He could not know how long that would take, or whether things would ever be better for this unfortunate family. But one thing he did know now, and he voiced it in a whisper. 'No! I can't go after my dad, and I won't go back. Like it or not, I'm on my own.'

Sighing deeply, he leaned his head on the railing. 'I'll

need to be away first light,' he muttered, 'I'm not sure which direction to take or where I'm headed, or what I'll do when I get there. All I know is I can't stay round these parts any longer.'

Worn by recent events and the crippling loss of his parents, he felt the tiredness laying heavy on him. But try as he might, he couldn't sleep. He shifted, and turned, fretting about the whereabouts of his father, and agonising over his grandad, knowing that he, too, must be feeling the pain of losing his family in such a devastating way. But what about me, Davie mused. Should he leave as planned and never come back? What should he do? Which way should he go? Sleep was elusive. The nightmare was real. Tormented and unsure, and so weary he could hardly breathe, he finally drifted into a shallow, troubled sleep.

The touch of a hand startled him awake. And when he instinctively clenched his fist to lash out, she closed her small hand around his fingers. 'I knew you were here,' she whispered. 'I went to sleep thinking it might have been you I saw running across the yard.'

'Judy!' In the soft glow from the lamp, he saw her face and was reassured. He smiled up at her. 'You gave me a fright. I thought I was being attacked. I was just about to tackle you.'

Judy's voice was soft as gossamer. 'I'm sorry, Davie. I didn't mean to scare you.'

Somewhat refreshed by the two hours or more that he'd slept, Davie was thrilled to see her. 'Your parents . . . still asleep, are they?'

She laughed. 'I could hear Daddy snoring as I came out.'

'That's good. I don't want them to find me.' Quickly, he tucked his shirt into his trousers and scrambling to his feet, he took her by the shoulders and drew her up to face him.

'I'm glad you're here,' he told her. 'I thought I saw you at the bedroom window but I wasn't sure whether you saw me. I daren't come too near the house in case your mam or dad saw me . . . I was afraid if they did, they might take me back to Grandad.' His voice fell. 'Did you know he told me to get out and never come back.'

Judy assured him, 'Your grandad is sorry that he threw you out. He wants to make amends.'

Davie was relieved at that. 'I'm glad,' he answered, 'but I can't go back yet, maybe never. What he did – well, it made me think.'

'What do you mean?'

'What I mean is, it made me realise how hard it must have been for him since we moved back in. All this time he's had more than enough to deal with, and he's been good to all of us, but now he deserves time to himself.' The boy felt somehow responsible, because of what his mother had done to the family. 'It's best if I were to get away from these parts altogether. Make a life for myself somewhere else.'

Yet, even now he wasn't sure if he could make it happen, or even if he was doing the right thing.

Sensing the doubt in his voice, Judy hoped she might change his mind. 'Your grandad was upset, Davie. The police had been and everything.'

Davie hung his head. 'So, you know what happened to my mam?'

'Yes, Davie, I know.' He was holding her two hands in his, and the warm, deep down pleasure was like nothing she had ever known.

'Did you know she came home drunk, there was a terrible row and my dad walked out?' The memory of it all was like a knife in his heart.

Judy nodded, 'He told us everything.'

70

Davie was silent for a minute. Letting go of her hands, he walked to where the horse was peering at them. He nuzzled his face against the animal's head, then, turning to Judy, he asked, 'Was Grandad told about what happened in the woods . . . with my mam?'

'Yes, Davie, he was told.'

'And is he all right, I mean . . . do *you* think I should go back?'

'That's up to you, Davie. You have to do what *you* think is right.'

He gave it a moment's thought, 'How is he?'

'He was in a poor state when we got there, but after a while, he seemed to be taking it well enough, I think. The neighbours had been in, and the woman next door is going to look in every now and then.'

'Is she . . . safe . . . my mam?' A great sadness welled up in him.

'Yes.' The girl tried to recall what her father had said. 'Daddy took her to the Infirmary, and they looked after her.'

Davie nodded his head. 'And Grandad?' Almost unconsciously he dropped himself onto a haybale. 'Will he be all right, do you think?'

Judy sat herself beside him, and slipping her hand into his, she told him honestly, 'He wants you home, Davie. He's really worried about you.'

When Davie remained silent, so did Judy. She didn't know what else to say, and she didn't know how to ease his pain. 'I'm sure he'll be all right, Davie. Like you say, he's been through a lot, and maybe you're right. Maybe he does need some time to himself.' Another thought reluctantly crossed her mind. 'Maybe you do too?'

'Right from when I was little, I thought my parents would

split up one day.' He kept his gaze down, so she wouldn't see the tears clouding his eyes. 'When Mam came home drunk in the early hours and Dad was waiting for her, they'd argue and he would always threaten to leave, but she always won him round in the end.' He gave a painful little smile. 'But not this time, eh?'

For a long moment he was silent, thinking about the past, wondering where his parents were at that moment; one gone away because he found it impossible to stay any longer, and the other gone to . . . ? When he was small and somebody died, they always told him that the person had gone to Heaven. Is that where she was . . . in Heaven? But she'd been bad, and they said nobody went to Heaven if they were bad . . .

'Davie?' Judy's voice broke through his thoughts. 'Davie, look at me.'

Raising his gaze, he looked at her.

'Your mammy's safe now. You do believe that . . . don't you?'

He nodded, bowed his head and thought about his mother, how pretty she once was, and how full of life. He recalled the times she made him laugh; the many occasions when she playfully chased him round the table, pretending to be the wicked witch, and other times, quieter and deeper, when she would tell him how she and his daddy truly believed that one day he would be a man to make them all proud.

'Davie?'

He looked up at her, his eyes dark with sadness.

'You're so quiet. What are you thinking?'

Not trusting himself to speak, he shrugged his shoulders, then when he did eventually answer, his voice was choked with emotion. 'It's all gone,' he murmured brokenly. 'My family, all the things I know . . . all gone. How can anything ever be the same again.' For the first time, the emotions tore through, and the tears broke away and now there was no controlling them.

Without a word, Judy wrapped her arms round him, and he clung to her, and after a while, when the sobbing was spent, and he drew away, she told him, 'You must try and get some sleep, Davie.' It was only then that she realised. 'Have you had anything to eat?'

He shook his head.

'Stay here.' She looked him in the eye. 'I'll just be a minute.'

As she turned to leave, he suggested, 'I won't go back to Grandad. But I could write a note, if you wouldn't mind taking it to him?'

Judy readily agreed. She liked the idea. At least this way, he wouldn't go away without making contact.

He watched her run across the yard. She looked so small and vulnerable in the fading moonlight; like his life he thought, like his whole world. But Judy was strong, and she was still here, still caring. And, as always, he considered himself fortunate in having such a good and loyal friend.

It wasn't too long before she was back. 'I brought you these.' Setting down the tray she pointed out the cheese and ham sandwiches, and the array of fresh fruit. 'For you to take with you,' she said. 'In case it's a while before your next meal.' She dug into her skirt pocket and bringing out a package, she told him, 'There's a pen and paper, and some stamps.' A shyness marbled her voice. 'So now there's no excuse. You can write and always tell me where you are and what you're doing.'

'I will, Judy. I'll write to you from wherever I am, I promise.' Cradling her face in his hands, he bent and kissed her on the forehead. 'You're special to me, do you know that?'

She was grateful that he did not see her blush bright pink. 'Eat up,' she said. 'And then you'd best get some rest.'

Together they sat and talked some more while he wolfed down the snack and drank the milk. Afterwards, he urged her to go back to her own bed.

'If I do, you won't sneak away before I wake, will you?' she asked.

He smiled. 'It all depends on what time you get up, lazy bones. I'll need to be away before your dad comes out.'

The girl was adamant. 'I'll be back long before that,' she said. 'Just don't go without seeing me.'

'I won't.'

'Promise?'

'I promise.'

When she suddenly threw her arms round him and kissed him full on the mouth, he was taken aback. 'What was that for?'

'I don't know. Because I'll miss you.'

'I'll miss you too,' he answered with sincerity. 'Nobody could ever have a better friend than you.' He looked into her eyes and thought how pretty they were. 'To tell you the truth, I don't know what I'll do without you.'

'Don't go, Davie.' She seized the moment. 'Please stay. Daddy will give you work and he'll pay you well. We have a spare bedroom, and you'll be able to visit your grandad whenever you like.'

For one tempting moment, Davie considered the idea. Familiarity. Safety. And friendship. The answer to all his problems. Living with the Makepeaces would be wonderful. But then he shook his head and said, 'No.' He knew it was not the answer. A clean break, a new life, and being responsible for his own actions, that was what he must aim for. 'I need to prove myself,' he explained. 'I know it's the right thing to do.'

'How can it be right? Where will you go? How will you manage?' When her tears fell, he wiped them away with the tip of his finger. 'If you go now, you won't ever come back.'

'I won't be gone forever,' he answered. 'And anyway, I've already said that I'll write to you, and every day I'll think of you.'

'Will you, Davie? Every day? Will you really?' Her smile brightened his world.

He laughed. 'I will, yes! Every single day.'

'And what will you think, Davie?'

'What will I think?' He wound his two arms round her and taking her to himself, he told her earnestly, 'I'll think of what you might be doing, and then I'll picture you every-where we've been together . . . climbing the oak tree down by the river or swimming in the canal, and I'll see you about the farm, cradling the newborn lambs in your arms and teasing the ferret out of its cage.'

Holding her away from him, he smiled down on her. 'More than anything, I'll always wonder how somebody like me ever deserved a wonderful friend like you.'

Judy had been thrilled to hear him say how he would always see her in his mind's eye. But when he called her his 'wonderful friend', it was as though her bubble of joy was cruelly burst. 'Is that what I am to you, Davie?' she asked tremulously. 'A friend?'

He nodded. 'The best friend of all,' he answered sincerely. 'If I was to travel the world, I would never find a better friend than you, Judy.'

She hid her disappointment. She wanted to be much more than a friend to Davie. In fact, although he didn't know it, and she was only just becoming aware of it, Judy Makepeace had already given her tender young heart to Davie Adams. There was as much pain and confusion in this secret giving, as there was pleasure.

'You'll need to be warm,' she told him hurriedly. 'It gets really cold in the barn at night.' Going to the hook on the wall, she took down a blanket and handed it to him. 'It smells a bit horsey, but he's only had it on his back the once . . . he doesn't like wearing blankets.'

Davie took it. 'Thanks. Now you go back to the house . . . go on. I'll be fine.'

A moment later, as she was leaving, Judy whispered, 'Get some sleep, Davie. And don't worry – I'll be back before my parents wake.'

She didn't want to leave him. She wanted to lie down beside him and feel his strong arms round her. Her feelings were all mixed up. She loved him for being here – but was angry with him for leaving her; most of all, she was saddened by the idea of waking up and finding him gone, and knowing she might never see him again.

Then she remembered his promise to write and to think of her, and her heart was warmed.

She got as far as the house when she wondered whether he was asleep yet. If he was intending to go right away to find work and somewhere to live, he might have to travel miles before he was settled. He needed his sleep. Oh, but what if he woke up, feeling sad and panicky, and she wasn't there? Or what if her father went down to the barn at first light, as he sometimes did if he thought the fox was about, and Davie heard him coming and sneaked away – and she wasn't there to say goodbye? A sob rose in her throat, along with a terrible premonition of loss. The idea haunted her.

Quickly now, she ran back, and creeping into the barn,

she called his name. 'Davie?' The lamp was out; there was no answer. She went on, deeper into the barn to where they had sat together, and in the glimmer of starlight through the window she saw him, snuggled deep into the blanket, fast asleep. For a moment she watched him, as she dried her eyes.

Carefully, she got to her knees and lifting the corner of the blanket, she slid in beside him. For a moment she just lay there, not daring to touch him for fear that he might wake. Instead, she looked at his sleeping face, and a tide of contentment washed over her. She took that moment to cherish him, and then she was pushing towards him, bathing in the warmth of his body, nervous that he might wake and send her away.

He didn't wake. Instead, in his slumbers, he must have sensed her there for he turned towards her and took her into his arms, and that's how the two young people lay, until fingers of dawn crept through the darkness.

~

Davie was the first to wake. And when he found himself holding her, he was shocked to the core. 'Judy, what are you doing here? How long have you been here . . . Judy?' She stirred, stretched her arms, but didn't wake.

Davie smiled. She was a funny little thing, he thought, his soft gaze sweeping her pretty face. She probably thought he would sneak off into the night the minute her back was turned. So she had come back . . . and he never even knew.

He looked at her a moment longer, at that small cute face and the long brown hair that teased over her shoulder; raising his hand, he moved a stray strand from her forehead.

My lovely little Judy he thought affectionately. I'll miss you so much.

He would miss *everything*, he thought – his parents and his grandfather, the sparsely furnished bedroom that on and off, had been his only real home these past few years, and the people of Derwent Street, with their familiar faces and cheery greetings.

He would miss weekends helping Tom and Judy on the milk-cart, and he would miss the long meandering walks through the local fields and woods. He would miss the joy of swimming in the canal in the heat of a summer's afternoon, and the all too rare visits into Blackburn Town, where he and his schoolfriends had wandered for hours amongst the brightly coloured market-stalls, clutching their saved-up pocket-money. His mam would never dig into her handbag again, he thought in sorrow, and fish out a threepenny bit from her purse, or, if he was lucky, a whole shilling. She'd give him a kiss to go with it, and a peppermint cream or a Spangle. His mam's handbag, full of bus-tickets, lipstick and tweezers and a packet of Park Drive, had such a lovely smell . . . For a moment, the boy was lost in memories.

Then his thoughts returned to the road ahead. Most of all, he would miss Judy, for she had not only been a friend to whom he could turn at any time, with her kind, warm nature she was also the loving, caring sister he had never had.

He spent another moment gazing at her, remembering, before reluctantly slipping out of the blanket, covering her over to keep out the cold, and finding the pen and paper she had brought him. He struck a match and lit the lamp low, and in its soft halo of light he began to write the promised letter.

Dear Grandad,

I'm going away now, and I don't know when I'm coming back. I don't belong in Blackburn any more, not after what's happened. I don't know where I belong – all I know is that I've got to get away. Please don't worry about me. Just look after yourself, and be strong. When I'm settled, I'll write to you.

I don't blame you for throwing us out. Mam had caused you so much trouble, and I know you were at the end of your tether. But she's gone now, and may God rest her soul. I shall pray for her every night. Will you tell her that, Grandad, when you visit her grave? I shall never forget her, never stop loving her. Will miss her forever.

If you hear from Dad, will you please let him know there are no hard feelings, and I hope we'll meet again someday. I shall be searching for him, every chance I get.

I love you, Grandad, but it's time you had your home back, and some peace and quiet. I want to find my way in the world. I'm nearly fourteen, and I don't really know what I want to do. I'm afraid, and I'm excited. There are so many things I need to find out, and new places I want to go.

I'm nearly a man now. And I need to prove I can do it all by myself.

So, take care of yourself, Grandad, and please keep an eye out for Judy. She has been my friend all of my life, and she's very precious.

Give me your blessing, Grandad. I give you mine.

Your grandson, Davie

A tear fell from his sore eyes. Folding the paper into itself, he knelt beside Judy. 'I've written the letter,' he told her.

Touching her gently on the shoulder, he raised his voice. 'I have to go.' Still no response. She was spark out! Laughing now, he gave her a little shake. 'Hey! Lazybones, wakey wakey!'

'Mmm?' Sleepily opening her eyes, the girl saw him there and all her memories came tumbling back. She began to scramble out of the blanket. 'Why didn't you wake me?' She looked out of the window. 'Oh no! It's morning.'

'JUDY!' Beth's raised voice struck fear into their hearts. 'Where the divil are you?'

Hurrying to the barn door, Davie peered out through the cracks. 'It's your mam,' he told Judy. 'I'd best go.' Running back to where she was brushing the horse-hairs from her skirt, he took her by the shoulders. 'It's time to say goodbye.' He handed her the letter. 'You will see that Grandad gets this, won't you?'

'You know I will.'

He gazed at her, feeling lonelier than he had ever felt. 'Thanks for everything, Jude.'

'Where the dickens is that girl?' Beth's voice was even closer now.

The boy turned and would have kissed her on the forehead, but suddenly Judy was kissing *him*, full on the mouth and with her arms round his neck. It was a fleeting kiss, but it spoke volumes.

'I'll write,' Davie said, as he clambered out of the window. 'Promise?'

His promise was the smile he gave her. And then he was gone.

CHAPTER SEVEN

'So, this is where you've been hiding out, is it?' Beth said angrily, hands on hips. 'What on earth d'you think you're playing at, Judy? You've had me almost out of my mind with worry. It's a good job I didn't wake your father and have him going crazy! The poor man needs his rest after yesterday's shenanigans.'

Tutting and fretting, but greatly relieved at finding the girl, she queried, 'I thought you didn't like the spiders in the barn – so what are you doing out here in the cold, at this time of morning?'

'Davie was here,' Judy said simply.

'Davie? Thank God he's safe.' Beth looked about. 'Where is he? I'm going to give him a big breakfast and a bit o' comfort, poor lad.'

'He's gone.'

'What – back to his grandad?'

'No. I don't know where he's gone.' It only now occurred to Judy that he had not mentioned any particular direction.

Beth was frantic. 'Is he all right? What did he say? Why didn't you wake us? Your father would have driven him home.'

'That's why we didn't wake you,' the girl explained. 'Because he didn't want to go back there.'

Beth considered that for a moment. 'I see. He can't forgive Joseph for throwing him out, is that it?'

'No. He's already forgiven him. Look.' She held out the letter. 'He wrote this to his grandad. He wants me to take it to him.'

Beth nodded. 'I'm glad for that at least,' she said. 'But how did you know Davie was here?'

'While I was pulling my curtains last night, I thought I saw a movement over by the barn, but I wasn't sure. And then I eventually decided it must have been him, so I came out, and there he was, making himself a bed in the hay.'

'So you helped him, did you, lass?'

'Yes. I made him a snack and gave him food for the journey. I hope you don't mind, Mam. He was so hungry and thirsty.'

Beth gave her an emotional hug and thanked God for this kindly child.

'You're a good friend, Judy. And so now he's gone, eh?'

'Yes, Mam.'

'And you don't know where he's headed?'

'No.' If only she knew, she might be more content. 'I don't think Davie knows either. He said he wanted to make a life for himself and not be a trouble to anybody.' She recalled his words. '"I need to prove myself", that's what he said.'

Beth gave a long, deep sigh. 'Well, it's understandable. His whole world's been turned upside down . . . I expect he needs to think his way through it all. He's nobbut a lad still and being on his own, he'll find the world more of a hostile place than he ever imagined.' The motherly woman believed he would have a change of mind once he was out there in the big wide world. 'I'll give him a week,' she said confidently, 'afore he starts heading back.'

Sliding her arm round Judy's shoulders, she drew her away, but then, catching a sniff of the girl's clothes, she pulled back. 'By 'eck, you stink to high heaven, lass!' she exclaimed. 'Anybody'd think you'd been sleeping with the old shire!'

When they got back to the house, Tom was up and at it. He had washed, dressed, and was already across the yard to feed the chickens. 'I'm off to see whether that damn fox has been at my birds,' he shouted to them. 'If there's any damage, the old sod won't get away with it this time!' He patted the shotgun slung over his arm. 'I'll be good and ready if he shows up.'

'Be careful with that thing!' Beth nagged him. She had never liked the shotgun. 'Like as not you'll get excited and shoot your toes clean off.'

'Away with you, woman,' he called back. 'There's nobody can handle a shotgun better than Thomas Makepeace!' With that he strode away, hellbent on a confrontation.

~

Inside the house, Beth set about cooking breakfast while Judy went off to get washed and dressed.

When the bacon and mushrooms were simmering nicely and still there was no sign of her daughter, Beth turned off the gas, covered the pan and went up to her room.

Judy was curled up on the windowseat, looking dreamily out across the land. 'Thanks, Mam, but I don't really want any breakfast,' she said.

'Don't want your breakfast!' Beth was astonished. 'But you're *allus* ready for your breakfast. During the day you don't eat as much as I would like you to, but you love your Sunday breakfast. I've cooked those new mushrooms your dad brought home. By! They smell right tasty. Come on now, Judy, get yourself downstairs, afore they spoil.'

'I'm not hungry this morning, Mam.'

Concerned, Beth came to sit beside her. 'What is it, my love?' She had an instinct that only a mother could feel. 'What's ailing you?'

'Nothing. I'm just not hungry, that's all.'

Beth persisted. 'Don't give me that. I know you far too well, and I can see there's more to it than that. Something's worrying you. Whatever it is, you know you can always talk to me.' Of course Judy would be worried about young Davie. But this was a deeper mood, and it wasn't in the girl's nature to be so sad.

There was a long pause, during which Judy wondered if her mammy could really understand the feelings that were burning inside her. 'Mam?'

'Yes?'

'If I ask you something, you won't laugh at me, will you?'

'Now, why would I do that, eh?'

'Well . . .' Embarrassed, she fell momentarily silent.

'Go on, lass.'

Another, longer pause, then, 'Mam?'

'Yes? I'm still here.'

'Mam, what does it feel like . . .' Judy took a deep breath '. . . when you love somebody?'

'Well, now . . .' Beth knew she would have to answer carefully if she was to keep the girl's confidence. 'It all depends, I suppose.'

'What do you mean?'

Beth took a moment to consolidate her thoughts, before saying, 'What I mean is, there's many kinds of love. There's the love you feel for your family, and the love you have for a dear friend. And then there's the other kind of love . . .'

'What other kind?'

'The kind that sweethearts feel for each other.'

'And is that really so different?'

'Oh, yes, lass. It's a very different love altogether.' Beth thought of her husband and the smile on her face said it all. She and Tom had met one market-day some twenty years ago. There was she, doing shopping for the doctor's house, where she worked as a maid, and there was he, behind the egg stall. She'd only gone and caught the edge of the table where the eggs were laid out, with her old-fashioned wicker basket, which was almost as big as she was, and knocked a couple dozen duck eggs to the cobbles. Eeh! She flushed at the memory of her clumsiness. But he'd been so kind, and in the midst of her confusion, she'd noticed the sparkle in his eyes. And that had been the start of it. And look at them now – a right Darby and Joan.

'You know straight off that he's the one you want to spend the rest of your life with,' she went on, and clutched her chest. 'You feel it in here . . . a kind of longing that you can't shift. You want to be with him every minute of the day and night, and when you're together, you never want it to end. I know you're only twelve now, but you'll soon be grown, and love like that will come your way, God willing.'

Judy was beginning to follow her reasoning, but she had another question for her mother to answer. 'And what happens if you love someone like a friend, and then it changes without you even noticing, and it's . . . different, and it hurts. And you don't know what to do about it?'

'I see.' But Beth wasn't quite sure what it was that she could see. Still, her darling girl was hurting, and she sensed that it had something to do with Davie. And the more she thought about it, the more fearful she became.

Reaching out, she hooked her finger under Judy's chin

and made her look at her. 'I've answered your question as well as I know how,' she said, 'and now I need you to answer mine. Will you do that for me?'

'Yes, Mam.'

'And will you answer truthfully?'

'Yes, of course I will.'

With a slow intake of breath, Beth prepared to ask what was on her mind. 'Just now, when I found you in the barn with Davie, how long had you been there?'

'I don't know . . . two hours, maybe more.'

'And were you just talking all that time?'

'Not all the time.'

'So, tell me how it was . . . right from the beginning.'

'Well, like I say, I was about to go to bed when I thought I saw a movement by the barn. I assumed it was the cats or something else, and I went to bed. But I didn't sleep very well. So I decided to go and see if it had been Davie, and it was.'

'All right. Then what?'

'We talked for a bit, and I went to get him some food and drink and I brought it back to him. He ate the food, and then I left and he promised not to go away without seeing me first.'

'But if you'd already left, how come you were still there when I found you?'

'I worried that if I slept too long, I'd miss him. So I went back.' She grinned at the memory. 'Davie was fast asleep and it was really chilly, so I got under the blanket with him. Pooh! It did pong, but at least it was warm.'

Beth's heart skipped a beat, and she did not smile. 'Judy, did anything happen when you were with Davie under the blanket?'

The girl gave her a puzzled look. She wasn't altogether

sure what her mother was saying, but nor was she so naïve that she didn't suspect the reasoning behind it. Being brought up on a farm, she knew all about the birds and the bees – and the pigs, cows and sheep, come to that. 'No!' Bristling, she sat upright. 'I know what you're getting at, Mam, and you're wrong!'

Springing to Davie's defence she declared, 'I know how Sheila Clarkson did wrong with that boy from the fairground and she had a baby, but Davie would never do a thing like that, and neither would I!'

Beth could see the truth in Judy's eyes and she felt a great sense of relief. 'I'm sorry, sweetheart,' she said. 'But I had to ask.' Reaching out, she took Judy's hands into her own. 'I'm a mother,' she murmured. 'One day, God willing when you're married and settled, with a good man and children of your own, you'll know why I had to make sure. So . . . am I forgiven?'

Judy nodded. She could hear everything that was said, and yet she hardly heard a word, because it was still Davie who filled her mind and held her heart in a way as never before. And it was the strangest thing.

'So, now that we've got that out of the way, will you tell me what happened . . . you said you got into the blanket to keep warm?'

More attentive now, Judy went on, 'I fell asleep, and the next thing I knew, Davie was ready to leave. He wrote the letter and then he was gone.'

'And was it then, that you realised your feelings towards him had changed?'

Embarrassed, Judy lowered her gaze. 'I've always loved Davie, like a brother really. But now, I don't know what's happened, Mam. It's all different, and I can't stop thinking about him.'

Taking the girl into her arms, Beth told her how love between man and woman was a strong, unpredictable thing. 'But I think the trouble with you now is that Davie has always been here and you never imagined he wouldn't be. You've seen him most every day since the two of you went to infant school. You were both only children, and we were all so happy that you'd found each other – Rita most of all, poor lass. She was thrilled that her Davie had you for his best friend. Now, suddenly, his life has changed, and because of that, so has yours. Happen you'll see him again, and happen you won't. But either way, there is nothing you can do about that.'

At the thought of never seeing him again, the girl burst into tears.

'I don't like it, Mam.' Her emotions were running wild. 'When I think about Davie now, it really hurts.'

'I know, lass, I know. But you must learn to live with the situation, because whether we like it or not, in the end everything changes. The years pass and nothing ever stays the same. You're bound to miss him. And I dare say he'll miss you the same.'

'Do you really think he'll miss me?'

'Well, o' course he will, lass.' Her heart ached for Judy. 'You're older now, and so is he. In fact, he was due to leave school soon and start work as a man. Like I say, things change. One day you wake up and what happened yesterday is gone; it's the past already. But the future is still in front of us. That's the way of things, and we have to accept it. And remember, your dad and I love you, and we'll help you get through this.'

For a time they sat cuddled up together, these two; one settled in her life and content with it; and the other still finding her way, unsure and afraid.

'Will he ever come back, Mam?' Judy was the first to speak.

'Who knows?' As ever, Beth was practical. 'Davie has a lot to deal with. Happen it'll be easier for him to do that from a distance. And then again, he may suddenly yearn for familiar things, and find his way home. All we can do is wait and see. Give him time, love, as much time as he needs.'

She gave her daughter a final hug. 'You stay awhile and think about everything,' she suggested kindly. 'If you need me, you know where I'll be.' She chuckled. 'I'll be over by the chickens . . . making sure your father doesn't run amok with that shotgun.'

~

In the evening, when dinner was over, Judy helped to clear the table and wash up, before excusing herself. 'I'm ready for bed now,' she said, gave each of her parents a hug and quickly departed the room.

'What's got into our Judy?' Tom was perplexed. 'She hardly ate any of her food, and if she spoke it was only because you or I talked to her first. Is the lass ill or what?'

'No, Tom, she's not ill – at least, not in the way you think.'

'Oh, aye, an' what's that supposed to mean?' he asked, going to sit by the fire for a read of the *News of the World*.

Choosing her words carefully, Beth told him, 'The thing is, our little girl is growing up fast. Right now, there are things going on inside her head that you can't begin to understand.'

'Oh, give over, woman!' Tom didn't take kindly to riddles. 'Just tell me what's going on, an' I'd like it in plain language, if you don't mind.'

'Hmm!' Beth smiled knowingly. 'What ails our daughter can't be told in plain language. She's a girl becoming a woman, and as I say, there's not a man on God's earth who could fathom that out, even if he tried.'

Tom tutted impatiently, but he had a smile and a comment. 'You're not wrong there. I've been trying to fathom *you* out long enough, Elizabeth Makepeace, an' I'm still no nearer than the day I put a ring on yer finger. Women!' he muttered. 'Damned if I can make head nor tail of 'em!'

'Stop complaining and read your paper.' Beth took out her sewing box and smoothed one of her husband's socks over the wooden heel she kept for darning. And while she threaded the biggest needle with black wool, she thought of her young daughter upstairs, alone with her dreams.

It didn't take much to see what was wrong with the lass, she thought, making a knot in the wool. All these years, Davie Adams and Judy had been friends through thick and thin. As small children during the latter part of the war, they had spent a lot of time over at Three Mills Farm, especially at weekends. Beth recalled her tiny daughter looking up at Davie with absolute love and hero-worship, following him around and ready to play any role he asked her to. She was cowboy to his Indian, batsman to his bowler, and they could spend hours in a corner of the farmyard, playing with their marbles and Dinky toys. With homemade nets, they'd fish for tiddlers and sticklebacks in the duckpond, and put them in jamjars, with string tied round, to make handles. And sometimes, Davie would push the battered old doll's pram around the yard, full of teddies and handknitted toys, while the hens squawked about them.

Beth sighed nostalgically. When Rita came to fetch him, the two women would enjoy a nice cup of tea and a bit o' cake and a natter. She missed those days, despite the constant fear of bombing. As a farmer, thank God, her Tom was exempt from service, although he did his share of fire-watching and the like. Often, when Don was away, Rita would stay, and they'd all play cards, once the kids were in bed. Then Rita was a different woman from the one who went out with her mother, all dolled up with a load of powder and paint on her pretty face and the pair of 'em up to all sorts of tricks behind their husbands' backs.

Those memories were best forgotten. Beth thought instead of the times she had helped the children with their homework when they'd gone off to the big school in Blackburn Town. She was canny at the arithmetic, was Beth – she'd needed to have a shrewd head on her shoulders, running the farm with her Tom, who was better at hosswork than headwork. Oh well. Davie had been due to leave soon, while her Judy had a couple of years or more yet. And now Rita was gone, and so was Don . . . and Davie had vanished into the wide blue yonder, just when Judy had begun to see her childhood friend in a different light.

It seemed that, with him leaving, their friendship, at least on Judy's side, had deepened into a more mature emotion. The girl had said it herself. She loved Davie in a new way – and it was a painful thing. Turning to her darning, Beth consoled herself with the knowledge that Judy was still too young at twelve to experience the stirrings of real love – the kind that robs you of your sleep and makes the day seem neverending.

She thought of Davie, and her heart ached. Where was the lad? Why didn't he come home, instead o' wandering the streets like some poor vagabond! She tutted aloud.

'What's that?' Tom peered over his newspaper. 'What did y'say?'

'I said, would you like another cup o' tea?' Beth asked, throwing off her anxious mood.

'Aye, go on then . . . and don't forget the sugar this time.'

~

Upstairs, Judy lay on her bed, her mind in turmoil. She was half-minded to go after Davie, but she knew her parents would be frantic with worry if she did so. And besides, which way would she go? Even Davie hadn't known where he was headed.

After a few minutes of trying to get to sleep, she went and sat by the window; she felt comfortable there, as though that great outdoors had the answer to everything. A trillion stars were dancing in the heavens, and from somewhere in the distance a barn owl was calling for its mate. How could everything be so magical, while she felt so sad?

She wondered if Davie could hear that same owl, or see the same stars in the skies. The idea gave her a small degree of comfort.

~

Davie was not as far away as Judy imagined.

Curled up at the foot of a tree trunk, he was finding it hard to sleep. Judy was strong in his mind, and stronger still was her impetuous kiss. It still burned on his mouth, her soft full lips against his. He wanted to see her again, but he knew it would be best if he didn't.

Soon, it would be time for him to leave this place for good. She still had a lot of growing up to do, while he felt a hundred years old. If they never saw each other again it would be a very sorry thing.

But maybe, in the end, that might be for the best.

For now though, he desperately needed to sleep. Rolling over, he wrapped the blanket she had given him closer about his shoulders. His bag, now a pillow, was lumpy, but he tried to relax. However, his thoughts were too alive with new feelings. Time and again, he brushed his fingers over his lips, remembering the urgency of her kiss; so unexpected and lovely; her nearness, and the warm, earthy smell of her hair brushing against his face.

After a while, he drifted into a shallow, troubled rest, haunted by recent events and the unknown road ahead. His mother's dying face, with its look of love, made him sob in his sleep.

Opening his eyes, glad to see it was almost dawn, he turned his thoughts to family.

Before he set out, there was one more thing he had to do. Then he would be gone from here, taking whichever path drew him away.

Not for the first time since that night, he wondered where his father might be. Had Don gone back to Ireland? Or was he still hereabouts, a mere few miles away? Or was he on a ship destined for foreign parts?

Davie needed him now more than ever, but he would never admit it out loud. All he wished was that his father should be safe, wherever he was, and wherever in the world his travels might take him.

He thought of his own situation and yes, the future seemed a frightening prospect. But the past was even more daunting.

And the sooner he put it behind him, the better.

CHAPTER EIGHT

T HROUGHOUT THE WEEK following Davie's disappear-
ance, news of his mother's untimely demise spread
far and wide. 'That silly tart got what she deserved,' some
declared callously. Others shook their head and found a
degree of compassion for a life lost, and other lives ruined.

'I expect we'll be the only ones at the church.' Beth had
been getting her family prepared for the ordeal of the
funeral on the Saturday morning.

Tom was more philosophical. 'I wouldn't be surprised if a
few neighbours turned up,' he commented, as he wound his
tie round his neck for the third time. 'Happen not for Rita's
sake, but for old Joseph. He's made a heap o' friends over
the years, an' he's never let 'em down when they needed
him.'

He cocked his head to one side, skenning downwards
through crossed eyes as he made a fourth attempt at taming
his rebellious tie. 'I reckon they'll not let *him* down neither,
especially not today of all days.'

Snatching the tie from round his neck, he threw it over
the back of the chair. 'I'm not wearing this damned thing! I
can't even fasten the beggar.'

Judy came to the rescue. 'Don't fidget, Dad,' 'she said,

sliding the tie round his leathery neck. 'And I think you're right. I bet the people will be there for old Joseph.'

'I'm not so sure.' Rolling the flesh-coloured stockings up to her thighs, Beth hoisted her skirt and hooked up the suspenders. 'Although we were friends, there was summat inside Rita that made her lose all control. By! She must have bedded half the male population o' Blackburn in her time. I'm just glad she never started on you, Tom. There must be a hundred women out there who'd like to dance on her grave, never mind come and pay their respects.'

As she spoke, she made the sign of the cross over herself. 'God rest her soul all the same,' she prayed.

Judy glanced across at her mam. 'Your seams are crooked.'

'What?'

Having looped her daddy's tie into a neat little knot, the girl pointed down at her mother's stockings. 'The seams are all crooked, see?'

'Oh, damn and bugger it!' As a rule Beth never wore stockings; she much preferred bare legs, or a warm pair of socks inside boots or stout shoes. She was a farmer's wife, not a townswoman.

Twisting herself round, Beth began tweaking the stockings, until the seams were as straight as she could get them. 'How's that, lass?' she panted.

Judy nodded. 'Much better, Mam.'

'Right well, it's time we were on our way.' Looking in the mirror, she dabbed a discreet shaking of powder on her face, then a touch of lipstick, and then came the hat – a small round, blueberry-coloured thing. 'How does that look?' she asked, spinning round to face them.

'Like a cherry on a cake,' Tom remarked, making his daughter smile.

Ignoring his cheeky comment, Beth asked of Judy, 'Do I look dignified, lass?'

The girl gave an honest answer. 'Yes, Mam.'

'And the hat – is it suitable for the occasion, d'you think? . . . And don't look at your father; he's got no idea.'

Judy gave her own opinion. 'You look really smart, Mam. Rita would be pleased you'd made the effort.'

Beth regarded her daughter with a critical eye; the dark flared skirt and fitted jacket, and her light brown hair taken back in one thick plait. 'You do us proud, so you do,' she said with a generous hug. 'Now then, are we ready or what?'

Tom was still tugging at the neck of his shirt; red in the face, he looked fit to burst. 'It's choking me, damn it!'

'It's *me* as'll choke you, if you don't stop yer moaning!' Turning away, Beth winked at her daughter. 'Look at our Judy,' she told her husband. 'She's quietly got herself ready an' not a word of complaint.'

Judy didn't mind their friendly bantering; she had other things on her mind. 'Do you think Don or Davie will be there?' she asked. She'd dressed up with Davie in mind, just in case by some miracle he turned up; had wanted to look her very best. She knew it was silly. He'd have his heart and mind on his mam, not her. And she worried about how he'd been surviving, these past few days. He hadn't been back to the barn.

'I've been wondering the very same,' Tom said. 'It wouldn't surprise me to see the lad there at some point. I mean, look how he stuck by his mam when everyone else turned against her. He'll not desert her now, not if I know the lad, he won't. As for Don, it's a crying shame. He'll probably not even know that the poor lass is dead.'

'If he does put in an appearance, do what you can to

persuade him to stay, Tom,' Beth said. 'Tell him he can have a home with us for as long as he wants.'

A few minutes later, with Tom lagging behind, still moaning because he was 'being throttled by this blessed tie!' the three of them made their way to the car. The old Morris Minor was in a bad humour today, and needed the starter-handle to get it going, by which time Tom had taken his tie off again, and had muck on his hands.

'I hope Joseph was ready when they came for him,' Tom said, breathing a sigh of relief as the engine caught. 'I don't expect he's had a wink of sleep.'

As they made the short journey to St Peter's Church, the conversation centred on Rita's father. 'You needn't worry about him not being ready,' Beth replied. 'When we popped in yesterday, Judy and I went through everything with him – the time the undertakers would be there to collect him, and what he would need to wear. He had it all set out on the sofa ready.'

'Aye, well, you never can tell with Joe. He's a stubborn old devil when he puts his mind to it.' Tom recalled his conversation with the older man. 'I said it might be best if he stayed with us for a few days, and that we'd follow Rita to the church from here, if he wanted. But he were adamant that she had to go from his house, and try as I might, there was no persuading him otherwise.'

'To tell you the truth, Tom, I never wholeheartedly agreed with your suggestion, kind though it was,' Beth said now. 'Joseph is used to his own four walls about him. Besides, I happen to believe he was right to insist that Rita was taken to the church from his house. It's the accepted tradition, and she was his daughter, after all.'

'And God help anyone who has a daughter like that!' As Tom thought of the poor young woman dying in his cart, his heart broke at the pity and waste of it, and for Rita's devastated family.

~

Over in Derwent Street, Joseph Davies took a last look in the mirror. His beard was neatly trimmed, and the night before, he had had a bath in the old tin tub. His shoes were shined and his fingernails trimmed. He had done his best for his daughter.

Turning to the photograph of Marie, his wife, he told her: 'Jesus promises us we'll be reunited with our loved ones, so I don't fear for Rita, knowing you'll be with her and our little baby Matty.' He sobbed as he spoke, then went on, 'I know that you and our Rita were good women; you never meant to do anyone harm. You both had hearts of gold – 'twas some strange quirk in your natures that made you run wild. I feel I failed you both, and now I long to be with you. If God is kind, He will let me join you in heaven. But first, I have young Davie and Don to look out for.'

Tears ran down his face, and he took a long, withering sigh. At that moment, he heard the sound of an engine, and pulling aside one of the curtains, which were closed throughout the house, he saw the hearse draw up at the kerb. Inside was a coffin, covered with the flowers he had ordered. This was the third member of his family he had seen to their last resting-place from here, and his heart cracked under the burden of his sorrow.

Bracing his shoulders, and saying a last, brief prayer, the old man went to open the front door to accompany his daughter to the church.

~

When the Makepeaces turned down Watson Street they were surprised to see several groups of people already gathering outside the church. 'Well, I never!' Beth was surprised at the considerable turnout. 'Look! There's Mr and Mrs Reynolds.' She'd never really taken to the couple. There was summat sly about the pair of them, although their son Lenny was a nice boy.

Today, the young woman was nicely turned out, her hair freshly washed and brushed loose about her shoulders and a touch of lipstick to her mouth; and with no children round her ankles, she seemed more relaxed and much prettier than Beth recalled. Patsy had four children, two girls and two boys – the eldest being Lenny. Not yet sixteen but already with his own little stall on the market, Lenny apparently made no secret of his intention to make a fortune by the time he was twenty. Beth thought he was a grand lad, hardly a chip off the old block, as Patsy's husband Ron was a tall, thin-faced man, a surly character, and workshy by all accounts.

Beth greeted them with a nod. 'I hardly recognised you without your childer,' she told the woman.

'When I've got my hands full with them, I never have time to make myself look nice,' Patsy replied. 'I've roped our Lenny in to look after the kids. That'll bring him down to earth with a bump!'

She turned to her husband, who returned a wry little grin. 'Yes,' he agreed, 'it won't hurt the cocky young devil to know his place ... keep him from getting above himself, if you know what I mean?'

Beth said in his defence, 'As I recall, your son looked a sensible, capable sort.' Lenny was a well-built boy with a mop of dark hair and a wary look in his eye. 'I imagine he'll cope with the children very well.' Bidding them good day, she moved on, feeling put out, somehow.

'I don't think that woman gets on too well with her eldest son,' she confided in Tom. 'I heard her going at him hammer and tongs that day at the house, and now they're talking as though he's a ruffian who needs to be kept under control.'

Tom was his usual self. 'None of our business,' he said, and the subject was closed.

There was a smattering of other neighbours, most of them Joseph's friends and old workmates, and others who were attending out of curiosity. There were also a number of younger men; these were Don's colleagues from the workshop, men who knew of Rita's reputation but never lowered themselves to be acquainted with her or betray Don. Together with their wives they were here to support the bereaved family, and show their respect. In Don's absence, they tried to represent him. The poor fellow would be devastated when he found out. It was a thoroughly bad do all round.

The others, the men who had used Rita and fought over her like dogs over a bone, they knew well enough to stay away.

~

No sooner had Tom parked his car than the organ started up and everyone began to file into the church. 'No signs of Don then?' Tom glanced anxiously about.

Beth had also been discreetly watching. 'Happen the police didn't find him, after all.'

'Poor devil.' Tom shook his head. 'So he'll not know his wife's gone and his son missing?' As he went in through the church door he kept his eyes peeled.

They shuffled into the pews and everyone got settled. 'Did you see anything of Davie?' Judy whispered to her mam. 'Is he here, do you think?'

'No, lass. Or if he is, I for one didn't see him.'

But the boy was there, crouched beside a huge woman in a pew to the rear of the church, where a large pillar cast a shadow. Scruffy, and thinner than ever, he strained to hear the priest's opening words.

A few moments passed, and then Joseph and three other men were bringing Rita in, and everyone stood and bowed their heads, or made the sign of the cross on themselves. For Judy, sitting with her family, it was a deep and sobering experience, for she had never attended such an event before. For Davie, in the shadows, it felt like his own death.

The service was all too brief. They sang the hymns and they listened to the beautiful sermon, based on the words of wisdom from Ecclesiastes, and they prayed for eternal peace for the soul of Rita Adams. And then it was over, and they were all filing out again.

As she emerged into the daylight, Judy was anxiously scanning the area for Davie. But he was nowhere to be seen. 'It's no use looking for him, lass.' Beth saw how anxious she was. 'The lad did all he could for his mammy while she was alive, and there's no more for him to do here.'

Knowing how Judy felt, the woman did not want to dash all her hopes. But sometimes, forever hoping for one thing means you will never get another, and that was not what she wanted for her daughter.

'I'm sorry, love,' she told Judy gently. 'I reckon your Davie is long gone by now.'

Having witnessed the conversation, Tom saw the sadness in his daughter's eyes and he wanted her away from this place. 'Come on, you two. We've paid our respects, so let's make us way home, eh?'

Beth was surprised. 'Are we not going up to Pleasington Cemetery then, to witness the burial?'

Tom shook his head. 'No need for that,' he replied in his no-nonsense manner. 'We showed up at the church, and to my mind, we've done our duty. Now, let's be off. I've umpteen jobs waiting to be done back at the farm.'

Judy remained on the look-out for Davie. In her heart she knew he was here somewhere, hiding.

~

It was while they were walking back to the car and her parents got waylaid by some old friends, that the girl saw him. 'Davie!' She went at a run towards the boy, who was chasing after the slowly-departing hearse.

At first he didn't hear her, so she went at a fast pace down the hill, and on to where the hearse was just beginning to pick up a dignified speed. 'DAVIE, WAIT!' Waving and shouting, she kept after him. And as he leaped onto the running-board of the hearse, he saw her.

'DAVIE!' Out of breath and fast losing him, Judy put a spurt on. But there was no chance of her catching up, and Davie made no sign of jumping off the vehicle. He had watched the service from the back of the church and hid while they put his mammy onto the hearse, and now he had to go with her and lay the wild posies he'd collected. Moreover, he needed to know where she lay, so he would never forget.

'GO BACK!' Davie's voice carried on the wind. 'Don't forget I love you . . . and tell my grandad I love *him!*'

As the distance between them grew wider, Davie let their images soak into his memory; his beloved father and grandfather, and Judy and her family, the kindest people he had ever known. And he wondered how he would manage without them. There was no telling where he might end up or how long he might be gone, and whether he would ever

come back to this place, where he had known both contentment and unhappiness in equal measures.

For now though, his future was not something that concerned him, because only an arm's reach away, his mother
lay lifeless, gone from his sight and from his life forever.

His father had been crippled by the burden he had carried
for too long, and there was a real possibility that he might
never see him again. But the boy wanted to see him. He
needed to tell him the way of things, and how neither of them
were to blame. At this moment in time, he longed for his
father's presence, more than at any other time in his entire life.

Yet even as he whispered Don's name, his eyes on Rita's
coffin, the piece of paper that his daddy had given him, with
the precious contact name on it, fell out of his trouser pocket
and was immediately whisked into a hawthorn hedge by a
passing gust of wind. And there it lay wedged, unread, while
the elements, seasons, and myriad hedge-dwelling creatures
reduced it to a sodden scrap. And father and son were lost
to each other, unless a kinder wind might blow them back
together.

~

Judy waved to Davie until her arm ached. And even when he
and the hearse were out of sight, she continued to wave at the
empty horizon.

When she climbed wearily back up the hill towards the
church, her parents were sitting quietly on the wall. The lane
was almost deserted, and the church was empty.

'Come on, sweetheart.' Beth came forward to slide a com-
forting arm round her daughter's shoulders. 'Your dad's waiting to take us home.'

~

As Tom drew away from the church car park, Patsy Reynolds climbed into the front passenger seat of a battered and elderly Ford, and lit a cigarette.

'Stuck-up bunch, them Makepeaces, ain't they?' she commented to her husband. Looked a bit shocked when we said about keeping Lenny under our thumb. None of their bleedin' business, anyhow.'

'I couldn't give a sod how shocked they were!' Ron's mood had darkened. He wished he hadn't taken time off from his job as a tram-driver to come here. But if they wanted to butter up old Joseph, they had to play the game.

Patsy dug him in the ribs. 'Hey, you know what?'

Scowling, he swung round. 'What?'

'I were just thinking.' A sly grin crept over her features.

'Oh, I see.' Thinking himself lucky, his passion rose. There was no one around, and it excited him, the thought of taking her here, on so-called sacred ground. 'Want some, do you?' he said huskily, and slid his hand under her skirt.

'Get off, you randy sod!' She pushed him away, and blew smoke in his face. 'I were just thinking about them Makepeaces, being shocked at what we said about Lenny.'

'So what?' Impatient, he started the car engine.

'Well, just you think about it.' She smiled, a look of devilment on her face. 'If they knew the truth, they'd have something to be shocked about, wouldn't they, eh?'

'What are you getting at, you silly moo?'

Nervously glancing about, Patsy lowered her voice to a whisper. 'It's as well they don't know the truth – about Lenny, I mean.'

Ron snorted. 'You're right. Mind, it would be a real treat to see the look on their faces.' Glancing at Tom's car as it travelled slowly along the lower lane, he shouted at the top of his voice, 'That's summat you didn't know, you miserable buggers

– the truth about the lad. Oh yes! Put the cat among the pigeons, that would.'

'Shut your bloody trap!' Patsy warned him. 'Just keep it buttoned! If the truth got out, we could end up in jail.' She punched her husband hard on the shoulder. 'You'd do well to remember that.'

As they hastily departed for home, the hitherto jovial atmosphere was quickly replaced by a moody silence, punctuated by the wheezings and bouncings of a vehicle that was well past its prime.

CHAPTER NINE

'WHY DO YOU think Annie and her mam didn't come?' asked Judy as her dad drove home, relieved to be away from the oppressive atmosphere of the funeral.

Annie Needham and Judy had hit it off right away, from their very first day at Elm Grove Girls' School. Although no one could take the place of Davie in Judy's affections, it was grand to have another girl as a friend; someone to talk things through with – things that she would have been too shy to mention to Davie.

'I'm not sure,' answered Beth. 'I think Mrs Needham helped Joseph out when his wife died some years ago – that was before Don and Rita and Davie moved back in with him. We heard she'd done a bit of shopping for him and the like. The Needhams rented a house in Jackson Street then. Oh well. Maybe she's just too busy with her own family. She's got an older boy, apart from Annie, hasn't she?'

'Yes – Philip. He's a butcher's apprentice and he's horrible. Gives me the creeps,' said Judy. 'Mam, could I go and see Annie, just for a bit? I'll come straight home on the bus, I promise.'

Annie was a strapping, dark-haired girl, the antithesis of Judy in many ways, being wild and rebellious, sometimes lazy and argumentative, and above all – flirtatious. But underneath all that, Judy had found her to be a caring and loyal friend. And when Annie wanted to fight the world, Judy's quiet nature and wise observations had a calming influence on the girl. Like the hand and the glove, these two opposites seemed to fit together incredibly well. And just at this lonely, confused moment in her life, Judy longed for her friend's no-nonsense approach.

'Aye, lass, why not. Might do you a power of good.' Beth thoroughly approved of Evie Needham, Annie's mother, who was an ordinary, hardworking woman, content with her lot, much like Beth herself. Evie liked a good old chat and was always ready for a laugh, although her husband was much shyer. However, Beth was not so keen on Annie herself, considering her to be a difficult girl, cheeky and insolent. What on earth Judy saw in her, she couldn't tell – but she liked to see her daughter being happy and so she kept quiet about her reservations.

'Dad will let you off at the top of Derwent Street,' she went on, 'but you must catch the early evening bus home. I don't want you wandering the streets alone at all hours.'

'All right, Mam, I will – I promise.' Judy decided to go into the corner shop later on and buy some toffee pincushions for her and Annie to share. The other girl loved them. She also had enough pocket money left to buy two bags of Smith's crisps as well. She enjoyed opening the little blue twist of paper containing the salt, and sprinkling it over the crinkly brown crisps.

As Tom turned into Derwent Street, the car began coughing and spluttering. 'It's time you treated yourself to a new vehicle,' Beth told him straight. 'This contraption was a bad buy when you got it, and if you ask me, it's on its last legs.'

'Give over, woman. This'll do me. Anyway, I can't afford no new vehicle,' he replied indignantly. 'I'm a farmer, and a milkman, to earn a few extra bob. I've got no fancy money to be changing vehicles.' He grinned wickedly. 'Now, if you were to talk about a new young bull to serve the cows . . . well, happen if I were pushed, I might find the money for that.'

'You'll do no such thing!' Beth gave him one of her stern looks. 'If you've got money to spare, you can get me a new bathroom. That's what's most needed, never mind bulls and the like!'

Seated comfortably in the back, Judy was kept amused by her parents' good-natured banter.

Annie Needham was playing hopscotch out on the pavement by herself when she saw them turn the corner. 'Mam, it's Judy!' she called in through the front door. Running to the kerb, she waited for them to arrive.

'This is a nice street, don't you think, Tom?' Beth had a liking for Derwent Street. Long and meandering, it was flanked by small square houses with high windows dressed in pretty lace curtains. There was a cast-iron lamp-post at either end; an ancient pub with bay windows on one corner, and a shop straddling the corner at the other end. 'If I weren't so happy on the farm, I reckon I wouldn't mind living along here.'

Her husband smiled knowingly. 'You're as likely to leave the farm as I am to walk stark naked through a busy market-place,' he teased. 'Anyway, why d'you think I married you, eh?'

Beth smiled at the idea of him walking naked past fat Lily on the fish-stall; bold as brass and twice as crude, she made no secret of her fancy for Tom. 'I've no idea,' she replied, 'but I'm sure you're about to tell me.'

'I married you, because you have the same passion for the land as I have.'

'Is that so?' Beth feigned indignation. 'So now the truth comes out, does it?'

'What d'you mean?'

'Well, here's me thinking you married me because you loved me, and now I see how wrong I was.' She winked at Judy, who knew her mammy was joshing anyway.

Tom, however, was completely wrongfooted. 'No . . . oh no! What I meant was . . . Oh dear,' he stuttered, 'it all came out wrong. I didn't mean it like that.'

'All right then. I forgive you.' Her face relaxed into a cheeky grin, and he knew she had been toying with him.

'Elizabeth Makepeace, you're a right little madam, that's what you are.' Tom was visibly relieved. 'You know very well I never wanted nobody but you . . . ever!'

'I know that, you silly old fool! But happen that's 'cause nobody else would have you.' She gave him a sound kiss on the face, and all was well.

'Hello, Mr Makepeace.' Annie stepped forward as he wound down the window. 'Mrs Makepeace.' She peeped into the car at Beth. 'All right are you?'

Beth thanked her kindly and said that yes, she was fine.

When Judy climbed out, still clad in her funeral clothes, Annie hugged her tight. 'I'm so glad you're here,' she said. 'Mam said you would have gone up to the church. I wanted to come too, but Mam wouldn't let me. She said as how it would be hypocritical, as she didn't approve of what Rita Adams had done to her family.'

'Give my regards to your mam,' Beth called as Tom pulled away, 'and don't forget what I said, Judy. You're to get the early bus back.'

Evie Needham appeared at the door just then, covered in

a dusting of flour and looking flustered. 'Cheerio!' She gave them a nod and a wave, showering the pavement with flour as she waved her hand.

'Nice woman,' Beth said as they chugged down the street. 'Attractive in a quiet way.'

'Hmh.' Tom gave her a sideways glance. 'She's only a little thing, isn't she? Meks you wonder how she ever had such a lolloping great lump like young Annie.'

Beth rolled her eyes. 'Tom! I must say, you have a wonderful way with words.' But she had to chuckle, because he was right. As always.

~

When the two girls walked into the kitchen, Evie was up to her armpits in bread making. 'We thought we might have a picnic down by the canal, Mam. Is there anything we can take with us?' Going to the pantry, Annie began delving for treats. 'Philip must have been in here,' she grumbled. 'The shelves are empty. I thought as there were a bit o' bread pudding and some cold ham and egg pie.'

Evie apologised. 'Your brother did take most of the food with him when he went to work this morning.' Wiping her hands on a tea-towel, she dug into her pinnie pocket. 'There's two shillings.' She gave the florin to Annie. 'You should get a few treats with that. It can do for your tea. And don't be back later than seven, Annie, or I'll start to worry.'

'OK, Mam – but I wish you wouldn't treat me like a kid. I'm thirteen now – nearly old enough to leave school.' All the way to the corner shop, Annie moaned about her older brother. 'Greedy bugger! Phil doesn't give a sod about anybody else but himself.'

'We'll be all right, Annie,' Judy consoled her. 'We'll get a bottle of pop between us, and a couple of meat and tatty pies. With the sweets and crisps that'll do us.'

Satisfied, Annie changed the subject. 'How did it go at the church?'

'All right, I suppose. Mam said there were more people there than she thought there'd be.'

'So, who else went?'

'Lots of Joseph's workmates and some others I didn't know. A few of his neighbours . . . Oh, and Ron and Patsy Reynolds.'

'Ooh, I really fancy that Lenny Reynolds,' Annie said wistfully, then she rolled her eyes, and gave a coy little grin. 'D'you know he's got his own market-stall, and the girls are all over him. He looks like a film star, and I bet he kisses really good.' She feigned a swoon. 'I'll bet me and Lenny could show that Vivien Leigh and Clark Gable pair a thing or two.'

'Behave yourself.' Judy couldn't help but smile. 'It's a good thing your mam didn't hear you say that.'

'Oh, I know. She would have given me one of her lectures, about not rushing my childhood and thinking of my future. She'd say I was too young to be worrying about boys and such.' In a temper, she kicked a mound of grass into the canal. 'I'm *not* too young! I'm fed up, that's what I am. D'you know, I'll be fourteen next year, and I've never had a boyfriend.'

Judy shuddered dramatically. 'Don't know as I want one.'

'Liar! I bet you wouldn't say no if it was Davie.'

With those tactless words echoing in the air, the conversation came to an abrupt end, with Annie wishing she could take back what she had just said, and the other girl feeling quietly bruised.

'Sorry,' Annie said awkwardly.

'It's all right.' Judy shrugged her shoulders.

'You think a lot of Davie, don't you?'

Judy nodded silently.

'And I've got a big mouth, which I always manage to put my foot in.'

'I won't argue with that.' Judy laughed. Annie was Annie, and she said what she thought.

'Was he there?'

'Who?'

'Davie!'

'No . . . well, yes he *was*, only we didn't see him at first. He must have sneaked into the back of the church before the service started.'

'So, what's happening with him? Has he gone back to his grandad?'

'No.' If only he had, Judy thought sadly. If only things could be the same as before, when Davie was never far away.

'So where is he then?' Annie doggedly pursued it.

'Gone away.'

'Where to?'

'I don't know . . . and neither does his grandad. I'm so worried about him, Annie.' Her voice fell. 'Maybe he won't ever come back.'

'Hmh!' Annie had seen Davie and Judy together a few times and she had sensed the affection between them. She believed it was more than just friendship. Just occasionally, Annie had caught Davie looking at Judy in a certain way. 'You do know that Davie loves you,' she said casually. 'I mean *really* loves you, and not like a brother neither.'

'Don't be daft!' A warm blush spread over the other girl's face and down her neck.

'I'm not being daft.' Annie turned into the corner shop and Judy followed. After Judy had bought the sweets and

113

crisps, it was her friend's turn. 'A bottle of pop and two meat and tatty pies.' She slapped the coin onto the counter. 'And if there's enough left over, we'll have two ounces of jelly babies.'

'Hey!' Leaning forward, the big man spread the palms of his huge hands on the counter. 'Lost your manners on the way here, did you?' he asked sharply.

Seeing that he wasn't about to serve them unless she asked politely, Annie grudgingly added, 'Please.'

'Hmh!' Taking a bottle of pop from the shelf behind him, he placed it on the counter. 'It really hurt you to say that, didn't it?'

Ignoring his comment, Annie cheekily reminded him, 'All I want are two meat and tatty pies – if you please. And some jelly babies.'

Delivering her a scathing glance, he served all of that, and a penny change into the bargain. 'You're a sullen little bugger,' he said. 'If you were mine you'd not stand for a week!'

'Oh, yeah? Beat me black and blue, would you?'

'Teach you a few manners, that's what.' He pointed to the door. 'Go on, be off with you!'

As Judy and Annie went out the door, his wife sidled up behind him. 'Right little madam, she is.' His wife was usually the one who served Annie. 'Such an angry child. I can't make her out.'

'She's no child,' he grunted. 'More like a monster in the making.'

'You're right, love.' Tutting and complaining, the little woman scurried away with a parting remark. 'How that nice Mrs Needham ever gave birth to that one, I never will know.'

~

'Why are you always so sharp with people, Annie?' Carrying the bottle of pop under her arm, Judy followed her friend down the bank to the canal.

'I'm not!' Having got to the canal edge, Annie threw off her coat and spread it inside-out on the grass.

'Yes, you are.' Taking off her own smart jacket, Judy did the same. 'Sometimes it's as if you want to fight the world.'

Annie shrugged it off. 'I bags first swig of the pop.'

Handing her the bottle of Tizer, Judy asked, 'Is there anything wrong? 'Cause if there is, you know you can tell me.'

Judy couldn't imagine there being anything wrong though, because Annie had a good home and a loving family. And as far as she knew, there was no one at school who gave Annie any trouble. In fact, they all seemed to steer clear of her, because of her troublemaking antics.

'There's nothing wrong!' Annie snapped, and she took a long drink from the bottle. 'I'm sorry,' she said lamely, handing the bottle back. 'I don't mean to moan and grumble, only sometimes I feel so trapped, I just want to take off.'

'But why? And where would you go?'

There was a long pause before Annie answered, and for a moment it seemed as though she was ready to impart something; a secret that haunted her.

'Annie, I know there's something you want to tell me,' Judy urged. 'If it's a secret, I won't tell anyone – you know that.'

Shaking off the dark mood that threatened to envelop her, Annie took hold of Judy's hand. 'There is something I need to tell you,' she said. 'It's just that – well, I want you to know that I could never be angry with *you*,' she said quietly. 'You're the only friend I've got.' Beyond that, she was not forthcoming.

Still convinced that Annie was harbouring something too

painful to speak about, Judy made a last attempt to get it out of her. 'Promise me, Annie,' she urged. 'If you're ever worried about anything, you would tell me, wouldn't you?'

Instead of giving a straightforward answer, Annie replied disarmingly, 'What is there for me to worry about?'

Judy gave it a thought. 'You're right,' she said. 'You're really lucky, Annie. You've got an older brother, and you seem such a close family. I wish I had a sister or brother, but there's only me, now Davie's gone. Sometimes it feels really lonely, especially at night when I go up to my bedroom, and there's nobody to talk to. Oh, I know I've got me mam and dad, and I love them madly, but it would be nice to have a sister.'

Annie hugged her. 'And instead you've got me,' she laughed. 'A loud-mouthed, miserable sod who wants to fight the world. Is that what you're trying to say?'

'You know that's not what I'm saying.'

'Well, consider me your sister. How's that?'

'That's just fine.' And now that it was settled, they sat down to enjoy their food.

For the next hour, they talked and laughed and exchanged confidences, about their favourite film stars and songs. Annie was dead smitten by Guy Mitchell, the handsome American vocalist. Both girls loved listening to *Two-Way Family Favourites* on a Sunday morning, when requests were played by Jean Metcalfe. You had to have someone in the Forces, though, to send in a request.

'Ooh, I could listen to him all day,' mooned Annie.

The two girls watched the barges go by, and waved to the man at the tiller, and when the food was finished, they picked up their coats and strolled along the canal towpath. 'Hey, look lively, you two daydreamers! You'd best move, unless you want trampling to a pulp!'

Leading the horse along the towpath, the bargee had nowhere to go but onwards. Shafted to a wide strong harness, the huge powerful shirehorse was bent forward, using his great strength to draw the barge along in the water.

Leaping out of the way, the two girls went up on the bank and remained there, until the horse had pulled the barge to a wider part of the canal.

Suddenly, a brightly coloured ball came bouncing past with a little boy chasing it, and behind him ran a woman who caught the boy by the scruff of his neck. 'What have I told you before, Charlie? You are not to run near the edge of the water.'

Her companion was obviously her husband and the boy's father; tall and pleasant-looking, he appeared to be in his early forties and in his smart, double-breasted overcoat, he had the air of a successful businessman. 'Charles! You listen to your mother and do what she tells you!' Taking the ball from the child, he gave him a stern though not unkind scolding. 'I intend keeping this until you learn to do as you're told. It's for your own good. Now get between me and your mammy.' He tempered his rebuke with a forgiving smile. 'You can still see the ducks without diving in amongst them.'

A moment later, with his mammy holding his hand on one side and his daddy holding his other hand, the small boy walked happily along the towpath.

Annie winked at Judy. 'He's a bit of all right, don't you think?' She gestured to the man. 'I'll bet he's not short of a bob or two neither.'

Judy didn't think the man was anything special. In fact, compared with Davie's dad, Don, he wasn't worth a second glance. Annie was right on one count though, because unlike Don, this man probably *was* worth a bob or two. But Don was far more good-looking for a man of his age; he was full of the Irish blarney, and he had a cheeky smile, just like Davie.

A fleeting thought crossed her mind. What if Don never found out what happened after he left, and what if he and Davie never saw each other again? She swallowed.

Annie linked her arm through her friend's. 'You don't like the look of him, do you?' she teased.

'No, I don't.' Judy gave a shiver. 'There's something about him that gives me the creeps.' A bit like your brother, she thought – but didn't say so.

For a while the two girls just wandered and chatted, about this and that and nothing in particular, until Annie suddenly got very excited. 'Look!' She pointed to a spot on the other side of the river, surrounded by trees and away from the madding crowd; quiet and secluded, it was a favourite place with fishermen. 'Isn't that Lenny?'

Seated on a three-legged stool and lost in thought, Lenny didn't see them. 'Hey, Lenny!' Annie's distinctive voice sailed across the water. 'Mind if we keep you company for a while?'

Looking up, Lenny waved them over. He had been feeling lonely, but the sight of the two friends brightened his day. He really liked Judy, though everyone knew she and Davie would be sweethearts one day. But now Davie was gone, and though he was sorry for what had happened to Davie, he was glad Judy was still here. And as she crossed the bridge towards him, his heart was lurching all over the place.

'Is there really a need for them to shout like that?' The woman and her son had heard Annie call out and their attention was drawn to Lenny. 'Such vulgar behaviour!'

As the girls ran across the bridge and through the field towards Lenny, the man discreetly slowed his step to steal another look at Lenny.

Sensing the man's eyes on him, Lenny raised his head.

For an instant they exchanged glances until unnerved, the man quickly looked away.

'Stuart?' His wife's voice cut through his thoughts.

'What?'

'Do you know that young man?' She had seen him scrutinising Lenny from a distance.

'Of course I don't *know* him, Janette.' The man was obviously irritated. 'Why in God's name would I know him?'

'Do you know the two girls then?' The woman's intuition told her that something was untoward. She recalled various other unsettling instances, when her husband had given her reason to doubt his word.

He scowled at her. 'What's the matter with you? Sounds like a blasted inquisition! I don't know that young man, and I don't know those girls. All right?'

'I expect so, yes. And there is no need to swear.'

'Good. So now can we get off home?'

As they walked on, Janette Fitzwilliam gave the impression that she was satisfied with his answer. But she did not believe him. She knew her husband too well. She saw how the colour drained from his face when he looked across the water and suddenly, what had started as a leisurely Saturday afternoon stroll in the park now seemed a frantic rush to get away.

Twice the man discreetly glanced back; his mind alive with dark, intriguing thoughts. His wife had her suspicions, he was sure of it. But for now, what she didn't know wouldn't hurt her.

~

As they approached Lenny, Annie and Judy slowed their pace. 'I really like Lenny,' Annie confessed. 'I've always liked him.'

Judy was not surprised. Annie fancied every single boy she ever came across.

'Does he know?' she asked.

Annie shrugged her shoulders. 'Don't think so.'

'Why don't you tell him then?'

'I will,' Annie retorted, 'when the time is right.'

'If you really like him, don't leave it too long, or some other girl will snatch him from under your nose,' Judy warned.

'Hmh!' Annie showed her a bunched fist. 'Just let them try, that's all.'

'You like him *now*, but I bet you'll fancy somebody else before the week's out.' Judy had never met anyone more flippant than Annie.

'I won't!'

'What about Ian Lacey?'

'What about him? Ow!' Tripping over a stone, Annie picked it up and slammed it into the water. 'Damned thing, I've stubbed my toe now.'

'I thought you and Ian had taken a shine to each other?'

'Naw.' She made a grimace. 'He's not my type, and anyway, it's *you* he's waiting for.'

Judy smiled. 'He'll wait a long time then!'

'You'll see,' Annie chuckled. 'One of these days, he'll start making his move.'

'Then he's in for a disappointment, 'cause I'm not interested in him, or any other boy for that matter.'

'Except Davie, eh?' Annie wouldn't let it go.

'Davie is my friend,' Judy answered loyally.

Annie sighed. 'All right, if you say so.'

'I do say so, and I don't want to talk about it any more.' She loved Annie. If need be, she would risk her own life to save her. But sometimes, like now, Annie could be really invasive. She didn't mean to be: it was just her way.

As they closed the gap between Lenny and themselves, Annie lowered her voice. 'Just look at him,' she whispered excitedly. 'Isn't he gorgeous?' Her eager eyes appraised Lenny's strong physique, and the way his thick mop of brown hair fell haphazardly over one eye as he bent to retrieve the keepnet. 'Who wants Ian Lacey when you can have Lenny Reynolds?' Annie said dreamily. 'Lenny's already finished with school, and he's really ambitious. He's already got his own fruit and veg stall on the market.'

She leaned over and whispered in her friend's ear, 'I've seen him on a Saturday morning. I hide round the corner and watch him. He's really good at selling. The customers like him . . . they keep coming back. One woman said she'll never buy her cabbages from anybody else, 'cause his are the freshest she's ever had, and the cheapest into the bargain. Oh, Jude, I really do like him!'

Judy was about to giggle about the cabbages, but was glad she didn't, for just then, Annie fell into a sudden dark mood. 'Lenny is kind and decent,' she said harshly. 'Different from some people who don't give a bugger!'

Her face contorted with rage, she quickly stooped to collect a handful of stones, which she then impatiently threw one after the other into the water, sending the ducks swimming away in all directions. 'Some people love to hurt others. They don't deserve to walk about free . . . don't deserve to live!' The last stone was hurled with such viciousness, it frightened the ducks into the air.

Reaching out, Judy took hold of her hand. 'Annie, please don't.' She saw how nervous the ducks were. 'There's no need to take it out on them.'

When she looked up, she was surprised to see that the other girl was actually crying. 'Who's hurting you?' she asked worriedly. 'What's going on that you can't talk to me about?'

'I've already told you – there's nothing going on.' Wiping her face with the cuff of her sleeve, Annie took to her heels and ran to where Lenny was collecting his fishing gear. 'Packing up already?' she complained. 'I was hoping you might show me how to catch a fish.'

'I might have done, but you've frightened them all away,' he chided light-heartedly. 'The ducks too, by the looks of it.' Like everyone else he knew how unpredictable Annie could be. Added to that, she had a frightening temper, which was why she had few friends, except for Judy, who was always there for her, loyal and protective. 'All right, are you, Jude?' His eager smile was for her and her alone.

Judy returned his smile. 'Yes, thank you, Lenny.' Curious, she looked into his keepnet. 'Did you catch anything?'

'A few tiddlers,' he replied. 'Nowt worth keeping.' At which he tipped the net into the water and watched the small fish swim away.

For the next half hour, the three of them sat and talked about Lenny's market-stall, and his plans to open a shop one day. 'I know how to buy cheap stuff and sell it out for a profit,' he said proudly. 'I learn summat new every day.' He helped himself to a couple of leftover jelly babies.

A short time later, the three of them took a lazy walk to the spinney, and when they came out the other end, they sat on a fallen tree by the river's edge and dipped their bare toes in the water.

'I love it out here,' Lenny confided. 'I'd like to build a house right in the middle of a field, somewhere nice and peaceful, with plenty of animals, and I'd put a great big fence round it, so no one can get in.'

'Except me?' Annie hinted hopefully.

He laughed. 'All right, except you . . . and Judy.' While he talked to Annie, he was thinking of Judy, and when they walked on again, he walked next to her, while Annie pushed up to him on his other side. But he didn't mind that.

'Has anyone heard from Davie?' he wanted to know.

'Not yet,' Judy answered. 'Although he was at his mam's funeral today. I didn't get a chance to speak to him, though. But I might be going to see his grandad tonight. Happen he's heard something.'

'I'll walk you there if you like?'

'I'll come too,' Annie offered. 'We could have fish and chips on the way back.'

'That would be nice,' Judy agreed, 'but I expect I'll be going with Mam and Dad.'

As always, Annie never missed an opportunity. 'You can walk me to the chippie later if you like?' she told Lenny. 'I might even buy you a bag o' chips.'

He laughed. 'All right, if you like. I've got nothing else to do, and I hate staying indoors.' *He had good reason for preferring to be outdoors. But he could not discuss that with anyone.*

Annie continued to flirt shamelessly with him, while he kept glancing at Judy. Annie seemed too intent on Lenny to notice, and Judy was lost in thoughts about Davie.

At the mouth of the river they went their separate ways. 'See you outside the corner shop on Derwent Street at six o'clock!' Annie wasn't about to let him forget. 'You haven't changed your mind, have you?'

'I said I'd be there and I will.' It would give him a chance to find out how Judy felt about Davie, he thought. Annie had a big gob on her, and she couldn't keep a secret. He said his goodbyes and took his leave. With his fishing rod slung over his shoulder, and his wicker basket swinging from his fist, he made a fine figure of a young man.

'He kept looking at you,' Annie told Judy. 'If I didn't know how besotted you are with Davie, I might have to fight you for him.'

When Judy looked taken aback, Annie flung an arm round her shoulder. 'Sorry. I wouldn't fight you, not even if you were to rip out my eyes and leave me for the crows,' she laughed. 'All the same . . . hands off Lenny. He's mine!'

'Annie?'

'What?'

'Where do you think Davie is now?'

'Dunno.'

'Do you think he's safe?'

Annie shrugged. 'Dunno,' she repeated. There followed a brief silence, before she added cheerfully, 'Look, I know how fond you are of Davie, but there are plenty more fish in the sea. You'll soon forget him.'

But having said it, Annie knew different.

Judy would *never* forget Davie.

Even if, in the whole of her life, she never saw him again.

PART TWO

~

Blackpool, 1957

On the Run

CHAPTER TEN

IT WAS A hot morning in late July, and the Everly Brothers' number-one hit 'Bye Bye Love' was blaring out all over the fairground as the maintenance team inspected the rides before opening to the public. On Blackpool's famous Pleasure Beach, Billy Joe's Fairground was a right crowd-puller with thrilling rides like the Dive Bomber, Cake Walk, Octopus, Jet Planes, Meteorite and Moon Rocket. But it was sheer hard graft to keep the machinery in tip-top order, and no one worked more single-mindedly than the youth the other men knew by the name of Davie.

'Dear God, man! Must you drive the boy so hard?'

Some people claimed that Eli Clements was as old as Methuselah, but no one knew his true age, for he never divulged it to any living soul. A man of wit and wisdom, he looked pitifully small; his frame was slightly bent and his homely old face was cracked and worn by the elements. His joints creaked as he walked and sometimes he had to stop and catch his breath. But for all that, he could still outwork *and* outthink any man there. Eli had been around the fairground long enough to know every nut and bolt on every ride, and when the machines broke down he fearlessly scuttled round and underneath these massive structures, as if he was born to it.

The other men employed at Billy Joe's respected him, and sought his advice whenever it was needed. What Eli didn't know, they said, wasn't worth knowing. As a general rule he did not interfere, though on this particular occasion, he could not help but speak out.

'You're hellbent on breaking that young 'un,' he told the foreman, Brian Moult. 'And he's never once complained about the heavy tasks you've set him. What's going on?'

The other man bristled. 'I think you'd best explain what you mean by that.'

Eli was not intimidated. 'What I mean is that we've had plenty o' young 'uns come and go, and never a worry. So why is it you've taken against this particular one?'

'Don't talk so much rubbish, man!' The foreman was clearly ruffled. There were things he didn't want uncovered, and he knew how once Eli put his mind to something, there was no stopping him. 'Your brain must be addled. You're imagining things.'

The old man stood his ground. 'My brain's no more addled than yours is,' he retorted. 'And I'm not the only one who's noticed how harsh you are with the lad.' He glanced across to where Davie was carrying a heavy girder across his shoulders. 'No man here could have done more than he has.' His voice stiffened with anger. 'What the devil have you got against the boy?'

Sighing exaggeratedly, Moult took a moment to look down on the old man. 'I've got nothing against him,' he replied drily. 'We all have to pull our weight here, and he's no different. He'll do what's asked of him, or he can take his wages and get the hell out of it. I'll soon fill his place. There's allus blokes looking for work.'

He lowered his voice to a more intimate level. 'Matter o' fact, old fella, *you* might do well to remember that.'

Eli was never one to cower and he didn't cower now. Instead, he squared up to the bigger man. 'Only a bully would pick on a young lad like that. You ought to be ashamed of yourself!'

Twisted in a cunning grimace, the man's face bent to his. 'Young lad, is it?' he growled. 'More like an escaped criminal. Where's he come from, eh, tell me that? Turning up outta nowhere, his arse hanging out of his trousers, thin as a twig and looking like he'd been living out in the wilds. Oh, he works hard enough, I'll give you that. But who is he, eh? And why does he never talk about himself?'

Eli rose to Davie's defence. 'He doesn't have to "talk about himself". Who he is and where he comes from is none of your business.'

'Is that so?' The big man gave another crafty half-smile. 'All the same, there's summat funny about him. He's far too secretive for my liking . . . doesn't mix in with the men and never lets it be known what he's thinking. I'll tell you this, matey, whoever he might be, I wouldn't mind betting he's been up to no good somewhere along the line. He needs to be watched and kept under, and that's what I mean to do. So, if you don't like the way I treat him, you can leave whenever you want.'

Eli enraged him by smiling. 'Oh yes, you'd like that, wouldn't you, eh?' he chuckled. 'You'd like to see the back of me, so you can carry on with your sly little deals. I know what you're up to. I've had my eye on you for some time.'

Fear rippled over the other man's face. 'What the devil are you talking about, you old crow? What little deals?'

Winking, Eli tapped his nose. 'Never you mind,' he said. 'All you need to know is that I'm watching your every move. I've said my piece and that's enough for now.'

'You'd best watch your step, old fella.' The foreman was

worried; how much did Eli really know? 'This is a big site.' His intimation was clear enough. 'Accidents are bound to happen now and then.'

'Is that right?' Eli glanced at the Caterpillar ride; a snaking, iron monster of a thing. 'Well, there's your chance,' he taunted. 'I mean, I could be spreadeagled underneath the workings, and then . . .' He clicked his fingers. 'One flick of the switch, and I'd be mincemeat.'

Before the other man could respond, Eli called on the young electrician as he strolled by. 'Isn't that right, Josh?' Satisfied that his remarks had been overheard, he registered the occasion in the electrician's memory. 'I was just telling the foreman here how easy it would be to shred a man, if he was ever caught underneath the belly o' one of these rides.'

'Mebbe somebody who didn't know what they were doing,' the electrican replied. 'But I can't see *you* ever being caught out. You're a canny old devil, Eli. You always make sure you've switched off the engines and put all the keys in your pocket.' That said, he walked on. Like everyone else on-site, he had no wish to stop and pass the time of day with the foreman, because if he did, it was a sure fact he'd find his wages short come Friday.

'See that?' Eli's little ploy had worked as he intended. 'It's well-known how extra careful I am when it comes to being safe. I dare say there'd be an enquiry if old Eli was to suddenly get careless.' He lowered his voice. 'And once these officials start poking about where they're not wanted, who knows what else might be uncovered?'

'Well, I for one would have no worries,' came the sharp reply. 'I've got nothing to hide.'

All the same, he was wary of Eli. There was no way of knowing how much he knew. But from what he was hinting, the old scoundrel knew something, that was for sure.

'You'd better watch your back, Eli,' he warned. 'There are more ways than one to be rid of vermin.'

With that ominous remark, he walked away, leaving Eli in no doubt but that here was a man who would go to any lengths to suit his own dubious ends.

~

For the rest of the day, they kept out of each other's way. But when the day's work was over, and the men drifted away, Eli made straight for the washroom, where he found Davie at the sink, stripped to the waist and swilling off the grime of the day.

With his mind on other things, Davie didn't hear him come in, and for a moment Eli stood in the doorway, waiting for Davie to finish washing, yet still scouring the walkways, in case the foreman should happen this way.

He glanced at Davie as he towelled himself, and was amazed to see how the lad had matured these past few months. Cold, hungry and bedraggled, he had arrived one morning, a mere boy of fifteen, with the look of a lost and desperate soul. The skin hung on his back, and his face had the gaunt look of an old man. And there was such pain in his dark eyes; deep-down pain which had still not altogether gone away.

Yet here he was now, his frame muscled and toned by the heavy labour he was made to do. He was capable and confident, and though he kept a discreet distance from them, he was respected by the men who worked alongside him. He was a quiet soul though.

A real loner.

Eli had always thought Davie to be a good-looking lad. At his age, with his thick shock of dark brown hair and the brooding eyes that seemed not to miss a thing, Davie should have been out on the town, or flirting with the girls and planning a future. But there was no sign of it. Moreover, he had made no friends outside of the men he worked with, and when they went off to town, Davie stayed in the caravan, reading, writing and seemingly content in his own company. Eli thought it was an odd, unnatural thing for a boy on the brink of manhood.

But then he reminded himself how he had no way of knowing what had shaped a boy like Davie.

'Davie?' Satisfied they were on their own, Eli made his presence known.

Surprised to learn that he wasn't alone here, Davie swung round. 'Oh, it's you, Eli! I didn't see you there.'

He quickly towelled himself dry and slipping his shirt back on, he walked across the room towards the old fella. 'I thought everyone would have gone by now.'

'Most of 'em have,' Eli replied. 'I hung back, so's I could have a quiet word with you.' He snatched a glance along the path. 'Davie, there's something I need to ask you.'

'OK, ask away.' Davie liked old Eli. In many ways he reminded him of his grandad.

Eli shook his head. 'Not here, son,' he told him. 'Walls have ears, and besides, you never know who might come in.'

The boy was intrigued. 'I'm going back to the caravan,' he said. 'We can talk there.'

'Won't the others be there?'

Grabbing his coat, Davie shook his head, 'Josh and Pete are doing some overtime to get the rides ready for morning so we'll have the place to ourselves for a few minutes.' He grinned. 'I'll make you a cuppa tea, if you like?'

Eli groaned. 'I recall the last time you made me a brew,' he reminded Davie. 'The cup was half-filled with the insides of the kettle. Tasted like iron it did.'

Davie laughed. 'That's because the kettle was worn out,' he explained, 'but I've got a new one now. And I make the best cuppa tea on site, or so I'm told.' In his first few days here, part of his duties was to run errands and make tea. But he didn't mind; he was glad of the work.

'Sounds good to me.' Eli accepted and so they set off together.

Situated at the back of the site, the caravan was small and cramped, but it was cosy enough. All the same, as they entered and Davie threw open the windows, Eli had to confess, 'I don't think I could share this poky hole with two burly navvies.'

He laughed aloud. 'I dread to think what it's like, the morning after they've been out on the town; unshaven, spewing up – and I know for a fact that Josh's feet smell to high heaven.' He shook his head. 'How in God's name do you put up with it?'

'I've got no choice It's either sleeping rough – and I've had more than enough of that – or it's bedding down in here. The men are all right. We have an understanding. I like my own company and there are times when I don't want to mix in with the general talk. But they understand me, and I'm grateful for that.' Having satisfied himself that there was water in the kettle, Davie set it on the gas-ring to boil. 'It won't take a minute.' He plumped up a grubby cushion and invited Eli to sit himself down. Which Eli did, albeit grudgingly; the couch was filthy and the cushion was covered in what looked like dried egg. At any rate he was glad the windows were open and the air was freshening a bit.

While Eli made himself comfortable, Davie got out two mugs, washed them thoroughly at the sink, and placed them on the drainer. 'What did you want to ask me?'

Before Eli could answer, the whistle of the kettle sang out, and for a few minutes Davie was preoccupied making the tea. 'There!' Placing a mug of steaming tea in front of Eli, he sat at the other side of the minuscule table. 'So, what is it you want, Eli?'

The older man wondered how he should put his thoughts to the boy, 'Might as well come out with it,' he said finally. 'What do you know about the foreman?'

'That's a strange thing to say,' Davie answered too quickly. 'What makes you think I know any more than you do? Anyway, why do you ask?'

'Because I don't like how he pushes you to your limit, I can't understand how he gets away with working you like a damned horse . . . labouring from six of a morning until whatever time he thinks he can keep you sweating. There's something not right here, and I'd like to know what it is.'

Leaning forward, he looked Davie in the eye. 'What has he got over you, son? How can he do this to you?'

For a moment, Davie fell silent, and now as he tried to speak, he was flustered and nervous, all the old fears returning. 'Nothing. I mean . . . I don't know. I'm not complaining, am I? I like the work. It keeps me out of trouble . . . keeps me busy. And besides, I need the money. I don't intend slaving for someone else all my life. I've got plans.'

Eli was adamant but gentle. 'Look, son, I'm not saying you've done anything wrong. I'm just saying that the way he treats you is nothing short of cruel. Oh, I know he can be a right sadistic swine, but I've never known him take against anyone the way he's taken against you. I need you to tell me the truth, Davie. And I'm not leaving this caravan till you do.'

With that he took up his mug of tea, helped himself to a biscuit, sat back on the couch and waited patiently.

Davie's heart sank. Realising that Eli meant what he said, he decided to make his confession.

'If I tell you something,' he began warily, 'will you promise that you won't ever repeat it to anyone? And you won't go to the boss, and cause trouble for me?'

'I promise,' Eli assured him. 'Whatever you tell me, will stay with me.'

So, Davie told his story.

He described how his mother had torn the family apart, and how, when they were homeless, his grandfather put them up. 'And not for the first time,' he told Eli. 'Y'see, Mam got mixed up in things . . . men and booze mostly. But it wasn't her fault. She was weak – she told me that herself. Her own mam was the same, and so I suppose it was in the blood.'

The telling was a difficult thing for Davie. All this time since leaving Blackburn, he had not spoken of it to a living soul. And now, with every word he uttered, it seemed as though he was unlocking a door that he had once firmly shut.

'The last time was the worst ever.' He relived the scene. 'We waited all night for her. Dad even went out looking, but he couldn't find her. She came home in the early hours, out of her mind with booze – in a terrible state, she was. Dad was waiting and he tried to reason with her, but she wouldn't listen. Then he told her he was leaving, that she would never change and he couldn't live like that any more.'

When the memories became too much and the emotion choked him to silence, Eli reached out and touched him on the shoulder. 'Go on, son,' he urged kindly. 'Sometimes it's good to get things out in the open. If you keep 'em buried deep, they'll only drive you crazy.'

It seemed like an age before Davie got up from the table and began pacing the floor, head bent and his heart aching. 'She tried to stop him from leaving, but he wouldn't listen.

He'd had enough. I thought he was being too cruel, but I've thought about it a lot, and I've come to realise how he must have felt.'

'So your dad left, did he, son?'

'Yes.' Davie nodded. 'Before he went, they had an argument on the stairs. Grandad was there . . . he lashed out in anger. Mam was fighting and unsteady, and then she just fell . . . tumbled all the way down the stairs. Dad tried to help her but she wouldn't let him. She seemed all right though . . . not hurt or bleeding or anything like that.'

In his mind's eye he could see it all happening, every small detail, hear every angry word. 'Grandad told her to go and stay with one of her boozy friends, because he was too old and frail to put up with her any more. He wanted me to stay, but I wouldn't. I wanted to be with her. We went to this man's house . . . she thought he would put us up, but he told us to clear off, that he wanted nothing to do with her.' Shamed, he bowed his head, and for a moment it seemed he might not go any further.

Coming back to the table, he sat down without a word. After a while, he looked up at the older man, his eyes haggard and tearful, and his heart turning over and over. 'Mam said we should go to the church – that someone would help us there. We got as far as the woods,' he whispered, 'when . . . she . . .' He dropped his gaze and composed himself. 'She died, Eli,' he said in a heartbreaking tone. 'My mam died, and there was nothing I could do.'

Suddenly, he covered his face with his arms and began to sob.

'My mam died,' he kept saying. 'She left me – and there was nothing I could do . . . *nothing*.'

Wisely, Eli made no move. Instead, he let Davie cry it all out. He watched and waited, and his old heart wept alongside the boy.

After a while, Davie wiped his face and gave a long, shuddering sigh. 'I'm sorry, Eli. I've always been able to keep it inside before.'

Eli brushed aside his apology. 'Then it's time you let it all out,' he said gently. 'No man can bear such grief on his own, let alone a young 'un like you.'

Feeling as though he had shed a great weight from his shoulders, Davie went on, 'For almost two years I went from place to place – looking for my dad, I think. I never settled anywhere, was always on the run, not knowing where I was going, or even who I was any more.'

'And did you find your father?'

Davie shook his head. 'No. I even went to Ireland, but it was like looking for a needle in a haystack.' He recalled the long, weary days when he trudged the streets asking questions and getting no answers. 'It's as though he disappeared from the face of the earth.'

'And then you found your way here.' Eli felt privileged that Davie was confiding in him.

Davie nodded. 'I couldn't stay with any job for more than two minutes,' he confessed. 'I just kept moving. Sometimes I didn't even know where I was.' He took a moment to relive those awful times. 'I became a thief, Eli,' he said shamefully. 'I stole food and clothes, and once I nearly got caught by the police. Then I got in with a bad lot. One night they promised me a lot of money to go with them and help break into this big house . . . The owner was away, they said . . . A pig of a man, they reckoned. They claimed that one of them had been beaten black and blue by him – put into hospital for weeks, they said.'

'I see.' Eli recognised how they were probably just using Davie – taking advantage of his situation. 'Older than you, were they?'

137

Davie nodded. 'By a good many years, I should say.' But he wasn't excusing his own part in what happened. 'I knew they were up to no good,' he assured Eli. 'But it didn't seem to matter at the time.'

'So you went with them, did you?' he asked. 'You broke into this man's house while he was away?'

Davie sighed. 'It all went horribly wrong. Mr Graham hadn't gone away at all; nor, as it turned out, was he an ogre. I found out later that he'd chased one of them off when he caught them hanging about the back of the house. So they had decided to teach him a lesson. They knew he'd be there, all right.'

'What happened?'

'They dragged him out of bed and beat him terribly, and when I tried to stop them, they set about me. Some time later, when I came round, the old man was lying on the floor . . . scarcely breathing.' Davie had a lump in his throat, recalling the panic he had felt at the sight of the old man sprawled beside him. 'There was blood everywhere.'

'So, what did you do?'

'I tried to help him, but he was so still, and he was cold. I put a blanket round him, but I didn't really know what I was doing. They'd kicked me in the head and I couldn't see out of one eye. I kept vomiting, too. Eli, I just lost my wits. I was terrified! I ran . . . I just ran through the house, and as I shot out of the door, the police were everywhere.'

At first he couldn't understand why they were there. 'I thought a neighbour must have called them, then I wondered if the others had shopped me. I tried to get away, but they caught me. I told them what had happened, but they said I'd have plenty of time to explain myself in court. They took my name and then they threw me into the car and drove me to the police station.'

'And when you went to court, they believed you, is that it?'

Davie shook his head, wincing. 'I never went to court. I jumped out of the car when we got to the police station. I could hear them shouting for me to stop, but I kept going . . . I just ran and ran, until I couldn't hear them any more.'

Eli was shocked that Davie could have gone along with those thugs, and even more saddened by the fact that a man had probably died. 'Dear God, Davie, what were you thinking of? You should never have run away. The best thing would have been for you to tell the court exactly what you've just told me . . . and then take your punishment.'

'I know that now. I was scared they wouldn't listen. Scared they'd hang me for murder.' He shuddered.

'So, where did you go?'

Pacing the floor as he talked, Davie went on, 'I travelled day and night, always looking over my shoulder. They knew my name . . . they knew what I looked like. I was afraid they'd find me. But then, when a year had gone by, I felt safe. I decided to get a proper job and that's how I came to be here.'

Putting two and two together, Eli asked, 'Does Brian Moult know all this? Is that part of the reason why he thinks he has a hold over you?'

Davie told him exactly what had happened, the day he arrived in Blackpool. 'I took a coach here, thinking that Blackpool was an ideal place to hide, full of holidaymakers and casual work. I was walking along the seafront, saw Billy Joe's and ducked in here to enquire about a job. Then, just as I was coming through the gates, I saw a police car pull up. Two officers went into the office and I saw them through the window, talking to Mr Moult. Then they came out and I waited for a while. I wasn't sure what to do. What if the police had somehow followed me here?'

'Hardly likely,' Eli said. 'Unless you told somebody where you were headed. Did you?'

Davie cast his mind back. 'I don't think so, but I can't be sure. Y'see, there was a farm some way back . . . I worked on the land for a time. The family there fed me and let me stay in the barn. I don't remember saying anything about my plans. I always keep myself to myself.'

Eli had noticed that, and he had been curious as to why a personable young fellow like Davie would want to keep a distance between himself and those around him; even though he shared a caravan, he was always out first and in last. 'You're a loner, son,' he said kindly. 'I sensed that from the start.'

Davie admitted, 'I've been on my own for too long, and sometimes I find it hard to talk with people.' Since that awful night at Derwent Street, followed by the death of his mother, he had been unable to communicate much with anyone. What was the point? They would leave him, wouldn't they? Sooner or later, everyone would leave. Best to keep yourself to yourself: expect nothing and depend solely on your own resources. If he didn't stick to that, he'd have spent every waking moment looking over his shoulder, waiting for the next big hurt to come along.

'So, even though you were worried the police might be on your trail, you still came into the office and asked for work?'

'I had no choice, and anyway, I made myself believe the police were here on some other errand.'

Eli had been thinking the very same. He wouldn't be at all surprised if Moult hadn't used the police against the boy for some devious reason of his own. And with Davie's next words, his suspicions were strengthened.

'I was starving hungry, and it was so bitter cold, I couldn't face the idea of sleeping outside again, and like I said, I couldn't recall telling anyone where I was headed. I didn't even know myself, where I might end up. So I took a chance and went after the work.'

He finished, 'I waited for ages, and when I thought it was safe, I went up the steps to the office, and as I made to knock on the door, I overheard a conversation between Mr Moult and another man. They were talking about some money they'd got stashed away. From what I could gather, they made it by cheating the owner of Billy Joe's . . . something about buying cheaper parts and such, and billing the company for twice the amount. They were saying that if they kept on the way they were and nobody any the wiser, they'd be able to "wrap it all up, and live a life of luxury".'

With a triumphant cry, Eli thumped the air. 'I knew it!' His suspicions were borne out. 'I had a feeling he was up to summat, but I couldn't quite put my finger on it. Then today, I bluffed him into believing that I knew exactly what he was up to. I was just stabbing in the dark. I didn't know anything, not really. Oh, but I do now!'

'Eli!' Davie was aware of the bitterness between the two men. 'You promised not to say anything to him.'

'And I won't,' Eli assured him with a mischievous grin. 'But like the man said, "there are more ways than one to be rid of vermin".'

'I don't want him riled,' Davie added. 'If he thought I was making trouble for him, he'd have me put away and no mistake.'

'So, go on then,' Eli urged. 'What happened, exactly?'

'Well, I heard them plotting and planning, and I had half a mind to sneak away and look elsewhere for work. Then the door was suddenly flung open and Brian had me by the collar. He dragged me inside and asked me what I'd heard.

I told him I hadn't heard anything, and that I just wanted work. But he knew I'd heard it all. I think he could tell I was on the run, from the way I looked. He told me the police had just been there, and that they were looking for me. They were turning the country upside down, and all he had to do was pick up the phone and they'd be straight back to take me away. I just panicked – didn't try to find out if it was true.'

'Bastard!' Eli was determined to teach the foreman and his partner-in-crime a lesson. 'So, he's been blackmailing you ever since, is that it? Making you do twice the hours and more than your fair share of work?'

Davie nodded. 'He said he'd keep quiet about me, if I kept quiet about what I'd overheard. But he wanted me here, where he could keep an eye on me. If I ever said a word to anyone, or tried to make a run for it, he swore that he'd track me down . . . said there'd be no escape. That he'd find me and keep me, until the police came and took me away.'

Eli was beside himself. 'Well, he won't get away with it, don't you worry. I'll see to that!'

'*No*, Eli!' Davie turned on him. 'Let it be. I don't mind the work, not really. Besides, you gave your word not to say anything.'

Eli assured him, 'Your secret is safe with me, although I'm convinced that at some stage you ought to turn yourself in and tell the police about that night. You can't live on the run for the rest of your life.'

'I will.' Davie had been giving it some thought, too. 'But not yet. I'm biding my time until I can go in search of the other two. I need them to come with me and tell the truth of what happened.'

The old man gave a wry little laugh. 'Sorry, son, but from

what you've told me about that pair, they're not about to turn themselves in. If that man died, they could be hanged for it.'

Davie turned deathly pale. 'So, what can I do?' He was frantic. 'I'm trapped, but I can't stay here like this for ever.'

'There'll be no need.'

'How come?'

'Well, now you've confided in me, it's given me a chance to turn the tables on that bully Moult.'

'But that would mean putting yourself in danger.'

Eli gave a knowing wink. 'That's where you're wrong, son. You see, there's nothing he can blackmail *me* with. But, given what I now know, I can make *his* life very uncomfortable . . . if I've a mind to.'

Davie was still concerned. 'If he knew I'd told you, he could cause all kinds of trouble for me.' He hoped the foreman hadn't seen Eli come to his caravan.

Eli understood Davie's fears. 'Tell me something, lad; if all this hadn't happened, would you still be scouring the country, searching for your father?'

The youth sighed. 'No, Eli, I wouldn't. I've given up. I've spent nearly two long years searching for him, and now, I think if I spent another two years searching I still wouldn't find him.'

His voice fell to a whisper. 'He gave me a piece of paper with the name of a man on it; he said if ever I wanted to contact him, I should get in touch with this man, because he would always know where to find my dad.'

'And did you?'

Davie shook his head. 'I never even read it. I were in that much of a state, I lost it. One minute I had it, folded up tight in my pocket, the next, it was gone.'

'And you've no other clue as to where he might be?'

'None. Unless he went back to Ireland.' He had long ago given up the idea that one day he would walk around a corner and there would be his father. 'It's been so long, Eli. He might have a whole new life – children and such. I can't help but wonder if he even *wants* to be found. You see, I didn't.'

It was the first time that the youth had voiced this truth. He hadn't even written to Judy, his best pal. Somehow, it got harder, the longer he left it. He'd been in shock, he knew now – a much deeper shock than anyone could understand – and it had lasted a long, lonely time. He hoped she would forgive him.

'Mebbe he does and mebbe he doesn't. And mebbe he hasn't got a regular woman nor children, and doesn't want them. Mebbe he's still in love with your mammy.' Old Eli felt for Davie. 'Look, son. You must never give up searching for him. In case he doesn't know, he has every right to find out what happened to his wife, because until then I don't suppose he can even begin to think about a new life.'

'You're right,' Davie said. 'That's why I need to find him. To tell him what happened after he'd gone, and to let him know that I don't blame him.'

'Good lad!' Eli was encouraging. 'It could be, now that some time has passed, your dad longs to see you as much as you do him. You just have to keep hoping and searching. I also think you should get in touch with your grandad. He may have heard something. Your dad may have contacted him. But first, and most importantly, you need to get right away from here.'

Davie was surprised that Eli could even put such a thing to him. 'It's impossible! How can I ever get away from here?' he asked. 'You know what Brian Moult is like. He meant every word he said.'

'You leave Moult to me.' Reaching into his waistcoat pocket, Eli took out a small pad and a pencil. He began scribbling, advising Davie at the same time. 'You must get a good night's sleep, then in the early hours while everyone's still abed, you're to quietly make your way to this place.'

Tearing off the top sheet of paper, he handed it to Davie. 'My old pal's name is Ted Baker. He farms some hundred acres outside of Bedford, in the area called Goldington. Greenacres Farm is the name of his place.' He smiled at the memories now flooding his mind. 'Years back, afore the war, me and Ted went from farm to farm, working the land and having the time of our lives; until the years caught up with us. When Ted was offered management of Greenacres, he jumped at the chance. Then he got married, and so did I, and in the end, we went our separate ways . . . though we never lost touch.'

He scratched his head. 'Mind you, come to think of it, I haven't heard hide nor hair of him this past year. But then I'm not concerned, because that's how it's been. We write every month or so for a time, and then it'll be a whole year before we contact each other again. Farmers are busy people, and they don't get too much time for letter writin'.'

'So, how do you know he's still there?' the boy asked.

Eli laughed at that. 'Because he's too deeply rooted in the land to do anything else. Farming is all he knows, and all he ever wanted. Old Ted has found his bit of Paradise. Believe me, son, he'll be there, you mark my words.'

He wrote a second note, and in it he told his old friend that Davie was the hardest-working young man he'd ever come across, and that he needed work and a place to stay. He explained how Moult had got his claws into him, and how, once Davie was safely out of the way, he intended giving the bullying foreman a taste of his own medicine.

He finished the letter by promising that he would make an effort to visit, sooner rather than later, and that he hoped all was well with his old friend. *We'll drink the drink and revisit the old days*, he wrote, and when the letter was finished, he folded it over and passed it to Davie. 'Give this to him,' he instructed. 'He'll help you – I know he will.'

Davie carefully placed both slips of paper into a neat box with a sliding lid that he had fashioned on his travels. After the experience of losing his father's contact's details, he was determined never to lose anything else.

Eli got up and said his goodbyes. 'My old lass will be wondering where I am,' he said. 'Don't forget to let me know how you're doing, lad – and don't concern yourself about Moult.' Again he gave that knowing smile. 'Putting that pipsqueak in his place will give me a great deal of pleasure.'

~

For a long time after Eli left, Davie lay on his bunk, thinking and planning, and hoping that the old man wasn't about to get himself into trouble on his account. Deep down though, he had a good feeling about it all. Eli must know what he's doing, he told himself. 'I could do worse than trust his judgment.' All the same, unlike Eli, he could not be certain that Brian Moult would let him go so easily. If the police became involved . . . Davie dare not even think about it.

When a mood of restlessness threatened to settle on him, he decided not to wait for the others to return. If he didn't go now, he'd never find the courage, he thought.

Throwing on his donkey-jacket and cramming his few belongings into a duffel bag, he opened the door and peered out. The machines had all been turned off and the crowds had gone. In the stillness of night, and from somewhere in the distance, he could hear his two workmates laughing and chatting as they made their way back to the caravan.

Now was his chance. Eli had urged him to get a good night's sleep, but Davie was too churned up for that. Right now, his instincts were urging him to leave, and to trust that wily old fella Eli to deal with the repercussions.

With the laughter of his two colleagues edging closer with every minute, he grabbed up his bag and left that place. Soft as a fox in the night, he crept away, down the steps and round behind the caravan. Then he ran along by the perimeter of the site, hoisted himself over the fence, and he was free as a bird.

'Did you see that?' Having enjoyed a drink or two in a lively seafront pub, the two workmen ambled along, delightfully drunk and disorderly. 'There's somebody there,' full of gas and booze, Josh belched long and hard.

Pete sniggered. 'Seeing things, are yer, mate? That's a bad sign, that is. You've got the gallopin' DTs!'

'No! I'm telling you. Look over there – somebody's climbing the fence.'

'You gormless bugger, there's nothin' out there!' Pete said, going to urinate against a tree. 'You must be seein' things.'

The two of them went away laughing. 'You never could take your booze, could yer, Josh. One sip of Newcastle Brown and your imagination runs riot.' Pete's raucous laughter echoed across the site. 'It'll be monsters coming out the sky next.'

'Ssh! Stop your noise. I'm taking over from the night-watchman in half an hour, and if that blasted foreman finds out I've been boozing, I'll be on me way, no doubt with you in tow, first thing tomorrow morning.'

The prospect of no work and no wages quietened them for a while. But it wasn't long before they were again poking fun at each other, helpless with laughter as they fell up the steps to the caravan; so addled with booze, they didn't even notice that Davie was long gone.

~

Doggedly pushing ahead, Davie wended his way to the open road, where he hoped he might cadge a lift south. He would not rest easy until he had put as much distance between himself and Billy Joe's Fairground as he could.

Having grieved to the full for his mother, and been unsuccessful in the search for his father, he was now more than ready for a new chapter in his life.

He felt as though, with this help, he had turned a corner, and maybe, just maybe, there were good things ahead for him.

With that in mind, and with every step he took, his heart felt lighter than it had done in a long, lonely time.

CHAPTER ELEVEN

THE JOURNEY WAS hard, and the weather was stormy. At times almost tropically hot, the rains soon came, and shelter was not easy to find. Hitching a lift was a nightmare as people pushed on, eager to reach their destination and wary of a young man standing by the roadside, bedraggled and wet.

After several uncomfortable days of working his way down the country, Davie was sorely tempted to seek more permanent work and to settle wherever he could lay his head.

But he had promised Eli that he would find his old friend in Bedford. With Ted Baker he had prospects of a new life, a safe haven, and regular money coming into his pocket. That was what he craved, and that was what he kept in mind.

So, he drove himself onwards, sometimes cadging a lift and at other times paying for transport. But with his limited funds, he was making slow headway.

Just when his spirits were at their lowest ebb, the stormy weather cleared, his humble stash of hard-earned money grew, and life was altogether more comfortable. He got a full three weeks of work in the market in Wolverhampton, before following the trail south-east again; but first he visited the second hand clothing stall to replace his boots and clothes, all of which had seen better days.

Never more comfortable than when he was outdoors, free and unencumbered, Davie stripped naked to bathe in brooks and rivers; he slept under trees and immersed himself in the privacy and seclusion he had long valued. Day and night, the skies were his umbrella and the wild creatures were his friends. And when he let his mind wander, it always went back home to Blackburn, to his grandad and Judy. He wondered whether his father had been in touch with the old man, and if he had, did he now know the truth about what had happened after he walked out on them? Did he want to find his son? And was he even now, out there somewhere, searching for Davie?

Disillusioned and cynical, Davie would sigh at the thought, and push it from his mind. He wasn't ready yet to make contact with Joseph, or even with Judy. Time had moved on, and so much was altered. He had spent many long months searching for his father, and Don was nowhere to be found. What made him think his father would be out on the road searching for *him*? And what if, by some miracle, they *did* find each other? Would they still be the same as before? Had his father changed? Would he find his son changed?

Would they be able to pick up where they had left off? And more importantly, would Davie be able to forgive how he walked out? Even now, Davie couldn't help but wonder . . . if his father *had* stayed, would his mother still be alive?

Davie was haunted by what might have been, but he did not apportion blame. It was simply a sorry series of events over which, it seemed, no one had had any control.

When he thought of his father, he was afraid of losing him, in the same way he had lost everything that was precious in his life. And when he thought of his mother, he was angry and sad, and filled with bitterness at the circumstances that had made her that way.

Day and night, these haunting thoughts never left him. They were part of his past and they shaped his future. And that future seemed a vast empty place.

When he thought of Judy though, his heart warmed. In his mind's eye he saw her happy bright smile, he heard the light, musical sound of her laughter. He saw her running across the paddock, long brown hair flying out behind her and no shoes on her feet. He imagined her sitting cross-legged on the grass, wide-eyed and full of wonder as she listened to his fanciful dreams and his excited ramblings. And oh, how she had cared; more than anyone else, it was Judy who had shared his impossible dreams.

She had been such a big part of his growing-up, and he missed her terribly. And he knew that, if he travelled the world over, he would never find a friend like her again.

One day though, he told himself, one day in the future, when his dreams were fulfilled and his roving at an end, he would turn towards home. He would see Judy and his grand-father again – and oh, the tales he would have to tell them!

~

One beautiful spring day, some nine months after leaving Blackpool, he hitched a lift into the outskirts of Bedford. 'Here you are.' Having stopped his wagon on the Cardington Road, the gruff, bearded driver waited for Davie to climb down from the cab. 'I hope you find what you're looking for,' he called.

Davie thanked him, closed the cab door and waved him on. And when the lorry was gone from sight, Davie was surprised and thrilled to see before him the wide, flowing

River Ouse, flanked on either side by banks of well-kept grass, and crossed at different points by numerous bridges, each with its own character.

Davie thought it a beautiful place. Majestic swans glided through the water; children played on the banks under the wary eyes of their mothers, and when the occasional canoe was driven out from beneath a bridge, the ensuing ripples created wider and wider circular patterns that broke into a trillion pieces as they came into contact with the walls at either side.

People on bicycles wended their way in and out of the age-old weeping willows that lined the pathways either side of the river; young couples lay on the grass, kissing and canoodling, oblivious to the passers-by. In the nearby cafés, customers sat and chatted, and from somewhere along the river floated the sounds of a playing brass-band.

The sun shone down and there was a sense of magic in the air. And for the moment at least, Davie was content to be a part of it.

So this was Bedford, his destination. He glanced about. Was this where he was meant to be? he mused. Was this where he would finally belong? He hoped so. He really and truly hoped so.

Feeling wearied by the long journey from his last stopover at Northampton, where he had done a fortnight's stint in a shoe factory, he headed for one of the small cafés overlooking the river. Here he settled himself as far away from the busiest area as possible; he could see the river from here, yet avoid the prying eyes of strangers.

'What can I get you?' The trim, middle-aged waitress was polite though unfriendly, and that was exactly how he wanted it – though what he didn't know was that she was quietly noting his crumpled clothes and wondering where he hailed from, and why he had chosen to sit here, when there were plenty of other, more suitable places – cafes where the workmen gathered to chat, or one of the many public houses in town.

But for all his scruffy appearance, she thought he seemed well-mannered and amiable, if somewhat uncomfortable around people.

'I'd like the biggest mug of coffee you do,' he requested, in a Northern accent. 'Oh, and a thick bacon buttie, with lashings of bacon, please.' The very idea made his mouth water; it was a long time since he'd had the taste of a good, genuine bacon buttie.

'I'm afraid we don't do bacon sandwiches, but I can offer you a ham and tomato roll.' And when he nodded, abashed, she said, more kindly, 'I'll make that two, shall I, sir?'

While she went to get his order, Davie made himself comfortable, determined to enjoy his moment of luxury and to savour the beauty of this idyllic scene. There would be time enough to go in search of the address Eli had given him. Meanwhile, he would sit and think, and make his plans for the future – though what his future might be, was anyone's guess.

He relished his snack to the full. Afterwards, satisfied and content, he ordered another cup of coffee and sat with it for a good half-hour, enjoying the treat; until finally he felt the urge to continue his search for Eli's friend.

At the counter he fished the relevant coins out of his pocket and paid his dues, even leaving a sixpence tip for the waitress. 'Thank you.' She actually smiled on him as he went.

Whether it was the sixpence that made her smile, or the sight of him leaving, the youth couldn't be certain.

Once outside and away from watchful eyes, Davie retrieved the slim wooden box from his duffel bag and took out the piece of paper with the name and address on it given to him by Eli. He found the older man's scrawl difficult to decipher:

Mr Edward Baker
Greenacres Farm
Goldington, BEDS

There were no further directions and no telephone number. 'Good God, Eli!' Davie said aloud. 'You could have drawn me a little map, or given me a list of directions to help me on my way.'

He stopped to ask passers-by, and it seemed no one knew the whereabouts of Greenacres Farm. 'Why not go to the bus depot and ask at the counter there,' suggested one helpful old dear. 'If anybody knows where it is, they'll be the ones.'

Following her excellent advice, he queued up at the ticket-counter of the bus and coach depot. 'I'm looking for a place called Greenacres Farm,' Davie explained hopefully. 'It's near here, somewhere around Goldington.'

The clerk knew of it. 'You'll need a number fourteen bus,' he told Davie. 'It won't take you to the door, but the driver will drop you off on the main street, then it's a walk along the lanes to the farm.'

Thanking him, Davie made his way across the boulevard, where he boarded a number 14 bus headed for Cambridge. He explained to the conductor where he needed to get off. 'You're on the right bus,' came the reply, 'but you'll have to walk three miles or so once we've dropped you off.'

Seeming to have no choice, Davie settled himself into a seat, where he was quickly joined by a small boy. 'Where are you going?' he asked of Davie.

Davie looked around, and seeing how the woman behind

was appearing to keep an alert eye on the child, he enquired of her, 'Is it yours?'

'Not exactly.' She appeared to be amused by Davie's description of the boy. 'I'm just looking after "it" while my daughter works the morning shift, she answered with a smile.

Davie nodded. 'Friendly young feller-me-lad, isn't he?'

'Is he troubling you?'

Davie would have preferred to answer yes. But when at that moment he looked down to see the little face uplifted in a cheeky grin, his heart melted. 'No, of course not,' he answered. 'He's no trouble at all.'

Satisfied, the woman sank back in her seat and left Davie to the chatter of her grandchild. After Davie was made to answer umpteen questions, about his destination, and why he was on the bus, and where his mum was, the child grew increasingly fidgety. 'Are you all right?' Davie thought the child was feeling travel sick.

'Have you got a hankie?' The little boy held out his hand.

Davie shook his head. 'No. Sorry, I haven't.'

'I need a hankie.'

Davie fished about in his pocket and as he thought, there was no hankie to be found, and behind him, the woman appeared to have nodded off. 'Got a cold, have you?' he asked the child.

'No.'

'So, why do you need a hankie?'

Lowering his voice, he made a face. 'I think I've plopped in my pants.' To Davie's horror, he gabbled proudly on, 'I plopped in them before . . . when Grandma took me to the pictures. She said I was a dirty little hound and gave me a smack.'

Horrified, Davie inched aside, his nose wrinkled in antici-pation. 'You haven't plopped now, have you?'

155

Wriggling and squirming, the boy dutifully felt the crutch of his trousers, his face crumpling as he looked up at Davie. 'Dirty hound,' he groaned. 'Dirty little hound.' The crying started as a kind of whining, which quickly soared to the pitch of hysteria. 'Want my grandma!'

'You little bugger!' Mortified, his grandma reached out, and grabbing him by the scruff of his neck, she hoisted him over the seat towards her. 'What did I tell you, eh?' Her voice sailed down the bus. 'Didn't I say, if you needed the toilet you were to ask me before we got on the bus – and now you've been and done a packet in your new trousers, you dirty little hound. Well, you can sit in it now, until we get home. And I hope it teaches you a lesson you won't forget!'

None of the passengers would ever forget it either, especially Davie, who got the full stench of the suspect 'packet' in the boy's trousers.

Relieved when they reached his stop, Davie scrambled off the bus. 'Which way to Greenacres Farm?' he asked the conductor before they set off again.

'Go left from here . . . down the lanes about three mile or so. The farm is on your left. You can't miss it.'

Davie thanked him and turned away. The end of his long journey from Blackpool to Bedford was finally within reach.

'Bye, bye, man!' The boy's cheery voice sailed after him.

'Bye, bye.' From a safe distance he turned and waved, chuckling heartily as he went. He hoped the little chap was not too uncomfortable.

Davie pushed on towards Greenacres Farm, in no particular hurry now his destination was so close. Instead he sauntered, pausing every now and then to take in what was all around him. The grass verges were alive with all manner of wild flowers, and above him the birds sang and courted, and in every field there was much to see; the cows and sheep, and the occasional fox that slunk its way along the hedge-rows, and just there, skirting the stream, was a moor hen with its babies trailing behind.

He wondered what Ted Baker was like, and suspected he would be made in the same mould as Eli . . . kind and honest, with a way of speaking out when he thought he was right.

In his mind's eye he pictured Ted Baker as a strong, ruddy-faced man, wrinkled by the elements, and possessed of a twinkle in his eye. No doubt like Eli, he too favoured a pint of the good stuff when it was available. All in all, Davie was looking forward to meeting him.

As always, after a time his thoughts turned to Judy. She'd have liked it here, he knew. He leaned on a gate and looked out at the lambs frisking in the field. She'd have been out there, talking to the lambs and paddling in the stream. He grinned, but then suddenly felt very lonely. 'You deserve everything good, my Judy,' he murmured. 'I hope you meet somebody who will look after you the way you deserve.'

He had never thought of Judy as a sweetheart, despite that wonderful kiss she had given him; to Davie, she had been more of a sister. But just then, imagining her in some other boy's arms, he felt a peculiar ache. It might be many years before they met up again, he knew, but they would do so one day, he was sure. Meanwhile, he wished her all the happiness in the world.

He was deep in thought when he was suddenly alerted by the thunder of horse's hooves, fast and furious, heading in his direction. Straightening up, he looked across the field and there it was . . . a huge black horse, bolting out of the spinney, with the rider clinging onto its back for dear life.

There was no time for thinking. Instinctively, Davie jumped the gate into the field and at once the rider was yelling at him to: 'GET OUT OF THE WAY, YOU DAMNED FOOL!'

Undeterred, Davie stood his ground; albeit with an eye for diving into the ditch, should he need to. Horses had always been his favourite animals; he loved and respected them, and through his many travels, he had learned so much more about their natures – knowledge that he prayed would stand him in good stead now.

With the rider in danger of falling and either breaking his neck or being trampled underfoot, Davie had to take action. As the horse neared, he opened his arms and looked it in the eye. 'Whoa, boy . . . whoa now . . .'

Wild-eyed and frothing at the mouth, the horse began to falter, yet continued to head straight for Davie and the gate, and the road beyond. And Davie knew if it got into the road, it could spell death and disaster for the rider, and his horse. 'WHOA THERE!' he repeated strongly. Though his heart was bumping with fear and he knew all the risks, Davie stood his ground.

At the last minute the horse turned, reared into the air and threw the rider to the ground, and for one awful minute it seemed as though its hooves would descend and beat him to pulp.

'Easy, boy . . . take it easy . . .' Davie's first thought was for the man who had landed awkwardly and was lying too still on the ground. The danger had not gone away, as the horse continued to snort and flail its legs in the air.

'All right . . . easy, boy. Come on, now . . . easy.' Several times Davie tried to calm it, but the horse was too agitated. With a final shake of its head, it galloped off across the field and back the way it had come.

Davie turned his attention to the man, who was now beginning to stir and moan. 'Damned bloody brute! Got spooked by a rabbit and took off as if all the bats in hell were after him!' Groaning in agony, he closed his eyes and lay still for a minute. 'As for you, what in God's name were you thinking of?' He vented his rage on Davie. 'You ruddy lunatic . . . you could have been killed!'

Wisely ignoring the stranger's reprimands, Davie sat him up; no easy task as he was a man of stature. Some fifty years old or so, with earthy-coloured hair, brown eyes and a quick temper, he did not take kindly to being thrown to the ground.

'Do you think you can stand?' Davie enquired warily.

'If you'll give a helping hand, lad, I'm sure I'll be just fine.' With Davie's assistance, the man struggled up, crying out when he tried to put his foot to the ground. His face was grey with pain. 'Something's wrong.'

Glancing down, Davie saw how the man's right foot was twisted into an odd shape. 'I reckon you've got a sprain,' he told him. 'Don't try putting any weight on it.' Sliding his arm round the man's waist, he took the considerable weight to himself. 'Where do you live?'

The man pointed towards the top of the field. 'Over the hill,' he said . . . 'A half-mile or so.'

'Well, there are two things I can do,' Davie explained. 'I can try to make you comfortable and leave you here, while I run for help. Or, if you're able and it's not too painful, I can take your weight and we can hobble you home. Which is it to be?'

'Get me home,' the man answered determinedly. 'And on the way you might forgive an old fool for cursing you, eh?' Through his pain he had a warm smile.

Davie spent a few minutes searching for a sturdy fallen branch to act as a crutch under the man's right armpit; while he supported him on the left, good side. The half-mile between them and the house seemed more like a hundred miles. The big man was a ton weight on his shoulder, and where he was clinging to Davie's neck, the strain was unbearable. 'Not long now,' he kept assuring the older man. 'Just

159

another few steps and we're there.' And not too soon, he thought, because in spite of his own strong, muscular frame, Davie feared he could not support the man's dead weight much longer.

As they neared the house, Davie thought how splendid it was. Constructed in red brick, with tall chimneys and long windows, it had acres of lawns and flowerbeds leading up to the driveway.

'My late father lived in the cottage through the orchard,' the injured man revealed. 'He always planned to build a grand house on this plot, but somehow the finances were always beyond his reach. Before he died, he gave the land to me, and I was determined to keep his dream. I built this place twenty years ago, just before the war. I named it "The Willows", after my late wife's favourite walk through the withy fields by the river.'

He took a moment to clear his throat and observe the house from its every graceful angle. 'It's beautiful, isn't it?' He turned to look at Davie. 'Do you have family?'

Caught offguard, Davie wondered how he might truthfully answer that. But before he could reply, there was another question: 'Do you have brothers?'

'No.'

'Sisters?'

'No . . . except there is a girl called Judy. She and I grew up together. I can never recall a time when Judy wasn't there. So yes, I expect you could say she's the nearest thing I have to a sister.'

'Mmm.' The older man nodded his head. 'Well, I've got one child, a daughter. Lucy is the light of my life – kind-hearted, hard-headed and even harder to argue with – so in my experience the best way is to let her imagine she's got the upper hand. What do you say to that, eh?'

Davie smiled. 'I'd say that was good thinking.' The smile was wiped away with the next question.

'Tell me . . . have you always been a good son?'

'I hope so, sir. I've always tried my best.' Sudden visions came to his mind – of his father walking out and his grand-father at the end of his tether. Oh, and the way it had been with his mammy! Rita's face as she lay dying flashed before his eyes, and a lump in his throat threatened to choke him. Would the memories ever fade? Or would they haunt him for the rest of his life?

'You have a wonderful place here, sir,' Davie said quietly. 'I was brought up in the middle of a busy town, with a street filled with people and more hustle and bustle than you could imagine. There were houses lined up on either side of us, and never a garden in sight. But for all that, I loved my hometown. I thought I might be there for ever.'

Then, realising he was giving away too much of himself, he caught his breath. 'It was just . . . well, something hap-pened and I decided to leave and make my own way in the world. I thought I might be homesick, and I was for a while. But I've worked my way across the land and lived in many different places, and everywhere I've been, every road I've trod, and whether it be early morning or late at night, the world is alive with excitement . . .'

Despite his pain, the older man was mesmerised. 'Good-ness me! It seems to me that you have a great passion for life, young feller-me-lad!'

'I'm sorry.' Davie was mortified. 'I didn't mean to go on like that. I'm not usually so talkative.'

'Oh, don't be sorry,' his companion advised. 'Never apolo-gise for what you feel inside. Any man, woman or child who doesn't have passion for life is not alive at all, that's what I say.'

He brought Davie's attention to the slight figure of a young woman strolling across the gardens. 'There she is! That's my Lucy . . . the loveliest creature you will ever lay eyes on.'

They were quickly spotted by the girl. Tall and slender, with long dark hair, she was dressed in a simple blue belted dress, and looked to be in her late teens.

At the sight of her badly limping father, she began running towards them. 'Daddy? What's happened? Has there been an accident? Where's Madden?'

The big man snorted. 'We gave him the right name, that's for sure,' he said. 'Madden suits him fine because that's just what he is . . . mad as a hatter.'

Glancing at Davie, he grumbled. 'And here's another mad devil – stood his ground with the horse coming full on at him. Damned crazy, the pair of 'em!' He yelled in pain when his foot dragged over a molehill. 'Jesus! I'll have that blasted horse sent for the chop, that's what I'll do!'

The girl rolled her eyes at Davie. 'He always says that,' she informed him. 'But he would no more send Madden for the chop, than he would send *me*.'

Her father laughed at that, but warned her all the same, 'I know I promised you could have him next year when you're eighteen, but I've changed my mind. That stallion is lethal. He's wild and unpredictable. I'm taking no chances with you, Lucy love. We'll get you another, calmer horse.'

'Dad, I don't want a calmer horse. I love Madden.'

In too much pain to argue, her father let it go. But his mind was made up. As far as he was concerned, his precious daughter would never be allowed on that black hell-devil's back. He would issue that same directive to all concerned, and after what happened today, the sooner it was done, the better.

CHAPTER TWELVE

'WHAT ON EARTH have you been up to now?' The elderly doctor had served the Thomson family for many years, and he felt the right to chide his patient for his foolhardiness. 'I told you that beast would get the better of you one day, and I was right.'

Raising Frank Thomson's foot to the stool, he set about cutting his sock off. When the full extent of the injury was revealed, he announced with some satisfaction, 'You've managed to break your foot, in two places if not more.'

To prove his point, he prodded a finger on the swollen arches, looking up through the edge of his spectacles when Frank cried out, 'Steady on, man! You're enjoying this, aren't you, you sadist?'

The doctor gave an aside wink at Lucy. 'Anybody would think he was in pain.'

Shaking a fist, the other man yelled and cursed, declaring, 'You're too old and crotchety to be a doctor! You are bad mannered and rough, and you relish other folks' pain. I reckon you should have been struck off years ago.'

Ignoring his rantings, Doctor Montgomery took charge of organising things, and within twenty minutes of his arrival, he had Davie in the front of his big Humber car, and Lucy and her father in the back. 'And don't start any of that moaning and complaining,' the doctor warned him. 'I need to concentrate on the road.'

'I'm not surprised!' Frank retaliated. 'You can barely see straight even when you've got your glasses on.'

'Behave yourself, Daddy!' Lucy had witnessed these two bantering for too many years, and now if they didn't do it, she would be worried.

Half an hour later they arrived at Bedford Hospital. Davie and Lucy helped Frank hobble to a seat, while the doctor went in search of assistance.

Frank's foot was now swollen to twice its normal size. To distract himself from the pain, he turned to Davie. 'It's as well you were there, my boy,' he told him. 'You did a foolish thing, though . . . turning Madden like that, and putting yourself in mortal danger.'

'There wasn't time to think about being in danger,' Davie said honestly. 'It was an instant reaction.'

'All the same, if you hadn't been there, I'm sure that mad bugger would have trampled me on the road.' Reaching out, he shook Davie by the hand. 'I'm very grateful to you. Thank you, young man.'

'I'm grateful, too.' When Lucy smiled up at him, Davie thought how lovely she was; soft-natured and with a smile warm enough to melt any man's heart. And just for the briefest moment, he thought of Judy. But it was a different kind of thinking; protective and caring, and feeling responsible, while with Lucy there was a stirring of something else – a sensation he had not experienced before.

'What were you doing around here in the first place?' Frank's voice cut through his thoughts.

'I was looking for a place called "Greenacres Farm".'

Frank looked surprised. 'Were you now?'

'Who do you know at Greenacres?' That was Lucy.

Taking out the box, Davie removed the piece of paper given to him by Eli and passed it to Lucy. 'I was told this man might find me work, and a place to stay.'

Lucy read the note and quickly handed it to her father, who cast his eye over it. 'So! You were looking for Ted Baker?'

'That's right.' Davie had noticed the look that passed between father and daughter. 'Do you know him, by any chance?'

Momentarily brushing aside Davie's question, Frank informed him, 'I own most farms hereabouts, *including* Greenacres Farm.'

'So you *do* know Ted Baker?' Davie was greatly relieved. 'Do you think he's in need of an extra labourer?'

'I don't think he needs anything right now,' Frank said respectfully. 'Ted Baker passed away last year . . . I'm sorry, son. The farm is now being run by another of my tenants. I've amalgamated the two farms, and as far as I'm informed, he has more than enough help at the minute.'

Seeing how the news had sent Davie into a sombre mood, he suggested, 'You obviously have a way with horses, so, if you're interested, I might have need of a strong young man myself.'

He quickly explained. 'I have six farms including my own. Five of them are tenanted out; of those, three of them are crop-producing and two are cattle-rearing. Mine does neither, because it's entirely turned over to breeding horses and, though I say it myself, it's one of the best studs in the country. My father started it in a smaller way some many years ago, and I was fortunate enough to have it handed down to me. It wasn't the biggest or the best then.' He smiled proudly. 'But it is now.'

'Everyone knows Thomson's Stud Farm,' Lucy added.

'Daddy's worked hard and sometimes he's been knocked back, but he's never been swayed from his goal.'

'Lucy's right.' Frank had not forgotten the bad times. 'There were moments when I thought I should give up.' He paused, then said, 'I lost my mother soon after Lucy was born. Some three years later, my father died too.' His loving gaze fell on his daughter. 'In that same year, my beloved wife Ruthie fell ill and never recovered.'

As Lucy's hand reached out to hold his, he told Davie, 'For a while, I could think only of what I had lost. My heart went out of my work, and things started to fall apart. But then I began to realise the wonderful things they had all left to me. My father left me his beloved farm, and the wisdom and experience he had learned through his life. My mother left me with a well of love and devotion that would carry me through every new day for as long as I live.'

He turned to smile on his daughter. 'And Ruthie left me with the most precious thing of all – my darling Lucy, the light of my life.'

Addressing Davie, he went on, 'Instead of thinking of what I'd lost, I suddenly realised what I had gained, and I began to count my blessings. And now I've done what I set out to do; I had a dream, and I stayed with it.'

He nodded, as though congratulating himself. 'Yes, it's taken a lot of work and courage to build my empire, and I don't mind saying, I'm proud of what I've achieved. I breed the best horses and I have a reputation for being a fair and honest man. Once Lucy left school, she learned typing and book-keeping, and she pulls her weight in running the business.' He squeezed her hand fondly.

Looking back for a moment, he was lost in the struggle he'd encountered in the early years. 'It's been a hard road,' he murmured. 'But I made it, and by God, I'm not finished yet!' Pride shone from his face. 'At the last count I had thirty-eight fine mares all in foal, and every foal already sold for a handsome profit. I have sixteen magnificent colts growing on for breeding stock; and I own twelve of the most prized and proven stallions you could find this side of Ireland or America.'

Davie was duly impressed, not only with Frank Thomson's determination, but also with the man himself.

'I admire you for what you've done with your life.' This was the first time Davie had met anyone who had actually realised their dream. 'Some day, I mean to build an empire myself.' As yet, though, he was still floundering in the dark. 'I'm not sure what direction I might take, or what it is I really want to do. All I know is, I need to make my mark on the world, and I won't rest until I've created something to be proud of.'

Frank gave no answer. Instead, he discreetly observed Davie, and knew instinctively that something must have happened in his short life, to make him grow up before his time. For someone so young he had a manliness about him; the kind of strength that only comes with pain and courage. There was a loneliness too, a deep-down loneliness that sets a man apart from the crowd.

He also saw the glint in Davie's eye and heard the passion in his voice, and he saw himself as a young man. 'Come and work for me,' he suggested quietly. 'I've an idea you and me will get on all right.'

Lucy had been surprised at how quickly her father had taken to Davie; she was pleased, as she knew he did not suffer fools gladly. She too had been drawn to take notice of this stranger who had entered their lives. There was something about him, something special and driven. He spoke with conviction and he had that certain way with him, that instinctively made you feel you could trust him. 'Are you very disappointed?' she asked. 'About Ted Baker?'

'I am, yes.' Davie could not deny it. 'It seems such a pity,' he answered thoughtfully. 'After Eli spoke so highly of him, I was really looking forward to making his acquaintance.' Coming all this way south, only to be told that Ted Baker was long gone, had been something of a setback. But here he was being given a chance to work, and that was some measure of compensation.

'You will come and work at the farm, won't you?' Realising she didn't even know his name, Lucy asked, 'What do we call you?'

'Dave.' He surprised himself by the shorter name he gave, and yet in that moment, here in this place, it was somehow very right. 'My name is Dave Adams,' he told her proudly.

The child 'Davie' was gone for ever. He was a man now. With a man's work ahead of him.

'I'm Lucy Thomson.' When she reached out to shake him by the hand, he instinctively hesitated. She was so lovely, so enticing, and he had never been more nervous than he was right now.

Gathering his courage, he shook her by the hand. He held that small soft hand in his, and his heart quickened.

'And I'm Frank – Mr Thomson to you.' The big man had a stern look in his eye. 'It's best you know from the start – I insist on respect from the men in my employ.'

'Not from the *women* though, eh?' Lucy laughed.

Her father gave her a scathing glance. 'If you're referring to Maggie, I'll have you know she's been treading a fine line; that woman is far too bossy for her own good.' He scowled at Dave. 'One of these days she'll get her marching orders, you'll see if she won't!'

Just then the doctor returned with a wheelchair in tow.

'Right, it's all in order.' Hands on hips, he looked down on his patient. 'We're off to the X-ray room.' And without more ado, he bundled Frank into the wheelchair and whisked him away.

'These are busy people,' he nagged. 'Think yourself fortunate they've managed to squeeze you in.'

As they turned the corner, Dave and Lucy could hear Frank ranting on at him. 'There's no need for you to stay. I've got my daughter here and she's more than capable of pushing me along the corridor. In fact, I'd rather hobble on my knees than have you treat me like a baby!'

'Stop your moaning and thank your lucky stars I'm taking the time to stay with you. There are far more important things I could be doing than listen to your moaning and grumbling.'

'Are they always like that?' Dave wanted to know.

'Always,' Lucy chuckled. 'Argue, argue, argue. If one says it's day, the other will swear it's night. They're worse than a couple of kids.'

'Known each other a long time, have they?'

'Yes, for ages and ages.'

'Who's this Maggie you spoke of?'

'She's our housekeeper and cook. She's worth her weight in gold. You'd have met her before, but she has gone shopping in Bedford today.'

'So he's not likely to send her down the road with her wages then?'

Lucy shook her head. 'Dad would never do that – he thinks the world of her. He might pretend to threaten hell and high water, but he couldn't do without her and neither could I. She's the salt of the earth, is Maggie.'

'You sound really fond of her.'

'I am – we all are.' She then explained, 'The man you

were looking for, Ted Baker who passed away – well, Maggie's his widow. When Daddy amalgamated Greenacres Farm with its neighbour, she was offered a cottage here and a job in The Willows, and now she's like part of the family.'

The girl had noticed how awkward the stranger seemed in the presence of others. 'You don't care much for people, do you?' she asked.

Dave shrugged. 'Never had much to do with folks,' he answered. 'I've always found my own company good enough.'

Now it was Lucy's turn to fall silent. She didn't know quite what to make of him. There was no denying she was attracted to him, and she was pleased that her father had taken to him. All the same, she got the feeling that Dave was not happy in close surroundings. 'You prefer to be outside, don't you?'

'I do, yes. The open roads and the countryside is where I belong.'

'Then you're bound to feel comfortable at the farm,' she assured him with a bright smile. 'As we're out in the middle of nowhere.'

Just then they heard the sound of the two men approaching. 'What a fuss!' That was the doctor chiding the patient. 'A grown man whimpering and complaining about being put under the X-ray machine, whatever next?'

'I was not whimpering!' Frank was at the end of his tether. 'Three times they had me on and off that damned contraption! It's bloody painful, I might tell you, being dragged from pillar to post, especially when your foot feels like it's parted company with your leg. Three times! God Almighty, you'd think they could at least get it right the first time!'

Ignoring his friend, the doctor informed Lucy, 'I have an urgent appointment to attend, but I've taken the liberty of ordering a taxi to run you back to the farm. By my reckoning, it should be waiting outside.' Considering his duty done for the time being, he then delivered Frank to his daughter, and was quickly gone.

'Can't get rid of me quick enough, can he?' Frank grunted.

'Could that possibly have anything to do with the fact that you are being so ungrateful and argumentative!' Lucy enquired, with a saucy wink at Dave.

Frank got back to the matter in hand. 'So, let's get down to business, young man.' He looked Dave straight in the eye. 'Have you thought about my offer? Are you prepared to come and work for an old codger like me?'

Lucy laughed. 'Not if he's got any sense, he won't.' Though she had her fingers crossed behind her back, and every nerve in her young body was aching for Dave to say yes. And when he did, she could hardly believe it.

'Thank you, Mr Thomson, yes – I'd like to come and work for you. But first, I'll need to find lodgings.'

Lucy was quick with an answer. 'I'm sure we can help.' She turned to her father, asking hopefully, 'We can, can't we, Daddy?'

Frank hesitated for the briefest moment while he discreetly scrutinised Dave; he had wanted a son, but it was not meant to be. He had wanted his wife to grow old with him, and now she was not here. But Lucy *was* here – and she was everything he imagined a daughter would be, honest and loyal, and born with the same fierce love of the land as himself. Whatever she wanted, he would give her, if he could.

'Daddy?' Lucy's anxious voice shattered his thoughts. 'We can find lodgings for Dave, can't we?'

'Well, yes, I imagine so.' He addressed the lad. 'First we need to get back, so's you can have a look around. I'll ask Seamus Macintyre to show you the ropes. He's my head groom, and what he doesn't know about horses isn't worth knowing.' He turned to Lucy. 'Isn't that so, love?'

The girl gave a small smile, and though her father missed the way she dropped her gaze to the floor, Dave was quick to notice the change in her manner. He couldn't help but wonder whether she had any liking for this man called Seamus.

'For all we know, you may not want to stay,' Frank was saying. 'The job may not be what you're looking for. And if it turns out that way, I won't hold you to anything. So – is that a deal?'

Dave was grateful. 'Fine by me, Mr Thomson.' And they promptly shook hands on it.

Lucy had a favour to ask. 'Will you let *me* show Dave round, Daddy? I know the stables and yards as well as Seamus.'

'All right, but don't make an issue of it with Seamus. You know how protective he is of his little empire.'

'I won't say anything,' she promised. 'But Seamus has a way with him, and I don't want him to make trouble for Dave.'

'I'm not sure what you mean by Seamus making trouble. If he seems worried by Dave being about the stables, tell him you've agreed it with me. As long as Dave gets shown the lie of the land, I don't mind who does the showing.'

'Good. That's settled then!' Hardly able to hide her excitement, the girl stood up, ready to leave. Right from the first, she had felt drawn to Dave.

And the longer she spent in his company, the closer she felt to him.

~

A short time later, with Frank seated in his office, his foot bandaged and propped on a chair, and going through the business of the day, Lucy set about showing Dave the ropes. 'We'll start with the kitchen, then the stables, and after that if you want, I can take you to the fields where we keep the stallions.'

'Sounds good to me.' Dave was surprised at how easy he felt in her company.

As they went through the house and on to the kitchen, where he was to meet Ted Baker's widow, Dave was amazed at the sheer size and beauty of this great house. Every room was flooded with sunshine, and he could imagine the laughter and joy that must have echoed from those walls. 'We used to have lots of parties, when I was little,' Lucy informed him as they travelled through, 'but not for a long time now.'

Dave assumed the parties must have stopped when Frank's wife was lost to them.

'This is Mummy.' As though reading his thoughts, she drew him to a beautiful painting hanging above the fireplace in the drawing room. For what seemed an age, she fell silent, looking up at the woman she had known for such a cruelly short time, and whom she still missed terribly. 'She was lovely, don't you think? Dad told me that in Hebrew, Ruth means "friend", like the Ruth in the Bible, and that's how I think of her, as my friend.'

When she now turned to him, and he saw the tears bright in her pretty eyes, Dave's heart swelled with sympathy. He knew how sad she was feeling, for didn't he feel the same way about his own mother?

In that peculiar, intimate moment he felt a great affinity with her; a need to hold and protect her and take away the pain.

~

'Lucy Thomson, you little devil!' Ted Baker's widow Maggie had never lost her strong Scottish accent. 'Whatever d'ye think you're doing! I've only just finished vacuuming that sheepskin rug. It took me ages to get the hairs standing on end again, and now you're crushing it all underfoot! Have ye no soul? Don't ye think I slave hard enough in this house, without you following on and undoing all my hard work? And who, might I ask, is your friend?' Her quick eyes pinned Dave in a shrivelling glance. 'I don't suppose for one minute, he wiped his feet at the door!'

Like a rabbit caught in the headlights, Dave couldn't take his eyes off her. With a voice like a Sergeant Major, he expected to see a burly woman with arms resembling tank-turrets and feet like shovels. Instead, this woman whom he assumed to be the dreaded Maggie, was remarkably hand-some, with twinkling light-brown eyes, a shapely, ample figure and only the occasional grey streak in her brown hair. 'I did wipe my feet,' he said lamely. 'Twice.'

'This is Dave Adams.' Lucy quickly stepped off the sheep-skin rug, while behind her Dave bent to brush the flattened areas where he and Lucy had been standing. 'He was the one who saved Daddy from Madden, and now he might be coming to work here.'

'Hmh! It's a pity he didn't let that lunatic horse carry your father over the hills and faraway. It might have taught the silly old fool a lesson.' With that she ushered them out of the room and falling to her knees, began a thorough inspec-tion of her precious sheepskin rug.

'Crikey!' Dave felt as if he'd been through the wars. 'For a minute there, I thought she was about to horse-whip the pair of us.'

Lucy laughed. 'When you get to know her, you'll find Maggie is more bark than bite.'

∽

His first encounter with Seamus was quieter, and infinitely more sinister.

Lucy was taking him round the stables when they fell foul of Frank's head groom. 'This is Molly.' Reaching over the stable door, the girl gently stroked the mane of the big chestnut horse. 'She's Daddy's favourite, and about to foal any day now.'

Dave watched as the mare paced the stable. 'She's magnificent!' he exclaimed. 'Can I get in with her?'

'I don't know if you should,' Lucy answered guardedly. 'She can be a bit temperamental, especially now she's in foal and near her time.'

'Best not disturb her then.' Through his travels, Dave had learned a great deal about horses, and she was the finest he had ever seen. The last thing he wanted to do was upset her.

On reflection, and considering how he had safely stopped the stallion in his tracks, Lucy told him to go in. 'She'll be fine, I'm sure.'

Slowly, and with great care, Dave went in with the mare. For a time he kept his distance, talking softly to her and holding out his hand. 'You're a real beauty, Molly,' he murmured. 'No wonder you're the boss's favourite.'

Slowly, slowly, the horse came to him, at first snorting and hesitant, but then trusting Dave implicitly, she stood before him, allowing him to stroke her neck and seeming to enjoy it.

'BACK UP, YOU DEVIL!' The sharp crack of a horse-whip startled them both, and when the whip was flicked over the horse's rear end, the pregnant mare went up on her back legs, lashing out at anything in her way.

Taken by surprise, Dave had neither time nor space in which to calm the animal, and with her being in foal, his best option was to scramble out of there.

'What the hell d'you think you're doing?' The man who

spoke was in his mid-twenties, thickset and strong-featured, with piercing dark eyes and a surly manner. 'Who in blazes gave you the right to go in there?'

'You crazy fool, Seamus!' Shaken, Lucy turned on him. 'It was me who told him to go in. You could have killed him, doing what you did.'

'How was I to know he was a friend of yours? I didn't see you in the shadows,' he lied. 'All I saw was this stranger in the stable with your father's favourite mare. What was I to do? If anything happens to Molly, your father will have my hide.'

'And he'll have your hide if I tell him how you flicked that whip against her rump! It's a wonder she hasn't harmed herself. She could even have lost her foal.'

'And will you tell your father?'

'I can't think of any reason not to!'

Lowering his voice, he told her to go ahead. 'And while you're at it, you'd best tell him how you let a stranger into the stable with her, unsettling her and making her jumpy. She was terrified – you must have seen how she was trembling?' Seamus was very clever with words when it suited him.

Taking an instant dislike to the man, Dave duly apologised. 'It was my fault, not Lucy's.' He sought to protect her. 'But you're not altogether blameless. It was you who sent the horse into a panic with that damned whip! Were you never told "whip a horse and you'll whip up the temper in him"?'

The groom laughed in his face. 'Wherever did you hear such rubbish?'

'From an old gypsy, who knew more about horses than you or I will ever know.'

Seamus gave a sly little smile. 'So, you're a gypsy, are you?' The smile gave way to a sneer. 'Why am I not surprised?'

'I'm no gypsy. Neither am I an expert. But I'm always ready

to learn from the masters. So, if I do come here to work, I won't be looking to *you* for advice on how to treat a horse.'

Seamus was taken aback. 'You, working here, in my stables? Huh! Not if I have my way, you won't.'

'That's not for you to say,' Lucy angrily intervened. 'Don't pride yourself on being anything but a hired hand.'

'I'll not forget this,' came the reply. 'In fact, I reckon it's my duty to tell your father what's been going on here.'

'Feel free!' With that, Lucy led the way out of the stables, leaving him quietly fuming.

Once outside, Dave muttered, 'I'm sorry. I seem to have caused trouble for you.'

'You haven't. Seamus was the one who caused trouble – he can't help himself.' Though he could be charming one day and moody the next, she had never seen him so incensed. 'Strange, that,' she murmured. 'He's not usually so aggressive to strangers.'

Dave had known immediately why Seamus had gone for him like that. 'He's obviously fond of you. Maybe he saw me as a threat.'

'That's silly!' Lucy was shocked. 'He has no reason or right to be jealous. Oh, he may have partnered me to our annual barn dance last year, but that's all. I've never given him any encouragement, and I never would.'

Dave wisely changed the subject. 'What if he tells your father about me going into the stable?'

'He won't. And even if he did, he would tell a different tale from the truth.'

'But would your father believe him?'

Lucy thought for a moment. 'He might. Dad has a great deal of respect for Seamus. He took him on about nine years ago, when Seamus was seventeen, and so far he's never put a foot wrong with the horses.'

'What would he say if he knew how Seamus had laid the whip on the mare?'

'He'd raise the roof – probably sack him on the spot.' She gave a worried little smile. 'But it won't happen. Seamus is far too clever to get caught out. He would spin such a tale, even I wouldn't be able to persuade Father of the truth.'

Dave was concerned, not for himself, but for Lucy. 'I can explain, if you like? I'll tell him how I went in with the mare, and that I did it without you knowing.'

Lucy was adamant. 'But that would be a lie. Look – it might be best if we just forget it happened. Thank goodness that Molly is all right. And besides, whatever we say, Seamus would still twist it his way. He's a nasty, cunning sort. Father doesn't know what he's really like.' She sighed deflatedly. 'I don't expect you'll want to work here now.'

'What makes you say that?'

'Well, because of Seamus and what's happened. If you do agree to work here, he could make your life a misery.'

'Oh, Macintyre doesn't bother me.' In fact, for the horses' sake if nothing else, Dave was ready to take him on. 'I've worked with nastier men than him.' Thoughts of Brian Moult crossed his mind.

'So, does that mean you'll be staying, after all?'

His smile confirmed it. 'Looks that way, don't you think?'

'Oh, Dave, that's wonderful!' Flinging herself into his arms, she hugged him long and hard. 'You won't regret it.' And neither will I, she thought, dreamily. Neither will I.

~

Seething with jealousy, Seamus skulked in the stable door-way. He saw how Lucy flung herself at Dave, and the way they held onto each other for longer than necessary . . . and his devious mind was frantically searching for a way to be rid of this intruder.

Since the first day he was taken on at Thomson's Stud Farm, there had been only one thing on his mind – to get his hands on Frank Thomson's millions; and in order to do this, he needed to win and wed the man's daughter.

He prided himself on having already bluffed his way into her father's good books. Frank Thomson openly liked him; after nine years, not only did his employer now trust him implicitly, but Frank was filled with admiration at Seamus's expertise with the horses.

With Lucy, though, he seemed to have got off on the wrong foot, Seamus thought irritably. He was too impatient and anxious to get his hands on the Thomson fortune. So from now on, if his well-laid plans were to amount to any-thing, he would have to play it crafty, watch his temper and create opportunities that would shine him in a new light.

He had worked hard and schemed to win a place here. And now that he felt the time was ripening for him to make his move, one thing was certain. One way or another, he could not allow some gyppo to snatch it all from under his nose.

PART THREE

~

Blackburn, 1960

Hand and Heart

CHAPTER THIRTEEN

R ETURNING FROM HIS self-imposed exile, Don thrilled at the sight of his old home town, with its huge Victorian station and sprawling boulevard and the ordinary folks going about their daily grind. The man was there as always, selling hot potatoes from his hand-cart, and strolling amongst the crowd, the flower-seller sold the last of her colorful blooms. 'I'm home!' he muttered with a surge of joy. 'Home where I belong.'

As the tram prepared to move out, the conductor caught sight of the man running towards them. 'Another minute and you'd have missed us altogether!' Pressing his finger to the bell button, he stopped the tram from leaving. 'Come on, matey – hurry up!' he shouted. 'We're already late.'

'Aw, thanks.' Don scrambled aboard. 'I thought I'd missed it for sure.' Wending his way down to the far end, he seated himself by the window. It was good to be back in Blackburn, he thought. He had been away too long, and with every passing day he missed his family more than he could ever have imagined. But when he went away, he had left in anger, angry at his father-in-law for having been weak just like himself in not taking Rita to task earlier . . . though he was deeply fond of that dear old man and ashamed that he had let him down.

He had been angry with his son, Davie, for wanting to stay with his mother, when time and again Rita had pushed them all to the limit, until in the end he could stand no more. But then Davie was fiercely loyal and independent, with a love for family that was deeply protective. Yet on that awful night, the boy's love and loyalty was torn all ways. That night, they all had choices to make; Rita to mend her ways or continue going downhill and taking them all with her; the old man had to decide whether he was prepared to go on accepting things the way they were, and Davie, just a boy with his world collapsing about him, was forced into choosing to stay with his father or defend his mother. Such a choice must have been the hardest thing for any child. So, Davie chose his mammy, and who could blame him for that? Certainly not himself, for he knew only too well how wonderful Rita could be, and how easy it was to love her. He only hoped his son had not lived to regret his choice, the way his daddy had done so many times.

These past years, he had half hoped that somehow his son would find him. When it did not happen, he was disappointed but not altogether surprised. Now, all he wanted was to reunite his family again, and pray they could build a better future together.

There were many regrets for the hurt he had caused by walking out. He hoped they would forgive him, especially Rita. She had been the love of his life and he could never see himself loving any other woman in the same way.

His deepest anger had been reserved for his wife. For it was she in the end who had split the family apart; with her wanton ways and her lack of remorse or shame, she had a great deal to answer for. His anger for this woman he had loved forever and still loved, had crippled him for a long, long time. And when at last it finally subsided, there grew in him a great sense of loss, more painful than anything that had gone before.

He missed old Joseph, and he missed his son, Davie, so very much. And for all her sins, he ached for Rita, his sweetheart, that bright, happy girl who had captured his heart with her first smile. Through all the anger and pain, and the time that had gone between, he loved her still. He had never stopped loving her.

And now he was back home, humbled and lonely, with a desperate need to draw his family back together and turn over a new leaf and God willing to help Rita do the same.

'All aboard that's coming aboard!' The conductor pressed the bell button for leaving; at the same time taking stock of his new passenger, who was tall and well-built, with a long, confident stride.

'You were lucky to catch the tram,' he told him now. 'Another minute and we'd have been gone, and you'd have had to wait a long time for the next one.'

Don thanked him again. 'I've been away,' he explained. 'I came in on the train. It was late, that's what held me up. But I'm here now, on my way home, and glad of it.'

'So, you've been away in Ireland, have you?'

'How did you know I was from Ireland?' Don asked.

'Ah, well, I've got a good ear for accents. But from what I can tell, you've lived longer in England than you have in your homeland, am I right?'

With a chuckle, Don quipped, 'The Irish girls wouldn't take me on, so I found me a Lancashire lass.'

'And did you ever regret it?' the conductor asked idly.

It seemed an age before Don answered, and when he did, it was in such a husky voice, the other man had to lean down to hear him. 'No, I don't think I ever did regret it,' he murmured. 'Though there were certain things I might like to have changed along the way.'

The conductor laughed. 'Aren't there always?' he answered.

'We love 'em and wed 'em, but there's none of 'em perfect, and never will be. But for all that, we'd rather not be without 'em.' Turning the handle of the clumsy machine strapped round his shoulder, he concluded the conversation. 'Where to?'

'I'm headed for Derwent Street, and as far as I can recall, the tram doesn't go there?'

The conductor shook his head. 'That's right. Sorry, matey. You still have to get off at King Street and walk up to Derwent Street.'

Don held out his loose change. 'King Street it is then.'

Taking the correct number of coins, the tram-conductor dropped them into the leather pouch around his waist, and proceeded to roll off the ticket. 'My own wife comes from County Cork,' he went on. 'Her grandfather came to England looking for work years ago, and the whole family followed.'

He sighed. 'My Rosie is a real beauty. When she was young, her hair was red as fire . . . it's faded a bit now, more's the pity,' he gabbled on. 'By! She's got one hell of temper, though. That's what they say, don't they? "Red hair, red temper".'

When Don held out his hand for the ticket, the conductor made no move to give it him. 'So, what about yourself?' he asked. 'Are you home to stay, or are you on a visit?' He then handed Don the ticket. 'Sorry. I hope you don't mind me being nosy?'

'No, I don't mind at all.' Though in truth, Don would rather be left alone right now. Friendly though the conductor was, he himself was not in the mood for talking. 'And to answer your question, I've lived away for some time, but now I'm back to stay.'

'Been away earning the money, have you?'

'You could say that, yes.' But none of it had gone to his family, he thought guiltily. They had had to manage without his wage for all these years.

'Do you have children?'

'A son.' Don pictured Davie in his mind. 'He'll be eighteen now.' His heart shuddered. It was some five years since he had seen Davie. Would he look the same? Would he want his father anywhere near? Had he forgiven him for leaving that night? And what about Rita? When they parted, it had been with bitterness, so how would she feel now, when he turned up at the door? Would she still be drinking and leading the life of Riley, or would she have settled down by now? And Davie would be out at work, keeping food on the table. Would he be in the same line of work as himself, Don wondered, recalling the hours they had spent together, making things for the house. He felt so excluded from their lives.

Realising he was not in the mood for chit-chat, the conductor prepared to move on. 'Good luck to you then,' he said, and approached his next passenger, a grey-haired, grey-faced woman. 'Hello, Mrs Armitage. And how are you today?'

While the conductor chatted, Don watched as the familiar streets opened out to him, and when the tram turned into King Street, his heart was full, the memories almost too much to bear. The sights lifted his spirits, and he felt like an exile returning to everything he loved. This was his home, his life – and oh, dear God, how he had missed it!

For the millionth time, all the old questions rampaged through his mind. Why had he run away? Why couldn't he have stayed and tried harder with Rita? Had she changed now? he wondered again. Had his leaving brought her to her senses? Or was she still gallivanting, bedding every man she met? Moreover, had she found someone to replace him?

Torturing himself, he began to believe the worst. So, had he done the right thing in coming back, or should he have left well alone and made a permanent life for himself, away from these parts, and away from Rita? It wasn't as though he himself hadn't had the occasional relationship, because he had. But there had been nothing serious, nor had he led the women to believe anything otherwise. They were mere time-fillers, until he found the strength to come home and make amends with Rita, once and for all.

And now here he was, worried and anxious about the outcome. Either she would turn him away, or, like him, she had been lonely, aching for things to be as they used to be . . . before it all went wrong.

As they travelled along King Street, he glanced out of the window. There was the picture-house and the row of shops. And now they were nearing the pretty narrow bridge in front of the greengrocer's. Suddenly the tram was stopping and he really began to panic. Should he stay on the tram and go back to tramp the hills and valleys of Ireland, where he had hidden away all these years? Or should he brave it out and take the consequences, whatever they were?

Yes, he should! He *had* to, or he would always regret it. And what of Davie, and the look on his young face as his daddy went out the door? What had the boy been thinking in that awful moment, and had he hated him ever since?

For one terrifying moment, Don's courage almost deserted him. Then he remembered how close he and his son had been, up until that shocking event when anger exploded and he burst out of the house. And then, after he left for Ireland, he had suffered from devastating loneliness, from days that never seemed to end, sleepless nights and the deep-down yearning that wouldn't go away.

His family were the most precious things on God's earth to him, and for these five long years, he had let his pride keep him away.

But he was here now, and come what may, this was where he would end his days. And if Rita didn't want him, he would make a new life nearby. He would work hard to win back his son's trust and love. *And never again would he desert him.*

~

'King Street!' The conductor's voice rang out as the tram shuddered to a halt. 'Good day to you,' he addressed Don with a cheery grin. 'Mind how you go now.' He watched him go down the road, occasionally pausing deep in thought. 'A troubled man, that's what you are,' he muttered. 'Whatever it is you're bracing yourself for, I'd rather be me than you.'

He was taken unawares when an elderly woman poked him on the shoulder with her walking-stick. 'Does this tram stop at Mill Hill?'

'Oh, sorry, darling, I was miles away!' He helped her aboard. 'Yes, it does stop at Mill Hill, and goes all the way to Samlesbury.'

When the woman was safely in her seat, he pressed the button to leave; with a last glance at Don's departing figure, he thanked his lucky stars that he himself led a simple, uncomplicated life. When his work was done, he went home to a hearty meal and sometimes, if his wife was in the mood, a bit of slap and tickle before he went to sleep. He was a contented man who worked hard and provided, and with a good woman to tend his every need, he wanted nothing more.

~

189

Unaware that his long-estranged son-in-law was on his way home, Joseph finished his pot of tea, put on his jacket, filled his pipe with baccy, and resumed his seat on the doorstep, enjoying the mild spring air.

Come rain or shine, he spent many an hour on his doorstep. In the winter when the fumes from the coal fire got down his chest, he would put on his overcoat and take refuge outside, while in the warmer weather like now, he would sit with his mug of tea and his pipe of baccy, and simply watch the world go by.

These days, it was the only real pleasure he had; save for when Judy would come by and they would talk about her young dreams, and he would tell stories about his own youth. These past few years, the girl had been his salvation, and he valued her for the genuine friend she had been to him.

'Good day to you, Joseph!' That was the lady from the corner shop. 'Don't sit there too long,' she advised with a wag of her chubby finger. 'They say it might rain later, and you don't want to be catching a chill.'

Returning her greeting, Joseph joked as usual, 'I won't mind a bit o' rain, Elsie.' He gave her a knowing wink. 'It'll save you giving me a bath later.'

'Away with you, Joseph,' she laughed aloud. 'Saying things like that will get the whole street talking!' And she trotted up the road feeling twenty years younger.

'Up to your old tricks, are you, Joe?' Having overheard the mischievous conversation, Lenny Reynolds paused a moment at the old man's doorstep.

'Aw, she loves a bit o' flirting,' Joseph chuckled. 'It makes her day. Besides, we might be old in the tooth, but we can't have folks thinking we're past it, can we, eh?'

'No, that would never do.' Lenny enjoyed his little chats with Joseph. After everything he'd been through, the man could still be very entertaining. 'And how are you today, Joseph – apart from chatting up the women?'

'I'm all right, thank you, Lenny. And how are you, lad?'

'Fine and dandy, thank you.' He threw off his work satchel. 'OK if I sit beside you for a while?' He always enjoyed the banter with Joseph, and besides, it was good to catch up with news of the lovely Judy Makepeace.

'Course ye can.' Joseph shifted along the step. 'Sit yerself down, young fella-me-lad.' He had a lot of time for Lenny. He had seen him grow from boy to man these past four years, until now he was a handsome, strapping fellow who, in spite of his disinterested parents, had turned out really well. He already had a thriving greengrocer stall on Blackburn market, and was saving up to buy a shop in the heart of town. Oh yes! Lenny Reynolds was going places.

'Tell you what,' Joseph clambered up. 'Come inside and you can tell me how the business is going.' He smiled into Lenny's brown eyes. 'Judy was around earlier. She's learning to drive, did you know that?' He wasn't surprised to see how, at the mention of the girl's name, Lenny's face lit up like a beacon.

As they went down the passageway towards the back parlour, the torrent of questions never stopped. 'When did she start learning to drive? Who's teaching her? Did she mention me? Will she be popping round again, d'you think?'

'Hold on, lad!' Joseph dropped himself into the chair. 'You can't give yourself a minute to breathe, what with Judy this and Judy that!' He gestured towards the kitchen. 'Go and put the kettle on,' he said. 'All them questions 'ave fair worn me out!' As Lenny went to the kitchen, Joseph called out, 'Oh, an' I wouldn't mind a drop o' the good stuff in me tea. You'll find it in the bottom cupboard. And don't be too stingy with it, neither.'

191

In a surprisingly short time, Lenny was back with two mugs of tea and the biscuit barrel. 'I found the brandy,' he told Joseph. 'I put a good measure in your tea, and there's still a bit left for a nightcap.'

Setting the biscuits and mug of tea down beside Joseph, he sat down in the other armchair and watched as his neighbour took a generous swig of the hot liquid. 'Aw, that's just what the doctor ordered.' Joseph smacked his lips. 'It might 'ave tasted even better if you'd tipped the lot in, but so long as there's a drop left to help me sleep, I'll not grumble. Thank you.' He raised his cup. 'You're a good lad.'

Though he had come to respect Lenny, Joseph had no liking whatsoever for the boy's parents. Devious crafty pair they were, he thought. They smiled and chatted to your face, while behind your back they were pure poison. He had never suspected how false they were, until one day he heard them talking in the backyard – about Joseph's family having left him to his own devices. 'We should keep him sweet while we can,' he heard that bitch next door say. 'After all, he's got nobody else to leave his few belongings to, and who knows? He might well have a bit of money stashed away somewhere.'

After that, Joseph had little to do with them. He nodded and smiled, and graciously declined their offers of help, and Ron and Patsy Reynolds were satisfied that he knew nothing of their expectations.

Lenny was a different kettle of fish. It was common knowledge that he didn't get on with his parents, and that they had little time for him. So Joseph befriended him, and sometimes the two of them would sit in his parlour putting the world to rights, and Lenny would confide in him – about how he had always felt as though he didn't belong to his parents. Sometimes he sensed that they resented him, and he didn't know why.

Joseph would reassure him, and he would go away less troubled, and in return for the bond of friendship that had grown between them, Lenny kept a wary eye on Joseph. When the old man was feeling under the weather, he would run errands for him, and make sure the house was warm and Joseph was eating properly.

For now though, Lenny sipped his tea and listened while Joseph rambled on, about how he missed his family, and how he wished to God he could turn the clock back, because if he could, then he'd happen be more tolerant and not let things get out of hand the way they had done on that particular night when it all ended in tragedy.

Lenny wisely made no comment. It was not his place to pass an opinion on Joseph's family, or the way it had been; though like everyone else down the street, he knew how shamelessly Rita Adams had behaved, and brought the family into disrepute.

Joseph went on, eyes down and staring at the floor, his hands relentlessly twisting round his mug of tea. 'I lost it all,' he said brokenly, 'my young grandson and my only daughter . . . and a son-in-law who had never set a foot wrong that I know of. That night though, he couldn't take any more, d'you see? It all blew up in our faces and there was nothing I could do. One minute I had a family all round me, and the next – I was standing in this very parlour, all alone. And oh, the silence after that terrible row. That's what struck me the most . . . the awful silence.' He gave a deep long sigh. 'They're all gone now, but not the silence. That's always there.'

The more he sipped of his tea, the more Joseph rambled on. 'One way and another we all suffered the consequences of that night. We all paid a price for my daughter's behaviour. She lost her life; Don went away and never came back, and as for young Davie . . . I daren't think how he must have suffered. Y'see, he really believed he could save his mammy from her bad ways, but in the end it were himself as needed the saving.'

He raised his red-raw eyes to Lenny. 'Not a single day goes by when I don't think about the lad. If *I* find myself feeling abandoned and lonely, what does *he* feel, eh? That's what I ask myself.'

He took a deep breath, as though the memories weighed him down. A long pause, and he was talking again. 'So where is he, my Davie? How is he surviving, or did he not survive at all? The police say they searched high and low for him, but I sometimes wonder if they were trying hard enough. After all, he were nearly fourteen. Happen they thought he were old enough to take care of himself.'

Lenny patiently let him talk away the memories, just as he had done many times since the departure of Joseph's family. Living next door to him all these years had made him appreciate just how lonely the old man must be. 'Joseph?' Exhausted now, old Joe was staring into space.

'What's that you say, lad?' Joseph was brought sharply to attention.

'I was just thinking. Is there anything I can do for you?'

Joseph shook his head, cleared his throat and thanking Lenny for his gracious offer, he answered with a smile, 'The only thing that can ease my pain is for my family to be here.' Though, after five long years alone, he had come to believe that neither Davie nor Don would ever come this way again.

Before emotion overwhelmed him again, he quickly changed the subject. 'Well then, young fella-me-lad,' he asked brightly, 'How's the business doing?'

'It's good,' came the proud answer. 'At long last I've taken on an assistant. She's hard-working and honest as the day is long.'

Joseph was duly impressed. 'An assistant, eh? And who might that be?'

'Annie Needham – and before you say anything, she's changed. She's not so bold and loud as she was. In fact, she seems to have grown up, all of a sudden. She came and asked me for a job on the stall, and I said I'd give her a week's trial. She worked like a trooper, and the customers really seem to like her. So I've made the job permanent. She helps me with the stall, she collects and delivers when I'm off buying, and if I need her to, she'll get stuck into the accounts, and from what I've seen I'd trust her implicitly.'

'Well, I never! And she's not disappointed you at all?'

'Not so far, no.'

Joseph was pleasantly surprised. 'At one time, Tom Make-peace forbade Judy from having owt to do with Annie. Said as how she was too keen on the menfolk, and the few times she came here with Judy, you could hear her halfway down the street. Gob on her like the Mersey Tunnel, folks used to say.' But for all that, he had taken a liking to Judy's friend. 'If she's changed as you say, then it can only be for the best.' He chuckled. 'One thing's for certain, it couldn't get any worse!'

Lenny admitted, 'I was nervous about taking her on at first. But she proved me wrong. In fact, I don't think I'd have got a better assistant if I'd scoured the whole of Lancashire. I can take off and deal with other things and leave her in charge, and when I come back, everything's in order and everything accounted for.'

Joseph congratulated him. 'That's wonderful news, lad. Well done, the pair of you.' He could always give credit where credit was due.

'I've got some other news that's even *more* wonderful.' Leaning forward, as though to avoid anyone else hearing what he had to say, Lenny lowered his voice. 'I think I've managed to swing it at last,' he confided excitedly. 'I've discussed a deal with the owner of that shop in the high street I mentioned the last time we chatted. The bank manager is right behind me, and so long as nothing comes along to clobber it, the deal is good as done.'

Joseph was thrilled. 'Aw, lad, that's grand ... bloody grand!' He shook Lenny by the hand. 'An' it's no more than you deserve ...' Laughing out loud, he tipped the rest of the brandy into Lenny's tea. 'This calls for a celebration,' he said. 'Here's to you, son – and may you go on to own a chain o' greengrocers right across Lancashire!'

'I'll drink to that.' Raising their mugs of tea, they clanked them together and downed the drinks in one go.

They talked awhile about the new shop. Once I've got the lie of the land, I plan to sell gift-wrapped baskets of fruit. I've just started selling them on the stall and they've increased my profit no end,' Lenny said proudly.

Joseph told him, 'If you keep on like this, I've no doubt you'll be a millionaire one day.'

'That's what Judy said,' Lenny said wistfully. 'I told her how badly I wanted the shop, but she doesn't know I've managed to do the deal.'

Joseph had long imagined Lenny and Judy making a go of it together. 'It would be good if you could find someone to share it all with, don't you think?'

'Yes, that would be good.'

'So ... have you found a sweetheart yet?'

'Not yet, no.'

'What about the girl you took out last weekend – her from Leyland Street?'

Lenny shook his head. 'She was good company, but that's all.'

'So, there's still nobody you like enough to put a ring on their finger?'

'No, there's nobody special,' Lenny sighed. 'I've dated a few girls, but it never comes to anything serious.'

'Ah, well!' Joseph was no fool. 'That's because you've only got eyes for young Judy.'

Lenny blushed. 'How did you know that?'

''Cause I've seen you!' the old man retorted. 'When she comes round to pay me a visit, you never tek yer eyes off her. Mesmerised, you are!' He gave a cheeky wink. 'Mind you, I'm not surprised, 'cause she's a real lovely lass.' He nudged Lenny in the ribs. 'Why don't you ask her out?' he suggested mischievously. 'Tek her to the pictures or summat.'

Lenny's eyes lit up. 'If I did ask her, d'you think she'd say yes?'

'Who knows?' On the occasions when Joseph had seen these two young people talking and laughing together, they were more like mates, with Judy seemingly content to leave the relationship as it was. But it was a well-known fact that a girl could always change her mind. 'If you don't ask her, you'll never know,' he warned. 'Anyhow, what have you got to lose?'

'Her friendship, maybe.' Lenny was afraid of taking that first real step. 'I don't want her to turn away from me altogether.'

'Aw, lad . . . she would never do that.' Joseph was certain of it. 'In life you meet all sorts o' folks,' he told Lenny now. 'Them as mek a good pretence o' being friendly, an' them as are friends to the last. Judy is a true friend. Through thick and thin, she would never turn away from you.'

Being made to think about it, Lenny was of the same

opinion. 'You're right!' he said. 'I'll ask her out, and if she says no, we'll just go on as before, being friends.' All the same, he would never lose hope that one day she might come to care for him, in the same way he cared for her.

'That's the spirit, lad. Tek the bull by the horns and see how it goes, eh?' Old Joe smiled. 'I recall when I were a soldier boy, fighting in Northern France, I had eyes for only one lass. She were more interested in me mate Wally, but I persevered, and I got her in the end. Brought her back home to Blackburn, I did. We never had a quiet marriage, mind. Oh dear me, no! It were up one minute, down the next, and there were many times when I wished I'd never got meself into it. But I did, 'cause I loved her, d'you see? An' for all her faults, I never stopped loving my Marie.'

He knew what a keen fisherman Lenny was. 'Going after a girl is a bit like being an angler,' he went on. 'You throw out a line, hoping the fish will bite, and you might land it safely. Another time you could throw out umpteen lines and still go away empty-handed.'

He tapped the end of his nose and winked. 'The thing is, if you don't throw out a line at all, you've no chance in hell of catching a fish – ain't that right?'

Lenny was fired with the idea. 'You're right! I might even take Judy to show her my new shop.'

'That's the fighting spirit!' The old man was thrilled. 'You do that, son!'

When the conversation was over and it was time to go, Joseph walked Lenny to the door. 'The next time you come and see me, happen it'll be arm-in-arm with our Judy, eh?'

With Lenny gone, Joseph walked back to the kitchen, where he set about washing up the empty mugs. 'Be gentle with his feelings, Judy, me darling.' He'd got into a habit of muttering to himself. 'You could do worse than link up wi' that young man.'

He almost leaped out of his skin when the knock came on the door, and as he ambled along the passageway, the knocking grew more urgent. 'All right, all right, hold your hosses! Now then, where's the panic?'

Flinging open the door he was shocked to his roots, for there stood Don, five years older and with a few strands of grey hair, but still the same well-built proud man he had always been. 'Good God Almighty!' Rooted to the floor, he stared at the man, unable to believe his eyes. 'Don!' Tears clogged his throat and he felt suddenly weakened, as though he'd been felled by some giant fist.

'Well, Dad, are ye pleased to see me or not?' Don smiled that familiar slow smile, his quiet voice belying the turmoil he felt at being back in this street, on the doorstep of this house, and there before him, his father-in-law, the man who had stood by him and Rita all those years. 'How are ye, Joseph?' The love in his voice was genuine.

When Joseph could hold back the tears no longer, Don took him by the shoulders. 'I'm sorry it took so long for me to come home,' he apologised. 'Things got in the way and suddenly five years had gone by . . . but I'm home now, and I mean to stay.'

Joseph looked up and he felt an incredible calm in his heart; but oh, there were such bad things he had to tell Don – about Rita, and young Davie. And he was afraid that such terrible news would drive Don away again.

Suddenly the tears brimmed over again, and when Don assured him once more that everything would be all right, he composed himself. 'You'd best come in,' he said shakily. 'We've much to talk about.'

Unaware of the awful news Joseph had to tell, Don stepped

inside, closed the door and followed Joseph to the back parlour.

'Are they home – Rita and young Davie?' Hungry for news, Don went on, 'Oh, but our Davie is a young man now, eh? Eighteen, and proud of it, I'll be bound. And my lovely Rita – I have so much to say to her. I'm frightened, Dad. Frightened that she's found someone else. Are they still with you, Joseph, or have they managed to find a place of their own?' Don was gabbling with nerves now. How could he have left them for so long? Panic crept into his heart. It was as well he couldn't see the old man's face, because the tragedy of what had happened was written all over it.

As they came into the parlour, Joseph gestured to the armchair. 'You'd best sit down,' he said sadly. 'I've news to tell yer.' Suddenly he was back there, on the day they came to tell him, in this very room, that his Rita was gone, and that his grandson had run off. 'I'm sorry, Don . . .' How could he say it? Maybe the best way was just to say it, and pray that his son-in-law could live with what he must hear. 'It's bad news, I'm afraid.'

With a pale-faced Don now seated, he eased himself into the chair opposite. 'That night, when you went away . . .' He cleared his throat. How could he go on? How could he burden this man with the truth? But he had no choice. The story must be told – and quickly.

'What is it, Joseph?' The man had a deep sense of foreboding. 'What are you trying to tell me?'

Joseph took a deep breath, and then he launched into the telling of it.

He told his son-in-law how, the night he left, Rita and Davie followed soon after. 'I lost my faith with her,' he said guiltily. 'She seemed more like the devil than the child I had raised. She wasn't sorry for what she'd done. I'd had enough,

Don. I knew then, that she would never change, and I couldn't take any more, so I asked her to leave this house.'

The shame of it would live with him forever. 'God forgive me, but I threw my own daughter out on the streets. She must have been hurt, poor lass, bleeding inside, mebbe, from her fall down the stairs, but she never said a word. Too damn obstinate as usual. I wanted to keep the lad here,' he explained, 'but young Davie felt responsible for his mammy, and when she went, he went with her. At the last minute I changed my mind and ran after them, but it was too late. They'd gone.'

When he paused, afraid of the next thing he had to tell his son-in-law, Don's soft voice rippled through his senses. 'Where are they?' he asked tremulously. 'My wife and son . . . where are they now?'

Joseph gulped, glanced up and, looking straight into Don's tormented face, he told him the whole story. He described how, for a time after they'd left, he'd sat in this very chair, hoping and praying they might come back, and everything would be all right. And then, some long time later, how there had come a knock on the door, and it was the police. 'Come to tell me a bad thing, Don. Oh, dear God, this will break your heart.'

When his voice quavered, Don urged him on. 'What, Joseph! Was there a fight? Did Rita cause trouble and they put her in jail – is that it? JOSEPH! You have to tell me!'

Hesitantly, the old man went on, 'You remember that night: how can you ever forget it? Rita was out of her mind with booze. She and the boy were headed for friends of hers, or so she said.'

'Go on, I'm listening.' Though with every word the old man spoke, Don's heart grew heavier.

Joseph described the events as he knew them. He told

how Davie had got his mammy as far as the so-called friend's house, where they had been turned away, then how they'd tried to make for the church. Almost carrying her by then, Davie had reached the shelter of the woods with his mam, who was becoming very ill and weak. It was here that she had collapsed. He told how Tom Makepeace was out on his early milk-round, when he heard Davie calling for help on the edge of the woods. 'When he got to Rita, she was hurt bad.'

Taking a deep breath, Joseph finished, 'Tom lifted her onto the wagon, meaning to drive her to the Infirmary. But they never got there because . . . she died . . . Oh, Don, I'm so sorry. *Rita's gone . . . she's gone.*' There! It was told, and now he couldn't speak for it was all too real.

For one shocking moment, the house was heavy with silence, all but for the old man's quiet sobbing.

Don was looking up at him, his eyes wide and shocked. Numbed by the weight of what he had just learned, he could only be still, as though he too had died somewhere inside.

Don knew, as well as Joseph, that they had both played a significant part in that night's terrible events. The combination of drink, temper, betrayal and blame had ended in a tragedy so profound, that both men would be marked by it for ever more.

Joseph knew how hard the news must have been for Don, and there was nothing he could do to ease it. So he stood up, and leaving the younger man to come to terms with it, he said helplessly, 'I'll get us a drink, son. I'm so sorry. I would give anything not to have to have told you that.'

As he walked away, he glanced over his shoulder. Don was just sitting there, staring into the fireplace and shaking his head, making small, unintelligible noises.

~

In the kitchen, Joseph quickly made a strong brew, and taking it back to his son-in-law, he was not surprised to see him, head bent, quietly sobbing and calling his wife's name.

On soft footsteps he went across the room, placed the cup of tea in the hearth and, sliding his arm round Don's shoulders, he consoled him, needing to give him strength, and yet knowing how futile it was, for news of that kind can break a man.

Moments passed before Don raised his head, and with both hands wiped his face. 'Where is she, Joseph? I need to see her.'

Joseph understood. 'First, just take a minute or two,' he suggested kindly. 'Drink this.' He handed him the mug of hot tea. 'I'll get myself ready, and I'll take you to her.' With every passing minute he waited in dread for the inevitable question, and when it came he was not prepared.

'Where's Davie?' Replacing the mug of tea in the hearth, Don waited for an answer.

Without a word, Joseph sat himself in the chair, his face grey with pain as he imparted the news to the younger man. 'Davie's gone. He ran away.' Before Don could speak, he went on hurriedly, 'Tom said he took it real bad. Y'see, Davie's mammy died in his arms. Afterwards, he just leaped off the wagon and ran into the woods. The police were out after him and everything, but he was never found, and he's not been in contact since, apart from a letter he wrote before he went away. I've kept it, Don. Happen it'll give you some peace of mind. He came to his mammy's funeral too, but that was the last we saw of him.'

The old chap ran a hand over his eyes. 'There have been times when I've driven myself crazy worrying about him, but summat tells me he's all right, and I have to believe that.' His voice broke. 'I have to believe it!'

Don was already up on his feet. 'Five years!' Beginning to pace the floor, he swung round, his eyes wild with grief. 'My God! He's been gone these five long years, and you say you've not heard from him in all that time?'

Joseph felt the guilt of it all. 'Not a word. I blame myself. If I hadn't asked his mammy to leave my house, the lad would still be here . . . and happen *she* would, an' all.' That thought would haunt him for ever.

Pacing the floor, Don tried to think as Davie would. 'Why in God's name would he run off? He must have been devastated! I can't understand why he didn't come home! With his mammy gone, he needed you more than ever.' He growled, 'He needed me too, and I wasn't there for him! Why didn't he contact me?'

Joseph tried to pacify him, like he had tried to pacify himself all this time, but it was not easy. 'Davie's a strong, capable lad, with a mind of his own. He's eighteen now, making a new life for himself somewhere. He'll be fine, I'm sure of it. Aw, look, don't fret yerself. You know your own son; you know how proud and independent he can be. Time and again I've asked myself why he'd rather run away than come home to me, his grandad. Happen it's because he's never forgiven me . . . and, it has to be said, happen he's never forgiven *you* for leaving. But he will, Don. One day he'll forgive and then he'll be back, you mark my words.'

There was no consoling the younger man. 'I should never have left. I just gave up and walked away, leaving my own wife and child. What was I thinking? Rita needed my help, not for me to desert her. Oh, my darling girl.' He sobbed. 'And my poor boy. I deserted him when he needed me the most.' Believing that it was he who had shattered the family apart, Don was desolate.

'What will you do?'

'What *can* I do?' Don's initial reaction was to go after him
– to leave now, this very minute – but common sense took
over. 'I'd go in search of him, but where would
I start? You say the police never found him, and you've had
no word of where he was headed – so if they couldn't find
him, what chance do I have?' He threw out his arms in a
gesture of helplessness. 'God knows, I would scour the
country inside and out, but there's no guarantee that I'd
ever meet up with him.'

Joseph agreed sadly. 'No, son. There's no guarantee that
you'd find him, and if you did, would he thank you for it?
No. Your boy will come home when he's good and ready.
And besides, you look done in. You're not fit to traipse the
country. You've come back to learn that your wife's lying in
the churchyard and your son's run off. For now, that's more
than enough for any man to take in.'

Crossing the room, he clamped his hand on the younger
man's shoulder. 'Give yourself time,' he pleaded. 'You
mustn't drive yourself into the ground. Try and live with
what you've learned, before you even think of taking off
again.'

Don was torn. 'I don't know what to do,' he murmured.
'Wherever Davie is, he might need me. And I need him,
Joseph . . . like never before.'

'So you mean to go in search of him, do you?'

Don shrugged. 'I think I owe him that much, at least.'

'Look, son, think about it. Don't rush into anything.
Stay here and take it easy for a time. Will you do that . . .
for me?'

Something in the timbre of the old man's voice made
Don realise what agonies his father-in-law must have gone
through. Now, when he looked up, he felt the raw pain in
the other man's eyes and the guilt was tenfold. 'All right,'

he said tenderly. 'I'll do what you said. It makes sense, and I promise I'll think about it. All right?'

Joseph's eyes were bright with tears. 'Thank you, son. It will be so good to have you near.' On impulse, he threw his arms round Don's neck. 'I've missed you,' he said. 'Never a day or a minute has gone by, when I haven't missed all of you . . . so desperately.'

~

A few minutes later, the two men left to walk the short distance to the churchyard.

When they got there, Joseph stayed back while Don went to his wife's resting place. Here, he fell to his knees and stroked the name on the headstone, all the while softly talking. Throughout the half-hour he knelt there, he sobbed helplessly, grew angry at what she had done, and then he begged forgiveness for leaving them behind. Then, getting up, he paced about, not knowing which way to turn or what to do for the best, and finally, he made his peace with her.

Stronger of heart, he returned to where Joseph was waiting. 'I'm ready to go home now, Dad,' he said quietly, and that's what they did.

~

In the evening, Don bathed and afterwards changed into some of his old clothes, which Joseph had kept. Later, the two men sat by the fire, talking and reminiscing.

Don confirmed his promise to Joseph. 'I've been giving it more thought,' he told him, 'and you're right. If I were to leave now, and spend the rest of my life searching for Davie, there would still be no guarantee that I would ever find him.'

He had plans, though. 'I'll go and have a word with the authorities and see what they have on their files. You never know, there might be a clue as to where he could be.'

Joseph was visibly relieved. 'I'm glad you're thinking that way, and not taking off again,' he commented. 'Matter o' fact, if you were to go out looking for the lad, he might well make his way back, just as you have done, and then you won't be here to welcome him home.'

'So, I'll stay awhile . . . if you'll have me?'

Joseph put up his hands in horror. 'We'll have none o' that!' he assured him. 'This is your home for as long as you want it – Davie's too.'

'I think you're right when you say Davie will be back.' Don had convinced himself of it. 'I'll get a job. I'll work hard, and save all I can. I'll give myself time to breathe, and if Davie still hasn't come home, I'll go after him. Meanwhile, I'll build a new life for all of us. What d'you say to that?'

Joseph laughed out loud. 'I say that's bloody wonderful!'

At long last the awful loneliness was over, and with two of them praying for Davie's return, who knew? Yes! With Don's homecoming, the old man really felt as though he had turned the corner.

Sadly, Rita was gone. But Don was here, and now Joseph was convinced that Davie would not be far behind. 'I reckon we should celebrate!'

With that he scurried off to the corner shop, in search of 'summat to warm the cockles'!

CHAPTER FOURTEEN

ALREADY, THE MAKEPEACE family were up and about, with Tom out grooming his shire-horse and his wife, Beth, pegging out the washing on this clear November Saturday; her tuneless voice uplifted in song and the dog whining at her feet.

Having tolerated it for the best part of five minutes, Tom could bear it no longer. 'For pity's sake, woman, will you stop that screeching. The poor dog will be a shivering wreck by the time you've finished!' All the same, he couldn't help but smile. He knew how she loved to torment the hound, and what was worse, unlike himself, the 'hound' seemed to relish every merciless minute of it.

'You get on with what you're doing.' Beth feigned indignation. 'Me and the mutt enjoy our morning song.'

'Huh!' Tom spoke directly to the horse, which seemed oblivious to everything but the juicy hay hanging from its teeth. '"Morning song" is it?' He sniggered. 'More like the sound of all hell let loose, if you ask me!'

Through her bedroom window, Judy heard it all. Scrambling out of bed, she went to the window, opened it and called down, 'Who's being murdered?'

'What d'you mean?' Beth looked up. 'You're as bad as your

father. No sense of music at all, the pair of you.' Collecting a bedsheet out of the basket, she put two pegs between her lips and at once order was restored; the screeching stopped and the dog rolled over at her feet in a fit of exhaustion.

'Thank God for that.' Tom was greatly relieved.

'You'd miss me if I wasn't here to sing you a lullaby.' Taking the pegs out of her mouth, Beth used them to secure the sheet to the clothes-line.

'Don't count on it,' he replied, though he felt a shiver of fear at the idea of her not being around. He had wooed Beth when they were both in their late teens, and they'd been together ever since. The thought that there might come a day when she wasn't at his side, was unthinkable.

'Your breakfast will be ready in ten minutes.' Taking up the clothes prop, she lifted the washing-line to catch the breeze.

'Any chance of an extra slice o' bacon this morning?' Tom peered out of the stable to see her going across the yard, a plump figure with a few strands of grey in her hair, but a pretty thing all the same.

'No chance at all,' she replied. 'You'll get one slice and think yourself lucky.'

Having witnessed the conversation, Judy dashed downstairs and promptly threw another couple of slices into the frying-pan. She knew all too well how her parents loved to tease each other.

Having left her clothes-basket by the back door, Beth came into the kitchen to check on the breakfast cooking. 'Morning, lass.' As always, her smile was bright and cheerful. 'You're up early for a Saturday.' Glancing at the wall clock, she noted it was still only eight-thirty. 'Couldn't sleep, eh?'

'No, Mam.' The girl tried hard to keep a straight face. 'I had this terrible nightmare.'

'Aw, pet.' Beth was quickly across the room, her chubby

210

arms outstretched to give her daughter a hug. 'Bad, was it?'

'Oh, Mam, it was just awful.' Keeping her composure, Judy returned her mother's embrace. 'There was this noise . . . a kind of unearthly wailing. I thought the devil himself was after me.'

And then she was laughing, and her mother too. 'You little sod, you!' Thrusting her away, Beth chided, 'You and your father have no appreciation of a good voice.' With that she grabbed the kettle, filled it with water and put it on the gas ring. 'Your dad wants a couple more slices of bacon.'

'Already done.' Judy scooped out the slices, along with four plump sausages, from the frying pan and transferred them to a dish that she placed under the low-lit grill. She then cracked the shells of four eggs, which were soon sizzling and spitting in the pan, while her mother washed her hands and made a start on the bread and butter.

A few minutes later, the table was laid; Tom's plate was dressed with two plump sausages, two slices of crispy bacon, and two eggs with swollen yolks ready for bursting. The remainder was shared equally between Beth and Judy.

'By!' Tom walked in just as the tea was being poured. 'Now, *there's* a sight to win a man's heart.'

'Is that the bacon, or me?' Beth asked with a mischievous grin.

'Both,' came the immediate reply. Then: 'Though if I was made to choose, I reckon the bacon would win every time.'

Judy shook her head. 'You two!' she laughed. 'You get worse.' No one in the whole wide world could ever know how much she loved them.

Over breakfast, they talked of this and that and Beth told her husband how Judy had fooled her. 'Said she had a terrible nightmare,' she tutted, 'and all the while she was taking the mickey out of my singing.'

'Oh, she heard it then?'

'Said it were like the divil himself was after her.'

'I know just how she feels.' Tom gave his daughter a sideways wink. 'Did you know that when your mam starts with the wailing an' screaming, you can actually hear the wild creatures run for cover?'

'Hey!' Beth warned him. 'You got your two slices o' bacon today, but I wouldn't count on 'em tomorrow, if I were you!'

'Oh, and why's that?'

'Because it's Sunday, and I've promised myself a lie-in.'

'What!' Tom was wide-eyed. 'That'll be the day. I've never known you have a lie-in through all the years we've been wed.'

'That's what I mean,' she retorted. 'So, like I say, you'll have to get your own breakfast, because it's time I gave myself a little treat . . . wouldn't you say, Judy?'

He caught her giving Judy a sly secret grin. 'Up to your old tricks again, are you?' he chided. 'If you're not careful, I'll turn you over my knee and slap your bottom!'

'Promises, promises. You'll be asking me to marry you next.' The kitchen was in uproar as father and daughter laughed at Beth's hilarious attempt to feign the shy maiden.

Afterwards, tucking heartily into their breakfasts, Tom asked Judy, 'How are you getting on at work, now you've been promoted?'

'I'm really enjoying it,' she answered. 'When I first started I was only allowed to show people in and out and take them to the fitting room . . . oh, and I got to work at the till that day Mrs Gregory was ill. But I was never trusted with anything too responsible.'

'And now she trusts you with all manner of things, isn't that right?' Beth was proud of her daughter's humble achievements.

'That's right.' Judy's excitement shone through. 'I get regular hours at the till, and help advise the customers while they're trying things on. Miss Maitland, the vicar's daughter, she told Mrs Gregory that I was an asset to her, and that she values my opinion because I seem to know what suits her best.'

'Good grief!' Beth was astounded. 'It's well-known what a difficult woman Miss Maitland is. I'm surprised she even noticed you.'

'Well, she did, and now Mrs Gregory lets me help her do all the things I've never been allowed to touch before. I get to dress the window with the new stock, and she's trained me up to create displays inside – and oh, we've just taken delivery of two new dummies. They have arms and legs that move, and Mrs Gregory lets me put them in any position I want.'

Tom burst out laughing. 'Is that so?' he said. 'It's just as well your mam isn't let loose on 'em, then 'cause she'd have the poor things standing on their heads, showing their knickers and all sorts!'

Beth chuckled at that, because it was true. She *was* ham-fisted, had no sense of style and she wasn't ashamed to admit it.

'Some time over the next month or so, Mrs Gregory is taking me to a trade show in London,' Judy went on. She had never spent a night away from home before, and the prospect of being taken to London had thrilled her. She knew her parents would take a little time to get used to the idea, so had waited until now before bringing up the subject.

Tom and Beth were delighted at the news, but worried all the same. 'London, eh?' Never having been to the big city, Beth imagined all kinds of horrors. 'How are you getting there?'

'We're going on the train.'

'And what happens at a trade show?' All Tom knew was farming and delivering milk.

Judy recalled what Mrs Gregory had told her. 'There'll be all the fashion people showing off their new designs and such, and all the buyers will be looking to take away samples or place orders. Mrs Gregory says if you don't keep up with the new fashions, you'll fall behind, and the customers will go elsewhere.'

'Important stuff then, eh?' Tom was impressed with the way his daughter was getting on.

'I'll pack you some sandwiches for the journey,' Beth announced with authority. 'We can't have you going hungry, now can we?'

'I won't go hungry, Mam.' Judy imparted her other bit of news. 'Mrs Gregory says she's taking me somewhere posh for lunch.'

'Ooh! Posh now, is it?' Beth's eyes opened like saucepan lids. 'By! It sounds like she's giving you the full treatment, lass.'

'You know what?' Tom was that proud. 'The way things are going, I reckon your Mrs Gregory sees you as a future partner. I mean, you're enthusiastic, and willing to learn, and there's nothing you won't take on. She could search the world over and she'd not do better than you.'

The girl's face broke into the widest smile. 'A partner? D'you really think so, Dad?'

'Well, she seems to have taken a shine to you, that's for sure. So, let's look at the facts.' He put his thinking cap on. 'We all know she's coming up to a certain age; her husband got killed on the railways some years back and as far as we know, they had no children. According to that nosy old bugger, Mavis Taylor, who cleans the surgery, Mrs

Gregory is in to see the doctor almost every week for this and that.'

Beth reprimanded him. 'That's none of our business, Tom, and I'll thank you not to discuss other folk's problems.'

'All right, all right, I'm sorry. But it's only the truth. Look now, she's already taken our Judy on because she couldn't manage on her own any more, and here she is, taking her to London, to the very heart of her business, and offering to treat her to a slap-up lunch.'

He now addressed himself to Judy. 'I didn't mean to be disrespectful to Mrs Gregory, but you do see what I'm saying, don't you, lass? She obviously sees you as someone she can trust. So, that said and done, she must be thinking along the same lines as I've said – training you up – and happen, if you meet with her expectations, she just might consider making you a partner at some time in the future.'

But the girl wasn't comfortable with her father's speculation. He was going much too fast for her. 'You're wrong, Dad. Mrs Gregory is not thinking of taking me on as a partner.'

'But why wouldn't she?' Tom was reluctant to relinquish the idea.

'She just wouldn't, that's all. She's very proud of what she's achieved, and she isn't about to share it with anyone – especially a girl not yet seventeen. She's just training me, that's all. She knows I love what I do, and she's showing me how it all works, so I can be even better at my job.'

Tom would not be dissuaded. 'Say what you like,' he told her with a wink, 'but you mark my words, lass, one o' these days – happen it'll be next month and happen it'll be some years from now – when she feels the need to take a back seat, I've a feeling your boss will be looking at you to take over the reins.'

Afraid to tempt providence and worried that she might soon be given her cards and sent on her way, Judy refused to discuss it further.

'I was thinking of going round to see Joe in a while,' she said instead. 'Unless you need me for anything, Mam?'

Beth gave her a reassuring smile. 'No, lass, there's nothing that won't keep. You go ahead and give Joseph our regards. In fact, he's very welcome to join us for dinner tonight, if he wants – Don too.' She paused, her mind going back a few months to when Don had turned up out of the blue. 'It's wonderful that Don is back,' she said. 'It seems to have given old Joe a new surge of life.'

The past six months had gone by so quickly, she thought. Don was working for an antiques showroom and workshop that had been set up adjacent to the auction rooms in town. Here, he repaired furniture and used his carpentry skills to wonderful effect. Working with wood again, in this environment, was like starting all over again, he had told Tom. But it wouldn't bring back Rita, nor his boy.

As Beth sighed, thinking of it, Tom broke into her reverie. 'Aye, it's made a world of difference to the old fella, but he still hasn't been persuaded to get back into the darts team. Look here, our Judy, you tell Joe that we're choosing the new darts team down at the Corporation pub on Wednesday. Say we're in need of a good player and there's none better than his good self.'

'I thought he gave that up some years back,' Beth recalled. 'Didn't he say as how staring at the board made his eyes sore?'

'That's what he said, right enough, lass. But I reckon it were more a sore heart than sore eyes. Ask him all the same,' he reminded his daughter. 'Joseph is still the best player we ever had. You tell him that, lass, will you?'

''Course I will.' Judy took the dirty crockery to the sink,

where she scraped the few leftover scraps into the special bowl: a treat for the pigs later on.

~

Leaving her parents chatting over the latest gossip from Tom's milk-round and Beth's recent visit to town, Judy went upstairs to get ready for the trip to Derwent Street.

When half an hour later she returned downstairs, her long hair brushed to shining, and her face scrubbed softly pink, Beth commented on how lovely she looked in her new cream-coloured dress. 'You made a good choice in that frock.' She noted how the calf-length skirt swung easily about Judy's slim legs, and she liked the way her waist was accentuated by the broad brown belt. 'Mrs Gregory is right to value you,' she remarked proudly. 'You have a natural instinct as to what suits and what doesn't.'

'You didn't say that last year when she came home in a pair of trousers and a flat cap,' Tom reminded her. 'You said she resembled a scarecrow from out the field.'

'And so she did!' Beth declared. 'Whatever Mrs Gregory was thinking of, when she dressed our lass in black flapping trousers and a big flat cap, I will never know!'

'We were just trying out the new fashions,' Judy grinned. 'And if you didn't like what *I* was wearing, it's as well you didn't see what Mrs Gregory had on.'

'And what was that?' Tom was intrigued.

The girl tried to describe it as best she could. 'It was a long red coat with split tails, a wide floppy hat with a bow, and a pair of high-heeled boots.'

'How ridiculous – especially for a woman her age!' Beth was not impressed. 'High heels indeed! I shouldn't think she was at all comfortable.'

217

Judy laughed at the memory. 'I didn't tell you before because I didn't want to be mean about her.'

'So, you can tell us now.' Though content in her old knee-length coat and a sturdy pair of shoes, Beth was always interested in what other women were wearing.

'Well, you know she took me shopping in Manchester, and she wanted us to come home in what she'd bought . . . said it would open folks' eyes?'

'Oh, yes.'

'Well, when we got back, we parted company at the Boulevard. I got on the tram and she walked over to the train station. It was pouring with rain and the wind had really got up. In a matter of minutes, the big hat was sailing down the gutter, her coat was up over her head, and she caught her shoe in a grating. Whipped the heel clean off, it did.'

'Well, I never!' Beth's face melted into a grin and Tom laughed out loud. 'No doubt she had summat strong to say about all that, eh?'

'She said it was all a matter of experience.' Judy shrugged. 'Nothing seems to ruffle her feathers.'

'Aye, well, fashions change and Mrs Gregory has to keep up with it all.' Looking at his daughter now, Tom was immensely proud. 'You look pretty as a picture, lass.'

'Well, it's a good job she doesn't tek after you, isn't it?' Beth was teasing again.

Tom would have none of it. 'Give over, woman. It's me she gets her looks from. My daughter comes from good stock.'

Judy giggled. 'You could be talking about one of your farm animals,' she said. 'Next thing, you'll be wanting to fatten me up for market.'

'Aw, my pet, you're the best thing me an' your mam's ever been blessed with,' he answered with a warm smile.

'You're just an old softie, Dad.' The girl gave him an affectionate hug, and the same for her mam. 'I'd best be off now,' she said. 'I'll be going straight on to Annie's when I leave Derwent Street, so I won't be back till teatime.' As an afterthought, she asked her mother, 'Is it all right if I bring Annie back for some dinner?'

' 'Course it's all right. I'll make a big shepherd's pie with enough for plenty more people, in case they all want to come.' Then, as always, Beth warned her to be careful about the traffic. 'The streets get busier by the day.'

With a decisive nod of his head, Tom agreed. 'We should consider ourselves fortunate to be living in the countryside.'

'The countryside isn't all that safe neither,' Beth said sadly, then: 'Not with you racing along the lanes in that rattly old milk-wagon and a horse that's going senile.'

'He never is!' Tom was shocked. 'That old horse has more sense than you and me put together.'

'That's not saying much then, is it?' Beth was determined to have the last word.

'Mam?' There was something else on Judy's mind in that moment, as in every moment throughout the day. 'D'you think Don might have got any news of Davie? Has he been trying to find out where he is?'

Beth could not pretend; it was not in her nature. She was not optimistic. 'I don't know, lass. You see, I reckon it's early days yet. Since he's been back, Don's had enough to cope with. He's found that new job, and he's also been taking care of Joseph. Five long years, he's been away, and there were a lot of things to put right. But don't worry, I'm sure he's got plans where Davie's concerned.'

Tom added, 'If Don had any news of the boy, we'd be the first to know.'

'I'd best get going,' Judy sighed.

'And don't forget to take your coat,' Beth reminded her.

As she set off down the lane, coat over her arm, the thought of Davie was strong in Judy's mind. Life was not the same without him. Day and night, she missed him so very much.

~

The tram was already at the stop, so she ran the last few hundred yards and clambering aboard, went quickly to her seat. The tram started forward and the conductor was soon round collecting the fares, and when he was gone Judy's thoughts returned to her favourite subject – Davie. She had never forgotten his face, nor his voice, and even now, she expected him to appear round every corner, but he never did.

Preoccupied with her thoughts, and oblivious to the other passengers, the girl was amazed when the conductor called out, 'Preston New Road . . . all off that's getting off!'

As the tram shuddered to a halt, Judy made her way to the step. 'Mind how you go now,' the driver called out. Having worked this line for the past six years, he was familiar with Judy and her friend, Annie. And like everyone else throughout the whole of Blackburn, he knew the story of Rita Adams and the family.

Judy disembarked, and made her way to the top of Derwent Street and down to Joseph's house. She knocked on the door and in no time at all, could hear him coming up the passageway.

'Aw, Judy lass, come in . . . come in,' the old fella said. He opened the door wide and allowed her to pass. 'I've just made a brew. There's plenty in the pot for two.'

Highly pleased to see her, he busied himself in the kitchen while she followed him around, merrily chatting and asking about everything; other than what she really wanted to know.

But Joseph sensed what was on her mind, and as they returned to the parlour, he bade her sit down. Handing her the cup and saucer, he sat himself facing her. 'I'm sorry, lass, but there's still no news of our Davie,' he said.

The girl's heart sank. 'What's happened to him, Joseph?' she asked quietly. There were tears in her eyes. 'Why haven't we heard from him, in all this time?'

Joseph shook his head. 'I only wish I knew.'

'Do you think he's all right?'

The old man took a moment to answer. 'I reckon so, yes,' he said at length. 'I've thought and thought, and deep down inside I've got a good feeling about him. Y'see, lass, our Davie were allus a sensible lad – made to grow up afore his time, what with his mammy behaving the way she did an' all.'

'So you really think he's alive and safe?' She trusted Joseph's instinct.

'I do, lass, yes, I promise.'

'And do you think he'll ever come home?'

'Well now, young Judith, your guess is as good as mine on that score.'

There were times when Joseph gave up hope of his grandson ever again setting foot in this house, and then there were other times when his heart and bones felt him walking down the street, tall and accomplished and grown into a man, ready to forgive those who had hurt him the most.

'Sometimes at night, when I can't sleep, he comes strong to my mind.' Joseph spoke his thoughts aloud. 'I worry about him all the time. Where did he go from here? Did he stay safe? And if he is safe, why did he never get in touch?' He gave an odd little shiver. 'I have to think that he made it somewhere safe. I can't let myself believe he did anything silly, or that he came to harm in some way or another. Y'see, if I let myself think that way, it would take away my hope and finish me altogether.'

The girl understood what he was saying, because didn't she feel the very same way?

'Joseph?'

He took a sip of his tea. 'Yes, my dearie?'

'Will Don ever go after him, d'you think?'

'Aye, lass, one o' these fine days he'll go after him, when he's good and ready.' He took another sip of his tea. 'Mind you, he's already been to the authorities ... trying to stir them into re-opening the search. The trouble is, it's been five years and more since Davie ran off. He were nobbut a young kid then, but now he's going on nineteen, and that does mek a difference. They tried to convince Don that Davie didn't *want* to be found – not then and not now. An' of course, it's no crime to leave home, is it, pet?'

'And do you believe that, about him not wanting to be found?' She had thought along those lines herself.

'I'm not sure what to believe,' he answered thoughtfully. 'Time and again I've tried to put myself in his shoes and think what *I* might have done.'

'And would you have made a new life away from here? Would you never want to come back?'

'Happen I would ... happen I wouldn't. All I know is this: if my father walked out on me, and my grandfather threw me out on the streets, I don't know as I could ever forgive them. And then to have his mammy die in his arms ...' Joseph's heart broke as he thought of what Davie must have gone through that night. 'Dear God, lass, what a terrible thing for a young lad to bear.'

For a time his words weighed heavy in the air, and in the silence, the two of them were carried back to that awful night when all of their lives had been changed for ever.

'Don is desperate to find him.' Joseph broke the silence. 'He's had a bad time himself, since he found out what happened. He's had no peace ... terrible nightmares, pacing the floor unable to sleep. When he's done with work, he's out on the streets at all hours, asking after Davie, talking to anyone who might listen – showing them a description of his lad, asking if they've seen him. Or whether they have heard of a boy on his own. But no one has, or if they have, they're not saying.'

'So he hasn't been able to find out anything?'

'Nothing whatsoever.' Joseph took in a deep, long breath. 'It's as if our Davie's fallen off the edge of the world.'

'So, what will Don do next?'

'Oh, he'll still go after him.' Joseph had no doubts about it. 'But he needs to build his strength up first. He needs to sleep regular and feel settled inside, afore he sets off scouring the country looking hither and yon.' Leaning forward, the old man confided in Judy, 'There were times soon after he came back, when I feared he was losing his mind. He woke me in the early hours, chiding himself, talking to Davie, pleading with Rita ... asking their forgiveness. He's still driving himself too hard, still blaming himself. I've told him: Rita had enough warnings and never once showed any remorse – not till it were too late, anyway! Any other man would have walked out on her years back, but my son-in-law won't have it. He misses her so much, is grieving so badly. And then he works all hours, hell-bent on saving enough money so's he can take time off work and go after his lad. He's worried about me an' all – says as how he has to make sure I don't go without while he's away. An' even now, after he's done his work and had a bite to eat, he's off till midnight, travelling miles on his old pushbike, asking the same questions: "Have you seen my son? Is there news of a young man on his own?"'

He paused a moment. 'I tell him to take it easy, to give himself time to breathe. But he doesn't know how to.'

Now that old Joe had given her the full picture, Judy was shocked. She had had no idea the situation was that bad. 'Wouldn't it be best if he went looking for Davie now,' she asked timidly. 'He could find work along the way, and could send you money every week, couldn't he?'

'I suggested that, lass, but he's got a first-class job here in Blackburn, and he's already building a little stash of money to see him through. A few more months, he said, and he'll be ready to leave.'

'I suppose he's right.' The girl could see the sense of it. 'Besides, Davie's been gone for so long, I expect his dad's thinking a few more months won't make any difference.'

'That's exactly right, lass. But still, he's like a cat on hot bricks. If he doesn't get his rest and stop blaming himself, he'll go under – and then where will we be, eh?'

He knew from first hand how guilty Don felt – for didn't he feel the same way, too? He wished there was more he could do to help him, but there wasn't. 'Much as I love Davie, I have to accept that he is Don's son and not mine. So I've come to the conclusion, it's best to leave Don be and let him do it his way. He has a fair-enough plan worked out, and it's only right that he should do as he thinks best.'

'So, when does he think he'll be able to go in search of Davie?'

'Like I say, he reckons on a few months. So what I think is, he'll work right through the winter until next spring, and then he'll up sticks and be off. I'll be lonely when he's gone, I can tell you that, lass. But if he's got Davie alongside him when he comes back, it'll be worth every minute I spend on my own.' He chuckled with delight. 'By! The day I see yon Don walking up the street with our Davie beside him, it'll be a sight for sore eyes, that it will.'

'Oh, Joseph, that would be so wonderful,' Judy murmured, her voice shaking with emotion. 'The best day of all.' She suddenly remembered her mam's message. 'Oh, and Joseph – Mam said you and Don were welcome to come round to supper tonight.'

'Tell your mammy she's a good kind lady, and I'd be there like a shot if I hadn't said I'd play cards with Elsie from the corner shop. Don will be off on his wanderings after an extra shift at the workshop today. So that's neither of us can come an' taste your mam's cooking. You just give her our kindest regards, love.'

Before she left to go on to Annie's, Judy gave Joseph a kiss on his leathery cheek. 'Take care of yourself,' she said. 'I'll come and visit again, if that's all right?'

'Goes without saying,' he assured her. 'The very sight of you in this house does my heart good. And happen the next time you come by, there'll be news of our Davie, eh?' He walked her to the door, where he gave her a hug. 'Don't you be a stranger now.'

'I won't.'

He watched her start off then he returned to his parlour and his armchair, and the dream of having his family all together under the one roof. 'God bless and forgive you, Rita,' he prayed. 'I can't stay angry with you, not when I know the fault started long ago, when you were little, and your wayward mammy was the worst example you could have had.' He nodded off, thinking of his beautiful Marie, and remembering her sitting up in bed, holding their newborn daughter in her arms. And for these precious minutes, his world was full of light.

CHAPTER FIFTEEN

J UDY WAS HALFWAY down Derwent Street when she heard her name being called. 'Hey, Judy! Hang on a minute!' It was Lenny. Panting, he caught up with her. 'Been to see Joseph, have you?' Coming out of the door to see her there was a lovely surprise. He, Annie and Judy were all the best of friends. Annie was always much calmer in Lenny's company, and Judy herself loved the straightforward and humorous nature of him. They all looked out for each other, and it was great.

As they walked on together, the girl told him what Joseph had said. 'Don is in a bit of a state,' she said.

'So I gather,' Lenny answered. 'I sat on the step with Joseph the other day, and he told me how Don took it real bad about Rita and his son. From what I understand, he blames himself for what happened.'

'I expect it will be a long time before he comes to terms with the death of Rita,' Judy commented sadly. 'We've had five years to get used to what happened, but it's all quite fresh for him, poor man.'

'You're right,' Lenny said. 'But when he's saved enough to carry them through, he'll take off after Davie. By that time, things won't be so raw, and Don will have a clearer mind.'

227

Judy felt content in Lenny's company. He was so kind and sensible. 'How's your business going?' she asked.

'Really well.' He smiled down at her. 'I'm hoping to complete on the shop soon. It's taken me ages to get the deposit, but the bank are helping me.'

Judy was pleased for him. 'Davie always said you'd go up in the world.'

'And what about you?'

'What d'you mean?'

'Did you think I'd go up in the world?'

'Of course. Everyone did.' She was utterly sincere, and his heart swelled with pride.

'Oh, Judy,' he burst out. 'I've got such plans. And Annie, you know, she's such a help. She works so hard, harder than any man, and all the customers love her. With her at my side, I'll be unstoppable! Before I'm done, I mean to have a chain of shops in every major town. I'll buy a big house on Preston New Road and fill it with beautiful furniture – made by Don.' And it would be all for her, he thought, if only he could make her love him.

Judy was so happy for him. 'You'll do whatever you set out to do,' she encouraged. 'I just know it.'

'Oh, and I'd love to see the world later on, see what it has to offer. I could put some responsible manager – Annie, if she's agreeable – in charge of my shops and take off for a whole year.'

'You might be lonely.' Judy had always seen Lenny as a shrewd, natural businessman. But he was homegrown and proud of his town and, as far as she knew, he had never strayed outside of Lancashire.

Summoning every ounce of his courage, Lenny took her by the arm and gently drew her aside. 'I wouldn't be lonely if *you* were with me.'

Taken aback, the girl was momentarily lost for words.

'I love you,' he whispered urgently. 'I've always loved you.'

She gave a nervous little laugh. 'You can't love me! Don't talk like that, Lenny.'

'But it's true, and I know you feel something for me, Judy. At least, I hope so . . . oh, I do hope so.'

Afraid of hurting him, she said softly, 'I like you, yes of course I do, Lenny, but as a friend.'

'You could learn to love me though, couldn't you?'

Unnerved and unsure, she walked on, and he went with her. 'Lenny, I don't know what to say,' she told him eventually. 'I never knew you felt like that about me, and I wish I could say I felt the same way, but I don't . . . I can't!'

Desperate now, he drew her to a halt again. 'Is that because you love Davie, the same way I love you? Is that why you can't love me?'

Judy took a moment to answer. 'I didn't realise how I felt about Davie, until he went away,' she explained. 'Davie was just Davie – part of my life, part of my growing up. He was always there, ever since I can remember. We were best friends, and then, after he'd gone . . . I felt different somehow. I didn't understand at first, but I do now. And yes, I do love him – in the same way you say you love me. I'm sorry, Lenny. Really I am.'

'But he might not love you in that way.' The words were harsh.

'I know.'

'If he did love you, he would have been back long ago.' Harsher still.

'I know that too.'

'Oh, Judy! One way or another, you're bound to get hurt,' Lenny warned. 'If he comes back and your love isn't returned, how will you feel then? And besides, Davie may never come back.' In a way, Lenny wished he wouldn't. 'But I'm here, and I'm not going anywhere. I'll always be here, loving—'

'Stop!' Putting her fingers against his mouth, Judy said, 'Please, Lenny, don't say any more. I don't want our friendship to be spoiled. I just want things to go on as they were . . . please?'

'I'm sorry.' He took hold of her hand and for a moment held it tight, before drawing away. 'I don't want to lose what we have either,' he told her, 'so I promise not to mention it again. But I won't ever give up.' He smiled, a quick bright smile that belied the bitter disappointment. 'Deal?'

She nodded. 'It's a deal.'

Reaching down, he gave her a fleeting kiss on the side of her face. 'See you later then?'

'Yes, Lenny,' she answered. 'See you later.'

Another smile, then he turned on his heel and was gone.

~

Her mind alive with the conversation between herself and Lenny, Judy hurried away to Annie's house. She could not rid herself of what Lenny had just told her. She went deep inside herself to find a response to his love, but there was nothing, except fondness and respect, and a long-standing friendship between herself, Lenny and Annie.

The thought of Annie brought her up sharply. Something about Annie's face whenever she talked about Lenny, who was her boss these days, as well as her friend, made her stop and think. But then she dismissed it, because Annie would have told her if she still had designs on Lenny in that way. Oh yes, three or four years ago, when they were still at school, she had had a major crush on him, had gone all moony whenever their paths crossed, but that was then and this was now. Annie was like a moth, flitting from one boy to another, an out-and-out flirt looking for fun, and as far as Judy could tell, it never went any further than that.

However, Annie did have a serious side, though she hardly ever showed it, these days. And for Judy, that was a troublesome thing, because she had always sensed another, lonelier Annie.

Where Lenny was concerned, had he really meant what he said, about loving her, or was it just a passing fancy? But then she recalled the depth of sincerity in his eyes and the tremor in his voice when he confessed his feelings. And she knew he was deadly serious.

What if he was right? Judy asked herself fearfully. What if Davie was never to come back, and she was destined to grow old and lonely without him? Could she learn to love Lenny? Was it possible to learn to love someone?

The answer had to be no. She thought of her own parents, and their deep affection for each other; the analysis of love that Beth had given her, the night Davie had slept in their barn. Besides, she had explained the way of things to Lenny, and he had accepted it. The air was cleared between them, and they were still best friends as always. Nothing lost. Nothing gained.

And now she was at Annie's front door about to knock, when her friend came rushing out, saying, 'Let's go!' She must have seen Judy coming.

Judy followed her friend as she went at a run up the street. 'What's wrong? Where's the fire?' she called out, hurrying after her.

At the top of the street, Annie slowed down, her troubled

eyes looking back towards the house. Judy thought she saw a flicker of fear in them.

'Annie, what's up? Are you all right?' she asked anxiously.

They turned the corner and Annie seemed to relax, though she was still lost in a strange and sombre mood.

Judy ran in front of her and blocked her path. 'OK what's wrong?'

'Dunno what you mean.'

'Yes, you do. You came out the house as if the devil himself was after you. Somebody's upset you, haven't they?'

Annie hung her head and for a moment it seemed she might confide in her friend. But when she looked up again, the smile on her face was radiant. 'Come on, you,' she told Judy. 'Let's have some fun, eh?'

With that she ran on and the other girl had no choice but to run after her. 'Hold on, you've got longer legs than me,' she panted. Even though Annie had already dismissed the incident, Judy knew very well that something sinister had been going on.

Annie kept running, faster and faster, until as they came onto the canal bridge, Judy had to stop. 'I've got a stitch!' she called out. Annie was bigger and stronger, and at the minute she seemed possessed. 'You go on. I'll catch up in a minute.'

Realising she had almost lost control, Annie came running back. 'I'm sorry.' Having tried and failed to rid herself of the torment she was in, she too was exhausted. 'I didn't mean to run away like that.'

Snatching at every breath, Judy found she was angry. 'Yes, you did! You're in some kind of trouble, and you can't trust me with the truth.' Uprighting herself, and taking a long gulp of fresh air, Judy led the way slowly towards the canal.

Annie followed without saying a word. Inside, she was

desperately wrestling with what Judy had said just now –
about not trusting her with the truth. For a long time now,
she had wanted to confide in her friend, but what she had
to tell was so awful, she could not bring herself to burden
someone else with it. 'Look,' she drew Judy to a stop. 'You're
right, there is something. But I can't tell you . . . not yet.'

'All I want to do is help,' Judy told her simply. 'You know
that, don't you?'

'Yes, I know, and I'm grateful.'

'It might be easier than you think, to talk about it,' Judy
suggested. 'You know what they say: "a trouble shared is a
trouble halved".'

Annie dismissed this. 'All it means is that you make somebody else worry, as well as yourself,' she said.

'Not if that someone else can see a solution.'

'A solution, eh? It's that easy, is it? Well, I can tell you now,
if there is a solution, it's me that has to find it,' Annie
asserted. 'So will you please let that be an end to it.'

'If that's what you really want.' Judy shrugged. She didn't
want Annie getting agitated again. 'I wish you could find the
courage to talk about it though.'

Suddenly, an odd thought crossed the girl's mind, taking
her by surprise. Some instinct made her wonder whether
this had anything to do with Lenny. Was *he* the problem?
'Will you answer something?' she enquired.

'Depends.' Annie was suspicious.

Judy took that as a yes. 'Annie . . .'

'Go on then, spit it out!'

'Do you have feelings for Lenny?'

The other girl looked puzzled. 'What kind of feelings?'

Judy felt oddly embarrassed. 'Well . . . feelings of . . . What
I mean is, do you love him? You know, the way you used to.'

Annie groaned. 'Bugger me, girl! Whatever gave you that

idea? I like him, o'course I do – otherwise I wouldn't be working with him, would I?' When she saw the look of relief on Judy's face, she realised what was going on in her mind. 'Well, I never! You think *he's* at the root of my troubles, don't you? Poor old Lenny – as if!'

'It did cross my mind, yes,' Judy confessed. 'I know you had a crush on him at school, and I know you love working with him. I just wondered if you thought more of him than you were letting on, that's all. I thought maybe he was The One.'

'Judith Makepeace! You've got a vivid imagination, that's your trouble.' Annie gave her a playful push. 'Besides, even if I did fancy him, it wouldn't do me no good.'

'Why not?'

'Because he's mad for *you*, that's why!'

'And has he told you that?'

'Not in so many words, no. But he didn't have to. I can tell. When we're at work, it's "Judy this" and "Judy that".' She laughed gaily. 'He's always talking about you. He sold a woman five pounds o' potatoes the other day, when all she wanted was a cabbage – an' that was because he was too preoccupied with singing your praises.' She looked sideways at Judy. 'Are you sure he hasn't told you how mad he is about you?'

Taking a deep breath, Judy blew it out with a sigh. 'Let's not talk about it any more.' She thought of Davie and said dreamily, 'All I want is for Davie to come home.'

'Hmh! If you ask me, you'll have to want on!' Annie didn't mean to be cruel. She was just being her usual practical, heavy-footed self.

'Why do you say that?' It was the second time today that someone had said something hurtful like that.

'I just think you're making a big mistake, waiting for

234

Davie,' Annie answered candidly. There was no easy way to say it. 'Think about it. He's going on nineteen now – all grown-up like the rest of us. I reckon he's either gone to the other side of the world, or he's found somebody he loves. Or he's dead. An' if that's the case, however much you might want to, you'll never see hide nor hair of him again.'

Annie knew her words would hurt, but they were not meant to. All she wanted was for Judy to realise that she could end up wasting her life, waiting for Davie. A lovely girl like her deserved love and happiness, of a kind that she herself would probably never know.

They stood on the bridge, leaning over the wall and chatting, and after a while they ambled down to the water's edge, where they sat on their coats on the grass bank and watched the barges go by. 'I went to see Joseph earlier,' Judy said sleepily.

'Oh, and how is he?'

'Bearing up as always. No news of Davie.'

'I'm really sorry.' And Annie meant it.

'Joseph is sure that Don will find him one day.' Judy then told her all about her meeting with Lenny. 'After I left Joseph's, Lenny came out of next door and we walked up the street together. He thinks like you – that Davie might never come home.'

'Did he tell you about the shop he's buying?'

'He did. I'm glad it's finally getting off the ground. It's taken a while but out of all of us, we always knew it might be Lenny who would make it rich.'

'Hmh! He's got a long way to go before he's rich.' Annie laughed out loud. 'Especially when a customer wants a cabbage and he sells her five pounds o' spuds!'

Judy had to chuckle at that. 'Lenny said you were an asset to him,' she imparted with a meaningful smile. 'He said you were a hard worker, that you knew the business as well as he did, and that the customers had taken a shine to you.'

Secretly thrilled, Annie brushed it aside. 'He's just full o' flannel,' she said smartly. 'That's why he'll do well in business.'

They sat for a while, plucking at the grass and throwing it into the water, while quietly observing the barges as they rippled past.

'I meant what I said, Judy.'

'What?' The girl swung round to face her.

'I said you were wrong in waiting for Davie, and I meant every word. You mustn't waste your life pining over something that might never happen; especially when you've got someone like Lenny falling over backwards to make you notice him.'

Ready for home, Judy stood up. It was getting chilly and the light would soon be going. 'He's always known my feelings for Davie,' she answered simply. 'It's Lenny who shouldn't waste *his* life on wanting what *he* can't have.'

Convinced of one thing, Annie had her say. 'He'll win you round in the end,' she predicted as they made their way back to the bridge. 'He loves you too much to let go, and like I said, Davie's been gone too long. I don't know of anyone who thinks he'll come back, and if his grandad and father were to tell the truth, they probably think the same. And even if he did come back, how do you know he's not already got someone? Face it, Jude – he could be engaged to be married, have you thought of that?'

The girl shook her head. 'It's not something I like to think about,' she said, turning away. But the truth was, ever since Lenny had made the very same comments, she had thought of nothing else.

~

At the bottom of William Henry Street, Judy tried to persuade Annie to come home with her. 'Mam says you can have dinner with us, if you like? She's making a whopping great shepherd's pie, an' there's plum tart for afters.'

Annie thanked her but said, 'I'd best get back. There are things I need to do.'

'Another day then?'

'Yes, that would be good, thanks.' She gave Judy a hug. 'And don't forget to thank your mam for me. My mouth is fair watering at what you'll be eating tonight. I think my mam is cooking tripe – ugh – but it's Dad's favourite!'

Giggling, the girls parted company, with Judy going one way and Annie the other. At the corner they turned and waved.

'See you later!' Annie's voice sailed down the street. With Judy gone, she felt incredibly lonely and bereft. 'I should have stayed with her,' she muttered.

She turned her thoughts to Judy and Davie. She so much wanted her friend to find happiness, but she doubted it would ever be with Davie. I didn't mean to say cruel things, she thought. It's just that I don't want her to be lonely. One of us being lonely is more than enough. This made her laugh wryly, though she felt more like crying.

She stayed for a few more minutes, letting the thoughts run through her mind – good thoughts, bad thoughts, and all of them disturbing,

'You were right, Jude,' she murmured. 'I do love Lenny. I love him so much it hurts. I work with him, I talk with him, and we laugh together – and all the time he's longing for you. He tells me how much he loves you, and I desperately want it to be me he loves, but it isn't and it never will be.'

Nothing in her sorry life was as bad as knowing she could not make Lenny love her. But if she couldn't have his love, she didn't want him to be hurt. 'Please love him back, Judy,' she prayed. 'I know you won't be sorry. You'll come to love him in the end, you won't be able to help yourself. I know how much you long for Davie to come home but with him gone, you will never find better than Lenny. He's a lovely bloke. He'll cherish and love you, and take care of you for the rest of your life.'

When tears threatened, she got up and walked on, in the chilly evening air. I'm no good for him, she thought sadly. I'm no good for anyone. Maybe I'm not meant to be happy. But I don't mind, not really. I've been unhappy for so long it doesn't matter to me any more.

'Hi, Annie!' Lenny had walked straight out of her mind and onto the pavement before her. 'I've been calling from across the street,' he said as he came towards her. 'You seemed miles away.'

Her heart racing, Annie managed a bright smile. 'Lenny!' He was the last person she expected to see, the first person she wanted to see. Her spirits rose immediately. 'What have you been up to?'

'Well, as it happens, I've been looking at the beginnings of my empire.'

She laughed. 'Oh, I see. You've been to see the new shop?'

'Yes. And this is the first time I've seen it completely empty. I didn't realise how much work needs doing. The storerooms upstairs are a disaster, and there isn't an inch downstairs that doesn't need attention – rotting wood, paintwork chipping, and in places it needs new floorboards. God knows what else I might uncover.' He made a little-boy face. 'I don't suppose you could give me a few ideas, could you – being a woman and all that?'

'What . . . you mean mop the floor and wash the walls,

and then if I've time, check the plumbing and happen fix a new sink in the back? Will that do, sir? Or is there more?' It was odd how her heart sang when she was with him.

He mimicked her mood. 'Well, we already know for a fact there's more to do than mop the floor and get stuck into a bit of plumbing.' He laughed. 'Why don't I let you renew the roof and rewire the entire place while you're at it?'

'All right then . . .' Annie got serious. 'What did you have in mind?' Whatever it was, it was nothing like what *she* had in mind, that was for sure.

'I just need to talk over my ideas with you, about colour schemes, shelving and layout – that sort of thing?'

'Well, yeah, o' course. I'd enjoy that. When were you thinking?'

His face lit up. 'If you're not doing anything right now, I've got the key.' Digging into his pocket he took out a long iron key and waved it under her nose.

'Wouldn't it be better if you asked Judy?' Annie said carefully.

'Not yet, not until it's all finished. I want it to be a surprise.'

'I see.' She could come and do the donkey work, but Judy wouldn't have to lift a finger. But Annie didn't blame anyone. It was only what she might have expected.

'So, will you come with me now and look it over?' he said eagerly. 'Can I steal a few minutes of your time?'

Annie didn't need asking twice. In fact, if Lenny wanted to 'steal' the rest of her life, it would be his for the taking.

They spent a full hour in the shop. 'You were right,' Annie said, stepping over a jutting floorboard. 'It is a disaster.'

But the two of them had great ideas, and taking out a pencil, Lenny drew a plan on the wall. 'I see it like this.' He sketched out his ideas.

Annie then sketched her ideas, and together they worked out the perfect layout for the shop. Afterwards he took her for a bite to eat and coffee at the nearby Wimpy Bar and the ideas continued to flow, until he walked her to the tram-stop, where they waved cheerio.

With Annie safely on her way, Lenny went to the pub, where he continued making notes and plans, and before he realised it, the time had run away with him. In jaunty mood, grateful for Annie's help and deeply satisfied with his day's work, he made his way home under the stars.

As he came up the street, yawning and ready for bed, Lenny saw the figure of a man climbing out of a car outside his home; in the lamplight, he recognised the tall man in the long dark overcoat. What was *he* doing here?

Over the past few years – ever since he'd left school, really, he'd become aware of this man taking an interest in him. If they passed in the High Street, the man would nod and Lenny would acknowledge him. But they never spoke. It was strange, the boy thought. Almost as if he should know him, although he didn't. Ron and Patsy (he no longer called them 'Mam' and 'Dad') had never mentioned him . . . Oh well, Lenny thought tiredly. It was one of life's little mysteries. He had enough on his plate at the moment, to bother worrying about that.

However, as he came further down the street, a deeper memory was triggered from his boyhood. This same man had called round to the house once. He could hazily recall his mother arguing with the man, and another time he had found them whispering downstairs. He remembered how nervous his mother became, when he asked her who the man was. From that day to this, he had never again seen the man at the house. Until now.

Instinctively, he backed into the shadows. There was no

mistaking him: it was the same man. Who was he? What did he want with the Reynolds family? Lenny's curiosity was heightened. If he had come to see Ron, he would be unlucky. When the visitor was let into the house, Lenny carefully started forward. Ron was over at a mate's house, helping him build a shed in the yard, and if he ran true to form, he wouldn't be rolling home for ages yet.

Suddenly, though he did not know why, it was important to Lenny to know why the man was here.

Taking out his key, he slid it quietly into the front-door lock and turned it; with trepidation he pushed open the door and softly closed it behind him.

Already he could hear raised voices coming from the sitting room. 'You'd best give me what I'm owed,' his mother was saying angrily, 'or I'll shout the truth from the rooftops – and then what will you do, eh?' She gave a low, harsh laugh.

The man's contemptuous answer was enough to stem the laughter. 'You silly bitch! You can shout and yell all you like, and I won't give a bugger!'

'What are you talking about?' Shocked by his defiance, she demanded, 'I want my money. That was the agreement, and as far as I'm concerned, nothing's happened to change it.'

'You bloody fool, you're not listening! Can't you understand what I'm trying to tell you? *She's left me.* Janette found the letters we exchanged and now she's gone – and she's taken young Charlie with her. Worse than that, she told her father and he's pulled the rug from under me. He's kicked me out of the family business, and taken back the house we've lived in all these years.'

'You're lying, Stuart. Now hand over my money!'

Lenny heard a scuffle. Then: 'LISTEN TO WHAT I'M

SAYING!' The man's voice broke in a kind of sob. 'I've got nothing – no family, no home and without references, no job. So don't ask me for money, because thanks to you, I've got none!'

There was the sound of another scuffle, and of furniture falling over. 'GET OUT BEFORE I TAKE THE POKER TO YOU!' Patsy roared. Her voice shaking with rage, she warned him, 'You haven't heard the last of this by any means. We had an agreement and by God, if you know what's best for you, you'll find what's owed me. I don't care where you get it. Just make sure you bring it before the end of the week.'

'And if I can't?'

'Well, now . . .' Her voice was slimy-wicked. 'It isn't just your wife and father-in-law who think you're the worst kind of scum. There's somebody else who might want to knock seven bells out of you when he knows the truth – or have you forgotten?'

'No. I haven't forgotten,' the man called Stuart said tiredly. 'In fact, that's the other reason I'm here.'

'What's that supposed to mean?' Lenny's mother sounded suspicious.

'It means I have to start again from scratch, and I don't like the idea of doing it all by myself. And besides, I've been watching him. He's a good strong fellow, with a clever head on his shoulders, and I understand he's bought the old tailor's shop on the High Street. Oh yes, I'm sure the two of us will work together very well.'

'So that's it. You're still the same cunning bastard you've always been!' Now, she was bundling him into the passage-way; though as yet neither of them had seen Lenny standing there against the wall in the shadow of the hallstand. 'It's not Lenny you're after at all, is it, eh? You've seen how he's making good, and you want a piece of it.' She laughed in his face. 'Once he knows about you, he'll be so disgusted he won't even want to shake your hand, never mind work with you!' She gave him a mighty shove. 'It were me as brought him up, wiped his backside and washed his smelly socks, and it's me who'll have first call on whatever fortune he makes. So bugger off, and don't come back, or—'

She was shocked to her roots when Lenny stepped out. 'My God, Len, it's you. Christ – you gave me a fright. I didn't see you there . . .' Flustered, she took the man by the arm, and smiled her best. 'This is Stuart Fitzwilliam, an old friend of me and your dad,' she told Lenny. 'He's just leaving. I'll see him out . . . you go inside, son.'

His face set sternly, Lenny blocked her way. 'Who is he, Mam?' His voice was ice-cold. 'What is he to me?'

'Nobody! Nothing' She had never seen Lenny look at her like that before, and she was shaken. 'Like I said, he's just a friend.'

Lenny addressed himself to the man. 'Who are you?'

'I think you know.' There was a certain satisfaction in the man's voice. 'I'm your father. I've come to take you away from her, back with me. You don't belong here, in this squalid dump. You never did.'

Lenny took stock of him, this respectable-looking, smartly dressed man with the sad eyes, and her, Patsy, beside him, bold as brass, her false smile hiding a multitude of sins. 'Is that right?' he asked of her. 'Is this man really my father?'

'No!' She was screaming now. 'Don't listen to him. Whatever he tells you, it's a lie – a downright lie!'

The man's voice cut in. 'We had an affair, and you were the outcome. Like Patsy, I was married, and though I've always regretted it, there was no place for you in my life. Since the day you were born, Patsy and Ron both agreed to keep you, as long as I paid. And my God, have I paid! I've paid through the nose to keep you in house and home, and more besides. Bled me dry they have, all these years. A few meaningless afternoons of sex with her, and I've been made to pay a million times over. But now, it's finished. You are my son, and I want you with me.'

He smiled like the cat who had the cream. 'We'll do all right, son, you and me together.'

When he made to lay his hand on Lenny's shoulder, the young man grabbed him by the wrist and held him off. For a long, revealing moment, he stared at the man, unable or unwilling to believe what he had just been told. And yet, deep down, he knew – and it was a blessed relief.

When he spoke, it was in a calm, collected manner. 'All my life I've never felt that I belonged. Somehow, I knew I was not a part of this family. For as long as I can remember, I've been rejected, unloved and punished, for something that was not of my doing. While you played Happy Families, I was nothing, a nobody. Alone, and made to feel guilty for being alive.'

His eyes hardened like bright marbles. 'You have no idea how it's been . . . no idea.'

Stuart Fitzwilliam stepped forward, a look of alarm on his face. 'But that's all over now, son. I've come to claim you. I've always wanted you, but it was difficult. You have to believe me . . .'

Lenny's confident smile belied the hurt he was feeling. 'All those years, and you never once acknowledged me. And now, it makes no difference whether you want me or you don't.'

Looking from one to the other, he informed them in a quietly controlled voice, 'It's too late, because I don't want you – *any of you.*'

His accusing gaze lingered on the woman he had always believed was his mother, but who had never loved him in that way. 'I came home tonight to tell you that I would be moving out in a week or so,' he said. 'But after what I've heard here this night, it's best if I go now.'

He spoke with pride. 'At long last I'm free of you – of all of you. From now on, there's no need for me to feel guilty or unwanted. I can be my own man.'

His voice hardened. 'As long as I live, I never want to see or hear from you again.'

'You ungrateful little toe-rag!' Patsy hit out, but when he caught her by the arm, she began to sob. 'You owe me for taking care of you all these years. *You owe me!*'

'I owe you nothing!' He brushed by them. 'Now get out of my way.' He ran up the stairs and into the room which he shared with his younger brother – half-brother, he reminded himself. He closed the door and sat on the edge of the bed, shaking his head and trying to take it all in. 'She's right,' he muttered. 'I *am* a bastard. I belong to nobody.'

And then he remembered Judy, and Annie too. 'Thank You, Lord,' he murmured, 'for the kind and honest people You brought into my life.'

Quickly now, he packed a bag and ran down the stairs; the man gone, the woman pleading for him to stay. He didn't hear; he wanted no more of it. So, without a word or backward glance, he fled from that place.

This house, these people, were his past. The future was out there, and he meant to grasp it with both hands.

PART FOUR

~

Bedfordshire, 1962

The Dark Horse

CHAPTER SIXTEEN

THE LATE MONTHS of December 1961 had been unusually hard in Bedfordshire, with days and nights of snowfall. Some drifts were so high they brought traffic to a standstill and made everyday life very difficult.

Winter had arrived with a vengeance, catching everyone unawares. People in isolated places were trapped, animals were lost in the far fields, pipes were frozen and schools had to close their doors to the children. And when the thaw came, it was with the same ferocity. The ice melted and the waters ran headlong down the banks and valleys and into the streets. Shops were flooded and emergency services were tried to the limit.

It had been a costly time, but now they were into the month of January, and chaos was replaced with normality. There were still cold, breezy days, but with the odd flicker of bright sunshine.

And the harsh months of 1961 already seemed a distant memory.

This particular Saturday afternoon was pleasantly mild, and having time to spare, Lucy strolled into the stable to see if Dave was there. She loved chatting to him. Humming her favourite Buddy Holly song, 'Listen To Me', she was feeling on top of the world, but her good mood came to a halt, along with the song, when she saw the expression on his face. Dave was checking the hooves of her father's best mare, Molly. 'I don't like the look of this,' he told her grimly. 'I saw her limping a few days ago when Seamus was riding her back from the fields.'

'Did you tell him?' Lucy came closer.

'Yes, but he rounded on me – said it was none of my business and that *he* was dealing with it. I took that to mean he'd already seen the vet and was treating it. But when I came in this morning, she was sweating badly. I suspected an infection, but I couldn't be certain until I took a look.'

Bending down, he raised the mare's hoof to wedge it between his knees; as he prodded it with the flat blade of the knife, he reeled from the stink that came up. 'Jesus!'

'What is it? What's wrong?'

Dave didn't answer straight away. Instead, holding his breath against the stench, he gently dug until he had located the culprit – a long bramble-thorn deeply driven into the mare's soft hoof. With that done he eased the iron-shoe away, reeling again when the pus was revealed.

'Well done, girl.' Patting her side, he carefully lowered the mare's leg to the ground and when in distress she hobbled over to the far corner, he burst out of the stable, securing the door behind him. 'Damn it!' He shook his head angrily. 'What in God's name is Seamus playing at? Why didn't he get the vet out to her?'

'Is it bad?' Lucy could see he was worried. 'Will she be all right?'

'Not if Seamus has anything to do with it. It's real bad, Lucy. The infection has gone right down into the soft flesh. There's a mass of pulp and the hoof was tightly swollen under the shoe. We'd best get the vet out straight away. She's in a lot of pain.'

Following him to the yard office, Lucy waited anxiously while Dave telephoned the vet; he was in the middle of describing the mare's symptoms, when Lucy's father arrived. Standing in the doorway, Frank Thomson listened to Dave's every word.

'By my reckoning, the hoof's been infected for some days now,' Dave was explaining. 'No, I've no idea why you weren't called earlier. Yes, I managed to dig out the thorn, and I prised the shoe off . . . lots of pus, yes. She's got a temperature. She seems in a bad way.'

He finished the conversation. 'Thank you. Yes, I will.'

Frank was at his side as he put the receiver down, his face hard and angry. 'Where's Seamus?' While Dave was talking, Lucy had told her father everything she knew.

'I saw him go off about an hour ago. He should be back soon.'

'Show me!' Enraged, he stormed out of the office.

Together with Dave and Lucy, he went straight for the mare's stable. Dave was the first in. 'Oh no, she's gone down!' Lying flat on her side and panting heavily, the mare was struggling to breathe.

Shouting instructions to them, Dave went inside. 'We need buckets of hot water and salt . . . plenty of salt, and towels . . . some cotton-wool. Quickly, Lucy. HURRY!'

While Lucy ran to get help, Dave tended the horse and Frank got to his knees, soothing the stressed animal and promising her that she would be all right.

By the time the vet arrived, Dave had drawn out as much of the foul-smelling pus as he could, before bathing the hoof several times in warm salt-water. Lucy was laying cold compresses across the mare's forehead, and Frank was in the office, having summoned two of the junior grooms, to satisfy himself that they had had no idea how bad the mare was. 'We're never allowed near her,' admitted the young girl. 'Seamus keeps us up the other end of the yard.'

Frank excused them, and when they were gone he slammed his fist on the desk. 'You've a lot to answer for, my man!' he growled. 'It seems you've forgotten whose yard this is!'

In the stables, the vet had concluded his examination. 'How is she?' Both Dave and Lucy were deeply concerned. 'Will she be all right?' Dave sensed the news was not good.

Scrambling to his feet, the vet slowly shook his head. 'Where's Frank?' He and Frank had known each other these past ten years and more.

'He's in the office, I think.' Before he could leave, Dave needed to know. 'Will she pull through?'

'I'm not sure. We'll have to wait and see.'

'But she's *got* to be all right!' Lucy was close to tears.

The vet explained, 'If the infection had been treated earlier, she would have had a better chance of recovering. But it's been left so long, there are complications. Her lungs are affected.' He spoke solemnly. 'I've done all I can; it's up to her now. All you can do is stay with her, keep her warm and calm, and hope the antibiotics do their work. But like I say, it's not good.'

'But when will we know?' Lucy asked brokenly. 'What else can we do?'

'There is nothing else to be done,' he assured her. 'The next twenty-four hours will be crucial.' He glanced at Dave. 'It might be as well if Miss Thomson waits inside the house.'

'No!' Lucy was adamant. 'I want to stay with Molly.'

'That's all right,' Dave assured the man quietly. 'I'll be here with her.'

'Well, if you're sure . . . Just do what you're doing – mop her face with a cool cloth, and keep her warm.'

Dave was desolate. 'What are her chances?' he asked once more.

'Fifty-fifty, I'd say. She's strong. She won't give up without a fight.' He made his way across the stable. 'I need a word with Frank.'

They saw the two men meet up in the yard; they saw Frank's face go pale as the conversation progressed, and when the vet was gone, Frank came across to join them. 'Molly is my best mare.' His voice was thick with pain. 'Aren't you, me beauty?' Gently, he stroked the horse's sweating sides.

'The vet says she's got a fifty-fifty chance.' Lucy had never seen her father so distressed. 'She'll pull through, Daddy. She's strong, you know that.'

Frank looked down at the mare, and he shook his head. 'I've seen how these infections can take hold,' he told her sadly. 'I hope you're right and she does somehow pull through, but she's got a hell of a lot of work to do, before she can shake this off. So don't get your hopes up, sweetheart. Let's just wait and see, eh?'

After a last whispered word or two of encouragement to the mare, he quickly left, his shoulders bent and his step determined.

A short time later, he saw Seamus arrive. 'I want a word with you, Macintyre!' He called him into the house.

'What's wrong, guv?' Bold and arrogant, Seamus confronted him.

For what seemed an age, Frank took stock of this man, a man he had trusted with his prized animals; a man who had callously abused that trust and might have cost him one of the finest brood mares in the land.

'Frank!' Seamus was blissfully ignorant of his boss's anger. 'You called me in. Mind telling me what I can do for you?'

His face fell when Frank snapped back, his voice low and trembling. '"What can you do?" You can go and collect what's yours and take yourself off my property. I never want to see hide nor hair of you again.'

The younger man was visibly shocked. 'What the devil are you talking about? What d'you mean, get off your property?' Even now, his arrogance blinded him.

Fixing him in his glare, Frank stepped forward until he was so close he could see the tiny red veins in the other man's eyes. 'I've been a fool,' he growled. 'I've trusted you . . . given you too much power, until now you act like you're lord of your own kingdom.'

'What on earth are you getting at?' Never having witnessed such rage in this usually tolerant man, Seamus instinctively stepped back a pace, his voice shaking with fear, his eyes wide and bewildered. 'I've no idea what you're talking about.'

Desperately controlling the urge to lash out with both fists, Frank continued to glare at him. 'If I were you,' he said, 'I'd get out of here as quick as you can, before I cause you a deal of pain – just like you caused that poor mare lying in the stables.'

When the head groom's eyes lit up with comprehension, Frank went on, 'Oh! So now you know what I'm talking about! You neglected a simple thing like a thorn in the hoof, and now Molly is down, and the vet doesn't give her a cat in hell's chance of recovering.'

'But I was onto it!' Seeing his cushy lifestyle coming to an end, Seamus began screaming. 'It was nothing – I would have got round to it. Damn it, she was fine when I left this morning. It's that fool of a boy you took on – he's the one responsible. Why don't you go and ask *him* what he's been up to? Meddling, that's what! He knows nothing about horses – nothing!'

'Dave is more of a horseman than you will ever be.' Frank was beginning to lose control. 'He knows every bit as much as you – probably more. And out of the two of you, *he's* the one to be trusted. So, like I say, pack your bags and get out of here, as fast and as far from here as you can.'

He thrust him away. 'If I were you, I'd go right now – because I don't know how long I can keep it together . . . if you know what I mean.' His eyes said it all, and the other man saw the violence there, yet still he was defiant.

'I want what's due to me! I'm owed three weeks' wages and severance pay. And I'm going nowhere without it.'

'You'll get nothing from me!'

'Then I'm not leaving!'

Frank smiled, which was more frightening than his temper. 'Is that so?'

With one lurch he had Seamus by the collar of his shirt. With the other hand, he took hold of the seat of his pants and with a mighty heave he threw him outside, where he landed hard on the ground, screaming and shouting and promising all kinds of retribution.

When Frank took a step towards him, he was gone . . . fleeing across the yard like the coward he was.

Having heard the commotion, Dave and Lucy had come to the stable door and witnessed the scene. 'It's no more than you deserve!' Dave called out, and fearing that he too would confront Seamus, Lucy called him back to the mare. 'She's trembling, Dave . . . she must be cold.' With great tenderness, she drew the blanket up and over the mare's flanks. 'There must be something we can do to help her?'

'You heard what the vet said, Lucy.' Realising that Molly had gone into convulsions, Dave took Lucy by the shoulders and spun her round to him. 'Go indoors,' he ordered quietly. 'This is no place for you just now.'

Realising something bad was about to happen, Lucy would not be persuaded. 'No, Dave. I want to stay here, with you.'

'No.' He led her towards the stable door. 'You have to trust me, Lucy. You really shouldn't be here.' Opening the door, he walked her outside. 'I'll call you if anything happens.'

'Promise?'

'I promise.'

With Lucy making her way across the yard, Dave returned to the mare. 'Easy does it.' He wiped her forehead with the cool cloth. 'Breathe easy, sweetheart. The fever's got a hold of you. Once that's broken, you'll begin to feel better.' But he was not hopeful, because now, her eyes were rolling and her whole body was shivering. He drew the blanket higher, and prayed a little. She didn't deserve this, but what was worse, it could all have been avoided.

Ever since he'd worked at the stud farm, Dave's love and respect for horses had grown, along with his knowledge of their ways. With the exception of Madden, the big, nervy stallion, the horses here were biddable, trustworthy creatures – a joy to deal with, and a deep balm to Dave Adams's troubled heart.

From across the yard, the shouting got louder. 'I HOPE SHE DIES!' Seamus was yelling shrilly. 'From the first time your boyfriend set foot on this yard I knew he wouldn't rest until he got it all – my job and you, you little whore. Oh yes, he wanted you all right, and by God he's got you now, hasn't he, eh? I expect the two of you have already climbed into bed, haven't you? Well? Answer me, you little bitch!' He raised his hand to slap her.

In minutes, Dave had raced across the yard to launch himself at Seamus. 'You bad-mouthed bastard, I ought to tear you limb from limb!' He swung a clenched punch which

caught Seamus between the eyes and sent him reeling backwards to the ground.

Before Dave could follow up, however, Frank had gripped
Seamus by the arm and was frog-marching him across the
yard, where he threw him out of the gates and into the lane,
together with his bag of belongings.

As he walked away he didn't look back, but Seamus's raised
voice carried across the yard.

'YOU'VE NOT SEEN THE LAST OF ME, ESPE-
CIALLY NOT YOUR SLUT OF A DAUGHTER AND
HER GYPSY BOYO. OH, I'LL BE BACK ALL RIGHT,
AND MARK MY WORDS, WHEN I DO, YOU'LL BE
SORRY, THE LOT OF YOU!'

His angry words flew towards them as they returned to
the stable.

One glance at the mare was enough. Dave looked at Frank
and the man took his meaning. Without hesitation he
guided Lucy out of there.

With Lucy sobbing on her father's shoulder, Dave bent to
stroke the mare's nose. 'Couldn't quite manage it, eh, old
girl?' There was immense sadness in his voice, and anger
too. 'What a waste! What a shocking waste!'

He stayed awhile, cross-legged on the straw next to Molly,
wondering how Seamus could have let this happen.

A few moments later, he covered her over and went into
the house. Frank poured them all a drink, while Dave telephoned the vet. 'There's no rush,' he told him sadly. 'She
didn't pull through.'

~

The following day, Frank asked Dave to take Lucy into town.
'A day at the shops will do her good,' he said. 'She's had a

bad night. We all have. Here. Take this and give it to her.'
The man handed him three ten-pound notes. 'She can treat
herself to a new outfit for the barn-dance next Saturday.'

'Whatever you say,' Dave answered respectfully. 'But if
you'd rather take her, I'll stay here and get everything
cleared away.'

Frank thought about the mare, and the task of having her
corpse removed from the stable, and for one brief moment
he was tempted to leave Dave here to deal with it. But then
he thought how Lucy would be better off in the company of
someone her own age than with himself; and besides, he
had seen the way things seemed to be going between them.
It gladdened his heart to think the two of them might get
together in a serious way.

'No, son, thanks all the same. You and Lucy get off. I'll
see to everything this end.'

When she heard they were going into town, Maggie begged
a lift. 'I've a new hat to buy,' she announced. 'I'm giving a
cookery talk next week at the Townswomen's Guild, and I need
to look my best. I can't be outdone by some fancy townsfolk.'

When Frank groaned and muttered, 'Women and hats!'
Maggie told him in no uncertain terms to mind his own
business.

'Men should be seen and not heard,' she said smartly,
with her rolling Scottish 'rrs'. 'You're not my keeper!'

'Not yet,' he murmured as he turned away. 'But one day
– who knows?'

It had been a long, lonely fifteen years without a woman's
loving embrace. The stud farm was his pride and joy, but
now that Lucy was grown into a woman, and his job with her
was nearly done, Frank Thomson had fallen in love again,
and the thought of putting a ring on Maggie's finger brought
a huge smile to his face, despite recent tragic events.

Ten minutes later, the three of them set off in Dave's Hillman-Minx, with Lucy and Maggie discussing shoes and hats, and which colour would suit the little woman best.

When they arrived in town, Dave parked by the church. 'Which way, ladies?' He didn't relish a day traipsing round shops, but this was for Lucy, and that was fine.

'I'm off to Taylor's hat shop,' Maggie told them. 'We can meet up later for a cup of tea if you want?'

So it was arranged. They would meet underneath the market clock at midday.

'Right!' said Dave. 'Where to first?' He thought Lucy strikingly pretty in her boots and long coat; the high collar drawn up to her chin to keep out the cold. With her hair loose about her shoulders, she had the vulnerable look of a child and, for one fleeting moment as she turned her back to say cheerio to Maggie, he was reminded of Judy Makepeace.

The thought both shocked and disturbed him.

For too long now, he had promised himself to go back, to see both her and his grandfather. But time had raced away almost without him realising, and then there was that sickening sense of fear deep down inside him.

Every time he thought of home it was there, swamping him; the lingering memories, the dark images, and the feeling of utter desolation.

By some unfair alchemy, Judy was caught up in it, had become part of it – almost something to be feared. With his rational mind, he knew that she was sweet, loyal, innocent – a friend for life – and that he had somehow betrayed her by disappearing, by failing to fulfil his promise to write. One day, all this would have to be faced – he knew it, but oh, dear God – not yet. Not yet.

There were times when he was acutely conscious of it, and

other times when he was able to thrust it all to the back of his mind. But day or night, it never went away.

Shaking off the melancholy, he turned his attention to Lucy. 'Come along, madam!' he teased with an easy smile. 'Chop chop!'

'Oh, there's no rush. Let's just wander.' She curled her arm through his. 'It's so nice to have you all to myself, without Dad monopolising you.'

As they strolled through the High Street, Dave thought how comfortable he felt with Lucy holding onto him. She was a lovely girl, and he had great affection for her. But he was shocked to find that the more comfortable he felt, the more he found himself thinking of Judy. His feelings for his employer's daughter were triggering other, long-buried emotions. Taking a deep breath, Dave returned to the present moment.

Lucy had a wonderful time going in and out of shops and taking Dave with her; though he felt embarrassed at the curious looks the sales assistants gave him in Etam and Marks & Spencer. They had fun listening to a couple of new records in a booth at the radiogram shop near Woolworths. Both of them were Cliff Richard fans, and Dave bought his latest EP for them both to listen to.

Dave was paid a good wage by Frank – enough to run a car and make regular payments into a Post Office savings account. It was the first time he'd ever had spare money, and today he enjoyed lashing out on a new shirt, shoes and trousers for best. Lucy naughtily tried to persuade him to get a pair of winkle-pickers, but as he explained to her, tongue in cheek, they would frighten the horses!

By midday, he and Lucy were loaded down with bags and boxes, and Maggie the same. 'Whew, what a rush!' She came stumbling towards them. 'I tell you what, my darlings,' she gasped. 'I'm more than ready for a cuppa tea.'

Fortunately, there was a café just round the corner. The trio found a table by the window and fell into the seats. 'I feel worn out,' Dave laughed. 'I'd rather shift a ton of bricks than do that again!'

'You might *have* to do it again when you're married,' Maggie chuckled. 'Wives need their husbands to carry the shopping.'

Dave was taken aback, while Lucy stared at her wide-eyed. 'Who said anything about getting married?' the girl asked, blushing.

'I'm a woman,' Maggie answered coyly. 'And we have a way of sensing things.' She tapped her nose. 'Now then, where's that waitress?'

After they had ordered a plate of sandwiches and some drinks, they started looking through their purchases.

'Now then, Lucy.' Maggie prised open the largest of her shopping bags. 'What d'you think to this?' Whipping out a mad creation of black lace and brown roses, she popped it onto her head.

'Well, I never!' Lucy was astonished at the change in Maggie. 'I've never seen you in a hat before. It really suits you.'

Maggie beamed with delight. 'What I want to know is, do I look like Dorothy Lamour?'

'Who's she when she's at home?' Dave asked.

'Good Lord!' Maggie was astounded. 'Are you telling me you don't know who Dorothy Lamour is?'

'Neither do I,' Lucy confessed.

The Scotswoman sighed. 'She's a film star . . . made a lot of films wearing a swimsuit, dancing in the water to music. But she sometimes dresses up all fancy. Yes, she is an amazing-looking woman!' She preened, and posed with her hat. 'So, do you think I look a bit like a film star in this?'

Lucy glanced at Dave who was thoroughly enjoying the conversation. 'What do *you* think?' she asked, straight-faced. 'Do you think that Maggie looks like a Dorothy Lamour?'

Before he could answer, the waitress was back with a big tray. 'Ooh, you do look nice,' she said, admiring Maggie's frivolous hat. 'I reckon you're the spitting image of Dorothy Lamour. I've seen a few of her films, and she's a right glamour-puss.'

Maggie almost swooned. 'There!' She gave Dave and Lucy a haughty look. 'I'm glad *somebody* knows who I'm talking about.' For a while after that, there was no controlling her.

While they enjoyed their lunchtime snack, they talked of Seamus and the way Frank had managed to keep his temper, most of the time. 'I'm surprised Frank didn't take a horse-whip to him!' Maggie said indignantly.

'I'm worried,' Lucy said quietly. 'It was a terrible thing, to lose Molly like that, and when Dad threw him out on his ear, Seamus promised all kinds of trouble. To me, he seems the sort to carry out his threat. I'm scared, Dave. Will he really come back, do you think?'

'He'll have to get through me if he does come back,' Dave promised. 'But Macintyre is all mouth and no substance, so I wouldn't worry about it, if I were you.'

Maggie wasn't so certain. 'I haven't said anything to your father about this, Lucy, but I think Seamus is a thoroughly bad lot. I've heard the way he talked to the stable girls, and once he came back late at night, drunk as a Lord . . . mad as a bull, he was.'

Hesitating, she hoped she was right in mentioning the following incident. 'The next day, young Laura from the top yard had an angry red mark across her face, as though somebody had slapped her really hard. I asked if Seamus had hurt her, and she denied it – got a bit upset at me asking. She made me promise I would not repeat that to anyone, or she would have to leave. And anyway, she insisted it was not Seamus, but a disgruntled boyfriend.'

'And was it – a boyfriend?' Lucy was horrified.

Maggie shrugged her shoulders. 'Well, it wasn't my right to question her. Anyway, in the end, I took her at her word and said nothing. But I regret it now, because if I'd spoken out and it was discovered that it really was Seamus who got rough with her, he'd have been sent on his way long ago.'

Dave could see how Maggie was blaming herself. 'You did what you thought was right,' he told her now. 'You believed Laura. Any one of us might have done the same.'

The woman wasn't so sure. 'The thing is, I've seen Seamus drunk before when he's come home late,' she confessed. 'I've seen him throwing things about. Once he kicked at the fencing and smashed it through. During the day he seemed always to be working, calm as you like – pleasant, even. He was a right Jekyll and Hyde,' she recalled his behaviour, 'because when he'd been drinking, he was out of his mind.'

'And you never told Dad any of this?' Lucy asked.

'No. Like I say, maybe I should have. But as far as I know, he never hurt anyone or did any real damage to speak of, and he was a natural with the animals.'

She gave an almighty sigh. 'I didn't think your father would thank me for telling tales, especially when he got along so well with Seamus. Frank trusted him as his head groom. Relied on him to keep that part of the business running smoothly.'

Dave agreed. 'You're right.' He could see Maggie working herself up to misery. 'If there was no real damage done and no evidence that he was not doing his work properly, Frank might well have given him the benefit of the doubt – and then you would have felt all the worse for telling.' He recalled how Frank had been oblivious of his daughter's reservations about Seamus, the day he had first come to the stud farm, nearly four years ago.

Maggie gave a sigh of relief, and took off her hat. 'Oh Dave, thank you. You've put my mind at rest.'

Lucy gave her a hug. 'So there you are, and now you can have a look at the shoes I've bought for the barn-dance this Saturday.'

With the confession off her chest, Maggie was her old self again. 'Go on then,' she urged. 'Let's see what you've got.'

When Lucy took out the shoes, Maggie oohed and aahed and said how pretty they were. The shoes were dark blue, with high heels and a peep toe, and where the foot slipped into the shoe, there was a darling yellow daisy. 'I'd never get my big clodhoppers in there,' Maggie groaned, 'but you'll look a picture in them, come Saturday.' She rubbed her hands gleefully. 'Put them away and let me see what else you've got.'

One by one, and much to Dave's amusement, Lucy displayed the articles. There was the daintiest pink crocheted bolero; a pretty blue, long-sleeved dress with a cinched waist and big belt, and a dark green skirt that hugged the hips and swung out at the hem. 'Lovely!' Maggie was beside herself. 'Wish I could get into them!'

Across the room behind the counter, the two waitresses drooled over Lucy's choice of clothes. 'Take down the name on the carrier bags,' one urged the other. 'I'm gonna save all me tips, and when I get me wages on Friday, I'm off to see if there's anything left worth having.'

CHAPTER SEVENTEEN

TWO DAYS LATER, Frank arrived at the stables early in the morning. Dave was leading in the stallion. 'Been going a bit mental again, has he?' Standing eighteen hands high, with a coat black as night and a temper the same, Madden was a magnificent beast.

'I put him in the back field as far away from the mares as he could be,' Dave answered. 'The trouble is, once he's got wind of them, even when they're not in season, he won't rest. He cleared two fences before I got to him, and we had the devil of a tussle, before I managed to calm him down.'

'You do well to handle him at all.'

Frank had scars where he had battled with the stallion at different times. 'He can be a bad bugger!' he exclaimed. 'But he seems calm enough now.' All the same, he was concerned. 'I didn't buy him straight off,' he admitted. 'I thought long and hard before parting with money for this particular one.' He recalled the day, years ago. 'It was the first time I let my heart rule my head. And, of course, I was wrong.'

Reaching out, he attempted to stroke the stallion's mane, withdrawing his hand when it got agitated. 'You can't deny he's a prime specimen though. He's got a pedigree a mile long, and his offspring are valued worldwide.'

'You're right, he is a beautiful animal,' Dave commented. 'But for some reason, he seems to have taken against us.'

Frank had his suspicions. 'There was one occasion when I had to reprimand Seamus for being too hard on the horse,' he told Dave now. 'The way this fella's been behaving, I'm beginning to wonder how many times that little bastard has taken the leather to him without my knowing.'

The very same thought had crossed Dave's own mind. 'The wrong treatment can turn a horse quicker than any-thing,' he agreed. 'And you must know yourself, once that happens, it's the devil of a job to bring them back – though I reckon with kind handling and the right attitude, we can get this fella round, now Macintyre has gone. *If* you'll give him a chance?'

'Mmm. Well, I value your judgment, Dave,' Frank told him earnestly. 'You've proved yourself to me, time and again. But I have to admit, I'm not so sure with this one.' He looked at the horse and thought what a waste it would be if they were to give up on him.

In his usual, brisk way, he made an on-the-spot decision. 'All right then. We'll give him a month. If he hasn't settled properly by then, he's out the door, and no argument.'

'I don't think he'll disappoint you.'

'I wonder if it might be best to get somebody else in, somebody who could just work with him alone. What d'you think, Dave?'

While they spoke, the stallion was fidgeting uneasily. 'There's no denying he's a powerful fella, and he will need a lot of time spent with him,' Dave answered. 'But if it's all right with you, I'd like to deal with him myself. Y'see, I've got to know him, and I reckon he trusts me.'

Frank smiled. 'Trusts you, does he? Well, that makes two of us. If you feel happy about that, then you have my blessing.

But, like I say . . . a month at the most, and not a minute more.'

Dave was relieved. 'That suits me.'

'Good. Now that we've settled that, I want to show you something.' Frank glanced at the tower clock. 'It's nine o'clock now. Meet me at the gate in an hour, saddled up and ready to go.'

'Go where?'

Frank would not be drawn. 'One hour. See you then.' With that he marched off, hands in pockets and a satisfied grin on his face.

Behind him, Dave quietened the stallion and made him secure, before searching out a capable groom. He found Laura in the bottom yard.

'The boss wants me to go somewhere with him. Can you keep an eye on everything?' he asked. 'I've no idea how long I'll be gone. Oh, and I need a mount. Is it OK to take Shamrock?'

''Course. It'll do her good. She'll be glad of the exercise.'

'Right, thanks. Oh, and if you need help with anything, get one of the younger girls to give you a hand.' He chuckled. 'Or you could always fetch Thomas from the fields.' He gave her a knowing wink. 'That should put a twinkle in his eye.'

When she blushed deep pink, he laughed out loud. 'I'd best go,' he said, 'before you come at me with the pitch-fork . . .'

There was time for a quick tidy-up, before he set about preparing the big Irish horse. 'Come on, my beauty.' He eased the saddle on. 'It seems we're going for a ride.' Taking a moment to encourage her, he then swung himself up onto her back. 'I want the best of behaviour from you,' he instructed; though he had no fear on that score, for this young mare had a kind and sensible nature. 'The boss will have his eye on you, and being as I've already sung your praises to him, you are not to let me down.'

When he arrived at the main gates, Frank was up and ready to go. 'I've been meaning to do this with you for a long time,' he told Dave. 'And there's no better time than right now.'

'Do what?' The young man was curious. 'Where are we going?'

'I'll tell you as we ride.' With a curt instruction he urged the horse on, leading the way through the gates and into the open fields.

Dave was already familiar with the layout of the fields, and as far as he was aware, there were no problems out there that had not already been dealt with.

'Is something wrong?' he asked, slightly apprehensive. 'I rode across the fields yesterday and everything seemed fine, except for the foal who caught her hoof in the brambles. But she's fine now – seen to and put back out to graze.'

'There's no problem,' Frank answered equably. 'I just want to show you my empire.'

'I thought I'd seen it all?'

The man shook his head. 'You may have seen the tip of it,' he answered, 'but you haven't been to my other farms, and I don't suppose you've yet managed to get out to Demon's Lake, have you?'

'No. I haven't got that far yet.'

Although he had been at Thomson's Stud Farm for a good while now, Dave's life was so busy that time flew, and his attention was mainly concentrated on helping to run the business. In his spare time, he did some woodcarving – mainly presents for this, his 'adopted' family, and helped in the house and garden.

'You need to familiarise yourself with every square inch,

and that's one reason why I'm taking you out today, to show you the extent of my business.'

'So, what's the other reason?'

'I need your opinion on a little project I've been considering.'

Dave felt very privileged; it was good to know that Frank trusted him enough to ask his opinion on one of his business ventures.

For the next two hours, they covered some 800 acres of land, part arable, mostly paddock. Then they were at the lake, a magnificent expanse of water, surrounded by spreading shrubs and trees. Even in the January starkness, it was a lovely place.

'Why do they call it Demon's Lake?' Dave was curious.

Frank was happy to tell him the story. 'According to legend, a young girl ran off with the bad boy of the village; they were in love and meant to get married. But the father came after them, pursuing their carriage like a man demented. The horses took fright and bolted, the carriage ended up in the lake and the lovers were both drowned. The carriage driver managed to leap to safety, but there was no saving the couple. It was a tragedy.'

'What about the father?'

'Ah, well . . . he's the demon they named the lake after. According to the driver, he was ranting and raving – calling on the devil to send the boy to hell. Then he threw himself into the water and drowned. The theory is, if he couldn't save his daughter from the bad boy, then he would haunt them both for ever.'

There was something about this tragic story that reminded Dave of the destructive passion of his parents' marriage – and of his grandparents', too. Tears stood in his eyes as he took in the serenity of the scene, all the time picturing the terrible sight of the accident, hearing the screams and terrified neighing, the surface of the lake heaving and then growing calm once again.

With the sobering tale of Demon's Lake strong in their minds, the men arrived at the furthest farmhouse. 'We won't call in,' Frank decided. 'If I arrive unannounced, they might think I'm checking up on them.'

As he gazed across the horizon, a look of wonder came over his features. 'I'm a fortunate man to have all this,' he murmured. 'Above all else, I consider myself to be custodian of this land.'

Seemingly embarrassed when he caught Dave looking at him, he pointed to the rambling house and cluster of out-buildings and explained, 'This was the very first farm I bought after Dad died. The farmer who owned it emigrated to Australia after the war. It was badly rundown, so I got it for a good price.' He grinned. 'Especially after I agreed to sign the tenancy to his nephew.'

'It's a grand-looking place.' Dave hoped the tenant was thankful, to have such a beautiful home.

'He looks after it well,' Frank said, as if reading his mind. 'I pay two visits a year to all my farms, once in the winter, and once in the summer. I find that's usually enough, though if I get wind of any farm being neglected or ill-used, I have the right to snatch back the tenancy.'

He smiled knowingly. 'A short-term contract with that kind of clause keeps the tenants on their toes.'

Dave was learning every day. 'You're a shrewd business-man, I'll give you that, sir.'

As they travelled on, Dave was increasingly impressed by the extent of Frank's business empire. Through hard work and dedication, he had amassed and lovingly tended an enviable piece of God's creation.

The land glowed with health; there were vast swathes of woodland, all carefully harvested, before being replanted and nurtured. Every square inch of prime land was kept fertile and protected, and each farm was a credit to both Frank and his tenants.

As he trotted down the bridle path, Dave had a sudden vision of his home town, of the mills and narrow streets of Blackburn. Of himself, as a boy, playing football with his pals on bomb-damaged ground. Of his mam, calling him in for a meagre tea. By contrast, this little corner of rural Bedfordshire, with all its abundance, was like the biblical land of milk and honey.

~

The last farm, and the closest to Frank's own place, was the smallest and by far the prettiest. Nestling in the valley, it was the nearest thing to a dream place that Dave had ever seen.

'This is Blueberry Farm.' Frank was visibly proud. 'What d'you think of it, son?'

'Of all the farms you've shown me, this is the best.' Dave had no doubts. 'Best spot, best layout, and every field fenced and watered.' He could see the stone water troughs shining in the fields. 'What more could a man want?'

They had reined the horses in at the very top of the hill, and from there they surveyed the property below. From this angle, the farm-stead was like the perfect jigsaw, every field fitting together; and right at the front of the house a long, wide paddock wrapped itself round the dwelling like a scarf.

'Would you like a closer look?' Frank was enjoying his day, and more particularly the surprise yet to come.

'I thought you didn't like turning up unexpectedly?'

'Oh, I'm sure no one will mind on this occasion.' Frank started down the hill. 'Come on! Time's a-wasting.'

Intrigued, Dave quickly followed.

As they neared the farmhouse, Dave could see how the building was in need of some repair. The white paint was faded and the walls were shot with fine cracks. The door was falling off its hinges, the windows were boarded up, and the gardens overgrown. Only the fields surrounding it were kept in pristine condition.

'Well?' Frank had seen the disappointed look on Dave's face as they neared the house, where the extent of its neglect was clearly visible. 'What do you think now?'

Dave was honest. 'I'm shocked.' He gazed about, at the broken windows and the leaning chimney, tiles missing on the roof and gutters hanging by a thread, and he could hardly believe it. 'How was it allowed to get into this state?'

Shame-faced, Frank explained. 'I bought this property for the land around it,' he said. 'I had no need of the house, which was already past its best anyway, so what with one thing and another, it seems to have gone unloved.'

Like Dave, he had instantly felt the beauty of this place.

'I had a mind to pull it down after I bought it,' he went on, 'but there was something about it that made me want to keep it, so I boarded it up to stop any passing tramp from setting up here. Time gradually slipped away, work rolled up on me, and nothing was ever done with the place.'

They lingered a minute, looking and both regretting that it had been so neglected.

'Let's see what the years have done to the insides,' Frank suggested.

The men dismounted, and while Frank was forcing open the misshapen door, Dave tied the animals securely to the fence-post, giving them long enough rein, so's they could crop at the grass without too much of a struggle.

The interior of the house seemed every bit as bad as the outside. 'It's a bit dark in here,' Frank said. He had fallen over rubble twice, and behind him, Dave hit his head on a low roof beam. 'If we rip down the boarding,' Frank decided, 'we'll be able to see a lot better.'

With that, the two of them began pushing out the boarding that covered the windows, and as each board fell, so the daylight flooded in, and the house came alive.

'Aw, this could be so lovely.' Dave wandered from room to room. The beams were thick and low throughout, but unlike the entrance porch, not so low as to hit your head. Every room had succumbed to the ravages of time, with the ceiling having fallen in, in places, and the walls torn and damp, but even then, there was still a kind of magic about this house.

They were in the kitchen now; a big square place with a higher ceiling and the beams open to the roof, it gave a feeling of height and space. At the far end was the most splendid range; a great creation of iron and brass, it was thick with dirt and dust, and stretching from side to side was the most beautiful cobweb . . . so perfectly formed and delicate in pattern, Dave thought it must have taken the spiders years to build it.

Deep in thought and lost in the arms of this lonely place, Dave was startled when Frank spoke right by his shoulder. 'What do you think I should do with it?'

Dave did not hesitate. 'I think you should bring it back to its former glory, sooner rather than later.'

Frank patted him on the back. 'A man after my own heart.' From the very first it had struck him that Dave was so much older than his years. It wasn't time itself that did that to a man. It was tragedy and loneliness, and a childhood lost.

Not for the first time, Frank was tempted to ask him about his past, but instinct warned him off. Dave was nineteen now, a fully-grown man, and his past was his own affair.

'Come on, son.' He urged him out. 'Let's get back. It's coming up to lunchtime, and Lucy will think we've been kidnapped. And there's no knowing what Maggie will do to us if we're late.'

~

First stop was the big barn, where preparations were already underway for the annual party next Saturday night. Family, staff on the stud farm, and neighbours from miles around came every January, to raise the barn roof and brighten up a very dull time of year.

The irrepressible Maggie was there, issuing instructions and overseeing everything. 'The music should be in that corner and the tables along that wall.' She knew her stuff. 'Oh aye, and make sure you put enough flooring down for a fair-sized dance area,' she reminded the beleaguered workmen. 'You know how folks like to get up and fling themselves about.'

As soon as she saw Frank and Dave enter the barn, she came rushing over. 'It's coming together a treat,' she said excitedly. 'All we want now is for the lanterns to go up and the barn to be dressed; the food is my concern, and I promise, it will be the best feast you ever laid eyes on!' At the mention of food, she caught hold of a workman hurrying past. 'I forgot to say, the trestle tables need putting up in the far corner. The food must be kept out of reach of children and gluttons, until I give the nod.'

Before rushing away, the workman assured her it would be done.

'You're a bully!' Frank loved every minute of it. 'Look at him run, poor devil.'

Maggie tossed him a withering glance. 'If you don't want me to organise the party, it's still not too late for *you* to take over,' she snapped. 'There's still a few days left. See if you can do any better, why don't you?'

'Hey!' Frank apologised. 'Don't be so damned touchy, woman.'

'Am I in charge or am I not?'

'Do you want to be in charge?'

'That's a silly question,' she retorted. 'Haven't I done it every year so far, and don't you know that very well, you old fox!'

'Whatever you say.' Frank assumed that he was forgiven. 'By the way, Dave and I have been out to the far reaches.'

She melted with a smile. 'Oh, Dave . . . did you see Blueberry Farm, love?'

'Yes, I did,' Dave acknowledged. 'I think it's such a shame that it ever got so neglected.'

'That's the master's fault.' Another mock-scathing glance at Frank, who by now was used to it. 'But to give him his due, he has had his work cut out in building this place up to what it is.' She went all dreamy again. 'Oh, but isn't Blueberry Farm the prettiest thing you've ever seen, and don't you think it's in the most magical spot?'

'I do, yes.'

'By the way, you'd best show your faces.' She had a habit of changing the subject at the drop of a hat. 'Lucy's in charge of lunch today, and she's been looking for the pair of you.' With that, she bade them cheerio. 'Got to go. Unlike you two, I've got work to do.' As she walked away, Frank exchanged a knowing smile with her. She knew what he was thinking, for hadn't they already discussed it earlier?

Dave had seen the discreet exchange between them, and chuckled to himself. It was never too late for love, he thought – and yet again his own thoughts were torn between Judy and Lucy.

But it was Lucy who came running to meet him. And it was Lucy who locked her arm in his as they walked on. It was a good feeling, but was it love?

Time would tell.

CHAPTER EIGHTEEN

T HAT AFTERNOON, THERE was work still to be done in the stableyard, with animals to be fed and bedded down for the night, water troughs to fill, and the yard itself to be left clean and tidy underfoot.

It was dark when Dave and Lucy started back towards the house. The air had become chilly.

'I'm not ready to go indoors,' Lucy said. 'Let's sit in the summerhouse for a while, shall we?'

'OK, but I can't stay too long,' Dave warned her. 'I need a bath and a change of clothes.' He grimaced. 'Your dad's taken me through woods and wilds today, and I've just forked over a huge muck heap. I'm sorry, Lucy, I must smell to high heaven.'

Lucy playfully sniffed the air. 'I can't smell anything, only the faint smell of roses.'

Dave laughed. 'Little liar!'

'All right then, we both stink. But there's time enough to sit and talk for a few minutes, isn't there?'

'If you like.' He was happy with that. 'I don't suppose half an hour would hurt.'

'And what then?'

'What d'you mean?'

'After half an hour – what then?'

'Well . . .' Like any man, he could never understand a woman's meaning. 'Then I'll walk you home, and I'll go back to my room over the stables.'

'And is that what you want?'

'Not in the long term, no. But just now it's all I've got. And like you say, there's no rush to get back.'

'So you're happy to stay here in the garden, with me?' She looked up at him, her eyes shining. With every passing day she loved him more. But she could never tell if he loved her the same.

'Lucy, I'm more than happy to sit here with you,' he answered. 'I love your company – you know that.'

'So, would you be "more than happy" to put your arm round me?'

'Now, why would I want to do that?' He loved to tease her.

'Because I want you to.'

'That's not a good enough reason.'

'All right then, I'm shivering. And I need you to keep me warm.'

Without a word he slid his arm round her shoulders and drew her close. 'Is that better?' When she didn't answer he gazed down on her face. 'You're not falling asleep on me, are you?' he asked softly.

'No.'

For a moment he was silenced by the dark uplifted eyes that gazed back at him. Then she whispered: 'Dave?'

'Yes?'

Giving no reply, she kissed him full on the mouth – a long, lingering kiss that woke too many emotions inside him, emotions that both frightened and excited him. Within them was guilt and passion. Guilt for this betrayal of Judy, and the passion of a youth wanting and needing to become a man.

They touched and fondled, and when the touching

became a frantic need, they made love right there on the floor of the summerhouse.

Both virgins, they followed age-old instincts to give and receive pleasure that was in turns wild and tender. And when it was over, they lay in each other's arms, still breathless, softly kissing, elated by what had just happened.

'Do you love me, Dave?' Lucy asked, and he answered that yes, he did love her.

The floor of the summerhouse was cold, and he helped Lucy to her feet. He was feeling a double guilt now, shame burning in his blood. What had he done. The rush of guilt was replaced by a deep-down need to make amends. 'Of course I love you, Lucy,' he repeated. There could be no other answer. Not now.

Adjusting their clothes, they strolled on, hand-in-hand. 'Are we engaged?' The girl asked innocently.

Affectionately, he stroked her face and smiling down on her, he asked, 'Is that what you want, my darling?'

Lucy nodded her head. 'More than anything else in the world,' she whispered.

He laughed softly. 'Then yes, we're engaged.'

'Can I tell Father?'

Caution set in. 'Let's keep it to ourselves for a while, eh?' he suggested. 'We need to get used to the idea, and besides, you'll want to choose a ring and all that.' He blew out a sigh. 'I hope you realise, it's a big thing . . . getting engaged.' Manlike, he dreaded all the fuss.

'You're not regretting it already, are you?'

He squeezed her hand. 'No.'

'I do love you so,' she assured him. 'I'll make you happy, I promise.'

He sensed her panic and the guilt was tenfold. But why? he asked himself. Judy was long lost to him. She was in his past, and Lucy was in his present – and his future. So why did he feel like crying – as though he should have lost his virginity to Judy, not Lucy? He was being foolish, he knew. He must pull himself together; thank his lucky stars for this girl's love.

'I know you will,' he answered. 'I'll do my best to make you happy too.' Lucy was a wonderful young woman who loved him without reservation, and there was more than a measure of love in his heart for her. People had been happy on less and besides, he had given his word, and he would keep it.

Dave wondered if this strange apprehension he was feeling had anything to do with his parents. They had loved each other with insane passion, yet even that was not enough to prevent the tragedy that followed. Yes, perhaps he was afraid of love. So maybe what he and Lucy had would prove to be stronger in other ways. And so much easier to control.

Shivering, he hurried bride-to-be towards home, a welcome fire, and a long, hot bath!

～

As good as her word, Lucy kept the news to herself; though there wasn't a minute when she didn't want to shout it from the rooftops.

'When can we choose my engagement ring?' she asked Dave on the day of the annual barn-dance.

'Let's get the do tonight out of the way,' he said, 'then on Monday morning we'll go into Bedford and start looking for your ring. After that, you can tell the world. Does that suit you?'

Lucy was more than suited, and for the rest of the day she walked around on cloud nine.

～

Down in the farmhouse kitchen Maggie was hard at work.

'I want all hands on deck!' She was drawing together all the last-minute details. 'In two hours folk will start arriving and there's still balloons to be blown up, straw bales to be laid out for the seating, and where's the banners? We always have banners!'

Summoning three of the stable lads, she set them to work. 'I've things to be doing myself,' she said. 'There's all the food to be seen to yet. And think on,' she warned. 'I'll be back in an hour, by which time I expect it all to be done and ready.' With that she marched off, chuckling to herself as she recalled how the three of them had been hiding in the stables. 'Lazy little hounds,' she told herself. 'Did they really think I didn't know where to look for them?'

Her kitchen at The Willows was a hive of industry; there was Lucy shifting the freshly baked bread rolls onto a cooling tray; little Peggy Henderson from the village flitting in and out of the larder like a headless chicken, and the cat waiting at the door for any stray titbits.

As always, Peggy was fussing, talking to herself in frantic clucks as she darted to and fro. 'Where's the ham shank? It was here just now when I got out the cream jug . . . Oh dearie me, dearie me!'

'Stop panicking!' Maggie came in the door and straight off she saw how little Peggy had already put one ham shank on the butcher's block ready for slicing. 'Look behind you, hinny,' she urged. 'In a minute, it will bite you on the backside!'

Peggy began giggling uncontrollably. 'Silly me,' she chirped. 'I must have taken it out earlier. There's so much to do . . . you can't think, can you?'

Maggie had an idea. 'We've all been working our fingers to the bone, and we're tired. I say we should stop for a few minutes and have one o' my delicious scones, with a cup of tea – then we'll get on with the sandwiches. What d'you say, eh?'

The girls were all for it. Lucy put the kettle on, while Maggie and Peggy got out the scones and cream, with a dish of strawberry jam made last summer.

No sooner was the table set for three, than the kettle was whistling and the tea was made, and they all sat down with a sigh of relief.

'What's tickling you, young lady?' Maggie had already noticed how Lucy kept smiling to herself, and when she wasn't smiling she was singing, and when she wasn't singing, she was looking out the window. 'As I recall, there's only one thing that makes a young woman as happy as you seem to be, and that's a young man.' And the only young man she could match with Lucy, was Dave.

Lucy's face grew pink. 'I'm saying nothing,' she remarked coyly. 'You'll know soon enough.' And beyond that she would not be drawn.

~

By 7 p.m. lanterns and fairy-lights had been switched on to light the way to the barn. There was plenty of space in an adjoining field for cars. About seventy people were expected, and the trestle tables, covered in white sheets, were groaning under the weight of party food for the evening's festivities, alongside barrels of beer, and cider, bottles of wine and pop for the teetotallers. To eat, there were platters of sliced boiled ham or roast ham shanks and fat beef sandwiches and pork pies enough to feed an army, plump chicken breasts and grilled sausages, and bowl after bowl of boiled potatoes, sprinkled with mint and herbs. One table alone held all the sweet things – trifles and tarts, and cakes to suit all tastes: chocolate, and fruit, and ginger, and plates of fancies.

'Good God above, Maggie!' Frank had come to inspect the barn. 'There's enough grub here to feed the whole of Bedfordshire.'

'Nobody ever goes hungry at *my* parties, that's for sure,' she announced proudly.

By the time people started arriving, the balloons were up, the banners were hung, and the trio of musicians – violin, squeezebox and flute, played the partygoers in.

Lucy was kept busy meeting and greeting, helping people with their coats and settling them in, while Dave remained by the door, watching out for one particular partygoer, and hoping against hope that he would turn up.

By nine-thirty the party was well underway, with the guests redfaced and merry, performing the old traditional country dances while the caller, a local farmer named Ned Kirby, nagged, cajoled and teased them through the steps.

Amid the gales of laughter, Dave went up to Lucy and said, 'There's still no sign of him. I don't suppose he got my letter. Or if he did, maybe he wasn't able to come all this way.'

Lucy was trying to console him, when suddenly Dave caught sight of a familiar figure coming through the crowds. 'Eli!' Small and wick, with a smile on his wrinkled old face, the old man had not changed.

Dave ran to meet him. 'Oh, Eli, it's so good to see you! I really thought you weren't able to make it.'

Eli gave him a big hug. 'Then you don't know me as well as you think ye do,' he said, his face wreathed in a delighted grin. 'It would have taken wild horses to keep me away. Mind, me car wasn't too keen on the journey from Blackpool, but it's having a good long rest in yon field.'

Lucy came up beside them. 'So, this is your friend?' If it hadn't been for the old fella, Lucy knew that Dave would never have found his way here, to her, and the good life he now enjoyed.

Eli looked at her with wide eyes. 'By, but she's pretty! This must be the young woman you told me about in your letter . . . Lucy, isn't it?'

He held out his hand in greeting, but Lucy threw her arms round his neck, thanking him for the help he had given to Dave. 'If it wasn't for you, we might never have met,' she said thankfully. Dave had told her all about his life on the run, and she knew that Eli had been a major force for good, helping to bring that way of life to an end.

Eli nodded. 'Brian Moult got what he deserved,' he told Dave, accepting a glass of beer and a plate of food from a stable girl acting as a waitress for the evening. Lucy left the men and went to help her.

'Not long after you took off, the truth got out about his wrongdoings. He was put away for some years – him and the other fella, and good shuts to the pair of 'em, is what I say!'

Dave was relieved, but curious. 'How did they get caught out?'

Eli winked knowingly. 'I expect somebody snitched on 'em, eh?' He chuckled wickedly. 'I mean, they must have made a lot of enemies, wouldn't ye say?'

Dave understood. 'You're an old rascal, but you're worth your weight in gold.' He would never forget what Eli had done for him.

Drawing closer to the lad, Eli had some more news for him. 'There's something you need to know,' he said. 'This is going to blow your socks off. By, you'll really be celebrating when you get a load of this.' He took a long swallow of his beer while Dave waited patiently.

'Your Mr Babraham . . .' he said unexpectedly, and when Dave went white, he leaned forward and grasped his arm. 'He didn't die,' Eli said in his ear. 'He lived – and was able to identify his attackers. It was in the local paper last week. The police had been looking for them ever since hc recovered from the incident. They found them when they committed a big burglary in Sheffield, and connected them with that other job. You're in the clear, lad. The police aren't looking for anyone else. I reckon he told them how you helped him, eh? Come on, now.' He looked kindly at the stricken young man. 'You need a drink. You can fill my glass up an' all while you're at it. There's a fair bit o' dust in me throat from the journey, so it's medicinal, mind.'

The old and young man went over to replenish their glasses, and then Dave, feeling light-headed with this wonderful piece of news, led Eli over to where Frank was chatting to Maggie. He introduced Eli as 'the man who saved my hide, more than once'.

'Well, Eli my man,' Frank shook him by the hand, 'you did us all a favour, and any time you're passing through these parts, you'll always be made welcome here. I hope you will be our guest tonight, and for the rest of your stay.'

Maggie reached forward and embraced the little man fondly. Her Ted and Eli had been best buddies for years, closer than any brothers, and she knew he had mourned with her when Ted had died. She herself had supported Eli, writing to him often when his missus had become ill and passed away, two years ago now. There was nothing she wouldn't do for him; he had a heart of gold.

'Come and sit down and have your food now,' she tutted. 'You must be worn out with that long drive down. Where did you stay overnight?'

'Oh, I stopped off in Coventry to take a look at the new

Cathedral,' he told them all. 'My goodness, it's a corker.' Truth be told, the old chap had enjoyed his drive down, had found so much to look at and admire. He'd been too long in Blackpool, that was for sure. And Billy Joe's Fairground had long since lost its attraction for him.

'What are your plans, Eli?' Frank asked, eyeing the visitor shrewdly.

'Watch him, Eli,' Maggie warned light-heartedly. 'Next thing you know, he'll be setting you to work on the stud.'

'Not me,' Eli announced. 'I'm past all that. I've rolled up my overalls, and now I mean to see some of the world, before it's too late. I've got a few bob in the Post Office, an' me feet are itchy.' He glanced out at the star-studded sky. 'It's a big old world out there, an' I'm getting no younger. The sooner I get going, the more I'll see of the Master's creation, before He calls me home.'

His prophetic words moved them to silence.

But it wasn't long before they were back in the thick of the celebrations.

~

The evening was a wonderful success. Frank and Maggie danced almost every dance; Eli found himself a partner and made a happy fool of himself, while Dave and Lucy swirled about the floor in each other's arms. At times, it seemed the barn almost shook at the foundations.

Maggie was thrilled to see all the lovingly prepared food disappear in record time. The guests had brought hearty appetites along, which was just what she wanted.

Towards the end of the evening, Frank took the stage and called everyone together. 'I have an announcement to make,' he said, and when they were all suitably attendant, he went on in grand voice, 'As you all know, Dave Adams came to us a few years ago, recommended by our good friend, Eli Clements. He has proved himself to be an important part of my business here. He gets on with everyone, and everyone respects him. He has taken to this work like a duck to water, and with Seamus gone, sadly under a cloud, I've decided to hand his job of head groom over to Dave.'

After the applause, there was more to come. 'I reckon it's about time that the new head groom had new quarters, so first thing on Monday morning, the builders are arriving to renovate Blueberry Cottage for him.' Holding out his hands to a shocked and delighted Dave, he told him with a warm, proud smile, 'Well done, son. Now, come and take your bow . . . you've earned it.'

The applause this time was deafening, because as Frank so rightly said, everyone had quickly come to like and respect this young man who had come to them years ago and joined their community.

Dave ran up onstage, knowing that, despite his shyness, he must acknowledge this announcement by Frank.

'I really don't know what to say,' he told all assembled, and turned to Frank and shook his hand. 'All I can tell you is, this is the best thing that's ever happened to me.'

Suddenly, Lucy was by his side. A bit flushed and merry from the cider, she kissed them both, before addressing the gathering, 'Like you, I'm thrilled for Dave, but I too have an announcement to make. You see, Dave and I are engaged to be married . . .'

Both Frank and Dave were taken aback by this development, but the crowd loved it. Shouts of congratulations went up, and the clapping and stamping made a right old din.

'I thought we weren't going to say anything yet?' Dave said in her ear.

'I couldn't wait,' she laughed. 'And anyway, I couldn't let Daddy steal all the thunder.'

Dave went along with it all, and when the crowd demanded that he kiss his fiancée, he gladly obliged; with Frank joking to the delighted folk, 'Looks like my daughter and I have both acquired a groom – the same one!'

The excitement was infectious, and everyone took their turn in congratulating Dave and Lucy.

'I suspected all your smiling and singing was because of a certain young man,' Maggie told Lucy smugly. 'You've been bursting to tell us the news, and now all I can say is . . . be happy, the pair of you.'

~

Lurking outside at the rear of the barn was one dark-minded creature who had only bad wishes for the couple. Although his ticket back to Ireland was already bought, and he was due to sail to Dublin from Liverpool in two days' time, Seamus Macintyre had no intention of leaving this farm with his tail between his legs. Oh, there were no shortages of jobs in Ireland, where the cream of the stud farms were situated, but it was the principle of the thing. He ground his teeth at the thought of the wasted years, spent waiting for a certain fruit to fall into his lap, only to see that gypsy brat run away with it.

He had taken his job, his girl – and the family fortune too, by the looks of it!

His evil mind alive with thoughts of revenge, Seamus crept silently away.

~

Inside the barn, people were beginning to leave. Everyone had an early start, the next day. The land never let you sleep for long; she was a hard taskmistress.

'Good night, and thanks for coming.' One by one, Frank shook the guests' hands as they came up to him, while Maggie and her team of helpers bustled about, collecting bits and bobs of discarded rubbish from the tables.

When everyone was gone, and the sound of car engines and merry voices had died away, Frank had a quiet word or two with Dave and Lucy, telling them how thrilled he was with their engagement, and promising to put on a wedding for them, that would be 'the talk of Bedfordshire'.

That said, he took Maggie by the arm, and announced that he was looking for a woman himself. 'What d'you say, Maggie?' he asked cheekily. 'Are you ready to make an honest man of me?'

'Ask me again in the morning,' she laughed. 'When you're sober enough to know what you're saying.'

Slightly inebriated from the cider she had downed, and contemplating the exciting future ahead of herself and Dave, Lucy took to the stage, where she twirled and danced, and sang aloud. The musicians had gone home, leaving their empty pint glasses perched on the bales. Wisps of straw littered the floor.

From the far side of the barn, Maggie and Dave looked on. 'Bless her heart, she's over the moon with it all,' Maggie told him. 'I've never known her so happy.'

Dave smiled. 'She's a lovely girl,' he said thoughtfully. 'I only hope I can do right by her.'

The Scotswoman was intrigued. 'And why wouldn't you do right by her?' she demanded.

'Love doesn't always mean happiness.' Dave said soberly. He paused, then added in a low voice, almost to himself,

'You can't know how it was – at home, with Mam and Dad.'

Like Frank, Maggie had always wondered about the boy's past, and once or twice she had almost raised the issue. But somehow Dave put up barriers and she never found the courage. Now, though, she spoke out.

'Why don't you tell me how it was?' she suggested kindly.

Seeing that Frank and Lucy were busy, Dave took a moment to consider and suddenly it was all tumbling out . . . how his father had been devoted to his mother, but she caused them so much unhappiness. 'I know she loved him, but she seemed hellbent on hurting him,' he recalled sadly. 'She was out all hours with the men . . . she even bedded my father's workmates. Money was nothing to her, even though she didn't earn much at the hairdresser's where she was a part-time stylist. Dad worked hard, and she spent his wages like water from a tap. Twice, we lost everything, and Grandad had to come to the rescue.'

The old emotions, of love, worry, and frustration flooded back and when he couldn't go on, she gently urged him, 'It's always best to talk about things, Dave. And you know whatever you tell me, I will never repeat it to a living soul.'

So, he went on and told her about the night when it all came to a head. He related how his father had walked out, and the subsequent events of that night. Not since he had unburdened himself to Eli, had Dave spoken of these matters. Finally, he explained how it all went wrong, and of how his mother's life slipped away while she was in his arms.

'D'you see what I mean?' he asked Maggie brokenly. 'She loved my father so much, and yet she still ruined his life . . . *all* our lives.'

Maggie was deeply shocked and saddened by the story. Dabbing at her eyes, she could now understand what the lad had meant when he spoke of hoping to do right by Lucy.

'You can't measure yourself against your mother,' she assured him. 'Because she spoiled your life and the lives of your father and grandfather, it doesn't mean to say that you might ruin Lucy's life. You are made differently, my lad.' She felt instinctively that there was something else, something he wasn't saying. 'Can I ask you something?'

'Anything.'

'Tell me honestly . . . do you love Lucy?'

Dave took a moment to answer. 'Yes, I do love her,' he said, 'it's just that . . .' He shrugged. 'I don't know what's wrong with me. I'm sorry, Maggie, I shouldn't burden you with all this.'

The woman persisted. 'Before you came here, when you were a boy, was there someone you felt strongly about?'

Judy came immediately, to mind. 'I had a friend,' he said. 'A girl by the name of Judy. We told each other everything.'

'A friend – is that all she was?'

Surprised by her question, Dave looked up. 'We were just children,' he said. 'Judy's father delivered the milk, and we played together. She was a lot like Lucy, kind and thoughful, and I loved her very much . . . like a sister, or a friend. Maybe more than a friend, Maggie – but we were too young to know about such things.'

His heart ached. 'Sometimes, when I think of home, I think of her and I miss talking with her. She knew what was going on in our house, and she understood. When there was trouble and I was worried, I could confide in her, and she would always listen.' He smiled fondly at the memory of her. 'Judy was my best and only friend.'

Maggie sensed his heartache. 'Of course you miss her,' she acknowledged. 'What happened to you, Dave, was a terrible thing. To have everything you cherished torn away from you, must have been unbearably hard.'

All the same, she needed him to be sure. 'I know you love Lucy,' she acknowledged. 'It's in your face when you look at her, and in the way you treat her. But it needs to be the kind of love that builds a marriage. To have that depth that binds you together for the rest of your lives. Don't compare what you and Lucy have with what your parents had. You mustn't be afraid, Dave. You are your own man, and you must draw strength from knowing that Lucy has promised herself to you.'

'I know all that,' he said. 'And I do love her. I want to protect her . . . to give her all the things she wants out of life.'

'It's *you* she wants.' Maggie wouldn't let it go. 'And that's wonderful – as long as you love her in the same way. Do you, Dave? Do you love her with every fibre of your being, the way a man loves his woman?'

'How can I know that?' he asked helplessly. 'All I know is that I *do* love her. Isn't that enough to build a life on?'

Maggie thought it probably wasn't. When he had spoken of the girl Judy just now, there had been something extraordinary in his voice – a certain magical essence that was lacking when he spoke of Lucy. But then again, she reminded herself, Dave had referred to this Judy as a sister, an only friend when his whole world was falling apart. Of course he would have special feelings for her – and besides, if it was anything deeper, he would have gone back for her . . . wouldn't he?

Lucy's voice cut through her thoughts. 'Dave! Come and dance with me!'

Excusing himself, Dave went to Lucy and, taking her in his arms, he moved her round the stage. Giggling quietly, they both sang the Elvis song, 'Are You Lonesome Tonight', and with her head resting on his shoulder, they were in a world of their own.

And from where Maggie stood, they looked as much in love as any other engaged couple she had ever known.

CHAPTER NINETEEN

GRADUALLY, ALL THE lamps outside the barn were being extinguished. The stable hands had gone off to their quarters, and a chill night wind had started to blow. The black sky was full of a million cold and distant stars.

Within the shadows of the stable block, a deeper shadow stirred, as Seamus crept about with a can of petrol. Murmuring to the horses, who whickered at the unfamiliar smell, he carefully poured some petrol into each stable. That done, he secured every door behind him, callously trapping the horses inside.

Lastly, he came to the stallion. 'Whisht there, Madden. Hello, boy,' he crooned. 'You're a real beauty, aren't you, eh?' Agitated and nervous, the stallion was beginning to fidget. 'We're the same, you and me,' Seamus said, talking softly. 'We're not loved or wanted by anyone.' He smiled. 'And we have the same dark nature . . .'

Hearing voices, he crouched low and listened. 'Ssh . . . ssh,' he whispered to the horse. He didn't want to be discovered now, not when everything was almost done, and all it needed was the stroke of a match.

Over by the big barn, Maggie was saying good night to Dave and Lucy. 'Good night, you two. See you in the morning.' Her distinctive Scottish burr carried through the night air.

Seamus peered over the stable door. Through the trees, he could see Dave and Lucy pressed up against a wall, kissing, too close, too passionate. He saw red. 'That spoiled bitch's father isn't the only one who needs teaching a lesson! Look at her, the little whore!'

Over by the wall, in Lucy's hot embrace, Dave was reluctant to let her go. He longed to make love to her again – but Maggie and Frank would be waiting to see her off to bed . . . Blood surged through him as he kissed her deeply, again.

'Bastard!' The Irishman, watching, could hardly contain himself. 'He stole my job, my woman and my future. I can't let him get away with it!'

Madden could sense danger in the air, and he fiercely resisted when the man saddled him up, ready for a ride. When the animal threatened to rear, Seamus gave it a hard thump across the head.

'Don't start your tricks with me, or you'll be sorry!' Taking a whip from the wall, he held it where the stallion could see. 'Want me to lay this across your back, d'you?' he growled.

Over by the barn, Dave thought he heard something.

'What's wrong?' asked Lucy.

'Ssh!' Dave quietened her and concentrated. 'I thought I heard something over by the stables.' His neck hairs stood on end. 'I'd best go and check.'

'I'm coming with you.'

'No!' If there was anyone lurking about, it was best for her to remain here, safe. 'Do as I ask. Stay here. Don't move, and don't make a sound.'

Sensing something bad, Lucy did as she was told.

Stealthily, Dave made his way towards the stable block. He was coming up the slight rise when all of a sudden, Madden burst through his stable door with Seamus on his back. Like a madman, the groom rode straight at Dave, the stallion beneath him wild-eyed and terrified, leaping and rearing at the sight of Dave running towards him.

'You're too late!' Seamus screamed. He struck the match against his boot, and for a second he held the flame high for Dave to see.

'Good God!' Dave realised with horror what he was about to do. 'NOOooo!' His frantic cry was lost as Seamus threw the match, and instantly there was a whoosh as the first stable was lit from within.

'Tell your best friend Frank there's more to come!' the Irishman bawled.

Dave didn't hear his threat as he ran to the stables, his shouts alerting everyone. 'FIRE! FIRE AT THE STABLES!' Shocked by the speed of the flames, he ran from door to door, opening them to let the horses out, desperate to save as many of the terrified animals as he could. But the fire was rampant, spreading so fast he was all too quickly beaten back by the heat and licking flames.

Having heard the pandemonium, they came from all directions . . . the stable boys and girls, Frank, still in his pyjamas with his dressing-gown thrown on top, and Maggie, her hair in curlers and her slippers on. And here was Lucy, yelling desperately for Dave to get clear.

Running up fast, the stable hands went in search of the horses that had fled in terror when Dave threw open the stable doors. Incensed that some of the horses had been saved, Seamus turned on Dave who, blackened and exhausted, was limping away from the inferno that was now engulfing the block.

'I couldn't save them all,' Dave almost wept to Lucy, who came running towards him. 'I couldn't save them, my love.'

Having been traumatised by the fire, the big stallion would go neither forwards nor backwards. Desperate to punish Dave, to run him down, Seamus was viciously wielding the whip, again and again. 'Come on, you bastard . . . move!' he roared, foam on his lips. 'MOVE, I SAY!' Another crack of the whip and the horse went up on its back legs, almost unseating its rider. Then, with a mighty thump it was down on all fours again, racing away, wanting only to run from the carnage and that pitiful noise of its fellow creatures, trapped inside the stables and roasting to death.

In the panic and confusion, Seamus finally managed to turn the stallion towards Dave. 'Time you got your come-uppance, gypsy boy!' He was laughing, his crazed mind shot by the turn of events. 'I told you I'd be back – that you hadn't heard the last of me!'

Things happened so fast, there was nothing anyone could do. Head down and driven by the devil himself, the horse careered towards Dave, and with no time and nowhere to run, Dave thought this must be his last moment on earth. When he heard Lucy crying his name, he knew she was too close; his heart dropped like a stone inside him. 'Go back, Lucy! For God's sake, go back!' he roared.

A cry went up and now Frank could be seen running forward, a look of desperation on his face. But it was too late. Seamus had what he wanted. He spurred the stallion into a frenzy, and when it seemed that Dave would die under its hooves, Lucy shot forward; the horse came down, and it was she who took the full force of the blow.

Shouts and screams turned to a deathly silence, broken only by the sound of burning wood and a horse's hooves as the stallion raced away out of control, the rider screaming for someone to help him. But there was no help. Only retribution.

Later the horse was found in the thick of the woods, so

badly injured it would have to be put down, and alongside him, the body of Seamus, almost decapitated when the horse careered into the overhanging branch.

~

Lucy lived, long enough to tell Dave and her father how much she loved them; and their grief was immense.

Lying in her bed, in the pretty bedroom upstairs in the farmhouse, the girl had looked so beautiful; a soft blush on her face and her hair spread out over the snowy pillows. But it was all illusion. Madden's hooves had caught her in the chest, causing massive internal damage, and beneath the lace nightdress, Lucy was bleeding to death.

Drugged by morphia, and with the light in her eyes growing dim, she whispered feebly to Dave, 'Remember the summerhouse . . .' Aware that she was dying, Lucy wanted him to know she was glad to have died a woman – *his* woman – body and soul.

'Daddy, I'm going to be with Mummy now,' she promised. 'Look after Maggie, won't you? And don't be unhappy. I love you and Dave so much.'

And then came the alteration in her face, and they knew that the Angel of Death was there at the bedside with them. As her father cried out, '*No! Dear God, no!*' she took her last breath and was gone from them.

In that last poignant moment, she smiled on Dave with such profound love, that as long as he lived, he would never forget.

~

A week later to the day, Lucy was laid to rest in the small churchyard down the lane.

Packed to the doors, spilling across the graveyard and filling the narrow lane, the mourners came from across the county; farmers, neighbours, townsfolk and a smattering of those who lived further afield but knew of the tragedy and wanted to offer their condolences.

After the burial, when no one remained but Frank and Dave, with Maggie standing back, her face swollen from crying, the two men stood in silence at the graveside. 'Why?' Frank was sobbing. 'Why my Lucy? What evil thing did I ever do, for her to be taken from me like that?'

In his own grief, Dave comforted him; he told him it was not his fault, that Seamus was the evil one, but that Lucy would not rest in peace, if her daddy continued to blame himself.

The profound words he spoke to Frank seemed to calm that good man, who had not slept nor eaten properly since the night he had lost his beloved daughter.

Quietly, Frank put his hand on Dave's shoulder. 'If it isn't my fault, then neither is it yours.' Head bowed, he walked away.

'He's right.' Maggie stepped forward. 'What happened was because of one man, so riddled with hatred and evil, that no one could have known the outcome.'

Dave slowly shook his head. 'I will always wonder if there was something else I could have done to prevent what happened.' Like Frank, he looked for the blame in himself. Had his secret doubts in some way influenced Fate? For here he was – free. A terrible sob rose in his throat, for Lucy, for his mother – for the tragic waste of it all.

Maggie walked back home with him. 'Frank's talking about moving away – says he can't bear to stay here, now she's gone.'

Dave was surprised. 'But Lucy was so happy here,' he said

huskily, wiping his eyes. 'And there are so many memories to help him through.'

'And what about you?' she asked. 'What will you do?'

Dave had given it no thought; the only task he had been concentrating on was seeing Lucy to her last rest. But Maggie had focused his mind. 'I don't know,' he answered sombrely. 'I think I can understand why Frank wants to move away, because if either of us were to stay, how could we take a single step and not be seeing her everywhere we look?' His voice broke. 'It's so cruel, Maggie. She was so young and vibrant, and so excited about our future together.'

He looked her in the eye. 'When it happened with my mother, I felt the same as I do now. Even though I loved my grandad, I couldn't go back. Mam was there, d'you see? And yet she wasn't there.'

Maggie understood his pain. 'If you really feel like that, then I think you should leave this place. You're still a young man, with a life before you. We must none of us make our life amongst the dead.'

She opened her heart to him. 'When I lost my darling Ted, I carried on living with him, in my mind and my heart, and in everything I did or planned to do. I know now, that I was wrong. I will always remember him, and I will always love him. But he's gone and I'm still here, and he would want me to have a life of my own.' She smiled fondly. 'If it hadn't been for Frank offering me the cottage and work in his house, I think I would have just withered away.'

Catching Dave by the arm, she slowed him to a stop, her tearful eyes uplifted to his. 'Do you understand what I'm trying to say?'

Dave did, and he told her so. 'But if Frank leaves here, what will you do?' he asked worriedly. 'Where will you go?'

Maggie's smile was radiant. 'I'll go with him,' she answered. 'He's asked me to marry him, and I said yes. Oh, it isn't the same kind of love I felt for Ted . . . no one can ever fill that place in my heart. But it's a kind of love all the same, quiet and good, and it gives me a feeling of belonging.'

She paused, before adding knowingly, 'I suspect it's the same kind of love you felt for Lucy, while she felt for you the same way I felt for my Ted. You see, Dave, there are many levels of love, and it doesn't make the loving any more or less . . . just different.'

They were at the gates now, and unable to hold the grief in any longer, Dave leaned against the gate-post, put his hands over his face and sobbed until he thought his heart would break. 'I wanted so much to love her back the way she loved me,' he said brokenly, 'but I couldn't, and I didn't know why. But I did love her, so much . . . I needed to protect her and be with her. I would have given my life for her, the way she gave her life for me.'

'She always knew that,' Maggie promised. 'And she was content.'

He looked up at this kind, wise woman and in his agony he asked, 'Why could I not love her back, the same way she loved me?'

Maggie knew; she had known for some time. 'Because you had already given that deeper part of your heart to another. Someone you knew as well as you know yourself,' she went on. 'Someone who helped you through the worst time of your childhood.'

She saw the truth beginning to dawn in his face. 'Yes – Judy.' She echoed his thoughts. 'She's the one I'm talking about. She's the one who came to your mind just now. I knew, as soon as you spoke her name, from the light in your eyes, the warmth in your voice. Without you ever realising, and long before you ever met dear Lucy, it was Judy who crept deep into your heart and soul.'

While Dave was shaking his head, still unable to grasp the truth of what she was saying, Maggie whispered in his ear, 'Go to her now, love,' she urged. 'Go back home to your Judy. She'll know how to bring you through this painful time.'

Before he could answer, to tell her that he wasn't ready, that he had so much grieving to do before he could even consider her suggestion, Maggie kissed him tenderly on the face. 'It's where you belong,' she told him. 'Live, Dave – grasp your life and live it! Lucy would have wanted it so – and you know in your heart that is true.'

With the tip of her thumb she wiped away his tears, and went to where Frank was waiting for her.

One last, encouraging glance back, and she was gone.

PART FIVE

~

Blackburn, 1963

A Man and His Dream

CHAPTER TWENTY

'L ESS THAN A week an' we'll be wed.' Dropping his fishing-basket on the grass, Lenny caught Judy by the waist and swung her around. 'Aw, sweetheart, you've made me the happiest man on God's earth!'

For what seemed an age he observed her every feature; the pretty grey eyes in a heart-shaped face, the long brown hair that reached down to her waist, and that slight figure which you could imagine might be blown away by the softest breeze. Yet Judy was strong; she had a temper that could move the heavens, and she possessed the fiercest of loyalty to her friends and family. And now at last, she was promised to him.

Lenny had to pinch himself. In two days' time, at eleven o'clock on Saturday, would they really walk out of St Peter's Church as man and wife?

He recalled the harshness of his childhood, and the times when he felt as though he was the loneliest person on earth. And then there was Judy, whom he saw as his future. He had lost count of the times he had asked her to be his wife, and the many times she had refused. 'Davie' . . . it was always 'Davie'.

But now, at long last, he had persuaded her that Davie Adams was gone for ever.

Kissing her long and hard, he thanked his lucky stars for the day when Judy Makepeace had finally relented and promised to marry him.

'Hey, you two!' Annie's heart weighed heavy at the sight of them kissing. Like everyone else, she knew why Lenny had left home in a hurry. Because of her own circumstances she, better than anyone, had an inkling of what he must have gone through, and how lonely he must have felt; and she loved him more than ever. 'Stop that, or you'll frighten the fish away!' she called when they carried on kissing.

Annie's light-hearted banter disguised her darker feelings. It wasn't just her friends' imminent wedding that troubled her; though seeing Lenny every day at the shop and being close to him in the delivery van, there were times when her love for him was almost unbearable.

But no. It wasn't just the thought of their wedding that haunted her. There was something else, some terrible secret that she still had not been able to confide to anyone. And the longer it went on, the more afraid she became.

Sometimes, God forgive her . . . there was murder in her heart.

Judy released herself from Lenny's arms with a smile. 'Got to go,' she told him. 'The dresses are due to be delivered this afternoon and me and Annie need to go into town for the final fitting.'

'Our mams are meeting us there,' Annie groaned, ' – and if we keep them waiting, they'll go off shopping and it'll be months before they surface.'

'Don't you believe it,' Judy joked. 'They'll be at the shop now, fussing and fretting, and giving the dressmaker what for. By the time we get there they'll have her so agitated, we'll end up with pinpricks from head to foot.'

Judy was right. As they went into the dressmaker's establishment, Annie's mother, Evie Needham, pounced on her daughter. 'Where the devil have you been?' This little woman could never understand how she had given birth to such a big, robust girl as Annie; though apart from the disturbingly quiet moods Annie often fell into, she would not want to change a single thing about her darling, spirited daughter.

'We've been to the canal,' Annie explained. 'I hope you haven't been upsetting anyone?' She gave a sly little glance at the assistant, who was wringing her hands together while calling the dressmaker from the back room.

Evie bridled. 'Upset anyone? What a cheek! Now, why would we want to do that?'

Judy's mother, Beth, had been on the far side of the shop, admiring a pair of blue lace curtains, which would look perfect at her bedroom window.

'I'll have you know, we've been on our best behaviour,' she declared with a smile as she came to give each of the girls a hug. 'We were beginning to get a bit worried, though. Still, you're here now, so happen we can get on, eh?'

'That's right,' Evie chipped in. 'There's a jumble-sale on at the Town Hall and we'd like to have a mooch about and find some bargains, isn't that so, Beth?'

'It would be nice,' Beth admitted, 'but we won't desert you, have no fear.'

The dressmaker emerged carrying two dresses; one midnight blue to complement Annie's strong nature, the other a melody of lace, cream silk and white.

The two women gasped with admiration. 'Ooh!' Evie shook her head. 'I've never seen anything so lovely.' As the dresses floated by, she stroked each in turn. 'Lovely!' she kept saying. 'Just gorgeous.'

Her own wedding had been a simple, hurried affair. Pregnant with her eldest child, Philip, it was a matter of getting a ring on her finger before her belly swelled for the world to see; though when he arrived five months later, there was no hiding the truth.

Beth was more intent on watching her daughter's reaction when she saw the wedding dress, and not for the first time, felt a sense of anxiety. She knew Judy too well to be fooled by the girl's quick smile of pleasure: it was no more than skin-deep. With only a few days to go until she made her vows, Judy should have been bubbling over with happiness. Yet underneath that layer of pretence, obvious only to her mother, Judy was far too quiet, too thoughtful. And before the day was out, Beth vowed to get to the bottom of it.

~

For her part, Judy was trying to get through the whole thing without letting anyone see how she truly felt. She had resisted Lenny's campaign for many months – but in the end, she was getting no younger, and if she couldn't have Davie, then Lenny was the only boy she would consider. After all, she wanted a home of her own, and children one day. Most girls of her age were married by now and pushing prams – except for Annie, of course, but then *she* preferred to play the field.

Lenny was good and kind – and handsome, too. He knew how to excite her when he took her dancing and they smooched during the slow records. He was a fabulous kisser, and more than once she had nearly given in and let him make love to her in the room he rented near his shop – when the landlady Mrs Denham wasn't around, anyway.

Judy's longing for Davie had lasted for eight long years, but there had to be an end to it someday. As she had matured, she had dreamed of giving him her virginity, of marrying him, but she realised now that this had been a childish fantasy. David Adams had disappeared into the wide blue yonder, without once contacting her, and for that she could not forgive him. Lenny would never do that to her in a thousand years. He was devoted to her – and she would soon be his wife. But if only it could have been Davie she was marrying . . .

Judy sighed at her own foolishness, a long withering sigh, and went to strip down to her stockings and bra in the fitting room.

~

The dresses looked beautiful on.

Annie must have merrily spun round a dozen times before the bemused dressmaker called her to, 'Stand still, please, Miss Needham! I can't make adjustments while you're twirling round like a top.'

Annie did as she was told; though she too, was hiding her real feelings. While her generous heart was happy for the bridal pair, she wished with all her heart that it could have been herself walking down the aisle with Lenny. However, after years of a different kind of hell, she too was adept at putting on a front.

'I look like Princess Margaret!' she exclaimed, admiring herself in the long mirror. 'Ooh, their eyes are gonna pop out when they see *me* going down the aisle.'

'Behave yourself!' Evie reprimanded her. 'It's *Judy* who's the bride, not you, and it isn't likely to be you neither, until you decide to settle with one young man, instead of flitting from one to another like a demented blooming butterfly.'

Annie was mortified. 'Oh, Jude, I'm sorry. I just got carried away there. 'O' course I don't want to stand out from *you*!'

'That's all right,' the other girl assured her. 'I'm so proud to have you as my bridesmaid. It means a lot to me, Annie.'

Annie was made up. 'I'll be the best bridesmaid you've ever had,' she promised, and both girls burst out laughing like a pair of hyenas. Evie and Beth exchanged disapproving glances.

'I've finished,' the dressmaker announced briskly. She was immune to pre-wedding nerves. 'So you'd best get out of these dresses, or they won't be ready for Saturday.'

'We'll be off then.' That was Beth. 'We've promised ourselves a new hat apiece, and a cup of tea with a scone afterwards.' She gave Judy a hug. 'You look a picture in that dress,' she told her with a beaming face. 'You too, Annie my love,' and then it was time to go.

Evie was having a quiet word with her daughter. 'I'm so proud of you,' she whispered fondly.

As she left, she glanced back, to see Annie gazing down at the floor, deep in thought. For some unknown reason, a sob rose in the back of Evie Needham's throat. The girl looked so lost and lonely. Was it because of the wedding? Seeing her best friends get married?

Lately, Evie had seen very little of her daughter. Out most nights and coming home in the early hours, she was causing her parents much distress, but nothing Evie or her husband Derek said, seemed to make any difference.

Annie had always been an unruly child, but these past few years, things had really got out of hand. Hardly a day went by without arguments and tantrums, and twice recently, Annie had packed her bags and stayed away overnight. The next evening, when she reappeared after work, she refused to discuss it.

There was something very wrong in the Needham household, but try as she might, Evie could not put her finger on what it was. Thank God for Philip, who was no trouble to them at all. He went to work, stumped up towards the house-keeping, and kept himself mainly to himself apart from one night a week at the pub, and one night out at his motor-cycle club. There were no surprises or tantrums with *him*.

Time and again she had pleaded with Annie to confide in her . . . to explain why she was so angry all the time. But Annie would have none of it. 'Leave me alone!' That was her stock answer, and unwilling to cause more trouble, Evie had given in and let it go at that.

~

That same evening, over in Derwent Street, Don and Joseph sat talking. 'So, you're off on the morrow, are you?' Joseph had known all along that soonever his son-in-law had saved enough money to take him far and wide, he would be away in search of Davie.

'You know I have to go,' Don replied quietly.

'Can you not stay until Saturday, and see young Judy wed?'

'Now that I've made up my mind, the sooner I get away the better,' Don said. 'I've explained to Lenny, who in turn will explain to Judy. Lenny is fine about it. He wished me well, so he did.'

'I know you're right, son,' Joseph conceded tiredly. 'It's just that I don't want to lose you again.'

'Aw sure, you'll not lose me. Didn't I always say I'd stay a few months, then I'd take off in search of my Davie? Well, now it's time to pack a bag and hit the road. But I'll be back.'

Joseph still wished it wasn't so. 'I hoped against hope that Davie would find his way home. But he hasn't, and I fear if you don't find him, we may never see him again.'

Don understood the old man's feelings. 'It was always in

the back of my mind, too, that one fine day I might see Davie strolling down the street, as if he'd never been away. But like you say, Joseph, if he's not coming home of his own accord, then it's up to me, his father, to go out and find him.'

'He's not a child any more, lad,' the old man cautioned. 'He might not want to come home. He suffered a bad time here, and who of us could blame him, if he's decided to leave it all behind once and for all?'

Don sighed with all the strength of the loss within him. 'Don't I know it, for wasn't it me who walked out on him and his mammy . . . and may the Good Lord forgive me.' He cast his mind back to that night, and the way Davie had stood his ground like a man. 'He'll have had his twentieth birthday now – be a young man, grown and changed – and who knows? He may even have a wife and child of his own!'

Joseph was not convinced. 'Somehow, deep down I don't think so,' he murmured. 'I've allus believed his future is here, with family and friends.' In the deeper recesses of his mind, the old man had always known that Davie belonged to Judy, and she to him. Sadly, he had been proved wrong, because now Davie was long gone, and Judy was promised to another. So if he was wrong in that, he could also be wrong in assuming that Davie's future was here.

With that in mind, he wondered if Don was right after all – and whether, in the years gone by since the family was split – Davie had set down permanent roots elsewhere.

His old heart sank at the thought.

~

'Why aren't you asleep?' Evie Needham popped her head round the bedroom door, to find Annie lying on top of her bed, gazing at the ceiling, and seemingly miles away. 'Annie!'

Jolted out of her thoughts, the girl sat up. 'Oh, Mam . . . thank God it's you.'

Evie entered the room and sat on the edge of the bed. 'O' course it's me,' she said. 'Who else would it be?'

Annie evaded the question. 'I was just thinking about the wedding, and everything.'

'There's time enough during the day to think about that.' Evie glanced at the bedside clock. 'It's going on midnight – I thought you'd be fast asleep by now. Come Saturday you'll have bags under your eyes the size of balloons. You've not slept properly these past few weeks. What's wrong, luv? If there's something playing on your mind, I'd like to know, so's we can put it to rest.'

Annie brightened her smile. 'There's nothing wrong, except I'm a bit nervous about being a bridesmaid. I've never done it before, and I want to look my best for Judy.'

'I expect it is a bit daunting,' her mother conceded. 'First-time bridesmaid . . . walking down the aisle, tummy a-flutter-ing and all eyes on the bride and you.'

Annie laughed out loud. 'Well, that's made me feel much better, I must say!'

Her mother laughed with her. 'Oh, I'm sorry, luv,' she chuckled, 'I didn't mean to worry you. But look, it'll be fine . . . wonderful! So long as you're properly organised. Are you?'

'Far as I know, yes.'

'Have you hung up your dress to keep the creases out?'

'Yes. Look for yourself if you like.'

'And are your new shoes polished?'

'Till you can see your face in them, yes.'

'And have you walked about the bedroom in them, so's they're not uncomfortable on the day?'

'Yes, Mam.' Annie showed her the red rubs on her big

313

toe. 'They were a bit tight at first, but they're all right now.'

'Good! Oh, and where's that little cloth flower I made for the shoulder of your dress? Did you put it in the drawer with your long white gloves, like I told you?'

'Yes, Mam.'

'And have you checked your appointment with the hairdresser, and don't forget you need your nails done. They'll happen organise that to be done, while you're under the dryer.'

'Oh, Mam!' Annie gave her a kiss to shut her up. 'Will you please stop fussing?' Much as she loved her mother, Annie wanted her gone. She had so much to think about, and right now she didn't know which way to turn. She desperately needed to confide in someone. But who? She couldn't tell her mam, because it would break her heart if she knew the truth – and on top of that, she might not believe her, and then what?

She had almost told Lenny in the shop the other day, but then a customer came in and she lost her nerve. Deep down though, she was relieved not to have told him; the shame of it all was too crippling. She couldn't tell Judy either, not with the wedding day so close. And even if she were to pluck up courage and confide in her friend, what could Judy do? *What could anyone do?*

No! It was her problem, and it was up to her to find a solution. The whole thing had gone on far too long. One way or another she must find the courage to put an end to it, once and for all, whatever the consequences.

With her mind racing on, she didn't hear her mother talking to her, until Evie gave her a shake. 'Annie! Are you listening to me?'

'Sorry, Mam.' Pushing the frightening thoughts to the back of her mind, she focused on her mother.

'No, lass, *I'm* the one who's sorry. You look dead beat.'
Evie gave her a hug, before standing up to leave. 'Come on.
Get into bed, now. Try and sleep.'

'I will, Mam, thanks.'

'There you are . . .' Drawing back the covers, Evie waited
until the girl had slithered into bed. 'Good night then, luv,
see you in the morning. We'll talk then, eh?'

Annie nodded gratefully, yawning until her eyes watered.
'Good night, Mam.'

With her mother gone, Annie closed her eyes and let the
sleep wash over her.

But, as usual, she slept lightly, on the alert, and it wasn't long
before the dreams came, and with them, the descent into true
darkness.

CHAPTER TWENTY-ONE

Don Adams was bone weary.

In the fortnight since leaving Blackburn, he had hitched several rides, not caring where he went, but heading south almost unconsciously. He had walked the pavements nonstop, studying each and every passing face; calling at shops, factories and any place where people gathered.

He placed notices in shop windows, asking if anyone knew the whereabouts of David Adams, and giving a description. He asked for people to please write to the Blackburn address below; there would be a small reward, he promised.

Anywhere and everywhere, he tirelessly enquired after his son. He showed the photograph of a teenaged boy, when in truth he was looking for a man. And at the end of the day, he seemed no nearer to finding him.

It was early one summer evening when a truck driver delivered him to a small village not far from Birmingham. Don tried knocking at several bed and breakfast places, and he didn't really blame the local landladies, with their pinnies and turbans and lovely Brummie accents, when they turned him down; for he'd been up with the dawn and on the road ever since, so it was no wonder he looked like a tramp. Moreover, the last place he'd searched was the local pub, and was it his fault if he'd sunk a few bevvies to lighten his weary heart? It was completely out of Don's normal character to do so, but tonight he was feeling very lost.

Darkness was closing in when he found himself down a country lane. Disillusioned and so tired he could hardly think straight, he was beginning to wonder if he would ever find Davie.

As he leaned over the fence, head down and eyes closed as he wondered which way to go next, the roughness of a warm tongue licked against his face. 'What the . . . !' Reeling backwards, he was pleasantly surprised to see a horse, her huge brown eyes staring curiously at this stranger who had dared to intrude on her patch.

Reaching out, Don gently roamed the flat of his hand along the mare's neck, ruffling the mane and taking pleasure in the animal's curiosity. 'You're a friendly girl, an' no mistake,' he said. 'A lot more so than some o' the people I've met along the way.'

As he climbed the fence and headed up the hill to the barn he'd seen earlier, the horse followed. Don chatted to the beast as they both climbed the grassy slopes. The stars shone down on two legs and four as they made towards the barn.

'Aw, yer a lucky lady, so ye are,' Don observed companionably. 'You're a big handsome beauty, well fed and watered, and pregnant too, by the look of it. I expect you want for nothing.' He stopped to stroke the horse's nose again.

'My guess is you've won a lot o' prizes in your time,' he hiccuped.

It was good to talk, and besides, the tongue was always looser when lubricated with the golden nectar. 'I'll have ye know I'm not a stranger to horses, oh no! Sure wasn't I born and bred in County Kilkenny.' Tripping over a molehill, Don quickly righted himself again. 'I'm not drunk – don't think that, my friend!' He laughed. 'Although I'll have you know, there was a time when I could outdrink and outfight any man alive.' He sighed. 'Oh, but that was a long time ago, when I was young and foolish, and desperate to impress the pretty girls.' His wife Rita came into his mind, and for a time he fell silent.

Having reached the barn, he pushed open the creaking old door. 'Is there anybody in there?' he called out, then answered himself: 'Nobody but me.'

Turning to the horse who was right behind him, he instructed her to, 'Keep a guard on me, will ye? Sure, I don't fancy anybody sneaking up an' catching me unawares.' If truth be told, he had never felt comfortable in the dark, more especially if he was on his own and, like now, in hostile territory.

Striking a match, he took a quick look about. 'Quiet as the grave!' He glanced outside and again inside, and when he was satisfied that the place was not already occupied, he stretched and groaned, and taking off his coat, he spread it out over the straw.

He then began shouting and yelling like a banshee, and beating the walls with his fists. 'Rats! Rats! COME OUT WITH YOUR HANDS UP!' The horse snickered in fright, but there was no sign of any scuttling creatures.

Satisfied, Don Adams bedded himself down on the straw and fell into a deep restful sleep.

~

When the dawn rose in the skies, he was rudely awakened by the sharp end of a shotgun in his ribs. 'Who the devil are you? And what d'you think you're doing in my barn?'

Don opened his eyes to see a small, shrewlike figure of a

man standing over him. 'What the . . . ?' For a moment, he was disorientated, but when he realised the danger he was in, he tried to scramble up. However, the man dug the shotgun into his chest and held him there. 'I want to know what you're doing in my barn!' For good measure, he gave him a light kick with the toe of his boot.

'I mean no harm, sir.' Fearing for his life, Don thrust his arms into the air. 'I've been travelling the road looking for my son, and I needed a place to lay my head.' If he had had a mind, he could have taken a chance and had the little runt on his backside, but there was no sense in arguing with the business end of a shotgun.

'Were you here to steal my horse?'

'No, sir, I wasn't, not at all, no.'

'Was it you who burgled my house last week? And don't lie or I'll have your head off and hung on a pole!'

'How could I have burgled your house when I only just got here last night?'

'Where from?'

'Up north. Like I said, I'm searching for my son.'

'Where is he?'

Don took discreet stock of the little man. Was he really as gormless as he seemed, or was he play-acting?

'I just told you – I've travelled down from the north to find him. I've no idea where he is, and my arms are aching, so if you don't mind . . .'

He began lowering his arms, until the man put the shotgun to his temple. 'I wouldn't if I were you!'

Don didn't quite know what to make of this little leprechaun. 'Sure I've done no wrong, other than sleep a few hours in your measly barn, with the wind whistling through the cracks and freezing the arse off me. And no, I haven't burgled your house, and I don't mean to steal your horse.

I'm here in this godforsaken place, because my family went through a bad time some years back; my wife died and my son ran away. I'm doing no harm here. So, all I'm asking is that you let me up and I'll be on my way.'

The man raised the shotgun. 'All right. Get up . . . but don't try anything, mister, because I'm watching you!'

Don got up, not surprised to see how he towered above the little creature, but the shotgun pointed straight at him was more than enough to keep the balance between them.

The farmer looked him up and down, and with his beady eye trained on the intruder, he lowered the gun to his side, though keeping it ever ready. 'Irish, aren't you?' he asked.

'That I am.'

'Hmh! I had an old aunt who was Irish. Daft as a bat, but she'd give you the shirt off her back.'

'I had one the same,' he said to keep the man sweet.

'Is that where you've travelled from . . . Ireland?'

'No. I've lived many years in Lancashire . . . a town called Blackburn.'

'Have you eaten?'

Surprised, Don shook his head.

'Come on then. I'll see what I can do.'

As they walked on, Don assured him, 'It really is like I said.' Taking a photo from his pocket, he showed it to him. 'This is my son, David. You wouldn't have seen him by any chance, would you?'

Stopping in his tracks, the little man took the picture and studied it. 'Mmm,' he kept saying. 'Mmm . . .'

Don grew hopeful. 'So – have you seen him?'

'No.' The little man shook his head. 'I don't think so. But he seems a nice young chap.'

Disheartened, Don retrieved the picture and slid it back into his pocket. 'He's older now, by a good few years.'

'So why are you showing that photograph, when like as not he doesn't resemble it one iota?'

The younger man shrugged. 'It's all I've got.'

They had arrived at the farmhouse – a scruffy place, but homely enough. 'It's nothing grand, but it's mine.' The little man bade Don to sit at the table. 'I care nothing for bricks and mortar, and fancy things. It's the land that I pride, and my beasts. As for that horse, she's my favourite of them all. I've been working with horses since I was knee-high to a gnat.' He laughed. 'Not that I'm much taller than that now-adays, though I say it myself.'

Cracking a couple of eggs into a frying pan, he slid it onto the stove and gave Don a sideways glance. 'I don't suppose you know much about horses, do you?'

'Well, I was brought up with them in Ireland, but that was a long time ago. I'm a joiner by trade.'

'Ah, but you might surprise yourself.' The little man had seen how his pregnant mare was patrolling the barn when he got there, and afterwards, as they walked back to the gate, she followed the stranger faithfully, even nuzzling him once or twice.

'Jenny here doesn't take to strangers easily – tetchy sort, she is.' He regarded the Irishman in a different light. 'But she took to you right enough.'

'So she did,' Don said. 'Oh, and by the look of her she's due to foal any day now, isn't she?'

'I thought you didn't know about horses?'

'I don't, but I know enough about the female species to realise when the belly is swollen with offspring.'

The little man nodded. 'Huh! Observant then, eh?'

'If you like.'

A few minutes later the meal was cooked to perfection – egg, bacon, black pudding and tomatoes, accompanied by a large pot of tea, and a pile of thick toast dripping with best butter.

'Do you need a place to stay?' The little man sat at the table with him.

Don wasn't sure. 'I've a mind to keep going, but I'm tired, to be honest, and I need to plan where to go next.'

'There's a cabin – not much, I'll admit – but it's got a bed and a stove and there's an old radio. You're welcome to use it, until such a time as you're ready to move on.'

Don chuckled. 'One minute you're calling me a thief and a burglar and threatening to shoot me, and the next, you're cooking me breakfast and offering me a place to lay my head.' He didn't expect something for nothing. 'All right! What's the catch?'

'There's no catch.'

'There has to be.'

The little man chewed his bacon and took a swig of his tea. 'Well now, if you mean, can you do something for me in return, there is one thing. Y'see, I'm a one-man band here, and with the mares in foal, it's a busy time.' He cocked an eye at Don. 'It'll mean handling horses, and you might be called on to bring one or two young 'uns into the world. So, what d'you say?'

'All right then.' Don could hardly refuse when he had been treated to breakfast and offered a place to sleep. 'But I won't stay long – a few days maybe – and then I'll be moving on.' He looked the other man in the face. 'I don't even know your name.'

'It's Jimmy – Jimmy Benson – and who am I talking to?'

'Don Adams, and my son's name is David.'

'Mmm.' Jimmy lapsed into deep thought once more. 'Mmm . . . Davie, eh?'

'Are you sure you haven't seen him?'

Jimmy looked up. 'Well, don't get your hopes up, but there was something about the picture of your boy. I'm not sure – it could be something and nothing. Y'see, I've got a neighbour with four lads, and they all look alike to me. I'm not good with children. Never had any, nor wanted 'em either.' He grimaced. 'Never met a woman who wanted *me.*'

Don sat up. Ignoring the last remark, he rapped out, 'Did you see him somewhere? Did he come through here? For God's sake, think, man!'

Jimmy shook his head. 'No, I must be mistaken. No, I'm sorry. Like I say, they all look alike to me. But I'll keep it all in mind, I promise.' As far as he was concerned, the subject was closed.

But not for Don. This was the first real glimpse of hope he'd had.

When breakfast was over, Jimmy said, 'Right! It's time you saw where you'll be working, and what I'm asking of you. After you've seen what it entails, if you want to change your mind, I won't hold you to your word.'

He led Don outside, through the barns and into the area behind the house. 'Good God!' Having wended his way through dilapidated buildings and pitted walkways, he was astonished to see before him the largest, smartest run of stables he had ever seen, and beyond that, the land opening out as far as the eye could see . . . acres upon acres of fine pasture, with a number of fine-looking horses contentedly grazing.

'Is all this yours?' Don looked into the little man's face and saw the answer written there.

'All of it . . . every square inch.' Jimmy suddenly appeared ten feet tall. 'Up to three years ago, I was just a worker here – fetching and carrying, putting the horses out, bringing them in . . . a general dogsbody.'

He had a story to tell. 'The old man who owned it had me doing all the dirty work. He hardly ever spoke, and when he did it was to bark out an order.'

He gave a grateful wink and a cock of the head. 'When he passed on, I found to my amazement that the old bugger had left me six hundred acres of land and that fine block of stables, complete with the horses that belonged in them. My master even wrote me a note to say how much he'd appreciated my loyalty over the years, and that he had issued instructions that, if any of his family should oppose his will, they were to be shut out of it altogether.'

He chuckled. 'I got plenty of black looks from the sons at the will-reading. But there was never a word said.'

As they walked the fields, he had more to tell. 'See that big house over there?' Pointing up to the property, he said, 'That was where my master lived. I was in the old cottage where I am now.'

'So, he didn't leave you the house then?'

Jimmy shook his head. 'No, and I wouldn't have wanted it neither. I'm a simple man with simple tastes. The house went to his daughter, a nice lady; very private since the divorce . . . keeps herself to herself. Yes, she got the house and gardens, and the two sons had all the money split between them.'

On the way back, Jimmy outlined his plans. 'I've been left some of the best horses you'll find this side of heaven – all mares, all top pedigree, and most of 'em in foal to a good stallion. It's a matter of balance,' he explained. 'The two sons were left the money but no land, whereas I've been left the land and horses but no money – which means I need to sell the foals so I can feed good foodstuffs to the mares, so I can breed more foals and make the money. From there I can start to build a future.'

Don had an idea. 'Why don't you just sell everything, lock stock and barrel – the horses and land, with your little cottage and barns. Then you can live out the rest of your life in luxury.'

Jimmy shook his head decisively. 'Don't think I haven't been tempted, because I have. The offers have been amazing. I've had offers from the best horse-breeders in the country, and from local farmers who would plough up the land and grow crops in it. Even the old man's two sons want to get it from me for a pittance, and sell it on for a fortune.'

He tapped his nose. 'They all think I'm a brick short of a load, but they don't know me. For the first and only time in my life, I've been given a chance to prove myself – a chance I never dreamed would come my way. I have such plans, Don – such ambitions! I've worked here long enough to know the ropes, and now I mean to make a name for myself. I want to show I can be the best. If I don't take the bull by the horns now, I never will, so I'm going for it, all guns blazing!'

He paused, a glint of fire in his eyes. 'Look here, matey, I know you want to go looking for your son, and so you should. But I'm asking you to consider if you could use this as your base – work one day, scour the area the next – until you've exhausted this part of the country. You could do it, Don; you could help me and still take time out to search for your son. It would be just for a while, please? I've never asked any man for help before, and I swore I never would. But I'm asking you this one thing. Will you consider it?'

Hands in pockets, eyes big and sad, he made a pitiful sight. 'If, after a few days, you change your mind, there'll be no hard feelings. Just give it a try, that's all I'm asking.' He paused, searching the Irishman's face for a hint of agreement. 'You see, I have a feeling you could help me realise my dream. Will you do it, Don? Will you help me?'

Don was fired by the little man's big ambitions. He also knew what it was like to be up against the money men, whose sole aim in life was to grab everything they could and send you on your way with nothing.

Yet although he wanted so much to help him, he had a dream of his own.

'All right, but I can't stay long,' he told Jimmy in a serious voice. 'In the short time I'll be here, I give you my word, I'll do what I can to help you achieve your ambitions. But remember, my knowledge of horses is vastly inferior to your own.'

Jimmy was not daunted. 'You're willing and able, and you have the heart for it,' he said proudly. 'And when it comes right down to it, that's all a man needs.'

The deal was done with a handshake, and back at the house, Jimmy filled two glasses. 'Here's to us,' he said, raising his own.

'No,' Don corrected him, 'Here's to you . . . *a man and his dream.*'

He would keep his promise to this brave little man. Then, God willing, it was back on the road to find his son.

CHAPTER TWENTY-TWO

'Y OU'VE MADE A wonderful job of this.' Judy wandered through the flat over the shop; completely renovated and carefully furnished to make the best of each and every room, it was now an attractive, comfortable home.

She herself had chosen the plain curtains and fitted carpets, which created a spacious feel, and Lenny had gone for the latest Italian furniture, with its clean strong lines. All in all, it was a pleasant and cosy home, a place where the two of them could be alone and spend many a contented hour.

Sliding his arm round her shoulders, Lenny sat her down on the new divan bed. He couldn't wait to be sharing it with her. 'In two days' time we'll be man and wife.' His hand reached out to stroke her hair. 'You could have any man you wanted,' he murmured, 'but you chose me.'

'You wouldn't let me *not* choose you,' she laughed, a little sadly.

'You don't regret it, do you – saying yes, I mean?'

Detecting the nervousness in his voice, Judy felt guilty and was quick to reassure him. 'I wouldn't have said yes, if I didn't want to marry you.' Cradling her two hands round his face she drew him down and kissed him full on the mouth, a soft and loving kiss that quickly aroused him.

329

'I do love you so.' Unbuttoning her blouse, he slid it over her shoulders, baring her small, pert breasts.

The knock on the front door startled them. 'Who can that be?' While Lenny went down to answer the door, Judy quickly buttoned up her blouse and went to put the kettle on.

It was Annie. 'Is Judy here?' she asked, and Lenny thought she looked as though she'd been crying.

Concerned, he drew her inside. 'Are you all right?'

Annie nodded. 'Yes. Look, I'm sorry to bother you of an evening, but tomorrow's the last day before the wedding, and there are things I need to go over with Jude.' She paused, her voice shaking as she added, 'I'm sorry, Lenny. I just needed to get out of the house.'

He took hold of her, could feel her trembling. Something tugged at him. 'I know there's summat wrong at home,' he said sharply. 'I've seen you go downhill for some weeks now, and I'm worried about you. Look, Annie, I care for you, and I want to help. But I can't do anything if you don't tell me the truth!'

'Annie?' Hearing voices, Judy had come downstairs, and she was shocked to see Annie there, looking so upset. 'Come upstairs, sweetheart.' While Lenny secured the door, she took Annie up to the sitting room.

'I'm in terrible trouble,' Annie burst out as they went in and sat down on the settee. 'I just don't know what to do any more.'

For a full minute she sobbed in Judy's arms, then when she became quieter, Judy gently urged her, 'Talk to me, Annie . . . Tell me what's happened to get you into this state.'

Annie wiped her eyes and sat very still and very quiet for a while, deep in thought and now bitterly regretting her weakness in having come here and worried the only two real friends she had in the whole world.

Raising her face and plastering a false smile on it, she declared in a bright voice, 'Look, you two need your privacy.' She stood up. 'I'd best be off.'

They were amazed. 'What are you talking about?' Lenny blocked her way. 'You're obviously very upset. Somebody's hurting you, and I for one want to know who. Come on, Annie. We're all friends together here; nobody else need know, if that's what you're worried about.'

She was adamant. 'I'm just a bit touchy at the minute, that's all,' she said. 'It's the wedding, I expect. My nerves are all on edge.' She laughed. 'Anyone would think it were me getting wed!' And oh, how she wished it was.

She refused the hot drink Judy offered, and she refused Lenny's offer to take her home in the car. She then made her apologies, and only a few minutes after arriving, she was gone.

Judy saw her away at the door. 'I know you're in trouble,' she told Annie, 'but there's nothing me or Lenny can do, if you won't confide in us.'

'Nothing to tell.' Annie gave her a hug and went away up the street at a fast pace. At the corner, she turned round and waved, and then she was gone from sight.

Upstairs, Lenny was pacing the floor. 'D'you think she'll really be all right?' he asked. Like Judy, he was very concerned.

'She seemed all right,' Judy sighed, 'but you never know with Annie. She can be very deep when she wants.'

'Do you think we should have a word with her mother?' he went on.

Judy shook her head. 'Annie wouldn't thank you for that.'

'So, what can we do?'

'We can't do anything.' Judy knew her friend only too well. 'We have to wait until she decides she can trust us. Until then, all we can do is keep a close eye on her.'

The mood in the flat was changed, and a short time later, Lenny ran Judy home.

~

Annie walked faster and faster until now she was running, tears streaming down her face and the fear so strong inside her, she could hardly breathe.

Cutting across the fields, she ran like she had never run before; brambles snatched at her legs and tore the skin, and when she stumbled, exhausted, she made no effort to get up. Instead, she lay face down on the grass, sobbing as though her heart would break. 'I have to do it!' she kept saying over and over. 'I HAVE TO DO IT!'

For what seemed an age she lay there as the afternoon turned to evening, making her plans, hoping she was doing the right thing; knowing she should not do it, but seeing no alternative.

Scrambling to her feet, she brushed herself down and combed her hair with her fingers. Fumbling in her pockets, she found a hankie to wipe the tears and dirt from her face. That done, she walked on, more composed, still afraid – but determined to go through with it.

When at last she came off into Montague Street, she started the long walk down to number sixteen. 'I can do it,' she told herself. '*I have to!*'

She made it as far as number sixteen. Outside, she paused and waited. 'Go on, Annie,' she told herself, taking a long, shuddering breath. 'You've got this far. Don't back out now.'

She was gathering all the courage she had when the voice spoke in her ear, making her jump. 'Are you all right, dear?' A wizened, goblin-like creature of advanced years was looking at Annie through tiny, quizzical eyes. 'Only you've been standing there ever since I turned the corner at the top. Are you lost, dearie? Tell me who you're looking for, and I might be able to point you in the right direction?'

Already nervous, Annie began to panic. 'It's all right,' she stuttered. 'It's . . . mmm . . . it's the wrong street.' She backed away. 'It's not Montague Street I want. No, not Montague Street at all.'

The little goblin watched as Annie went away down the street at a quickening pace. 'Strange lass!' She shook her head and trotted along to the corner shop, where she had a snippet of juicy gossip for her old friend, Enid. Girls and young women were always coming to number 16. Nurse Pomfret lived here with all her cats – nasty, smelly things they were. No one along here liked the woman, or her blessed animals. But no one dared to say any more than that.

~

Having got as far as King Street, Annie sat on the wall outside the picture-house. Her knees were shaky. She thought of making her way back to Montague Street but her courage was shattered for today. 'Tomorrow,' she muttered. 'I'll go tomorrow.' Determined though she was, the fear had still not gone away.

~

With Lenny gone, and her father off to his bed, for the milk-round still had to be done early in the morning and Tom wasn't getting any younger . . . Judy made herself and her mother a mug of cocoa. For a time, she quietly watched as Beth took a sip of her drink before carrying on with her knitting, then another sip and another row of stitches, and another sip then another row, and Judy could hold it in no longer. 'Mam!'

Looking up, Beth placed her knitting on the chair arm. 'Sorry, sweetheart, I was concentrating. I've got to the sleeves and they're always the trickiest part. You know how your dad likes his jumpers to be loose about the arms.' She looked over at the girl. Her daughter seemed unusually agitated. 'Are you all right?' she enquired. 'You seem a bit on edge.' She smiled reassuringly. 'Oh, you don't need to worry. You'll see, everything will go exactly as planned on Saturday.'

'I wasn't really thinking about that, Mam.'

'No? What were you thinking about then?'

'I was thinking about Annie.'

'What about her?'

The girl took a moment to consider her words. 'I think she's in some kind of trouble,' she said eventually.

Beth grew anxious. 'What kind of trouble?'

Judy shrugged. 'I'm not really sure, only these past few weeks, she's been like a cat on hot bricks. She hardly ever laughs any more, and when you talk to her, she seems miles away. And tonight she came round to Lenny's flat and she was crying, and when we asked her what was wrong, she said it was nothing, but I know she's lying. And I'm really worried about her.'

'Hey.' Beth came and sat on the sofa beside her. 'You're her best friend, sweetheart. If Annie ever had a problem, she allus came to you. If there was anything wrong now, she'd tell you, I know she would.'

The girl shook her head. 'There have been a few times lately, when she's started to tell me something, and then she clams up.' She looked to her mother for an answer. 'Has

Mrs Needham said anything to you? Is there any trouble at home that you know of?'

Beth gave it some thought. 'No, not that I can think of.' She pursed her lips in that peculiar fashion she had when concentrating. 'I reckon I can tell you what Annie's problem is,' she went on sagely. 'It's the wedding. She's afraid she might let you down somehow. She's probably convincing herself that something's bound to go wrong and that it will be her fault.' She tutted. 'You know how she is – allus looking to blame herself for everything.'

Judy saw the sense in what her mother was saying. 'Oh Mam, do you really think that's all it is?'

'I do, yes.'

'But she's got nothing to worry about, and besides, if anything was to go wrong, that doesn't make it Annie's fault.' A shiver of fear went through her. 'Nothing will go wrong, will it?'

' 'Course it won't, lass! Now drink your cocoa afore it gets cold.'

~

All the same, and in spite of her mother's reassurances, come the early hours, Judy was sitting on the edge of her bed, wide awake. Maybe her mam had hit the nail on the head, she thought with a yawn, then slithered between the sheets and pulled the blanket over her head. Maybe Annie really was nervous about the wedding. She closed her eyes, thinking sleepily, Because the closer it gets, the more nervous *I'm* getting, too.

When warm and wonderful memories of Davie came to mind, she made herself think of Lenny, a good man, soon to be her husband. Her heart should be singing for joy, she knew.

Instead, she was anxious and worried, and she couldn't help feeling that something was in the air, something unexpected.

Something completely out of her control.

~

It was two in the morning in the Needham household.

Annie had been sleeping soundly when she was awakened by the touch of a hand against her face. 'Wake up, darling. Ssh . . . come on, my beauty, wake up.' The voice was rasping, but soft, and close to her ear.

Before Annie could cry out, his hand was over her mouth. 'Now, now . . . don't start carrying on. Just relax and we'll be finished in no time at all.' His hands were all over her. 'You know you like it. Yes, you love it, don't you, you dirty little bitch!' He gave a low, wicked laugh.

'GET OFF ME!' Terrified, and amazed at her own strength, Annie lashed out, knocking him off-balance. The spell that had kept her quiet for so many years, enduring the abuse in terrified silence, had finally broken. 'I'm pregnant! You bastard . . . you made me pregnant!' She screamed. 'MAM! MAM, HELP ME!'

Her frantic cry echoed through the house, bringing her parents running into the room. 'Philip! What are you doing in here? What the devil's going on?'

A quiet, private sort of man, Derek Needham usually kept out of things. He loved his family and provided for them, and that was his role in life. But when his sleep was disturbed, that was another matter.

Evie looked from her daughter to her son. 'Somebody had better explain, and quickly!' Her eyes fell on Philip. 'You're drunk, again! I wish you'd stop going out to that blasted public house, if you come home in this state. Now go back to your own room. Next door! You've frightened the living daylights out of your sister, look!' She assumed he had wandered into Annie's room and startled her.

'Mam, didn't you hear me?' Annie wailed, redfaced and out of control. 'I'm *pregnant*! Look!' And she pointed to her swollen stomach. 'It's Philip's fault, Dad. He attacked me – he's come into my room at night ever since I was a kid. I asked you for a lock once and you wouldn't let me have one – I wish I'd told you why, but I didn't think you'd believe me. Mam, Dad, *I'm pregnant and you've got to help me.*' She was having hysterics now.

As Evie and Derek looked on, too shocked to speak, their son spoke up, far too cunning to be caught. 'Ask her what's going on,' he retaliated. 'Yes, go on. Before you take any notice of her load of old rubbish, ask her what she's been up to, carrying on with that gypsy boy from the fair. Oh, I see you didn't know. Well, he's made her pregnant, and just now she called me into her room and had the gall to ask me to help her get rid of it. Well, I won't! I'm too ashamed of her, my own sister . . . sleeping with every Tom, Dick and Harry, as you well know, only you won't admit it, and now made pregnant by a gyppo off the fairground.'

Her legs too shaky to hold her, Evie sank into a chair. 'Oh, dear Lord . . . Oh, Annie, is this true?'

Always a proud man, Derek was deeply ashamed. 'She's the worst kind of trollop! That's what she is.' By now, he knew, the neighbours would have heard the row, and it would be all over the street tomorrow.

Outraged, and at the end of her tether, Annie screamed at them, 'Yes, I am pregnant! But it wasn't by any gypsy!' Pointing at Philip, she shouted, 'It was my own brother. The first time he raped me, I was eleven years old. I've kept quiet, even though I often felt I was going mad, and tonight I just couldn't take any more. That's why I shouted out for you.' And then, at their continued silence: 'Do you hear what I'm saying? IT WAS YOUR OWN SON WHO MADE ME PREGNANT!'

'She's lying!' Philip was a past master at deceit, and like a rat when cornered he was at his best in that moment. 'I can't believe what she's saying.' He was incredulous. 'It's like I told you. Just now, she heard me on the landing and called me in. She told me everything. And now you know what kind of a daughter you bred.'

While Evie didn't know what to think, as she was still in shock, Derek was determined. 'I want her out of this house, and I want her out this very night!' He looked at Annie through narrowed eyes. 'You've allus been one for the fun and games,' he said harshly, 'but now you've got your come-uppance, and I'll not have you bring your shame down on us.' With that, he stormed out of the room.

Dejected and frightened, Annie went down on her knees before her mother. 'You believe me, don't you, Mam?'

Her mother didn't answer. Instead she bowed her head in her hands and sobbed as though her heart would break.

Annie looked at her brother. With his hands in his pockets and a confident smirk on his face, she knew he had won the day. All the fight went from her.

Going right up to him, she said not a word, but looked on him with disgust. If ever there had been murder in her heart, it was now.

But even though she was innocent, she had lost. And he had won.

Quickly, she dressed and left, with nothing more than the clothes on her back.

Where she was going, there was no need of anything more.

~

For what seemed an age, Annie Needham walked the darkened streets. There was no one about at this late hour, and she was glad of that. She needed to think. She thought of Judy, and Lenny, and her parents, who had so easily been taken in by their son. Why was that? she asked herself time and again. Why did they believe him over her? She recalled her mother, broken by the lies Philip told, and her father hurt and angry, beyond reason.

'You didn't believe me,' she said to the night. Their disbelief had shocked her. 'Why could you not believe me?' But her father had been right. She had flitted from one boy to another, looking for Lenny in all of them, and finding only emptiness.

All these years, reeling from what her brother had done to her, and fearful that if she told her parents they would not believe her – the very thing that had happened tonight – she had gone from boy to boy, feeling used and dirty, not to give of herself, which she had never done, but with a need to feel wanted. Sexually active from far too young an age, her innocence plundered and mocked, she had let herself be used time and time again.

All those boys . . . they were simply another means of trying to forget.

'Yes, all them boys, Lenny,' she murmured. 'And not one of them fit to lick your boots.' She smiled to herself. 'I think I've loved you forever, but you never saw me like that, did you, eh?'

She gave an odd little laugh. 'However much you love somebody, you can't make them love you back.' She wondered if God was listening to her. Nobody else was. She was alone on this earth, but no matter. It would soon all be over.

When her wanderings brought her to the canal bridge, she stood there awhile, gazing down into the darkness of the water. Just for a minute or two, no longer.

Then she climbed onto the wall, closed her eyes – and in that moment when she let herself fall, it was as though all the weight of the world simply floated from her shoulders.

~

'Did you hear that?' Locked in passion with his girl in the alley-way, the young man broke away and listened. Then he was running, up the rise and on towards the bridge.

'Steve!' His girlfriend ran after him. 'Where are you going? Come back, you idiot!' She started laughing, thinking he was playing a game, teasing her as usual.

'Jesus!' Looking down at the water, he saw Annie, arms out, floating face down. 'There's somebody in the canal!'

Stripping off his jacket, he yelled, 'Run back to the pub and wake someone up and tell them . . . Get help! Go on! Hurry!' As she set off, he dropped his jacket to the ground and leaped, feet first, into the murky water.

CHAPTER TWENTY-THREE

Donal and Jimmy had been up since the early hours. It was now 6 a.m. All but one of the horses were turned out into the field. The one horse remaining was the same mare, Jenny, who had befriended Don on his arrival in Bedfordshire.

While he let down the door to the horse-box, Jimmy gave the animal another grooming. 'This is my first show,' the little fella said, grinning from ear to ear. 'I've been to countless sales and shows in my time, but this is my first show as an owner. I can't wait to see the looks on the faces of the other breeders when they see the quality of this mare.' He clicked his tongue and smiled. 'This is a day to remember.'

Eventually, he laid down the brush, slipped on her headcollar and led the mare into the trailer. 'Come on, Jenny, my girl! We're off to show the other buggers what we're made of.'

Don shut the trailer door behind her, and the two men climbed into the cab, with the little fellow driving; though to Don's amusement, he could hardly see over the steering-wheel.

The journey took an hour and a half, and when they drove into the field, there were already any number of horse-trailers and boxes parked up. 'Looks like it might be a busy day.' Climbing down from the cab, Jimmy looked about. 'There's Rob Goodman – he's been at this for as long as I can remember, oh, and Maisie Billington.' He chuckled. 'Better than any man, she is,' he said. 'Carries a shotgun everywhere and wouldn't think twice about using it if she took agin somebody.'

Don had never been to a show of this calibre. Here, before his eyes, were magnificent specimens, their coats gleaming like coal-dust, manes meticulously plaited and hooves polished to a brilliant shine. There were huge stallions and graceful mares, and the folk who paraded them were every bit as fine and dandy as their prize animals.

When it was their turn to unload the mare, Jimmy led her to the enclosure, heart and soul taller and prouder than everyone around him.

'There are some fine animals here,' Don said in awe. Though he was not an expert, he recognised quality when he saw it.

Jimmy went to the entry cabin and gave his name as James Benson, owner of the bay mare, name of *Sunday Best*. This was Jenny's official title.

Soon, it was time. 'Wish me luck.' Jimmy crossed his fingers. 'She's far and away my best horse. If she wins the trophy, her value will go through the roof.' He was shaking with excitement. 'It'll mean I'm in with the big boys,' he whispered. 'They'll be clamouring for her young 'uns and they won't mind parting with their cash, neither.'

The competition was on. The animals were paraded in their finery, and with every horse and owner lined up, the two judges walked up and down with their clipboards and their top hats, and as each horse was eliminated, the line shrank, until there were only five remaining.

One of the five was Jimmy's mare.

From where Don stood watching, he could see the little fellow's hand shaking on the rein. 'Chin up, Jimmy!' he muttered. 'You're looking good.'

The judge stopped at Jenny then; he ran his hand down the animal's fetlock, then along her back, and now he had the mouth open and was examining her teeth. He then stepped back, took another, longer overall look, made a note on his clipboard and moved on to the next hopeful.

Jimmy caught Don's eye and gave him a cheeky wink.

The Irishman smiled. 'You're still in there, boy,' he muttered through his teeth. 'Still in there!'

At long last, the moment was here.

The judges called out the prizewinners in reverse order.

By the time they called number three, the two remaining contenders for the title of Best Mare were a fine eighteen-hands-high palamino by the name of *Golden Girl*, and Jimmy's seventeen-hands bay mare, *Sunday Best*.

The judges conferred, the decision was made and, clutching the prized trophy in his hands, the chief judge began his walk towards the winner.

Jimmy was trembling in his boots. If he came first, he would surely faint, he thought, but if he came second it would still be a good result and his name would be known in the right circles. But if he came first! Oh, God above! If he . . .

'The winner is *Sunday Best*!' The voice echoed through the grounds, and when the judge handed Jimmy the trophy, he laughed out loud.

'Thank you, sir!' he said. His throat was choked and the tears filled his eyes, as Don ran forward to take the trophy from his quivering hands. 'I've won!' Now he couldn't stop the tears, but he didn't care. 'I've won the trophy!' And everyone around him was just as thrilled, for they knew of

343

Jimmy the ex-groom, and the legacy he'd been left, and to a man, they were proud of him.

Like Jimmy said, it was 'a day to remember'.

~

He talked about it all the way back to the horse-box, and he talked about it while they loaded the valuable animal, and even when the door was shut and the mare safe, Jimmy couldn't stop talking.

'I beat the lot of them!' he kept saying. 'I've got the best mare and she's worth a fortune, and I won the trophy.' He didn't want to let go of it, and as the folks gathered round to congratulate him, Don went away to the refreshment tent to purchase two pints of the best in celebration.

If he himself didn't deserve it, little Jimmy certainly did.

When he started on his way back, a pint in each fist, Don was amused and pleased to see one or two people still lingering, talking to Jimmy and patting him on the back.

As he approached, they wandered away. 'There you are.' He handed the little man a pint, from which he took a long, thirsty gulp.

'Did you see them come and talk to me?' Jimmy said excitedly. 'Some of the best horse-breeders in the land and they came to congratulate *me*!' He took another swallow of his cool pint. 'See that man over there?' He pointed to a red-faced man of large proportions. 'He's considered to be the richest owner of all . . . sends his foals all over the world, he does. Mind you, since old Frank Thomson got wed and retired a couple of months back, he's had it more or less his own way.'

'Who's this Frank then?' Don asked, out of no particular interest. 'Good breeder, was he?'

'Good!' The little fella almost choked on his beer. 'Frank

Thomson was the best ever!' He pointed to where a group of men were talking together. 'See that young man over there? Well, he turned up at Frank's place one day a few years ago – much like you did with me, as a matter of fact. Well, anyway, Frank took him on as stable lad. Then the yard manager committed a misdemeanour, got sacked, and to cut a long story short, that young man there, well . . . he took over his job.'

He paused, his excitement at winning somehow over-shadowed by what he now told Don. 'This young fellow and Frank's daughter recently got engaged. There was a party. The previous yard manager, jealous as hell, came back and set light to the stables.' He shook his head. 'Such wickedness. In the chaos, many horses died, along with the man who did it. The girl, poor young lass, was trampled underfoot. Frank was inconsolable. A short time later, he and his long-time housekeeper moved away and got married. And that young man there, well, he took off, but he stayed around these parts. Helps out where he's wanted, beds down with the horses. Oh yes, he knows his way round horses. Frank knew he was good, or he would never have taken him on. Dave, his name is. Dave . . . Adams.'

Electrified he stared at Don, who had turned to stone, a question burning in his eyes.

~

Dave was deep in conversation. 'This is my last horse fair,' he was telling an older man. 'I'm ready to move on. There's an old grandfather back home in Blackburn who I haven't seen in ages . . .'

When the older man raised his gaze to look beyond Dave, at the two men who were staring at them, seemingly entranced, the young man stopped talking and slowly turned around too.

For the longest, heart-stopping minute he didn't recognise the man coming towards him. But in that split second of recognition when their eyes met, he gasped aloud, the words catching in his throat, so he could hardly breathe.

And then Don was running towards him, and the emotion was too much to bear. 'Dad! . . . It's my dad!'

Don caught him in his arms, and they hugged and cried, and when the hugging was done, Don held his son at arm's length, his eyes shining and his heart full.

'I always knew I'd find you,' Dave told him.

And all Don could do was nod.

Together they went to Jimmy. 'This is the boy in the picture I carry,' Don said emotionally. 'This is my son, and I've found him at last.'

Jimmy could find no words; his heart was too full. Oh dear, he'd known it all along – that Frank Thomson's head groom was called Dave Adams . . . but the memory had stayed beneath the surface. This was what age did to you, he thought savagely, clutching his trophy. It made you about as much use as a piece of hay from a horse's nosebag, blowing in the wind!

'And now, we're going home.' Dave looked at his father. 'We are, aren't we, Dad?'

'Yes, son.' At long last, Don was at peace. 'You and me . . . we're going home.'

~

That same evening, they said their goodbyes to Jimmy. 'You will come back and see me, won't you?' The little chap was sad to see them go.

Don promised that he would, and so did Dave. 'Mind you get in touch with the two people whose names I've given you,' said Dave. 'They're about the best you'll get, to help you build a business. What they don't know about horses isn't worth knowing.'

Jimmy thanked him, and as the two men walked away, he knew that the goodbyes were not forever.

~

On the train to Blackburn, Dave asked after his grandad, and the friends he had left behind. 'As far as I know, everyone's all right.' Don had no knowledge of the recent events that had happened while he was away.

'And Judy?' She was the one uppermost in Dave's mind. 'How is she?' It was eight long years since he had last seen her, but her picture was bright in his mind's eye . . .

Uncertain as to how he might take the news, Don informed him, 'If my memory serves me right, I reckon she and Lenny are already wed.'

He didn't see how the news had shocked Dave, because at that moment a lady entered their carriage and they had to shove along the seat.

'She'll be thrilled to see you, so she will,' Don went on, in a low voice. 'As will your grandad. Oh, just wait till he sees you, he'll be over the moon, the dear old fella!'

At that moment, the lady's small suitcase tumbled from the luggage-rack, scattering its contents all over the carriage floor, and her dog, a small Jack Russell, yapped so shrilly that further conversation was impossible.

However, to Dave's yearning heart, the train wheels were rhythmically singing '*Travel-ling home! Travel-ling home!*'

Home. What was there waiting for him? The house in

Derwent Street, his beloved grandfather, eight years older, and a parcel of memories, to which he would now bring his own. But he could get through it all, he knew, if only *she* were waiting for him, too.

CHAPTER TWENTY-FOUR

Annie was not drowned.

Thanks to Steve, the young man who dived into the canal to save her, she was still alive when they rushed her to the Infirmary, where her life was saved. The baby was lost, however, and though she was desperately sorry that such a terrible thing had happened because of her own cowardly act, Annie had come to believe that it was meant to be. The poor mite, child of her own brother, had been cursed from the start. As she recovered, very slowly, from her ordeal, Annie prayed daily and nightly, for her baby's soul, and she shed many a healing tear.

Since Annie had been admitted, Lenny and Judy were never far away. They were there now, though Judy had gone to get a vase for the flowers they'd brought. Their wedding arrangements had been cancelled. Neither of them had the heart for it while their best friend was recovering from a suicide attempt.

Lenny sat by the bed, holding Annie's hand. 'I'm so glad your parents keep coming in to see you.' Annie had told him and Judy about the falling-out at home, although she withheld the full truth. 'We've all been so worried.'

Suddenly Annie was crying – bitter, guilty tears that

wouldn't stop. 'I'm sorry!' she kept sobbing. 'I'm so, so sorry.'

'Hey!' Instinctively he took her in his arms. 'Cry if you need to,' he murmured. 'I'm here for you. We all are.'

He misunderstood her reason for crying. 'You mustn't blame yourself,' he told her tenderly. 'It's a terrible thing that the baby was lost, but who knows . . . maybe it was meant to be?' It seemed a feeble thing to say in the circumstances, but he was truly thankful that Annie herself had not been lost along with the child. Because something had happened to him.

When the news came through that Annie had tried to drown herself, and that if it hadn't been for the young man, she would have perished, he was devastated. Not only because she was a dear friend, as he thought. But because he knew then, that he loved her. It was Annie he wanted for a wife, and though he loved Judy, it was Annie with whom he wanted to spend the rest of his life. How could he not have seen this before? He had been too intent on pursuing the dream of winning Judy's unwilling heart, to recognise the truth before his eyes.

'Lenny?'

'Yes?'

'I need to tell you something.'

'Go ahead.'

So Annie told him everything: how it was her brother Philip who had repeatedly abused her throughout her childhood; how he had raped her and left her pregnant, and how she had alerted her parents and told them the truth. But they would not believe her.

'My God!' Lenny was devastated. 'Your own brother!'

Annie went on. 'They didn't believe me,' she said brokenheartedly. 'He lied and made them believe *him*. He said I had gone with a gypsy boy from the fairground.'

Lenny understood. 'And that's when you went out and tried to end it?' He was filled with rage at what Philip had done. 'You *must* make them believe you! He *has* to be punished!'

'No!' Annie drew him to her. 'I've seen how ill and tired they look,' she said. 'My parents are good people. If they were to believe what he did . . . it would cripple them. I can't do it, Lenny. I can't punish them for what he did.'

Returning with the vase, Judy saw Lenny with his arms round Annie; she saw how Annie clung to him, and she knew in her heart that it was love, and not friendship.

And she was glad.

'Here you are!' She arranged the flowers in the vase and stood them where Annie could see. 'There's something to brighten your day,' she said cheerfully, as Lenny released Annie from his embrace.

Just then, Annie's parents appeared.

'We'd best be off now,' Judy said tactfully. She and Lenny each gave her a kiss, and as Judy walked on, Lenny whispered in Annie's ear, 'Do what you think best, sweetheart. Your secret's safe with me.'

Smitten with guilt, Annie's parents were at her bedside most every chance they got; today was no exception. 'Will you tell us the truth, Annie?' Evie asked, sitting down. Now that her beloved daughter was out of danger, and on the road to recovery, Evie Needham was determined to get at the truth. She couldn't eat, couldn't sleep, couldn't look her son in the eye. Life was an ongoing nightmare. '*Was* it the gypsy boy who made you with child, or was it . . .' She could hardly bring herself to say it. 'Was it our Philip?'

Annie looked at her mother and saw how sad and frail she appeared of late, and her father, standing at the end of the bed, a look of pain and confusion on his homely face; and she knew they must suffer no more.

351

'Philip was right,' she lied. 'It *was* the gypsy boy from the fairground.' She knew she had done right when all the pain seemed to ebb from their faces. 'I'm sorry, Mam . . . Dad. I don't know what I was thinking of, to blame Phil like that.'

Evie held her tight. 'It's all over now,' she said brokenly. 'Let's put it all behind us and start again, eh?' When she looked at Annie as she did now, she could only see her child, her darling daughter whom she had nearly lost, throwing herself and her unborn child into the deep, dark waters of the canal.

Reaching up, Annie wiped her mother's tears away. 'No more tears,' she said. 'A new start, that's what we've been given.'

'Good girl.' Derek came forward. He made no move to take his daughter in his arms, but he did the next best thing; he held her hand and squeezed it. 'We all of us make mistakes,' he said. 'I'm sorry about the child, but sometimes God works in mysterious ways. Happen it were for the best, eh?' For a second, it almost seemed that he might know the real truth of it all.

When Annie nodded, her gaze enveloping him with such daughterly affection, he leaned down and kissed her face. 'You'll do,' he said quietly. 'That's my girl.' He added something else too, while his wife poured out a glass of water behind him. 'There's a lock on your door now, pet.'

~

That night, Lenny found Philip in the pub, boasting loudly about his latest conquest – a girl of seventeen from a troubled background in Accrington. He was describing what they'd got up to, in the most obscene and foul language.

'Step outside, will you?' Lenny's dark voice put a stop to his tale.

'Like hell I will!' Every instinct in his useless body warned him that the truth was out. 'You bugger off, Reynolds, you bastard!'

The words were hardly out of his mouth when he was lifted from his feet and taken at a run out the door. Lenny held him by the collar up against the wall. 'I know what you did, you filthy scum!' he said.

'Oh, yeah! An' what's that then, eh?' the youth said cockily, although he could scarcely breathe.

'Don't come that with me!' Lenny tightened his grip on him. 'You know what I'm talking about. And all I'm saying is this . . . I want you out of Blackburn. I want you as far away as a man can travel. And if I *ever* see hide nor hair of you again, you'll rue the day!'

Like the coward he was, Philip was soon persuaded to leave, but not without complaint – and there was his big mistake. 'She deserved it, the little cow! One bloke after another . . . always looking for excitement. Well, she got it and—' Lenny's flying fist closed his mouth for him.

With blood running down his shirt, he ran as if the devil himself was after him. 'Mad bugger!' he shouted as he ran. 'Who wants to stay round these parts anyway!' He stopped, bent double to vomit up his ale, and Lenny, still panting from the encounter, turned and walked away, wiping his hand clean against his jacket.

~

Three days later, on the Saturday morning, Lenny and Judy were on their way back from a visit to the Needhams', to see how Annie was settling in back at home. Beth had given them a half-dozen freshly laid eggs and a pot of home-made bramble jelly to take with them.

As they strolled together down the track towards the gates of Three Mills Farm, Judy knew it was time to put things right.

'Do you love me, Lenny?' she asked him.

'Of course I love you!' He was startled, spoke too quickly. 'What makes you ask that?'

Placing her hand on his arm, she drew him to a standstill. 'But you love Annie more.' Her smile was knowing. 'It's all right,' she said gently. 'I think I've known for some long time – and then the other day, when I saw the two of you together in hospital, I was never more certain.'

Lenny was mortified. 'Oh, Judy, I'm so sorry,' he said, grabbing her hands and holding them tight. 'I didn't even know myself at first.'

'I believe you, and I can promise you that I'm happy for you both. D'you know what, Len? I reckon that you and Annie are made for each other. It was funny, our wedding being delayed. It wasn't meant to be, was it? I'll always love you as a friend, Lenny, and now I'm going to set you free.'

It was so good, to have the truth out in the open. 'I love Davie,' she went on, 'I always have.' She shrugged, then smiled and turned away. 'I always will.'

They walked on in silence, both coming to terms with this change in their lives. At the door, he told her, 'I won't come in, if that's all right?'

She gave him a warm, friendly hug. 'In the morning, you must tell Annie. You two . . . you belong together.'

She stood and watched as Lenny walked back down the track, his head held high, a free man. Judy was glad: she had done the right thing. Even if she remained a spinster for the rest of her life, it didn't – *couldn't* – matter. Her heart belonged to Davie.

∼

Inside, a young man stood and watched from the window. He had heard what was said, and he dared to believe there was a chance for him.

'Come away now, Davie!' That was Beth, fussing. 'Your tea is getting cold.'

Instead, he ran and opened the door, to greet his Judy.

There was a shocked and palpable silence; which only lasted a few seconds, but in that profound pause, so much occurred. Girl and boy drank in the sight of each other – Dave the sweet maturity of the grown-up Judy; she the handsome, slender strength of her childhood friend grown into a man. A million messages passed between them; and were answered. And then, as each took in a new breath, they felt the world falling into its rightful place.

The spell broke as he moved forward and picked her up, swinging her around.

'I'm back,' he announced. 'And I'm here to tell you that I'm yours if you want me.' He laughed out loud. 'I'm asking you to marry me, Judith Makepeace, and if you don't accept right now, I'll go away and I will *never* come back!'

Her answer was to kiss him full on the mouth. 'Don't you dare go anywhere!' she said.

The miracle she had prayed for had come to pass. He was home. Her Davie was home. And at long last, they were together.

$\sim$

Two months later, David Adams watched as Tom walked his daughter Judith down the aisle towards him. A picture of loveliness in her new white gown and pretty mother-of-pearl headdress, she glowed with happiness.

Behind them, Derek looked every inch the proud father as he accompanied Annie. Instead of a bridesmaid gown, Annie wore the dress which Judy had chosen when planning to marry Lenny; it had taken a yard or so of material and some alteration, but she looked, as Derek said huskily, 'Pretty as a picture.'

No one remarked on Philip's absence from his sister's wedding.

The double wedding service was doubly joyous, and the party afterwards, in the Top Meadow at the farm, was a success in every respect; with dancing and music and laughter ringing across the fields.

Davie could not reach Eli, but he got a message from him the day before the wedding, to say he was travelling in Europe, and having a wonderful time, and he hoped to see them all in the spring.

Frank and Maggie turned up, tanned and healthy and ready to dance a noisy Twist along with everyone else, making the cows nervous in the next field.

Old Joseph made an exhibition of himself by gyrating along with Annie – the bride demonstrating how to do it, with her veil flung back. When he'd done, everybody clapped. He bent to take a bow, pulled his back, and had to be carried to the beer tent to recover. But that was no hardship, as little Jimmy was already there to keep him company, 'testing the booze' as he put it.

~

Derek and Tom got a bit merry, and after escaping from the noise and chaos, they sat on the garden bench, enjoying their well-earned pints. 'Here's to the women!' Tom said, clinking his glass against Derek's.

'And here's to the men who will always love them!' Derek replied.

~

Judy found herself being taken to a quiet corner by her new husband. 'I love you so much, Mrs Adams,' Dave said. 'I'll make you the happiest woman on God's earth.'

'I'll keep you to that,' she laughed.

~

Davie kept his word, over forty-five years and three children – all girls, all with the look of their mother.

CHATTERBOX
The Josephine Cox Newsletter

If you would like to know more about Josephine Cox, and receive regular updates, just send a postcard to the address below and automatically register to receive Chatterbox, Josephine's free newsletter. The newsletter is packed with exciting competitions and exclusive Josephine Cox gifts and merchandise, plus news and views from other fans.

Chatterbox
Freepost
PAM 6429
HarperCollins Publishers
77–85 Fulham Palace Road
Hammersmith
London
W6 8BR

Alternatively, you can e-mail chatterbox@harpercollins.co.uk to register for the newsletter.

Also visit Josephine's website – www.josephinecox.co.uk – for more news.